P9-EKD-911

Bella Maura

DAWN DYSON

CREATION
HOUSE
A STRANG COMPANY

BELLA MAURA by Dawn Dyson
Published by Creation House
A Strang Company
600 Rinehart Road
Lake Mary, Florida 32746
www.strangbookgroup.com

Design Director: Bill Johnson

Cover design by Justin Evans

Library of Congress Control Number: 2010931342
International Standard Book Number: 978-1-61638-202-5

First Edition

10 11 12 13 14 — 9 8 7 6 5 4 3 2 1
Printed in the United States of America

To the girls of uta.
I have no thing to offer you, save one—
God was there, too.

The abuses of those who abused you fell on Me.

—Letter of Paul to the Romans, 15:3

Without heaven above its head, without its life-breath around it, without its love-treasure in its heart, without its origin one with it and bound up in it, without its true self and originating life, the soul cannot think toward any real purpose—nor ever would to all eternity.

—George MacDonald

Deamhan Paidir Naid

The devil's plan be thwart, my Lord.
Devil call go unheard—my Angels, sing!
Devil's tears be fallen, not mine nor theirs, my Savior God.
Da wicked one day say, King!

For one hundred thousand souls be saved,
Save me—
My sea from fauther dead,
No mother heart within 'er bled,
No one on the earth hear me.

My voice, 'tis me…, Beautiful Mary, come through,
Said she—
No deamhan paidir be heard, my God,
No words be spoke but true undoubted laud.
No time be given Satan's breathin' out,
No lands find 'im creepin' in.
No souls the night found be sleepin',
No saint on earth be still.
And for my God, my Holy One, only be done Your Will.

—A sample prayer as recorded by Jonathan Driscoll
spoken by Bella Maura Driscoll
aged five years, eight months, and eleven days

chapter one

ᗷROWN CLAPBOARD HOUSES stagnantly lined the shore like giant tree trunks without levity. Well past the beautiful and genteel portion of winter, the actual trees appeared as lifeless sticks, black and twisted and strung up oddly in a sea of ghostly white sand and dead saw grasses. The scenery had been blank and colorless for miles; the only thing it inspired was a general malaise behind eyes passively partaking of it—that, and a vague sense of fear, of trepidation regarding the ocean of things yet unknown, the icy depths of which could make a body grow numb—the remote chambers of a mind go still.

As the gray fog of the day turned black into evening, the dreary shore road seemed an endless test of jagged rock and sleety drizzle. Sienna was exhausted, her neck stiff. She had planned to be there by now. She had a familiar CD playing low for comfort and she took a deep breath as she moved her head from side to side easing the tension. Not the best night driver in the world, she began straining (and partially praying) for Jeffers Street immediately upon entering the edge of the small town. Shortly thereafter, she made a right on it under a soothing lamp glow of yellow haze. She released a breath she hadn't known she'd been holding as she mentally reviewed Cheney's hasty directions blurted to her over the phone more than a week prior. It was safe to say they felt a bit sketchy at this point. She rounded a bend as the vacant village receded in her rearview mirror and more expansive vacation homes emerged. The blacktop took yet another turn along the inlet coast. The darkness and water beneath threatened to swallow her Audi whole should she deviate from the glossy pavement edge one inch. She never thought she'd miss the straight gravel roads and endless cornfields of her past, but she imagined them spanning out into the unknown rather than the mystic lapping water.

She didn't know the sea yet. They were certainly not friends.

After another dangerous curve and more deserted, veiled, and looming houses, somehow—she believed by the grace of God—the gold-plated numbers jumped up as her headlights swept over them. *Thank you, God!* she muttered under her breath, then, *Finally!* She was amazed she'd found it since every house appeared identical—especially in the blackened, misty night. As she pulled up the drive, she noticed the house itself was completely devoid of warmth. It was extremely uninviting for such an exquisitely built structure. The question arose regarding the possibility of its being haunted and hovered amidst its historical bones and century secrets, before she quickly dismissed the ludicrous thought with a smile. She chalked it up to her writer's imagination but she still couldn't quite put her finger on why she suddenly felt so uneasy. She swallowed back some anxiety as she scanned the strange neighborhood, finding it eerily silent in its off-season existence and fully assuming the slanted characteristics of neglect like an abandoned ghost town, albeit a very wealthy one. The spirit within its space and border seemed to openly resent her human intrusion and so her attempt to stifle her uneasiness failed. Rather, it multiplied, climbing up out of the pit of her stomach, and lodged solidly in her dry throat. Her mind sharpened against the salty midnight air, her senses heightened toward something too close to fright, her tongue tasted the sour words within; *This could prove to be a very big mistake...*

She hadn't seen Cheney for fifteen years. Even back then, they weren't what one would consider close. This journey had been more of a mercy call than anything, and now she wondered if she had followed God's voice or her own. She recalled the desperation in Cheney's voice as it trembled on the other end of the line. It was something near terror, and Sienna would never forget the sound. When Cheney had made the call the week before, it had been in the middle of the night and completely unexpected—the first contact between the two since college. And it was, simply, very odd.

Sienna knocked timidly at the front door. No one answered.

"Cheney? Cheney, it's Sienna," she called, waiting, watching hopefully for a light to come on. It never did.

She knocked again to no avail, not knowing what else to do. She glanced back at her car, suddenly feeling every ounce of exhaustion from the trip. She got a blanket out of her trunk, then turned up the heat and locked the doors. After one last scan of the surreal neighborhood surrounding, she fell asleep almost instantly upon saying a short prayer.

⁂

While tossing through a terrible sleep full of strange disjointed dreams, the length of which Sienna couldn't determine, she awoke with a start to the sound of slurred voices. As she was forcing herself to become more alert, she slowly recognized Cheney's laugh as it filtered in through distant memory and connected. She saw two figures approaching the front door of the house, both of them stumbling as if severely inebriated. She wiped a circle of vapor off the car window with the cuff of her sleeve, and confirmed to herself it was indeed Cheney out there, leaning heavily into the man next to her and trying to give him a kiss. She fell against him instead, limp as a rag doll and obviously passed out. Sienna watched as the man, not much better off himself, let her body slide to the cold, wet stoop, apparently contented to leave her there for the remainder of the wickedly frigid night.

Jumping from her car Sienna shouted, "Hey, you! Hey! Wait a minute!"

The man's delayed reaction was one of gradual surprise and he clumsily stumbled off, escaping into elongated shadows and overgrown shrubbery. A thick and creeping sea fog seemed to emerge instantly, rolling in off unkind currents, circling and overlapping itself in rotational undertones like displaced waves. It completely snuffed out the light from a nearby street lamp, and Sienna's body was suddenly overcome with chills. She strained through the black liquid air, quickly making her way to her friend's side.

"Cheney, what have you done to yourself?" she murmured through a heavily-laden sigh.

As she knelt down, she bumped Cheney's handbag with her knee. She pulled it open, felt around inside for a house key, and fingered smokes, a matchbook, a lighter, drug paraphernalia, condoms, and a tube of lipstick—but absolutely no keys.

"Good Lord," Sienna whispered as she quickly deduced Cheney's lifestyle.

She ran back to her car, switched on the headlights and returned, intently looking down into Cheney's lurid face. Thin skin stretched over sharp and jutting bone. Dark blue veins protruded oddly through pale, ghostly white and sunken temples. Mascara had streaked—dripped into a coagulated black. Purple shadow of grave sickness and cover-paint dispersed. Foundation was swept into premature crevices and haggard, splintered lines that seemed to come out from, and lead to, nowhere. It was the face of someone half-dead and barely breathing. And no matter how hard or how long she'd been trying to hide it, her demon's face was coming unmasked. Its parasitic nature was unleashed, unearthed; its hellish corpse, nearly, completely, exhumed. It was latterly exonerated by a soul lost to its own vast freewill and earthly dependency—whatever form therein, unremarkable. Sienna couldn't help herself—she rolled up the jacket sleeve of Cheney's left arm. The flesh was dotted with fresh pinholes overtop layers, and layers of stacked purple scars that told of irreconcilable years hard-lived like the weeping rings of a severed tree.

"Sweet Jesus," Sienna gasped, bringing both hands to cover her mouth in shock while her eyes remained wide open and fixed, locked in on the all-telling arm lying limply on the cold hard ground. She didn't say it, she barely let herself think it, but moving in segregated words shifting in and out of her tolerantly stifled yet inherently judgmental mind, was the kind-hearted, sick-hearted notion that this particular resurrection of life was an outright impossibility, a blatant improbability at its mildest—these thoughts lingered in the secret spaces between heartbeats and breaths taken, they mixed in through the air in her blood along with the phrase, *too far gone* . . . and they stayed, just as deep as her veins.

Just then a hooded man in a dark sweatshirt rounded the corner. He was moving so fast, Sienna sprang to her feet and jumped back a step in reaction, suspecting him to be the bearer of harm.

"You gonna leave her here again?" he accused her piercingly.

His Irish accent was thick, his tone most unpleasant. She stared into his back as he turned it on her and momentarily walked away. He unlocked the door with his own set of keys, pushed it hard and letting it slam against the wall inside as he flipped on a light.

When he returned, she tried her best to explain, "I'm not—what I mean is—I'm trying to help her. I'm her friend."

He stopped for a moment as if resting upon her very words, letting the drizzle surround his rounded shoulders, the crystalline droplets collecting one-by-one, then fading into his hood, uncountable. Along with the dampness, he absorbed into his being the notion of a decent person standing before him, with the possibility that behind her voice might actually lie something called the truth. He stood there motionless in the silence between them as if completely unaccustomed to hearing someone sober—or sane—for that matter. When he put his body back in motion, his demeanor had softened, if only just a little.

"Let's get her inside," he instructed.

He picked Cheney's languid body up effortlessly as if used to the drill. He laid her out on the living room couch then checked her pulse and temperature mechanically as if this bizarre interaction between them were rote.

"She's nearly frozen," he finally said, no emotion evident in his voice.

And without looking at Sienna—he hadn't made any eye contact with her at all—he requested dryly, "Would you mind starting a bath? It's upstairs, first left."

"Sure," Sienna replied softly, politely exiting the scene with a bowing humility and an awkward reverence normally reserved for someone's funeral.

As she climbed the stairs, her body seemed unnaturally heavy, the spirit within her overwhelmed by the sense of sadness, the utter helplessness, she imagined that she felt emanating from that man. She took a deep breath and shuddered to find there wasn't any air. The house seemed like a vacuum, or an underground tomb, vacant and simply waiting on a death to fill it.

The stranger below started a fire in the fireplace, got a pot of strong coffee brewing, then he carried the limp woman up stairs he seemed all too familiar with. His countenance was similar to that of a man walking the gallows with the weight of the world in his hands. He entered the bathroom without a word, stepping sideways through the door. Sienna stepped into a corner of the small room, trying, as much as humanly possible, to not be in the way. After he perched Cheney on the toilet lid, he slapped her on the cheek as gently as possible, yet firmly enough to wake her up a little. She groaned and her head rotated ungracefully then fell forward into her chest. A curse word dribbled out of her mouth as he began to disrobe her. Sienna felt nervous and awkward, not knowing if she should leave or stay, trust this man, or call the paramedics.

Without turning toward Sienna, the man sensed her discomfort, primarily because it was his own. He shook his head shamefully and said quietly in her direction, "I'm sorry..."

He lifted Cheney and placed her body gently in the steaming water while giving Sienna directions, "All you have to do is keep her head up so she doesn't drown herself. She usually wakes up about a half an hour in. Make her drink a cup or two of coffee before you fall asleep. If anytime she stops breathin', call 911. I'm right next door, to the north."

He stopped talking for a moment, wiping wet strands of hair away from Cheney's face with his thumb.

"Give me your hand," he said, holding his out in the air for Sienna.

She took it without hesitation and he steadied her as she knelt down beside him.

"Just hold her chin up like this." He showed her kindly, with his hand over hers. His touch was warm, his hand strong. He looked into Sienna's eyes for the first time that night. He looked into them for a long, unapologetic moment; at first, to gauge whether or not she seemed trustworthy—and he quickly surmised that she did; and secondly, to look more deeply into her as a person, to thank her. He was clearly relieved that someone else was there with him, that someone else could see what had become of his life. Something inside him exposed the fact that he was glad that someone was her. His eyes seemed to communicate that he wanted to talk to her for hours, his heart, coming straight through them, seemed to say that he wanted her to know more of his story. But he broke the gaze, looked down, looked within, and instead he simply asked her without inflection, as if it weren't really a question at all, "You gonna be okay here?"

"Yeah, I think so," Sienna said weakly, not really equipped to save a life.

And with that he disappeared just as quickly as he came.

Sienna was suddenly overwhelmed with immense responsibility. She literally held Cheney's life in her hands. The stranger's assertion proved right. Almost thirty minutes later, on the dot, Cheney began to come around. And as she slowly came back through varying degrees of coherency, she arrived with a full-blown vengeance. She hurled curses, accusations, and slanderous abuses in between her indecipherable sentences and shrill screams with fervent slapping and clawing. In the midst of this emphatic mess, she finally caught a glimpse of the person in her bathroom. And she had no earthly idea who it was. She stared through blurred vision, blinking at Sienna, focusing for a long quiet time, not really placing her. Her mind just wasn't working yet—it wasn't moving, cooperating, or connecting with anything at all.

"Cheney, it's me—Sienna. Remember me...from college...Sienna?" she repeated, and getting nowhere, offered, "You're okay, Cheney. You're gonna be just fine."

Sienna was out of breath, wet and sprawled out on the slippery tile floor. She stood up carefully then started looking in the cabinets for disinfectant and a bandage. Her arm had gotten scraped in the struggle and was beginning to drip blood.

"Oh, Sienna…Si, I used to call you, right?" Cheney stammered, slowly adjusting to the name.

She watched nonchalantly as Sienna did her best to tape up her own arm.

"So what are you doing here?" Cheney finally asked, clearly having forgotten inviting her.

"Never mind, let's just get you into something warm, some pajamas or something? And then we'll go downstairs and get some hot coffee. How does that sound?"

Cheney followed Sienna around like a spiritless shadow, going through all the motions without conjuring the energy or wit to supply another outburst. Once downstairs, she drank some of the intensely black coffee—vomited it right back up and curled up on the couch in front of the fire—all without so much as a single word of thanks. Sienna grabbed a garbage can to place beside Cheney and covered her with a frayed patchwork quilt. As she sat down in the old recliner next, sheer exhaustion settled into her bones and stayed. An antique clock somewhere in the house laboriously chimed three times.

"Three a.m.," she said aloud.

She looked over at Cheney who was softly moaning in pain.

"God, why do people do this to themselves?" she thought, "and what am I supposed to do about it?"

She asked her questions sincerely but didn't get an answer to either one—nothing more than the soft crack and hiss of the hungry fire consuming itself beside her. Her eyes flowed out the window into the cold liquid night, into so much blackness, blankness, and depth moving forth that her soul couldn't hold its answer. So she let it all go. Just then she noticed the light on the nearby porch coming on. Its sweet glow dispelled the darkness surrounding and let loose every ounce and trace of her secret fears beholden. It gave enough warmth to be her blanket, enough security with which to start her on toward rest. It stayed steadily on all through the night season as night seasons do steadily creep. It promised a clearer and lighter tomorrow, and in that promise she found comfort to sleep.

And it belonged to the house to the north.

chapter two

*T*HE NEXT MORNING, Sienna awoke to a heavenly light streaming in. It was peaceful, warm, and uplifting and had transcendently placed the house in a much less dreary land. As she stretched her arms overhead, she noticed that Cheney was still sound asleep on the couch, snoring rather loudly at intermittent times, with her body twisted and contorted most unusually. The clock on the stove read 10:46 a.m. As Sienna started a fresh pot of coffee, she was pretty sure she could have slept a few more hours with no problem because she fought with the filters as they declined to separate, she scattered an entire scoop of coffee grounds across the counter and she fumbled her empty mug, finally catching it against her stomach just before it fell to the floor. She rolled her tired eyes back in her head, then her gaze levitated to a merciful sky beyond the ceiling. "God, I'm going to need some extra help today," she thought.

After being adequately caffeinated, she took the liberty of unpacking her things in a spare bedroom. She showered, changed into fresh clothes, quickly cleaned up the bathroom and then decided she'd see about breakfast. As she made her way through the unfamiliar kitchen cabinetry, she realized there was nothing more than coffee, soda, liquor, and half a loaf of stale bread. She then set herself to doing some of Cheney's laundry, but there wasn't any detergent to be found. Clearly, she'd have to do some shopping, so she made herself a list. It ended up being ridiculously lengthy since apparently shopping was not one of Cheney's strong suits.

She went around the house opening as many blinds as possible. The sun was glorious that day, the trading seasons hinting of their spring, and she wanted to take full advantage of every transitional moment. She was intent on finding some birdsong cheer, of borrowing some life from nature and breathing it back into the old-boned house that seemed to know through timely wisdom that it was hiding secret sins. The gloominess that clung to its foundational makeup slowly lifted as Cheney rose looking about as lively as a vampire awakened at high noon.

"Close the blinds, would ya? I've got a headache," she snapped through her grogginess.

"Good morning to you, too, Cheney."

"Yeah, whatever…so you really drove all the way here? I was just kiddin' with ya, I didn't think you were serious about coming."

"You asked me to come, so here I am."

Sienna sat down on the couch next to her old friend. She tried not to sound condescending, nor look judgmental, when she said, "Look, Cheney, I have a good idea what's going on here. And I don't think you called me out of the blue for nothing. I just want you to know that I'm here to help you in any way that I can, but only if you want help. If you're not serious about changing, I won't get caught up with you in this. I'm here to help you get out of it and that's it."

Sienna knew it sounded a little harsh, maybe too straightforward, or too "AA", but after all she'd been introduced to the night before, she couldn't help it. She had to be honest for her friend's sake and firm for her own.

"That's cool, Si. Don't have to look so serious. Your face might get stuck that way—you know?"

Sienna smiled and nodded agreement. It was a start between the two reconnecting friends.

"I've got to go shopping, you okay here?"

"I'm not a baby, Sienna. Go. Do your thing. I'll be here when you get back."

"Okay," Sienna said weakly, pretty certain she couldn't believe a word Cheney said.

She scanned her shopping list one last time before adding, "By the way, I'm a really good cook if I do say so myself. By the looks of you, you could use some fattening up. What do you like to eat? Just name it and I'll make it for you."

"I don't know, Sienna. I'm not really hungry right now."

"Later on you might be. So what sounds good…pasta, meat and potatoes, you a vegetarian…what?"

"Pancakes."

Sienna smiled as she grabbed her purse and keys. "Pancakes it is. I'll be back soon."

Just as soon as Sienna's car left the driveway, Cheney shuffled to the kitchen and wrapped her skeletal hand around a bottle of booze. She slowly made her way to the bathroom, closing several of the blinds Sienna had opened. She stared blankly into the mirror, peering out at a stranger she didn't know and didn't like. The disconnect between self and soul, between her mind, heart and body, could have spanned a dozen oceans or linked a million worlds. She blinked back the vacant image that was reflected there, tried to erase her own face which looked like a shriveled mystery specimen in a laboratory jar—something hideous and locked inside a crypt that should never have surfaced—should have never been seen. She splashed water on her unfeeling skin then headed back to her bedroom, a place to disappear from reality's shore, to separate from her own life-breath, and its unelected existence. She slumped down on the unkempt bed, angry at herself for calling Sienna in the first place. As she unscrewed the bottle cap, she recalled that something had been seriously wrong with her that day—the day she called her ex-friend. She'd woken up in someone else's bed, realized she was someone's mother but couldn't remember the little girl's name, and something inside her snapped. She began to panic because she couldn't remember her daughter's name. A voice in her head told her to pick up the phone and call Sienna. And to this day, she had no idea how she'd gotten Sienna's current phone number; it had been years since they'd spoken.

"What was I thinking?" she mumbled, taking a hefty drink before curling up and falling back into a sleep not nearly deep or permanent enough to escape her sallow and torturous, rotating dreams.

Sienna drove back down the same curvy road she'd arrived on the night before—which seemed like weeks ago already. The drive this time was absolutely beautiful. The sea was a deep blue, the houses warmer, friendlier. "What a difference the sun makes," she thought. She turned up her CD and sang along to a few songs before entering a larger, neighboring town with familiarly named shopping centers. She enjoyed the shopping, both the people and the break it gave her from the awkwardness between Cheney and herself. Sienna knew something about addictions—that everyone has them in some form or another. And she figured Cheney was in a war with herself and, in all probability, only called Sienna during a momentary lapse. But Sienna reassured herself that the Lord works in unique and mysterious ways, and she believed she was where she was supposed to be. She would just take it one step at a time, one day at a time, and God would show her the way.

Back at Cheney's house, Sienna was pleased to find the door still unlocked. She made a mental note to ask Cheney for a key. As she entered, she found the couch unoccupied, so quickly searched the house, finding Cheney fast asleep upstairs. She commenced to unload the groceries, leaving pancake mix and everything necessary for dinner there on the counter. She started a load of laundry and waited. It was now nearly 5:00 p.m. and her stomach was rumbling. She decided on a fruit salad and ate it slowly and alone—just herself and that big, rambling house. Around 6:00 p.m. she put the pancake mix, eggs, milk, and butter away.

Cheney didn't come out of her room at all, not until the next day.

chapter three

𝒯HE MORNING HAD passed peacefully, uneventfully, and every bit as slowly as time could pass for a human being, with the borders of their life preeminently dictated and held in an hourglass hidden in the palm of God's hand. Not at all accustomed to an empty agenda, beholden solidly to the notion that every moment of life should be lived to the fullest and its overflow used as blessing seed, Sienna was lying on the couch, staring up at the ceiling and going increasingly stir crazy with each gradation of the rising light. More than just a little homesick, she sprung up to phone the stable back home to check on her horse, Ira. Barbara, the stable manager, assured her he was fine but added that he was starting to get restless and seemed to be wondering where "his girl" was. When Sienna hung up, she realized the phone call only made her miss him, and Barbara, more. Here, so far removed from her world of layered aspirations, she couldn't help but feel she was wasting her allotted time on earth.

Her fingers restlessly tapped the counter as she thought about Ira. Ira was a big deal to Sienna. Ira was a big deal to a lot of people. Reserve Champion Hunter Under Saddle at the Quarter Horse Congress in Ohio last year, he was a leggy, black gelding with exceptional breeding and disposition. Many offers had been made to buy him. Some of them were outrageous sums of money, but Sienna wouldn't dream of selling him, and Ira wouldn't think of being someone else's horse. They made quite a team. Watching them together was often described as a dream, a living art form of movement, balance, and beauty. Sienna loved riding almost more than anything else in life, and she always had, ever since she was a little girl. Now that she couldn't ride and was so far from home, she wished she'd at least brought one of her dogs for company.

Suddenly, something outside glimmered like a diamond, and her gaze was drawn out the window to search after it. Her eyes followed the mirage into that mysterious and roving sea that seemed to make a mockery of counted days and human plans. It swallowed time down whole and threw back to shore its own choice of allowed seasons. It rotated its rainbow reflections through warped tunnels of change and age. The voyages of space and distance—the passages of circumstance and chosen elect—determined with its own holy order the hour, revealed in its own century seen like Truth unwinding as a masterful clock before the dumbstruck learned. The mesmerizing effect it had on the "whosoever will" watching, the universal pull under the moon which held its power over human mood, its force behind destiny's course and the soothing womb of mother-earth sound that made it all okay, made it all just go away, was astounding to her. In its secrets, it seemed to hold nothing if not true equality. It seemed to be the father of opportunity, the mother of second-chances and the kind-hearted judge of acquittal from every failure occurring on land—holding something of the nature of God in its waters, something of Him and of His Final Rest as its heavens were reflected, magnified to show all that might look up what they sought, as they be found seeking still.

She wanted to run along its borders, laughing. She wanted to tell it her name, to smile out and greet it and taste its salted air on her tongue as would an unhindered child. She wanted to cry into it her most sorrowful shame, the most atrocious witness of earthly sin, so it could cleanse her eyes from it and erase the stinging memory. And she wanted it to salt her soul, become a pillar to hold her up, to keep her from ever repeating sin, to help her do her best and to remove from her all her living pain, as far as the east is from the west.

But Cheney's emergence abruptly interrupted her prism-like and polar-balanced thoughts. And for the first time since Sienna arrived, Cheney actually seemed pleasantly normal, if one could set aside the stringy red-dyed hair, the bloodshot eyes, the spider-webs tattooed up and down her white pin-holed arms. If one could look past all that and still focus on the original person beneath, they'd see Cheney's smile, if only for a fading, liquid moment in time.

"Pancakes?" Sienna offered.

"Pancakes would be great, sure."

Cheney flipped through the channels on television for a while and decided on a game of college basketball.

"Who's playing?" Sienna asked, trying to make conversation.

"Heck if I know. I just like the noise, ya know. I can't ever stand it to be quiet. I gotta have somethin' goin' on all the time, ya know?"

"I used to be like that," Sienna said thoughtfully.

She poured out the first bit of creamy batter, and the griddle sizzled.

"Hey...," Cheney started, then hesitated a bit, saying the rest rather reluctantly, "some friends of mine are going out tonight. You wanna come?"

"No thanks, Cheney. And I'm sorry, but I don't think you should go either. I don't think it's a good idea at all."

Cheney looked contemptuously at Sienna, but Sienna continued on anyway.

"You might want to consider changing who you hang out with, Cheney. I mean, if you're serious about sobering up.... You might not want to be around anybody for a long time. Give yourself some time to get to know *you* again, you know what I mean?"

Sienna placed a stack of steaming pancakes in front of Cheney and met her glare dead-on. *Here it comes*, she thought.

"You kinda turned out to be a know-it-all, huh, Si? If you think you're gonna come in here and tell me how to live my life, you can just leave now. I don't need you or anybody else telling me what to do."

Sienna took a deep breath and softened her expression; she purposefully took on a soft tone to try to defuse the situation.

"Cheney, tell me what happened here. Tell me what happened to you. After you left college, what went wrong? I mean you ran off with that guy, what was his name?"

"What guy?"

"The guy you dropped out of college for, the one from Tennessee?"

"Sienna...," Cheney drawled with exasperation beneath an emphatic eye-roll, "I have no idea what you're even talking about. That was so long ago."

Cheney shook her head disapprovingly in an attempt to make Sienna feel stupid and small. It didn't work.

"So was I, Cheney. Our friendship was a long time ago and you remembered me."

Cheney pushed her plate of pancakes out of the way and leaned on the counter assertively, defiantly.

"Sienna, let me explain something to you. I'm a drinker and a smoker, and I do most everything else illegal if you want to know the truth. I do a lot of things—most of them I don't remember. That's just the way I am. I don't know why I called you. Obviously it was a mistake. Now, just go on home so we don't have to do any of this. Sorry I called you."

Cheney left her pancakes without touching them. She went into the fridge, grabbed another bottle of booze, and started up the stairs

"Cheney, the other night you just about died," Sienna called to her. "If your neighbor and I hadn't been here, you'd be dead."

Cheney stopped mid-stride on the stairs and slowly turned back around.

"He was over here, too? You people seriously need to get a life."

The next thing Sienna heard was the bedroom door slamming shut. As she turned off the griddle, a single tear rolled down her cheek. *What happens to people?*

In college, Cheney was wild, yes, but no different than a lot of college students. She didn't do drugs, not that Sienna knew of anyway, just drinking and hanging out with guys. Cheney had been adopted reluctantly by distant relatives at the age of ten—not because her parents died, but because after their divorce they simply decided neither of them wanted her anymore. Sienna always thought that was deplorable, and she knew it was unspeakably hard on Cheney. To make matters worse, Cheney's adoptive parents were very religious at church, but were not what one would call peaceful at home. They didn't make Cheney feel very wanted or loved. So, as could be expected, Cheney ended up on the rebellious side with a built-in aversion to the church, and most unfortunately, with God Himself.

Sienna's ideals were too disarrayed and her values too premature back then. She hadn't had the personal trials to tear her apart yet, nor the experience of God's hand putting her back together, so she simply couldn't put anything useful into words. She would have liked to relate to her friend that the church—the building and the religious form—reflected people's idea of God, not necessarily a true reflection of God. She wished she could have told her that the true Church wasn't about the people, but the Holy Spirit within them. But they were both so young, so Sienna, not equipped to do much else, just stood by Cheney as best she could.

Cheney was always reserved about private things, but her true feelings escaped through her music, often without her knowing it. Cheney's music was a raw art form, full of pain, hate, and an alternate soft, even strength. There was definitely something there—that "it" factor. Sienna loved to listen to her sing and play the guitar and was patient while listening to Cheney fight with herself and her past through the torture of writing great songs. They didn't come easy. Then one day Cheney was gone without a word. Someone said she'd run off with a boy from Tennessee. Sienna didn't get a chance to say goodbye—she knew nothing about it. She boxed up Cheney's things and hadn't heard from her at all until the recent phone call.

Sienna wiped the remainder of a few more fallen tears, realizing she still had some of Cheney's old boxes in her garage back home. She wondered if Cheney would want them. She finished cleaning up the kitchen. While she was at it, she found every alcoholic beverage and poured it down the sink. She threw away three packs of cigarettes. She gathered up all the day's trash and found a garbage can outside. The afternoon sky was a bit overcast, but the temperature was pleasant. She decided to take a walk along the shoreline. She went back inside to grab a sweater and her car keys (just in case she got locked out of the house), she found an old pair of rubber boots that she pulled up overtop her jeans, and she headed off toward the coast. She was really starting to feel miserable, wondering if she should just head back home. As she moved slowly across the crisp and shell-coated sand, watching the seagulls land and take off in front of her, she prayed for direction but heard nothing but the answer of the waves. She walked a bit more then prayed for comfort and peace so her feelings would quiet down, and she could receive and welcome the direction, should it come. And it did. Suddenly the sky opened up, the sun shone upon her, and as she felt its fleeting warmth, she knew she should stay. But that was it. No more, no less. The clouds gathered again and the sun was masked, but she was not saddened anymore. She was even somewhat hopeful. She did, however, still crave to be near her horse, or dogs, or barn cats—anything familiar. She was really beginning to miss home and the comforts that filled it. She turned around and headed back, the remnants of the winter wind falling sharp and strong against her fair skin.

Closer to the steps by the pier, she felt safe enough to turn and look out into the expanse of the sea. It was all revolving shades of gray. It reflected the mood of the sky, and she really had to concentrate to tell where they separated and let go of one another. After a time, it seemed they didn't. Her black hair softly swirled around her face in youthful curls; it matched the deep color of the slated rocks behind her. Her freckled and light ivory skin blended into the grains of sand countless upon the shore. Her gray eyes entered deep into the mystic colors of the sea she was so enamored with. She was oblivious, there as she was looking at God's cold beauty, thinking that it was beauty still, that she was indeed a part of that beauty and that it was a part of her.

And that They were watching her, too, with the same sense of vastness and captivating awe.

chapter four

"HEY."

She didn't know she wasn't alone and she jumped a bit—leaving her feelings lying naked on the ground before her and exposing beneath her the rather odd reaction as it lifted like a cloud, or vaporous fog into his eyes. And as it did, his unforgettable voice grabbed hold of something sacred and reserved inside her. Its warm beauty, its strong comfort, its sweet recognition of who she was, echoed down through the chambers of her soul, sinking into her like mist to bone. He had a gift with it, she knew—and she knew this instantly. With a voice like that, he could break generational curses, gather great tribes for the day of reckoning, call forth to night action secret societies that protect the innocent world, or, simply, capture her heart as he drew it slowly in, back over his sweet initial conveyance. He could summon and pull out from her (and from countless others just as easily) aspiration and outright belief, thoughts so profound they birthed everlasting meaning through the host that conjured them forth with the borrowed energy of his hallowed inspiration—and all this through his sound alone. How this could be possible, she didn't bother to ask because she knew where all holy gifts come from—she had one, too.

But truth be told, he wasn't trying to do any of that. He was simply talking to her with an intent that shifted down through her very soul, separating the degrees of her truth like grain from chaff. And if amazing novels, universal myths, and actual bloodlines could be traced back to stories told of true love—if these things could be thought to exist with an origin found within the tiniest seed of truth—theirs became as good as planted on this day. It was sealed unto all history from one singular moment as an angel, colored as their world, lifted between them and watered with the word what they'd planted there between them. On his voice, on her wings they fluttered. And the timeless breeze coming off those wings, his voice, connected them in spirit, and it had crossed oceans to find them.

"Sorry, I didn't mean to scare ya," he continued, layering his voice like a song without words; only soul utterances, universal, within it.

He could have said nothing, or everything, in any single word he chose to speak to her and it would've all meant the same thing—he was enamored by her completely—and he was completely disinterested in taking the long road toward a destiny he'd already seen.

He'd been watching her walk all night, all the wee midnight to morning hours and today, all day. He'd been watching her out on the shore, getting lost in the secrets of the sea and he'd lost himself, equally as much, in the mystery of her. When he'd startled her with his warm greeting, he was casually leaning against the railing of his back porch, wearing a charcoal sweater-coat, jeans and black boots over a body that couldn't be hidden by anything. He was very beautiful. In fact, one could say he was so beautiful, he was intimidating to look at. And he was that shockingly handsome to everyone, but it had become a sort of handicap that kept people at a distance—girls felt out of their league and guys didn't want to compete. Although attractive, he was oblivious to it, and he was a hard person to get to know. He was an introvert, the starving-artist type with a foreign accent, and he figured that was why people seemed to treat him so aloofly. And on top of this, he had somewhat of a controlled tragedy going on beneath his eyes. *Everything* was in his eyes, not like some people—people whose eyes reveal absolutely nothing about them. No, this guy had eyes that revealed his entire heart and soul, told whatever he was thinking and feeling as clearly as if someone had written it on a billboard. And she couldn't stop looking into them because they reminded her of all the things she ever wanted to say, to tell the whole world, but could never find the words for.

"Hi, I'm Jonathan." He smiled at her, a somewhat guarded, sideways smile, his eyes searching hers. "If I had any manners at all, I would have introduced myself the other night."

"Oh, that's okay...I mean, considering the circumstances and all," she said as she reached out her hand, "Hi, my name is Sienna."

He shook her hand gently then held on to it for a moment.

"Sienna...I like that," he said and let go of her hand. "Sorry, I didn't come over sooner, but she doesn't want me around."

"Oh."

They both glanced remorsefully in the direction of Cheney's house, then

27

their gazes dove down toward the ground in front of them. Sienna's hands went in her pockets and she began moving a twig back and forth with the toe of her shoe.

"Hey, look...Sienna," he offered quietly, "You can come over here if you need somebody to talk to. I've been dealing with her for a long time."

"I understand. And thank you for that. The fact is, she just called me out of the blue. I haven't seen her for fifteen years. I really don't even know her anymore. Honestly, I don't know what I can do."

He looked at her, studying her countenance, her eyes, her lips, then he seemed to follow her words out to the sea, gazing after them for a long mournful moment, and saying nothing at all. The sadness seemed to flow back into his eyes as if he had no desire to say anything else. To her it seemed an awkward silence. To him it seemed perfectly natural to have nothing to say about something to which there are no answers. She started to say goodbye.

"Well, I'll just be going then...."

"Sienna?" he interrupted her, almost urgently.

"Yes?"

He glanced over his shoulder, back toward his own house, then his eyes fell to the railing in front of him. He nervously tapped out a rhythm with his hands as if playing the drums, then he abruptly stopped them, looked up, and asked her his question, Irish charm in full play.

"So, do you like hot chocolate, then?"

She grinned, looking down to kick her twig one last time, "It's actually my favorite."

He smiled back, a tired smile, but it stayed until their departure.

"Tonight then, whenever you come over, I'll make some for you. It's the best in the world so I've been told. I always make some for my girl. She won't mind the company, I'm sure."

"Oh, okay...that sounds great. I'll see you later, then."

"Yeah...." He lingered thoughtfully, then nodded with, "See ya," and a final tap on the rail.

He disappeared into his house, and she moved on toward Cheney's. Sienna wondered what he meant by "his girl." She wondered if he had a girlfriend or a wife, though he didn't wear a ring. She really didn't want to be a third wheel. When she got back into the house, Cheney was roaming around half-dressed getting ready for her big night out.

"You decide to come?"

"No, Cheney. I meant what I said earlier."

"Look, Sienna. I shouldn't have asked you here. There's no reason for you to be wasting your time. You can leave whenever you want. If you stay for a while, that's up to you. But I don't really hang around home much. Oh, by the way, here's a spare key. If you decide to go, just leave the key and lock the door. Okay? And we'll keep in touch—is that cool?"

"Yeah, I understand. Be careful tonight, Cheney."

"I will. See you, Sienna. And again, I'm sorry for bothering you after all this time."

With that she was out the door. All Sienna heard was party-type laughter and yelling and the screeching of tires. Suddenly she felt very tired, and the recliner seemed to be calling out to her. Intent on sleeping for a half-hour, she woke up two hours later. It was almost dark. She turned on a table lamp and read a bit of the Bible and prayed for a few moments more. As she said amen and opened her eyes, she noticed Jonathan's porch light come on.

She freshened up a bit and headed over to his back porch. She knocked on the screen door feeling very self-conscious like a girl in high school. She hadn't felt that way in years—nervous over a cute boy. Suddenly the main door to the house opened and a little girl came through it. Sienna opened the screen door.

"Hi, I'm Bella."

"Well, hi there, Bella! What a pretty name you have. I'm Sienna."

"Come in. Daddy's going to make hot chocolate for us," she said, grabbing onto Sienna's hand and leading her inside.

chapter five

*H*IS HOUSE WAS unashamedly lived in and all the more inviting because of it. Centered in the great room was a large stone mantle containing a well-established fire—it was lightly sparking and emitting comforting warmth and sound. Two sets of boots, one large, one very small, were drying on the hearth. The living area, kitchen, and obvious music area were all together in one vast, open space with stairs leading to the more private areas of the home. The furniture was sparse but usefully placed, comfortable and equally sturdy, displayed about the room as timeless pieces of history that had done as much traveling as staying put. Numerous hand-knit pillows and throws in the fisherman pattern were scattered, piled and draped everywhere as if created and sent monthly by loving relatives from across the ocean.

"Where is your daddy, Bella?"

"He'll be down in a minute. Come and see my playroom."

Behind the kitchen was tucked a secret and rather large space that would be the envy of any young child. A pink, oversized doll house with Victorian trim was against one wall. Books, pillows, toys, puzzles, and games were strewn all through the middle atop a huge area rug. A child's easel with brushes and canvases and paints were in the far corner. It was tempting for Sienna to dive into it all herself. She noticed there was no area for music just as he stepped in the space.

"Hey," he smiled shyly at her. "It's good you're here."

"Well, thank you for having me. I couldn't miss this famous hot chocolate I keep hearing about. Right, Bella?"

"Right. Daddy, *when* are you going to make it? I've been waiting," the girl complained.

"Well, we can't keep princesses waiting, now can we, girl?"

And he scooped her up, tickling her belly while moving back toward the kitchen. It was obvious they were close, that they had a very special bond. Bella laughed and hugged her dad's neck as he put her down. When they were so close together like that, smiling into each other's eyes, it was obvious how much she not only looked like him, but emulated his mannerisms exactly.

"That is an amazing play area back there," Sienna said to him. "I used to be a teacher. It probably sounds strange, but it brings back so many good memories. Some of the books you have I used to read to my kids."

He looked into her eyes for a moment as if noting the emotion she was feeling through that memory. He chose not to ask questions about why she no longer taught school, he was just glad that her memories about it were good.

"So now, before this all starts, I must warn you. When we say hot chocolate, we mean Irish hot chocolate. It's a little strong, if I do say. And then when you consider how Bella takes it—it's Irish hot chocolate you can stand a spoon up in. It's like chocolate soup, really."

"I'll give it a try. I'm sure it is wonderful," she grinned.

"Well, if you don't like it, I'll put a nip of Irish Crème in it. That helps it go down, trust me," he chuckled. "Bella was born asking for chocolate milk, weren't ya, Bell?"

"Daddy," she playfully scolded.

Just then an old yellow lab made his way to greet Sienna. After that, he meandered directly to his familiar place in front of the fire where he circled and collapsed into memorized comfort.

"Fierce beast, that one," Jonathan remarked as he cracked some eggs.

"Oh, he's beautiful though. I miss my lab back home. He's a black lab."

"If you don't mind me askin', where is that—home, I mean?"

"Connecticut, now. But I grew up in Nebraska, lived there most of my life."

"Nebraska," he repeated thoughtfully as he stirred in some heavy cream.

The name of the state sounded almost humorous in an Irish accent, made it feel even farther away. Again he asked her no "why" questions, which had a calming effect on Sienna. She really began to relax in his company. She distinctly felt the refreshing freedom of not being judged, while at the same time being wholly invited in. Both Jonathan and Bella were incredibly welcoming and accepting.

"Here you are, my little lady," he served Bella in a small dessert cup. "And Sienna...Now, if it's bad, I'll get you something else."

"I love to cook," she said. "I could tell by the eggs and cream that it must be more like a custard, right?"

"Yeah, my mom's recipe."

He waited for her to taste it then asked, "Do you like it?"

"This is fabulous!" she answered with a smile, "This is the way to a woman's heart, for sure."

He looked directly at her and said, "Ah...so you can see right through me, then, can't ya?"

Sienna went a little red in the cheeks and didn't quite know how to reply.

"This *is* the way to a woman's heart, Daddy," the little girl blurted out through chocolate covered lips.

"Good Lord help us, Bell," he smiled weakly at his daughter while rubbing his forehead in an attempt to soothe a sudden headache, "I think we can wait a few years for you to be talkin' like that, can't we now?"

Sienna chuckled under her breath and his eyes quickly met hers, a look of weariness mixed with humor running through them.

As Bella smacked her lips and scraped her spoon loudly against her dish, he confided in Sienna like they were already best friends, "I'm doing my best to keep her from growing up, but I think I'm losin' the fight."

"But I'm supposed to grow up, Daddy," Bella contradicted. While Sienna nodded her kind agreement to the child's notion, her eyes were full of empathy in regard to his parental angst.

"I know, sweetheart," he conceded, "I know ya are. And you're doin' a fine job of it, too. They just don't tell dads how we're supposed to handle these painfully obvious things."

"I'll help you," Bella offered sweetly.

Jonathan said nothing, but his smile was a beautiful thing—unpretentious, unrehearsed, completely genuine. And Sienna was a witness, pleasantly blessed, as he leaned in to kiss his child's face.

When they had all finished their hot chocolates, Sienna offered to help him clean up, but he insisted she find a book that she really liked instead, that they'd read it, the three of them, just as soon as he had finished. She picked *Brother Eagle, Sister Sky* by Susan Jeffers and Chief Seattle. It was her favorite of all the children's books she'd had while teaching.

"Oh, I love that book," Bella exclaimed as Sienna sat down beside her, "I love the ponies in it."

"You like ponies?"

"I *love* ponies. When I grow up, I want a pony of my very own. I want a red one, a black one, and a yellow one with blonde hair."

"They sound beautiful. I bet someday you'll have one of your own."

Bella's eyes widened with wonderment as she whispered, "You think so?"

"I do. If you want one bad enough and if you'll take very good care of it, I'm sure one day there will be a pony out there for you to love. And I bet he'll love you, too."

"Really?" she asked, studying Sienna's face intently as if memorizing it.

"Really."

"Go brush your teeth, sweetheart, then we'll read your book," Jonathan called out from the kitchen.

"Okay, Daddy."

With a freshly brushed and smiling Bella in the middle, the three sat together on the sofa as Sienna revisited reading the book she loved so much. Bella commented on the horses, and Sienna added knowledge as to which horses were called Paints, which were Palomino, which were dappled gray, and so on. Bella soaked it up and so did Jonathan as an onlooker, his heart overpowered by how the two related so naturally as if they'd known each other for years. Their connection was almost a force, as if Sienna could be Bella's own mother. He wouldn't admit it, but it scared him a little. He didn't know Sienna's situation at all, he didn't want to get too attached too soon, but as to what he knew of Sienna, the person, it was already too late.

chapter six

$\mathcal{B}$Y THE END of the story, Bella was fighting the sheer weight of her eyelids and losing. Jonathan gently cradled his daughter in his arms, excusing himself from Sienna with an endearing look. And as she watched him carry Bella upstairs, she couldn't help but think, *What a great dad.* While he was gone, Sienna found herself getting butterflies, she was getting increasingly nervous about being alone with him. She found the humor in someone her age having what certainly felt to her like a crush. He was so calm and confident, at ease with himself and welcoming to her, that she felt more peace with him than she'd felt in years around anyone else. So how this fact could make her anxious, she had no earthly idea. Maybe it was because she felt so comfortable with him *so soon.* She got up and paced a bit, went over by the fire and stood by the slightly snoring dog. She glanced next door, Cheney's house was dark. Sienna doubted her friend would be home before two or three a.m. Just then Jonathan quietly moved up beside her and for a moment nothing was said, she just listened to the fire, but mostly to his breathing. She didn't know what brand of fragrance he was wearing, she just knew he smelled really, really good.

"Thank you for the beautiful story, by the way," he said, "Much more interesting than my version, I'm afraid."

"You're welcome," she began sheepishly, "but I should be thanking you for inviting me over."

She nodded toward the window facing Cheney's house and finished, "It would have been pretty lonely over there, waiting for her to come back, wondering if she's okay...you know?"

He stared into the fire, and that familiar sadness that dogged him crept back into the lines around his eyes. It seemed to cloud his entire vision. He stood there in complete silence, and Sienna felt that urge rise up prompting her to leave, but based on their encounter before, she remembered the possibility that awkward silence could be just silence, the awkwardness being nothing more than her insecurity or impatience. So she let them drop, she stood silently beside him, not rushing the moment at all, and to her pleasant delight, she found the silence between them to be a gift. She felt the nearness of him to be purer, more genuinely known without the weight of words between.

"Do you have a minute?" he forcefully asked, as if pushing the words out of his chest. "I mean, I know I said if you needed to talk to come over...but I think I lied a bit. I think I'm the one needin' to talk. To you, if you don't mind."

"No, I don't mind at all," she said kindly.

"Should we sit then?"

"Sure."

They went back to the sofa. She grabbed a wool-covered pillow and hugged it under one arm. They faced each other. He looked into her eyes with a painfully uncertain expression, wondering if he could, wondering if he *should*, do this.

"When I say I'm needin' to talk, what I mean is, I haven't ever really talked to anyone about it. It's been years that I've waited to really tell someone. I haven't found the right person to tell. But I'm thinkin' that person is you. And if you don't want to hear it, just tell me. You don't have to listen to me, I mean, it's not your problem, is it?"

He began to fidgit a little, then a lot, then he had to stand up and pace a little. He ran his hand through his hair in evident frustration.

"It's okay," she looked at him reassuringly. "I know we don't know each other very well, but I understand the hard things in life. I've been through some things. Please, just relax and say anything you want. It'll be all right."

He stopped pacing and thanked her with his glance. He sat back down.

"Have you ever gone through a nightmare with someone and stayed?"

He didn't explain what he meant any further, he just waited for her reaction.

"Yes, I have," she said simply.

The way she said it and the certainty of expression she used when she looked at him washed over him like a cleansing flood. And he instantly believed her.

"My friends don't understand," he continued. "They all get divorces and move halfway around the world and start over and drag all their loose-ended children behind them clanging their heads. I didn't want to do that, ya know? I didn't want to *be* that. I didn't want my little girl looking at me through lost eyes all her life. I didn't want that for her. I didn't want her to have to ask me 'why' in the way that she walks or to have to breathe those cursed questions 'who am I?' or 'where do I belong?' through her posture. No—I want her to always carry herself like she is loved."

He looked over at her. He shut his mouth and the water gates at the edges of his eyes started to open. He didn't want to cry. He swallowed it down and grew a hard shell, and the second he did, she saw where the sadness lived.

"Cry if you need to," she said, "I'll tell no one else."

She held out her hand, held it out in mid-air between them, gazing into his eyes. He considered the gesture for a long moment, looked back into her face, grasped her hand and felt it, the weight of it, its softness and its warmth. He ran his thumb over the back of it thoughtfully.

"We were married," he glanced toward Cheney's house. "We were young. We were in a band. Believe it or not, we were really good. We made some real money. But with real money came the drugs. She got hooked. I didn't. When we found out she was pregnant, I basically imprisoned her, sat on her while she was cleanin' out her veins. I held her hostage eight months, didn't let her out of my sight for a second. I got kind of crazy, ya know? The band tanked. I didn't even know if the baby was mine. And I wasn't any saint in those days either—I mean we were all young and stupid and success came way too fast—everything came way too easy. The minute she got out of the hospital, after Bella was born, I didn't hear a thing from her. I got the divorce papers, that was the only way I knew she was still alive. A buddy of mine found her through some old musician friends of ours a couple years ago. She was strung out, half dead. I couldn't just leave her out there, ya know? She had nothin'— was livin' on the street. I mean, I'm not in love with her, but I love Bella with all my heart. And that's Bella's mother."

He was still holding her hand. Silence rested between them again. Finally she replied quietly.

"So you're trying to save her."

"Yeah, I guess."

"Same as me."

"Yeah."

"There's only one problem..."

Silence.

"...neither one of us is Jesus Christ."

He wasn't sure if she meant it as a joke, but he chuckled anyway and she was glad he did. It certainly lightened the mood.

"No, I for one am definitely not Jesus Christ," he replied, "although at one time I was cocky enough to claim otherwise."

"Does Bella know Cheney's her mom?" Sienna asked.

"No. When Bella was born, Cheney didn't want her. I don't think she ever even saw Bella or knew her name. All she could think about was getting back into drugs and away from me."

"I see."

"And...I bought the house next door two years ago. I was thinkin'...since we're both older now, maybe I could help her. I don't know. I thought she'd see Bella and want to change...but there's nothin'...there's nothin' in her eyes when she looks at Bell. So I keep them apart. I don't want Bell gettin' hurt. I just try to keep watch, ya know? I try to keep her from killing herself. I don't know what else to do."

Sienna nodded understanding, and silence settled in for a moment more. Sienna took her time and formed her words of encouragement as best she could.

"You know," she began, "I don't always have an answer for everything right away. It takes me some time. And sometimes the only answer I find is that I have to figure out a way to live with the 'I don't knows' in life. Not just exist, but really *live* even with the wrongness surrounding everything—like if a garden is neglected and the weeds take over, the flowers—they still bloom. And they keep blooming year after year. Sometimes I think we have to be like that. We have to continue to thrive on purpose, regardless of our circumstances. Because, who knows? Maybe someday someone will come along and see what somebody else left behind and think it is perfect, they'll think it's a dream come true. And they'll value it all the more for its tenacity through all those abandoned and lonely years."

He was stricken silent by the heartfelt picture she painted. He'd never heard anyone talk like that before. She smiled sheepishly at him and continued, a bit more down to earth.

"And I wasn't kidding about the Jesus Christ thing. I've been through enough to know I can't live without Him. And I don't want to live without Him. To put it plainly, without Him, it's just not really life at all. I want to help Cheney, but I'm not up for playing God. The only thing I can do is pray for her, pray for God to make Himself known to her, and let God work through me as much as I am able. She's in God's hands. I told Cheney I'm not going to get so caught up with her or her problem that it steals my life, but I'll do what I can, for as long as I can. I've got to remember that it's ultimately Cheney's choice. She has freewill and I can only mess with it to a point and that's it.

"It's tough when you see someone struggling so much to just stand by and watch, isn't it? I guess everyone has to walk their own road, and none of the roads are easy.... Anytime you need to talk about anything, Jonathan, I will be here. I want you to know that I care. And I can be trusted."

He leaned back into the sofa absorbing everything she said. After a time, he smiled over at her, taking the liberty to softly study her sweet face. He was finding the introduction to her mind easy, smooth like her porcelain skin. She was so open with her thoughts—with her heart. She was direct and decisive, and powerful. She gave him her confidence, lent it freely for him to borrow. He was comforted by all of her words. Her experienced, yet patient attitude behind them calmed him. Her steady voice soothed his worries. And as for a confidante, she was a most excellent choice, the only choice for him, he knew. He could think of nothing better than a kind word from a pure heart at just the right time, and that's exactly what she gave him. Finally, he felt the drops, small beginnings of peaceful liquidity filtering into his dry soul and flushing out the confusion. He found those humbling in-dwellings, places of sacred rest built upon rock, infiltrating throughout his weary body and finding within him a nestling stone, a home for himself, within himself. And he imagined—because it had been so very, very long—what it must be like to be at complete peace with oneself, to have an active conscience that was pleasantly appeased, to have within one's chest the Holy Spirit and finding Him smiling, at rest, comfortable, and permanently stayed as would be a temple, its puritan walls hurling no offense within, without.

"Thanks," he said and squeezed her hand. He held a look in his eye that hinted of relief and renewal. He released a slow breath, the familiar tension locked inside his mind let him go.

"And thank you for being so good with Bella tonight," he continued. "I think she needs it, you know, to be around a caring person like you—a caring woman. It means a lot...it means so much to both of us."

"You're very welcome and thank you. I really wasn't looking forward to spending all evening alone. It is nice to have someone to talk to."

"I wasn't too intense for ya, then?" he smiled through the question.

"No, you weren't too intense. But I have one more thing to say before I go."

"And what would that be, Sienna?"

She liked the way he said her name. He said it like a song title, one he was practicing for life. Before she continued, she made note of its sweetness which lingered in the air like the melody of a meadow bird following the dewdrops at dawn.

"I've never seen a girl as loved as that one, Jonathan," she said and motioned toward the upstairs where Bella was sleeping.

As she got up to leave, Sienna continued with a voice of assured truth as she walked toward the door. "She knows who she is. She knows where she belongs. And she carries herself like love is the most natural thing in the world."

They said their goodnights rather quickly, rather in the middle of a new mystery neither one truly wanted to part. And as soon as he shut the door, the tears finally escaped his eyes though he was smiling wholeheartedly beneath them.

He was in awe of the force that had brought him this woman, on this very night, at the most pivotal point in his life. He went to the window, touched the cold glass with the palm of his hand, made sure she got safely in, and waited until she turned on her light before he shut off his. And the words he was thinking on were two that when whispered together in shadow somehow made their own light, made their way from the mystic darkness of night to the commonplace of noonday habit. Two words to transform the secrets of youth into ancient stories of separation and loneliness bleeding into the sweet ever-after, told of a garden-like place that goes on beyond any earthly grave; tiny words which together make universal, experiential sense of the meaning of One.

The words he thought on were but two. They were *soul* and *mate*.

chapter seven

 IDNIGHT CAME AND went with no sign of Cheney. Sienna was curled up on the sofa, contemplating all that had transpired since her arrival when soft sounds drifted across her thoughts. Familiar with the writing process, she gathered that the stray repetitive chords she heard from Jonathan's house were the humble beginnings of a new song. In her mind's eye, she watched Jonathan's strong hand etch words and symbols down on paper, no sooner scribbling some of them out. She saw several rumpled pages float to the floor until, upon the last page, flowed acceptance of a ribbon of meaning. Creativity that might be shared with another soul, he would reach out with this one and offer it to the world to trample on or adore. She eventually fell asleep as she was recording the evolved melody in her mind. She remembered thinking it was quite good, its sound reminding her of an uncomplicated memory or a beautiful dream from her childhood.

Some hours of sleep passed before she was awakened by someone beating at the door. She hastily rose from the couch expecting Cheney, but found Jonathan.

"She's not back yet," he blurted.

His body language clearly communicated his frustration and worry. He paced the small stoop, turning to peer out into the night for a brief moment before facing Sienna again.

"Sometimes I ignore it—ya know?—If she's gone all night. I mean, it's none of my business anymore. But tonight I have a feeling. I don't know what it is. I just think I should go look for her. Will you come over and watch Bell for me?"

"Sure...let me grab my keys."

On their way over to his house he continued talking to her. "I usually get the lady next door, but it is so late I didn't want to bother her. She's in her seventies. Mrs. Hopkins is her name if you need anything. I have her number on the wall by the phone. My cell is on there, too. Call me if you need anything at all. The places I go to look for her—well, they're drug dens, basically—over in the city. My hope is that everybody's passed out by the time I get there. Most of those people don't even know their own names. But they all think you're a cop...it's a bloody mess."

They'd reached the back porch and he turned to go.

"Jonathan?" Sienna touched his arm to stop him.

"Yeah?" He gave her the moment she was asking for. He gave her his full attention, looking right into her.

"Be careful."

She gravely delivered the words. Her gray eyes contained a visible storm of predicted consequences. She wanted him to weigh his choice heavily. And as her grip tightened slightly around his arm, he began to view this decision as a mother would. He began to truly think about why he was risking his own life when he had a little girl to take care of. He couldn't stop himself, however, from leaving. He still felt responsible. And he didn't know why.

"I'll be back," he said, and as he turned to go something inside him made him grab Sienna up in his arms and quickly hug her.

"I will. I'll be back."

She watched his outline fade as he ran toward the blackened street.

⚮

The blacktop was shiny from the dampness of the night. His SUV glided over the curves and held the road surprisingly well considering how fast he was driving. Sienna's eyes kept haunting his thoughts. He didn't understand his compulsive need to watch over Cheney, to save her. He felt the pressure of the situation building, and he knew things were coming to a head. He couldn't shake the feeling that something terrible was going to happen—he had no idea what—other than Cheney's inevitable death. He was afraid she was going to kill herself and that it would be sooner rather than later. He was scared of losing her. Knowing himself as he did, he guessed he would torture himself for the rest of his life for not being able to save Bella's mother. He'd do anything for his little girl.

He drove through the diseased and severed limbs of the city, by crack houses, shivering prostitutes, and homeless people sleeping over the grates in the sidewalks. He got out and started walking. Stray people glanced through him with vacant holes for eyes, like they had lost their own souls and wandered around nights trying to find them. He crossed the street a couple blocks in advance to avoid what he assumed was a gang of sorts gathered around a street lamp. They were loud and drinking, thankfully occupied with themselves. He disappeared around a corner, to the back of an abandoned warehouse where he'd found her once before. This time it was completely empty.

"Where the blazes are ya?" he angrily muttered the words to himself under his breath, running his hand through his hair as he did when he was overly stressed. He punched the wall with the side of his fist. He'd given up trying to think like her years ago when he realized she didn't think. She didn't think at all. He made it back to his car and started off toward another place, a party house on the back side of a college campus. When he arrived, he felt hopeful. Obviously they'd had a party that night. The lawn looked like a landfill that had had enough and simply thrown it all back up.

As Jonathan moved closer he noticed the once modish old house appeared beaten and sick—a type of sickness brought on from long-term abuse. He related to it completely, and in his thoughts continued a type of exchange with it. He mused that if a house could be thought to have a soul, this one emitted a feeling of sorrow so clear he swore he could hear it weep. It breathed out from between its boards whispers of apology for still existing. It was doing its best not to remain standing, to decay from within with its mismatched and torn curtains floating secret screams out gaping windows, but there was no escaping its foundation. Graffiti told its story, bled curses onto its sagging skin which nobody, except the writer, ever read. As a structure, it so closely resembled the shells of bodies passed out inside that one would think the house would eventually fall down or burst into flames, but it didn't. It just continued to be how it was: awful, sinful, wasted, and at that—Jonathan's thoughts became pure confusion—because the house, like the zombies within, shouldn't be. Not for so long. Nothing else could survive this self-abuse, but somehow they lived on—not a life, but a sentence, year after year after year. Somehow they stayed alive on, and stood for, absolutely nothing at all.

He walked right in since there wasn't a front door (if there had been, he'd have ripped it off the hinges himself). He began stepping over people, trying to find an arm flopped out and marked with her tattoos, trying to find that fire-red hair and ghostly eye makeup. As he looked at the incoherent faces, he began to wonder whose daughters these were—whose sons were these? They were all...lost...nameless...fatherless. He started coming to a realization that perhaps in some strange way he was trying to save Cheney to keep this from happening to Bella. *Dear God. . . .* He was ashamed that Cheney, that Cheney's so-called friends, made their money and supported their habits by playing to younger and younger kids—college kids with spending money—high school kids just looking for a place to fit in—even unsupervised middle school kids. It infuriated him.

He went upstairs, found her in the last bedroom at the end of the hall. He dressed her in the clothes that he could find, thought about beating her so-called boyfriend nearly to death, then remembered how close he had been to doing the same thing with his own life. He carried her out. No one even noticed he was there. After he laid her in the backseat of his car, he went back into the house and dialed 911, said nothing and let the receiver hang. On his way out of town, he passed several squad cars. He knew where they were going, and he hoped Cheney's friends would be tied up for a while.

He began to drive her back home but decided to take her to the hospital instead. He didn't know how bad off she was—he never did. He just knew he was tired, and this addiction of hers was getting too big for him to handle. He filled out her paperwork, explained the situation, and left.

On the way back home, he pulled over onto a highway lookout point and got out of his car. The moon was full overhead, its light glistening across the black sea. He ran his fingers through his hair and knelt down; he hurled a rock out over the water and started to cry before it dropped. He wanted to take Bella and escape, to go back to Ireland and forget everything about this place. He didn't know what was stopping him. His career was writing and selling songs; he could keep his connections through e-mail and the Internet. He could make it work if he really wanted to. And his girl was young, she'd adapt to Ireland quickly; she'd probably fall in love with it, carry it with her always and everywhere, every bit as much as he had. He supposed the answer to be buried someplace beneath the stone-cold fact that he was ostentatiously stubborn and morally old-fashioned. He never intended on getting a divorce—ever. And he didn't want to just leave the mother of his child for dead. The only thing he knew for sure was that the waiting—waiting for her to die or waiting for her to clean up and change—was making him old. Waiting for her to be a mother was exhausting. He never understood why Cheney didn't love Bella. Bella was love. How could she not want her? He hated Cheney more than anyone else in his life. He hated just as much to admit it. But this was the first step toward repentance. It gave him the freedom found only in truth. He hated her because he didn't understand anything about her. He never did.

The sky, its firmament spread out awesomely before him, was beginning to lighten in shifting gradations and come down. Its pastels blanketed the softly quaking sea, floated to him with coasting layers of the haunting realization that the admittance of failure was a strength. This admission was an accomplishment—a true north on a rotating compass rose gone still—gone to guide on toward truth and bearing like it should, in a manner much like that of a guilt-ridden conscience wiped clean (how it can easily find the eastern horizon above the looming border wall). The light reflecting in his eyes told him it was almost dawn inside, outside. He started to sing an old Irish song without thinking; he'd known it since he was a boy. Tears ran down his face—a small sacrifice that flowed into the waters of many. He offered it freely. He sang it into the dawn—a type of prayer and connection to his homeland. He dearly missed both God and country. As the sun rose, he felt freedom and effortless peace as he soaked up the sun's rays without effort. And he felt it as a source of comfort and blessing along with the personal, earthly responsibility to give comfort and to bless back. And he knew, somehow, that God was listening to his song because he knew, humbly, that God had given it to sing. Suddenly, a renewal of energy surged warmly through his blood—just enough to make it home.

chapter eight

$\mathcal{S}$HE WAS CURLED up on his couch, and he watched her soft outline slightly rise and fall with each breath she took. He moved closer to her, his desire being to hold her close and to be held in return, but he hesitated. He stood over her for a silent moment more instead, not wanting to disturb whatever rest she might be in need of.

"Jonathan . . . thank God," he heard her say, her body beginning to shift and turn beneath the blanket.

She sat up on the sofa and looked up into his face. Blinking at him through tired eyes, she determined that he was as exhausted as a human being could be.

"Are you okay?" she asked, her obvious hours of worry returning to their former place and state, torturous emotions reclaiming their expressions, familiar with the facial skin and line that formed them.

"I'm fine, thanks," he said and fidgeted—partly in an attempt to stay awake, but mostly because he wasn't sure if he just lied to her or not. "I think I'm gonna go lie down for a while. Bella's still asleep, is she?"

"Yeah, she's upstairs in her room. She's fine," Sienna said, standing up next to him.

He reached over to her, gently touching her arm. He rubbed it affectionately as he spoke.

"I put Cheney in the hospital. She'll be there for a few days. Thank you so much for your help. I appreciate it . . . ."

As his sentence dropped off into silence, his hand moved up to her shoulder and stayed. His eyes seemed to pick up the conversation. They told her that he didn't want her to leave, but he didn't want to offend her by asking her to stay.

"I could stay," she offered, "Bella will be up soon and you probably need some rest."

He smiled his thanks at her, but didn't move on toward anything else; he just lifted his hand to her neck, tracing over the soft skin along her jaw line with his thumb. This time she couldn't tell what he was thinking, his beautiful eyes veiled his true thoughts and hid his secret questions, which were these: *How long could you stay, sweetheart? Could you stay forever? Would you even want to?*

"Bella likes Frosted Flakes for breakfast, usually," he said, putting his hand back at his side, squeezing it and letting go. "She hates it, but try to get her to eat some fruit, too, if it's not too much trouble."

"Sure, no problem."

"Are you sure you want to stay? She can be a handful, sometimes."

"We'll be fine. Get all the sleep you need. I'll take good care of her. And I don't mind, really."

Sienna could see he wasn't listening very well; she figured it was because his mind was still at the hospital. Little did she know it was entirely on her.

She put her hand on his cheek and looked directly into his bloodshot eyes, "Rest, Jonathan. You don't have to worry about anything. Just rest."

He smiled slightly but looked so beaten down with concern. He expressed his thanks to her and quietly made his way upstairs. She didn't see him again until late that afternoon.

∞

Sienna and Bella spent the day roaming the shoreline, making sand castles, drawing self-portraits with sticks, playing hopscotch and generally dreaming out loud. Sienna was exhausted by noon, but did her best not to show it. The little girl was so full of life and imagination, her creativity didn't seem to have an end. She told stories, obviously told to her by her father, and they were really quite good. Any one of them could have contended as a children's bestseller. She quoted poetry, or song lyrics—Sienna couldn't quite tell which—and prattled off Irish prayers in the original language, and God seemed to be present for all of them. She was the most engaging child Sienna had ever met.

As late afternoon approached, they gathered up plastic pails and scoops, shook out their sand-filled sweaters and headed back toward home. Bella had grown silent, and Sienna was wondering what she should make for dinner. She was concerned about Jonathan, too, and she began to offer up a prayer of her own, but was interrupted.

"Sienna?"

"Yeah, sweetie?"

"Are you somebody's mother?"

Sienna usually felt a swift kick to her gut upon hearing that question, but not this time. This time she didn't feel any pain, she simply answered, "No, I can't have any children."

"Why not?"

"Because God had other plans for me."

"Oh," Bella said thoughtfully. They walked on quite a ways in silence before she added, "That's okay. I don't have a mother. God must have other plans for me, too."

The comment softened Sienna's heart. It was one of those moments she wanted to savor and make certain she'd absorbed its meaning fully.

"That's right, Bell. He does. And He loves you very much."

Just then Sienna felt a tiny hand grab onto hers, and she heard a sweet voice say, "You would have made a good mom."

∞

As they arrived at the house, Sienna caught sight of Jonathan sitting on his back porch steps, empty coffee mug in his hands. Obviously he had been watching them for a while. A misty look of peace was draped across his smiling eyes. He was wholly intent on taking in Sienna, as much of her as he could. He barely looked at his child as she climbed onto his lap. He moved over to make room for Sienna to sit beside them.

"You must be tired. You didn't get much sleep last night either," he commented.

"Yeah, I'll admit it. I'm kinda beat, but I had so much fun today with Bella here. I loved it."

"I had fun, too, Daddy. Sienna, can you come over again tomorrow?"

"We'll see, sweetie," her father interrupted. "Let's give her a chance to catch her breath first, okay?"

"Okay," Bella said agreeably.

Sienna was impressed by how gracefully and thoughtfully the child took her father's correction. She was equally impressed by how tenderly and gently her father gave it.

"You ladies must be hungry...Would you like to have dinner with us, Sienna? It's the least I can do."

The look in his eyes suggested a mild pleading of sorts, indicating that he really wanted to spend some time with her later on that evening.

"That sounds good. What time do you think?"

"In an hour or so?"

"That'll give me just enough time for a hot shower and a good nap."

"Me too," spouted Bella.

Jonathan laughed and as he got up to go, balancing Bella in his arms, he leaned in next to Sienna and kissed her lightly on the cheek and whispered, "Thank you for today."

∞

Sienna showered until the hot water ran out. She tried to take a nap, but was too excited to sleep, so she got up, put her hair up into an informal twist and pulled on her favorite pair of jeans and the softest cashmere sweater she'd brought with her. She opted not to put on one of Cheney's perfumes and chose a mildly scented lotion instead. She felt truly refreshed, comfortable, and relaxed as she headed next door.

It was almost dusk; time had crept into another evening soon gone—she hoped it would be a memorable one. The sea air smelled wonderful as it wafted up the beach, something like the subtle beginnings of a spring rain as it had blessed her childhood fields. It was a calming, pleasant smell that made her feel young, yet wise. As she made her way up the stairs, he opened the main door and stepped out onto the porch to greet her.

"Hey." He smiled, and actually took her hand and kissed it as he drew her into his home saying, "Come in. You must be starving. Bella's down for a nap at least...maybe for the night, I don't know."

He took her jacket and her bag.

"I wondered if I should have brought her in for a nap this afternoon, but she didn't seem tired," Sienna said.

"Oh, she'll be all right. She had a great time today. She couldn't keep quiet about you. I think you've made her fall in love with you already." He winked at her and pulled out her chair for her.

"Thank you," she said, rather mystified as he scooted her in, not recalling another single, solitary time in her life when she'd been treated this well. She'd bought the con that chivalry was entirely dead. As she watched him, her cheapened ideals of dating evaporated one by one right out of her head. She watched as he lit two candles and poured her a glass of wine before seating himself, smiling bashfully like a schoolboy as he reached across for her plate.

"I hope you like Italian?"

"Love it." She smiled, her eyes shining at him.

When they had finished, he insisted she leave the dishes for him to do later.

"Would you like to go outside then?" she asked. "It's a beautiful night."

He helped her with her jacket, got the door for her, and grabbed a blanket on the way out. They sat on the stairs and looked out over the water that had crept up the shore erasing all the artwork of the day.

"Sienna," he said, "do you want to get away from here for a while?"

"What do you mean?"

"Well, I've been here for two years straight. I haven't gone anywhere. I think that's part of the reason I put her in the hospital, so I could get some time to myself. But the more I think about it, I'd like to have some time with you— to get to know you."

"Where do you want to go?"

"Ireland," he said and chuckled, "but we've only got a few days until they release her. And who knows if she'll even come back here... Is there anywhere you would like to go?"

"There sure is." She smiled. "Do you like horses?"

"Horses...," he said the word reflectively, as if remembering something way back in his youth.

"My horse is my kid, and he's back home in Connecticut and I miss him."

"Okay, let's go—tomorrow."

"That would be great." She beamed.

"Good." He was thrilled to see her smile. She had a gorgeous smile and beautiful smile lines that sprung in around her eyes like a sweet surprise.

"You're beautiful," he said, looking directly at her.

She smiled bashfully staring down at her shoes, tapping them together.

"You are," he said again. "You're beautiful."

She eventually lifted her eyes to his and accepted the compliment silently. They sat for a while, marinating in mutual happiness until a stray thought crossed his mind. He felt awkward for saying it, but it needed to be said.

"Sienna?" he asked sheepishly.

"Um-hm?"

"Your horse is the only one waiting for you in Connecticut, right? I mean, there's no one else? I mean, no another guy is there?"

"Well..." she teased. "You'll have to duke it out with Calvin and James—my dogs—they do get pretty jealous sometimes."

He nodded, relieved and apologetic for the question at the same time. A cool breeze began to blow in off the sea water. He opened the blanket and wrapped it around them both, draping it over her shoulders and leaving his arm around her, too. He invited her to lean in against his chest.

"Jonathan, do you speak Ireland's ancient language, Gaeilge?" she asked.

"Yeah, I do."

"That is one of my favorite things in the world," she said. "My grandfather died when I was two. I didn't know much about him, but I know he was Irish and I have always loved hearing that language. You can say anything you want, and I'll have no idea what you are saying, but just say something, please...anything."

"Well, you know I could be cursing a sailor's streak and saying all sorts of things that would make you blush if you ever found out."

"I guess I'll just have to trust you," she said and then laughed.

And he told her stories he'd heard as a boy, and he told her the things he missed most about his country and his youth, and he told her things he didn't have the courage to say to her yet. She didn't understand the words, but she knew when he was happy, when he was a younger version of himself, when he was terrified, and when his heart was breaking from sorrow. In his tones she could separate dreams from reality. She could be healed in the silent spaces between. But her favorite part was when he was speaking about love—it seemed to span oceans, continents, generations, and it seemed to swallow what is known of time. And it seemed to define infinite freedom, and it seemed, most importantly, to include her—all of her past—all of her future. He talked to her, about her, as she listened not only to his voice but also his heart which beat strongly with stories of its own. She fell in love with the expanse of his soul, with the layers and depth and warmth of him. She didn't want to leave him ever, or ever forget his voice.

He'd just gotten to the end of one of his many stories as Bella toddled sleepily outside and interrupted him with a request for chocolate milk.

"Ah, *not* down for the night, I see." He smiled, kissing the top of Sienna's head. "Which means you're probably up for the *whole* night, ay, Bell?"

He looked to Sienna and said, "I hope you'll be okay with driving some of the way tomorrow?"

"Sure."

"Okay, baby girl, chocolate milk it is," he said getting up then and helping Sienna to her feet. "We should have bought one of those chocolate cows and put it out back."

"Daddy, there are no such things as chocolate cows."

He went inside to make her chocolate. When he returned, Bella and Sienna were engaged in a whimsical discussion about which color of pony to purchase first.

"Your milk is on the counter, Bell, and your cartoon just came on."

"Bye, Bella. See you later, okay?" said Sienna as Bella jumped up to leave her.

"Okay, bye!" Bella replied, and then went into the main house to drink her chocolate milk and watch SpongeBob.

Jonathan and Sienna were left standing on the porch. Not exactly knowing what more to say and definitely not wanting to engage in the obvious, Sienna was about to leave, to pack and get rested for the next day. More importantly she wanted to remove herself from temptation…but there was something in the way he was looking at her that made her hesitate. It spoke to her and held her like his generational stories. It was too important to dismiss. Here was something that she had been searching for since she was born, but hadn't known it. She looked directly into him, softly questioning his beautiful eyes that spoke of the painful experiences of his life. He was looking at her in such a way that she could feel his heart—for his little girl—for her—for his disconnected past and everyone in it. She was finally recognizing how big his heart actually was. She finally acknowledged the vastness of his capacity to love. It overwhelmed her because it was so real. She was sharing his emotion and more importantly, his abandonment of the past pain and his turn toward hope. And it was happening with *her*. For a moment, she was overpowered by the unmistakable connection between them and she broke the gaze. She could hear it shatter like glass. Fragility, she learned, is not always a sign of weakness, but a standard by which only those who love large enough to stretch themselves beyond their own skin can measure. Sometimes the other person, the loved one, lets it drop. She wasn't about to miss it now. She began to move into him and he reached up, his hand warm against her cheek, not breaking his intense plea for her to engage—to notice him. To share with him this thing called life. He was inviting her in to all of it, into this sacred journey that is both a wretched and a beautiful mess. Both hands held her face tenderly, almost desperately, asking her to stay with him in this experience. He stayed like that for a time, until that moment when she just knew. And he was sure she knew—that she understood and committed to all that it meant. Before she'd see any tear fall, she knew they were there, just under the surface. He moved close to her and kissed her with a grace, power, and passion she'd never felt from any other man. She could feel his energy, his being, his soul—he enveloped her. He would have been too intense for someone not made exactly the same way. It was a heavenly match, better than home, to be this understood, to be this known.

Dear God, I thought this didn't exist, she said to herself. She gave Him a whole-hearted *thank You*. She smiled at the humor of God. *Leave it to You to give this to me now—when I wasn't looking for it, when I thought I no longer needed it. Here it is—in all it's glory. Love is the biggest thing there is. Love is God. God is love.*

And this was it—the real thing—and they both knew it.

When he pulled away it was to look at her face, into her welcoming gray eyes. The smile that progressively pulled on his lips was priceless. Happiness, relief, calm, and comfort filled it. He leaned his head back and laughed with pure joy. She'd never witnessed anything that beautiful.

He kissed her on the forehead, closed his eyes, put his forehead to hers, rocked her gently for a moment, and then looked at her again with pure love. He held her and she listened to his beautiful, warm heartbeat until SpongeBob was over and Bella returned for her dad. It was the best half-hour of television ever.

chapter nine

Mrs. Hopkins toddled in through Jonathan's door and went straight to the sofa without introduction. She made no apologies for lying down and covering herself with a blanket. Her eyes promptly shut, which was understandable, since it was nearly four o'clock in the morning.

Jonathan whispered, "She's great—just makes herself at home. I wish more people were like that, ya know?"

He smiled at Sienna for a moment then quietly asked, "Are you ready?"

"I think I am."

"Then let's go, baby."

As he kissed her forehead and she felt the warmth of his body, she wanted to hang onto that moment with him, but when the moment passed to their present endeavor and plans, she felt that warmth dissipate into the stark morning chill. By the time she opened her eyes he'd grabbed up most of the luggage and was reaching down for his black guitar case. Sienna gathered the two smaller bags remaining and remembered and went back for the thermos on the counter. The air was brisk, typical of the cold coastal mist, and went right through sweater and skin directly down to bone. She shivered as they hastily threw most everything in the trunk of his SUV, with the exception of Sienna's handbag, a couple extra sweaters, a map, and their travel mugs, which she wasted no time filling with steaming coffee.

He cranked the ignition, but he didn't put it in drive for a while. He just stared blankly at his house then, as if all the air left his chest, he whispered, "Dear God, I already miss her."

Sienna met his eyes with a look of empathy and he chuckled at himself, shaking his head at his own pathetic show of sentiment, but Sienna could see the genuineness underneath and was thankful she had witnessed the display.

He tried to explain, "That little girl is like the air that I breathe."

"I can see why," she said, missing Bella already herself.

He pulled out into the quiet street, checking his rearview mirror while asking if she wanted to stop by the hospital before they left.

"Actually, I have a card for Cheney in my bag. I could at least drop it off at the front desk. I doubt they'd allow visitors at this hour."

⁕

Sienna asked after her friend at the front desk and was told, as she expected, that no visitors were allowed until ten o'clock. A doctor on early morning rounds overheard the conversation and took Sienna aside.

"I thought you might want to know about Cheney's condition. Are you family?" she asked.

"No, just a friend," said Sienna.

"Well, she could probably use one of those about now. We are extending her stay for at least a week due to complications with her liver. And she's also severely malnourished. But between you and me, it might give her enough time to clear her head and make some better choices. I'm recommending she check herself into a long-term treatment facility. I haven't mentioned it to her yet, but I will in a couple days. If she cleans up now and starts taking care of herself, she might make it through health-wise. But I'm sure you are aware that if she keeps up her current lifestyle, she won't be so lucky next time. There's only so much a body can take."

"I understand. And thank you, Doctor...?"

"It's Dr. Lewis, and you're welcome."

Sienna dropped her card off at the desk and turned to go when she heard Cheney calling her name.

"Sienna, is that you? Come down here!"

"There are no visitors until ten a.m.," the nurse repeated, in a tone suggesting the beginnings of an outright irritation.

"Please let me talk to her," Sienna pleaded. "I'm going out of town for a few days and won't have another chance to see her."

The nurse eyeballed her for a moment then reluctantly conceded.

"All right, but just for a minute," she said. "And stay in the hallway so you don't bother her roommate."

"Yes, we will. Thank you."

Sienna rushed toward Cheney who looked tired and frail, even from a distance. She was standing alone at the end of the dark corridor, looking very small and significantly underdressed in her flimsy gown and cheap slippers. She was leaning against the wall, using the IV stand to keep herself upright.

"Cheney, should you be up?"

"Hi to you, too."

"Sorry. Hello. But seriously, shouldn't you sit down at least? Here..."

Sienna helped her to a vinyl, outdated chair then pulled up another one beside it.

"So how are you feeling?"

"How do I look like I'm feeling, Si? I feel like crap and I'm freezing. And let me guess how I got here—he did it, didn't he? Two things I hate—hospitals and him."

Sienna followed Cheney's glare back down the hall to Jonathan who had just come in from parking the car. He waved slightly to Sienna but came no further knowing full well that Cheney would attack him verbally, if not physically, blaming him for everything.

"He did it because he cares about you, Cheney," Sienna stated as she took her sweater off and covered her friend with it. "...and because you're Bella's mom," she added.

"Oh, come on, Si, I'm not her mom and I never will be. He always wanted me to be but that doesn't make it true, does it? I know who I am and I know what I am. You would think by now he would see it, wouldn't ya? You would think one of these days—one of these years—that he'd wake up and finally see me for what I am. He must be a special kind of stupid, don't you think?"

"No, I don't think that," Sienna said sternly. "I think he's been hopeful, not blind, Cheney. He's been giving you time and chances, he's been saving your life over and over again hoping one day you'll wake up—"

"—And be a mother," Cheney interrupted.

"Yeah...maybe...or maybe he just wants you to be all right for you. I know that's what I want."

Cheney looked down at her bruised hands, vacantly scanning the various places they'd stuck her with IV needles. She absentmindedly peeled back the tape securing the current one, replaced it, and then peeled it back again. Sienna became a bit squeamish watching her do this again and again. She had to be moving the needle, but she seemed completely immune to the pain. Finally, to Sienna's relief, she stopped.

"What if...," she said dreamily, but landed hard, "someone's only wish was to disappear in peace. Is that so terrible?"

"No, Cheney. It's just sad because you are worth so much more than that. And for some reason, you can't see that right now. You can't see what everybody around you sees—that you are so worth fighting for! You are so worth it."

Cheney looked vacantly down at the cold, hard floor.

"Cheney," Sienna said softly in soothing, comforting tones, "maybe you just need to give yourself some time. Don't decide right now if you want to disappear or if you want to stay. Just give yourself time, give yourself space and distance. Just linger here for a while. Ask me some questions, talk to me if you want to and, if not, just be silent. You don't have to go anywhere right away, do you? You don't have to disappear *right now*, do you? What if the very day after you disappear, everything changed? And if you'd just given yourself one more day here, you would have seen it. You would have found whatever it is you've been looking for. What if that happened, Cheney?"

"What if...," Cheney mumbled, sarcastically rolling her eyes back into her head.

"Yeah, what if something wonderful happens?"

Sienna placed a hand on her friend's arm, emphasizing the words she'd just spoken. Cheney smiled a weak and tired smile in return, partly longing for that something wonderful to happen and partly cynical, but it was there at least.

"And, Cheney, this life of yours is between you and God. No one else gets to vote. No one else gets to have an opinion. He created you because He wanted you. Your parents don't get to override God, Cheney. Your pain and your addictions do not get to override God. You have every right to be here, you have every right to be you. You have every right to breathe and be happy, Cheney.

"We all get into this chaotic, tragic existence at one time or another. And we all come to the point that we just can't take it anymore, not if we want to get beyond survival and to truly live well. I think everyone who has ever lived cries out for peace sooner or later. We claim we would give anything just to have some peace, so we step back, get right with God, and become open to changing our ways. To tell you the truth, it can be a little boring. Days, months, years go by and it seems we've accomplished nothing. There aren't any self-destructive adrenaline rushes anymore. We're not having near death experiences anymore; nobody seems to notice us anymore. But here's the secret: you take on the boredom, the loneliness, and you embrace your time with God and let Him do the talking for a change. You discover your God-given gift and start developing it. Before you know it, you start to understand the tremendous life-power in that gift. You finally know what it's like to feel alive as God would have it instead of how the world would have it. The world, if you let it have its way, Cheney, would want you adding to the problems or it would have you dead—either one. But when you live in peace, yeah, it's a slower pace, but it is so beautiful and so worth it, like growing your own roses as opposed to buying them at the grocery store...."

Cheney's face took on a twisted look of confusion, but at least it indicated that she was listening, so Sienna continued.

"Your own roses live forever. They outlive you if you take care of them. They bloom, unfold slowly, and they do so repeatedly through the seasons and years. You get to watch the whole thing happen—it's almost like their life is moving through you. The store-bought rose is already dying when you get it—you know? Do *your* thing, Cheney, not the cheaper version the world is trying to put off on you, because that's already dying when you get it. You are one of a kind, an original, authentic creation. Do the thing that is uniquely yours, not anybody else's, because that's *alive* and it always will be.

"And you say you want peace, that's good. You have to have peace in order to have the energy to fulfill the call on your life, to carry out the true thing you were put here for, in this exact time. It took me thirty years to figure out I write novels and it's slow, it's beautiful, it's what I was made for and I know that beyond a doubt. And I also know, Cheney, that you write songs. God needs you, Cheney. He needs you here, He needs you now, He needs you to be available to do what you do and to do it well. There's nothing better than that anywhere. You just have to get out of your own way."

Sienna looked into Cheney's glazed-over eyes, searching for one ounce of verve that she had perhaps roused from behind the deception, confusion, and the all-out catatonic sickness coating the woman's mind.

"You get what I mean here, Cheney?" Sienna finally asked in a tone indicating that her communicative efforts were spent.

"I get ya, I get ya, I get ya. I think I've heard it all before on TV, on an info-mercial or somethin'. And I don't mind tellin' ya I don't like to be preached to, but you are some kinda preacher, Si. You could probably make some money at it, the way you get all wound up about hearin' yourself talk. People like that kinda crap. And I gotta hand it to ya, you almost have me—*me* convinced that there's a reason to get up in the morning."

Sienna smiled at her. "There is."

Cheney stared blankly at the far wall, not saying anything, sort of falling into a stupor. Sienna sat next to her, quietly, watching the moments passing by them like choices left unmade. She felt the surges of blood flowing through her veins. She heard the seconds ticking on the clock that was timed within her Creator-given heartbeat and thought; *we only get so much time to decide these things, don't we?*

She looked over at her sick friend, scanning her person for a sign of hope so small like the eye of a needle in her arm she'd have to go through or a cloud the size of a man's hand in her smoky mind she'd have to think.

"It's been since before Bella was born," she said finally. "I haven't written anything. I don't even own a guitar anymore. Tell me something, Si. Do I have the right to quit if I want to? I mean quit everything, just stop it all. Do I have the right to escape? Permanently, I mean. What's wrong with that?"

Sienna's throat had gone dry, her palms were clammy, and what she wanted to say she didn't. What she wanted to talk on was the very subject of hell—that Cheney mentioned so flippantly, and what she wanted to ask was, "Cheney, have you ever looked down into the mouth of a volcano? Have you ever seen lava churning?" And, "Do you think God's a liar?" What she wanted to say was, "Then don't chance it, Cheney. Don't be stupid."

She wanted to say these things but she didn't. She bit her lip instead and considered Cheney's world. It was a world of hate, cruelty, and of cold-hearted, neglectful authority. And suddenly she knew, beyond a doubt, that Cheney needed to be brought into God's love, not hear about His judgment—which humans know next to nothing about.

"Yeah, you do have that right, Cheney...the right to quit," she said, "God gave you freewill—He's not going to force His will on you. But remember one thing for me, will you?"

"What's that?"

"Don't exercise your right to do anything unless you are in complete peace with God about it. And don't assume to know God without giving Him as much time as you've given the world."

Cheney stared at Sienna for a long moment.

"That's a long time."

"Yes, it is."

Sienna swallowed. She waited. She looked up at the Styrofoam ceiling, imagining the heavens beyond it. And she closed her eyes, breathing out slowly a silent prayer that her words had landed upon this lost one with grace and wisdom, power and enough love to save Cheney from herself.

Cheney's mood seemed to lift a bit, giving her enough energy to ramble.

"You're somethin' else, Si. You know that?" she said. "I remember the night that I called you. I was into it pretty heavy. My skin was crawling. I was out of my mind. I felt like I was giving birth to a baby and I have no idea why. I can still remember the pain—I mean physical pain to the point that I must have passed out. I remember waking up and I felt like I just had a baby but then I couldn't find her, like she was dead or stolen, maybe. I was in and out of consciousness, I guess. I remember that I woke up again still looking for her and I saw a little girl running and I knew she was mine—knew she was the baby I lost. She was running away from me and I opened my mouth to call out her name, but nothing came out. I didn't know what to say. I just started to scream because I didn't know my own child's name, Si. I couldn't remember her name but I could remember yours. My screams just started to turn into your name. I kept screaming your name over and over and over. I just kept calling for you until I must have passed out again. I still have no idea how I got your phone number. I don't remember dialing it. I was thinking about that last night, because I can't get any sleep in this place. I was up all night thinking about why I called you.

"A couple years back I heard from Mac—you remember her? Mackenzie—with the blonde hair?" asked Cheney.

"I do." Sienna nodded.

"She got in touch with me and we were talking about some of the people back at college and where they are now. She told me about your not having kids and about your husband. I'd forgotten all about it 'till last night, Si. It just didn't make any sense before, but I know the reason I called you, now. And you'd better listen to me. I'm only gonna say this once. I'm not even sure why I'm saying it now, but anyway....

"I didn't call you so you would save me. I called you because you are supposed to be Bella's mom, Sienna. I'm not her mother, Si. You are. Get it?

And Jonathan, well…he needs somebody like you. He's so loyal…to *me*! Look at everything I've put him through and he's still looking out for me! I'm embarrassed for him. He makes a fool out of himself every single day. Just stands there wide open with his heart all exposed and lets me knock the crap out of him. It's cruel what I've done to him. But he just takes it.

"And that girl of his…I mean, I'm not a mom, Sienna. One night, while I was pregnant, I threatened Jonathan that I would kill us both—the *baby* and me—if he wouldn't get me my fix. And I meant it, Si. Do you get it? I meant it and I was completely sober. I'm not a mother. But you—you are. I remembered you with your horses. I'm surprised you didn't sleep in the barn. And that stray dog you found in the campus parking lot? You'd take in anything and take care of it. Don't you get it, Sienna? You are the only good thing I can leave behind. You are the only thing I have to give Bella after I'm gone.

"And you are going to have to pay Jonathan back for me, for all the years I hurt him. I know you, Si. You're the only one who can. He's probably a royal mess by now, but will you do this for me? Tell me you will, Sienna. You need a family and they need you."

Sienna's breath had escaped her lungs and she was scrambling to remember how to take in another. She glanced at Jonathan who was still standing down the hall, intently watching them both from afar, and she knew, in that instant, that Cheney spoke the truth. It was just like her songwriting. She couldn't string two words of depth or meaning together in daily conversation to save her life. Months would go by and Sienna would wonder if the girl even carried a soul, she was more like an empty hollowed-out shell. This would go on like an endless drought until, out of the clear blue sky Cheney would have written the most amazing lyrics ever heard. The dorm room floor would be flooded. Papers, broken pencils, and guitar picks would be strewn all over like a cyclone had hit. And then she'd sing whatever amazing thing it was that flowed through her to the arid world like a summer rain. Pure truth hit like lightning, splitting soul tree to the ground, leaving an impossible fire line of wet black ashes and long soaked lashes upon the face of the one standing in awe because they'd been targeted personally, like the song had been written just to them. And the chances—the odds—of their hidden secrets being splintered and exposed, of their sculpted identity being stripped and left naked in the open air, had to be a million to one.

It was absolutely unforgettable to Sienna. The experience lingered long after; its sound leaving its mark on her memory like a brand. It would haunt the listener's ear forevermore, but it was odd, downright spooky in fact, how Cheney could forget them as though they'd never been. She'd simply move on, to something else, to nothing at all. She'd play them once, maybe twice to absolute perfection, and then they'd be gone from her forever—abandoned like the beautiful motherless child. When asked to repeat the song, she could barely hum a few notes of the melody, and then horribly off-key.

When Sienna roused herself from these memories of her college experiences, she found Cheney rubbing her head like she had a bad headache.

She mumbled, "I don't know what is wrong with me today. Must be some kinda medication they've got me on...God only knows what they're pushin' in these places."

And just like that, whatever divine revelations Cheney had held inside her had vanished. And Sienna just watched it evaporate from between them like morning fog beneath the sun. She didn't know what to say to reclaim it, so she just let it go.

"You never did miss it, Sienna," she said, "Any of it. Everybody else wanted to know what the songs meant, wanted to know where they came from. They wanted to get obsessed with them and take them in a perverted direction or they wanted to suck all the blood out of them and boil it down for cash, but not you. You were the only one who just listened, and waited, took them for what they were and let me toss them away. And you didn't miss any of them, Si."

Sienna took her opportunity, knowing Cheney was fading away.

"No, I didn't, Cheney. And—I want you to look at me—you're not done, Cheney. You are nowhere near done. Your songs are not all written yet. Do you hear me? You're the only one who can write them and so help me God, I am going to prove it to you."

Sienna hastily got up and jogged toward Jonathan, said something to him and he left. She quickly returned to Cheney and helped her back to her room and into her bed.

"You know why I forgot them, Si?" Cheney asked weakly. "Do you know why I tossed the songs away when they were done with me?"

"No, why?"

"They weren't mine to keep. They were never about me."

"Well, then I'm glad you called me, Cheney, if for no other reason than to put a guitar back in your hands. You need to write *your* song. Write the one about *you*."

Sienna did her best to smile encouragement, and Jonathan entered without looking at Cheney. He put his guitar in the corner and Sienna's Bible on the bedside table. He left the room as quietly as he came in.

He waited in the hall just outside the door and listened as Sienna spoke these words, "Cheney, do you know what it feels like to have finished a song, but there's no one there to listen to it? You know how it feels like the song doesn't really exist until somebody hears it, that it isn't really done until somebody gets it? That's how I feel when I finish a book and I'm waiting for it to be published. I feel like I'm suspended in mid-air and I can't hit the earth and walk again until it finds a reader. When it's finally placed in someone's hands who will read it, I can take my next breath at that point, ya know?"

"I do, I remember. That's what you did for me—you were my listener."

"Well," she went on, handing her Bible to Cheney, "God created this for us. There are songs in here that are so beautiful they make you cry and laugh at the same time. There are novels and stories and truth and dreams in here; there are turns of phrase and beautiful lyrics that have withstood hundreds of translations and have come out transcendent of language. Could you imagine creating this? But it's not done until it's been read. It's not finished until it's been heard, until somebody gets it."

Cheney held the Bible to her chest and nodded. "Thanks," she whispered as her eyes closed.

"Fight, Cheney," Sienna said and covered her lost friend with a blanket.

As she left the room, and met Jonathan in the hall, she felt little in the way of hope, but she knew she'd done her best.

It was a good thing that Sienna left the room when she did. The Bible remained unopened. Cheney's hands fell open; her arms slid down to her sides, the book plummeted to the floor. Special notes, collections, and a photo escaped their safe-keeping and scattered. Cheney's eyes opened wide, frozen in fright towards the ceiling. She couldn't move for there it was again, playing in her mind—that same song...the same...the same...the same as it had always been....She raised an arm, feeling her scars coming open, craving juice to bring the silence, having none, the song just grew louder. And this title was hers to carry—just as it had always been. She'd never sung her song out loud, couldn't quite get the first word out—the one preceding her name. It was *suicide*. If she could have found any other word for that one, she'd have replaced it, sang it out and been dead a long time ago.

And it was a good thing that Sienna didn't see this. Cheney sat up and she sang it anyway, shaking in terror and sealing her fate. Having nothing in the way of poison to kill it, she said the word. She said the word spoken to her since she was a girl. She said it as if reading the tombstone looming over her grave. She sung it as the title on a door in a thirty-year room where she could find no other way out.

Having nothing in the way of induced sleep to silence it, she sang the chorus out as if on a dare. It was a demon prayer. And knowing nothing in the way of spiritual warfare, she melodically condemned her own soul. Satan's use of God's gift by coloring it twisted, unraveling it backwards, displaying it as something segregate and splintered from the whole had cheapened her salvation just as the fatherly lie had been told.

Sorrowfully, to the utmost degree of all human sorrow, that's all it takes for these most precious, delicate things to come undone. So if it be a question at all, the answer is yes, yes, and yes. All people's souls are in eternal need of a Savior, and there be only One.

Cheney's hospital roommate made charitable use of her damnable state and made elderly haste, at that. The old woman had listened in quiet desperation and in paralyzing horror to that wicked, forsaken song. She had listened with tears innumerable falling down. And she didn't say a word—there was nothing to say to this—but she knew, whatever precious few moments, days, weeks she had left in this world, that she'd not take another breath in peace as she was. So she pushed a button, several panicky times. She grabbed the nurse's hand urgently—pulled the nurse close and she told her, "Dear God, young woman, please summon me a priest. Pick the Bible up off the floor and hand me that crucifix there on the wall. I want to hold it. I want it near me. Young woman, do as I say, please!"

chapter ten

ONATHAN AND SIENNA walked down the long, dark corridor in silence. They walked out into the misty morning drizzle, into the gray. He opened the car door for her, and once inside she consciously tried to stop shaking. She ordered herself to *just breathe*...as she held her trembling hand out level before her. She clenched it into a fist and dropped it, thinking about that cold and drafty hospital and its generic take on life. It was a stagnant place generally void of human compassion with its white sterile walls. Its white cloaked staff too accustomed or immune to death. But Sienna wasn't. Not at all. She shivered and rubbed her own arms briskly, trying to create heat. She'd left her sweater with Cheney, but she knew she wasn't trembling from the temperature anyway.

Jonathan got into the driver's seat. Next, he pulled out and draped one of his sweaters over her shoulders. He kept his arm around her and gently pulled her against his chest. He stared up at the blank hospital windows, wondering about the many lives hanging in the balance behind them. His arms, his chest, his heart absorbed the fear from Sienna. He knew exactly how Sienna felt. He didn't need to ask her to know that she felt Death itself breathing down her neck, sending chills down her spine and ice through her veins. He didn't need to ask her to know she felt herself to be an incompetent adversary. She had but moments in time to talk some sense into Cheney, but Death spun its lies constantly inside its victim's mind—day and night—asleep or awake. He didn't need to ask her to know she felt heartsick. Cheney had a way of making good-natured people feel like that.

Finally he spoke, softly and with care, politely pardoning the silence as if to ask its permission to step up alongside it.

"I won't ask you if you're okay because I know you're not," he said as he kindly stroked her hair.

"I know what it feels like to try to convince somebody to live. You feel like *you* are the thread they're hanging by. And sometimes you think you're gonna snap."

She didn't want him to see her crying, but she couldn't stop the tears. She stayed hidden there against his chest, and he let her, waiting 'till the last one fell away.

⚭

They stopped at a roadside diner just finishing its noon rush. There were still stray fries, crumpled—ketchup smeared napkins and an occasional dehydrated pickle or soggy potato chip stuck on the carpet. Their waitress looked a bit disheveled but had a pleasant demeanor as she asked, "What'll it be?"

They ordered and waited for their drinks to arrive. Jonathan called home and spoke with Bella for a while about graciously accepting Mrs. Hopkins' chocolate milk even though the woman made it very weak. Sienna couldn't help but laugh when she heard Jonathan's warnings, "No, Bell, you will not climb up on the counter to get the chocolate mix yourself. Do you hear me? Put Mrs. Hopkins back on the phone...."

"Mrs. Hopkins? Yeah...yeah, I know...No...Yes, that's fine. Yes, she probably does get a little rambunctious if she eats too much sugar but.... Yeah, okay....Okay. Okay. Thank you, Mrs. Hopkins. Okay, goodbye."

He rolled his eyes, shook his head and released a sigh, all while running his hand through his hair.

"I'm kinda glad I'm not there right now. The chocolate milk discussion never ends with Bella losing, I can tell you that."

His eyes were smiling as they met hers.

Wow, he's beautiful, Sienna thought to herself then managed to say, "I can fully understand that—girls and their chocolate. You can't mess with it."

Their lunch arrived and Jonathan mumbled a polite thank you to the waitress but didn't take his eyes off Sienna. He reached across the table for her hand.

"Sienna, you've been pretty quiet. I just want to make sure you're all right with this trip—I mean, being with a stranger and everything."

"I'm fine, really. I'm just tired. And I don't consider you a stranger, by the way."

She smiled up at him and he looked relieved.

She went on, "I guess I'm thinking about Cheney. Some of the things she

65

said, well…they're hard to forget. And I'm wondering about you, if you'll still like me after you see what I'm all about."

"That's one less thing to worry yourself with. I can guarantee that I'll like you always," he said simply.

"How do you know that? I mean, how can you be so sure when you really don't know me that well?"

Sienna started to pull her hand away, remembering the pain of severed past relationships, recalling her disdain for unfulfilled promises better left unmade, but he looked at her in such a way that it made her feel known and accepted. And it was suddenly clear to her that he knew more about the two of them, about their relationship and future, than she ever would. He already knew her frankly better than anyone else ever had, or ever would. They were a perfect match, too close for doubt to find a way in. It was an impossible reality that comforted her—someone to follow, someone fit and worthy of being the leader of another child of the King.

She had questioned him because she wanted to see the things he could, but that wasn't her gifting. Her judgment, her discernment, was clouded compared to his. There simply was no other way to walk beside him other than to trust him—with everything she was. He just seemed purer of soul than she, more honest and less complicated, and noticeably unmolested by the opinions and former approaches of the world—as if he'd made a conscious choice on the matter a long, long time ago.

He wasn't afraid of getting hurt, he wasn't afraid of it because he wasn't planning on it. And she was, though she'd hate to admit it. She still had marks of terror on her soul that she tried to ignore, that she tried so hard to erase. She was not aware that he could see the percentage of her life they'd taken, the exact scope of the memory they occupied, the present perception they distorted.

He hadn't removed his hand from atop hers, and when he spoke she felt heat release from it as he told her, "Give me all of you. Give me everything. I'll get to know you every moment of every day—and I'll never assume to know you completely, no matter how many years go by. People do change, Sienna, but not that much if they know who they are from the beginning—and I do—and so do you. I can tell.

"What I'm trying to say is, I'll never get tired of getting to know you. Ever. You fascinate me and you always will."

She didn't know what to say to that. He leaned forward, looking intently into her searching eyes until they landed on his and stayed.

"Sienna," he whispered, "I'm not going anywhere. And if you trust me, give me some of your time, you won't want me to. Okay?"

She nodded and smiled and he gently squeezed then let go of her hand.

"And just so you know," he added, "I'm not interested in your past. I'm interested in you and who you want to be."

She took the time to completely acknowledge what he was saying, and she found herself amazed that his disposition hadn't changed, not at all, since their first kiss. He was committed to her for life—she just couldn't believe she finally found what she'd searched for her entire lifetime. He was stable. He was self-assured. He was selflessly giving.

He changed the subject as he started to eat, and asked her, "So what is it that you believe in?"

She hesitated for a moment, trying to recall if anyone her whole life had ever asked her that question. She could think of no one.

"Well," Sienna said thoughtfully, "God. The desire to find true love on the earth, or a taste of God moving through man, you know—here—now. I don't think we are supposed to only find it in heaven, after we die. You know what I mean?"

"I do." He smiled.

"I believe God is moving," she said, "Always. And I believe each person is born with a God-given gift and most of them know what it is when they are like five years old, ten at the most. But the world sort of comes in and takes over and snuffs it out, but if people would stay in that gift and perfect it, they'd be happy. Passionate. Interesting. More alive. They'd never be bored or dissatisfied."

"I agree," he said thoughtfully.

"And I believe in butterflies..."

"Butterflies...?" He lifted a brow inquisitively.

"Yeah, butterflies as a demonstration of the redemption process."

"What do you mean?"

"Worm is unsaved man, right? Wallowing around blind in the dust, not accomplishing much but having plenty of company, eating all the "crap," should we say, the world has to offer and getting sick on it. The cocoon is when your life crashes in around you, you think you're dead—that it's all over.

You're wounded, completely alone, separated, in the dark. You completely liquefy. You completely turn to water, you completely change. You struggle for life, each breath is a challenge. And finally you emerge completely changed and beautiful—saved. And you can fly. You can see everything from above."

"You've gone through that, I take it."

"I have. You?"

"Yeah, at least in part, but I've never heard it put like that before."

"I have a much more eloquent version written down somewhere, like most die-hard writers, I can't speak incredibly well. Most of the time I don't talk at all."

"I think you're doing fine," he encouraged, "What else you got?"

"I believe our lives are so much better with God in charge."

He had quit eating and was staring at her.

"What?" she said, feeling sheepish.

"Nothing," his eyes darted down as he shook his head.

"Something," she replied.

"Well...I've never heard anyone talk like you do. I've only asked a few people what they believe, and they say something general like 'peace' or 'love' or 'death and taxes.' I've never found anyone who actually *knew* what they believed in. It's...refreshing—that's what it is. But in all fairness, I should warn you."

"About?"

"I use conversations."

"You 'use' them—to write songs?"

"Exactly."

"So this means you're going to write a song about me."

"Already have."

She started to laugh and he joined her.

"That's better," he said.

"It is much better. I'm starting to feel better. Thank you."

"You're welcome."

The waitress refilled their beverages and left the bill behind.

"Okay, in all fairness, I get to ask you a question now," she said.

"Anything."

"When am I going to get to hear it?"

"I'll let you know," he smiled and ate a fry.

"Okay. Here's another one. How did you come up with Bella's name?"

"Ah, now you're gonna get me misty eyed." He smiled, looking inward to a fond memory.

"Well, it was just the two of us against the world. She was so small I was afraid I was going to break her. I was wondering how this tiny person was going to survive. I was walking with her and introducing myself to her and figured I'd better find her a name, so I asked her. I said, 'What's your name, sweet baby girl?' And just then the church bells rang and I looked out the window and the sun was just coming up over the steeple. It was beautiful. But—here's the most astounding part to me—I heard her voice, ringing in off those bells. I had no idea then what her voice would sound like, so I know I didn't make it up. I remember it like it was yesterday—she said her name to me in her voice, *Bella Maura*. Bella Maura, which I later found out means beautiful, wished-for child. And what you were just saying, about how most people know their God-given gift at five years old?"

"Yeah...?"

"Bella Maura Driscoll. Driscoll means interpreter or messenger, so her complete name means beautiful, wished-for messenger. And here's the thing, Bella can pick up on languages unlike anyone I've ever heard of. Most people think I teach her those Irish stories, but I don't. She just knows them. She just knows the language. I mean words I usually don't speak? She says them, in her stories, and they're right. I mean she just *knows* them. I've never told anyone that."

"I believe you. You know that day at the beach, when I was watching her? She was saying prayers, Irish prayers, then she'd tell me in English what they meant and they were advanced—like very mature, adult prayers. They weren't memorized. She has a gift."

"God-given, right?"

"Absolutely. She's fearfully and wonderfully made."

They had arrived at the end of the conversation. Their souls were light. They'd found in each other validation of personality, identity acceptance, in other words, a home. For so long, they'd had conversations like these only within their own minds. No one else proved trustworthy enough to encourage such openness. No one else could relate, but, now, here they were, effortlessly communicating together. Pretences had fallen away and were gloriously useless.

Jonathan paid the tab and left a tip. On the way out he held the door for Sienna.

"By the way, Bella really likes you, Sienna. She feels safe and accepted with you. She must because she hasn't ever opened up like that, you know? She's never told her stories to anyone but me before."

chapter eleven

EW HAVEN WAS more beautiful than Jonathan had anticipated. Several turns down unfamiliar streets eventually led them to Sienna's house which was nothing like Jonathan had envisioned.

"Wow. This is yours?" he asked, wide-eyed as he got out of the car.

"It is." She nodded. "I've been very blessed. Oh . . . and I'm sorry in advance for all the women."

"What?" He smiled with a hint of uncertainty.

"If it gets to be too much for you, I've got a big back yard you can escape to anytime. Come on, I'll show you around."

She led him through meticulous landscaping, down a curved brick and lighted path, toward a huge timber frame, two-story stone house with a copper roof. There were several small, wrought-iron balconies around walk-out doors on the upper level. An attached greenhouse projected off one side of the square structure. The main door was substantial to say the least, oversized and made from solid hardwood that had been stained to a rich umber tone. She turned her key in the lock and opened up for him her world. Inside were warm hardwood floors and ceiling beams, a tremendous window-scape and a large stone fireplace. There was a vast open space and a large staircase which led to a balcony lined with doors leading to several bed and bathrooms. The furnishings were elegant and comfortable and dotted with books and blankets. End tables were decorated with lamps, glasses half-full, notepads, and bottles of nail polish.

Two muscular dogs rushed to greet Sienna who dropped her share of the baggage aside to scratch them behind the ears.

"These are the dogs I was telling you about. The Lab is James and the Rot is Calvin. Don't worry, he only looks mean, but he's really a teddy bear."

"The spike collar really says 'teddy bear' to me," Jonathan joked.

Four young women entered the room then and started hugging Sienna in turn, all of them talking at once. Their shrill voices and excited energy set the dogs to barking, and the noise the group created steadily broke down the advertized tranquility of the furnishings and impeccable design.

"Oh, girls," Sienna found a slim opportunity to interject, "let me introduce you to Jonathan Driscoll. Jonathan, these are my girls. This is Mia. Mia is studying foreign language, she knows Irish and she is also a five-star chef, if you ask me."

"Sienna, I'm not that good," said Mia.

"Yes, you are. You should cook something while Jonathan is here."

"I'd be an honest judge, I promise," Jonathan said while shaking her hand.

The other girls giggled and looked at each other in regard to his accent and his looks.

"And this is Jackobie," Sienna continued. "Jackobie has been with me the longest. She's a brand new M.D. We are very proud of her."

"Nice to meet you, Jonathan," she offered.

"And then we have Katarina, or Kat as we call her, who is a biology major. She's the one responsible for the landscaping and the greenhouse looking the way it does. She's amazing. And this...." Sienna paused for a moment, a look of pride in her eyes, pulling the girl forward almost against her will. "...this is Aurora. She's a musician, too. She's very gifted so I suspect you two may want to get together to play and discuss music. Jonathan is also a musician, sweetheart."

"What, no guitar?" Aurora asked haughtily from beneath a cocked head of pink and black and white-blonde punk hair.

"Well, I did have one but—it's a long story, I guess. Maybe you can lend me yours?"

"We'll see," she said and then she retreated into the kitchen.

"Never mind her," Katarina offered. "She warms up eventually. Must be the hair."

"Yeah," Mia seconded. "It's the hair. It's like a full-time job. Sometimes it makes her cranky."

They all chuckled.

"Well, girls, we're going to get settled in. We are both pretty tired after the drive."

"We'll take your bags up, then we'll disappear for a while and give you two some alone time," Kat teased.

"Nice to meet you all," Jonathan said.

The girls giggled and departed, one of them saying, *He's soooo cute,* under her breath.

"I'll show you to your room. You can stay in Katarina's room. It's got its own private bathroom," Sienna said.

"Are you sure she won't mind?" he asked.

Shaking her head "no" Sienna explained, "Kat's getting married this summer, so when she's not at school, she spends most of her time with her fiancé and his mother, who just happens to be a professional wedding planner. Very exciting—compared to being here, I'm sure—so you should have plenty of privacy."

"Okay."

"I'm going to get cleaned up. I'll meet you downstairs in a bit if you want? We should have the place to ourselves for a while anyway."

"Sounds good," he said and pulled her into a warm hug. "Thank you for having me."

⬳

Curled up on the sofa in front of the fire, Sienna was doing her best to read a novel but found it hard to concentrate knowing Jonathan was in her house. Her dogs were both napping by the hearth. It was so good to see them, she'd missed their comforting presence over the last week. She was anxious to see her horse but would have to wait until the next day because she was just too exhausted to drive out to the stables—and of course, Jonathan *was in her house.*

She superficially read another paragraph and, having absolutely no recollection of a single word or concept, she tossed the book aside and took a sip of red wine. As she peered over the rim of her glass, she caught sight of him walking across the balcony. He was in a sleeveless white t-shirt and jeans. His meticulously cut hair was still wet from showering and slightly spiked. The sunset had magnified the colors of the evening sky to a luminescent peach and the windows behind him served a remarkable highlight to the beautiful way that he moved. He caught her staring at him, and he smiled a certain sideways smile which indicated that he lacked no confidence in the way that he looked. As he navigated his way down the incredibly long staircase, particular features of his stood out to her one by one, such as his beautiful eyes and their soft sweetness, his high cheekbones with their pride and curvature which lead to a strong and determined jaw line. She followed the tanned skin of his muscular shoulder down his arms, sparingly tattooed and amply defined with natural curve and line, all the way down to his strong and patient hands—hands that held his baby, held a guitar, held a pen for hours—scribbling creatively, hands that held on to promises made no matter what they cost, no matter how long ago they were made; hands that were left empty, holding nothing but the question of reaching out again.

Simply put, she couldn't take her eyes off of him because his body was amazing. The way he carried himself was sublime, with sweet and kind nobility and a directness that was unapologetic for making her think the things she found herself thinking. But as he came closer to her and looked into her, it was the man inside—it was his kind heart and his selfless generosity that stole away her breath.

He reached for her glasses, gently taking them off her face and placing them on the end table. He kissed her forehead, he kissed her mouth, and then more passionately again, somewhat losing himself and then stopping. He pulled back apologetically, his forehead resting against hers. He took a slow breath then he smiled and sat down beside her, holding her in his arms. They watched the fire silently for a time.

"You're an amazing person, you know that?" He whispered it into the back of her hair.

He closed his eyes for a long moment, genuinely opening his heart to her, feeling it happen—it had been a long, long time. "You're beautiful," he said, "You are. You're beautiful to me. Thank you for letting me follow you home."

She stared into that mesmerizing fire and found a knowing there, like a message decoded from the century center of that deep forest tree befallen, now hissed as heated voice released; like a soul whisper that cometh on the midnight breeze independent of the summon and the wished star, irrefutable in its holy directness, unfathomable calendar and its target lands, a timely wisdom sent out a thousand years yet afloat and emergent as liquid on one knight's crying stone and written on tablet, carved and branded, bleeding ink treasure for the history book be made. And in this mystic conversation through the embers of that fire and those deepest in the hidden recesses of her soul, she felt the man at her back had always been waiting somewhere in her future and the reason why was more than the human heart could comprehend.

All of that, plus one other thing it told her. *In the vastness of these things there can be made no room for fear....*

Not knowing what else to say, she said this in a whisper, "I'm glad you're finally here."

She turned toward him, looking steadily, seriously into his eyes. He held her gaze without question. He just waited on her like he had for years.

"I hope you are brave," was all she said and he felt her sweet intention, fearful, timid, but willing to find out no matter the road. She was starting to trust him, she was starting to follow her heart, almost as if she didn't have any other choice.

"I might surprise you on that," he said sweetly. "The one thing I am is brave. Me brother says it's the same thing as havin' no common sense. I don't know, he might be right—though I don't want ya tellin' him that. Have we got a deal?"

Slowly, her stone-serious expression turned upwards into a smile and she agreed, "Deal."

He kissed the back of her hand then gently rubbed it introspectively.

"I'm wonderin'," he said, "if maybe you'll keep me, then? Maybe if I pass the test with your girls here?"

He looked up to her with pleading, almost boyish eyes. There were no games with him, no pretensions whatsoever. She'd never met anyone that open and vulnerable while being completely aware and intelligently unashamed. And it worked. Completely. There was no way it could fail. Pure honesty, knowing oneself thoroughly, has a drawing factor about it. He possessed a comforting appeal greater than that of a conqueror of many lands or the inheritor of any amount of worldly wealth.

"I've been wondering the same thing," she told him.

"You have?" He smiled.

"Don't worry, these girls will all love you. They will."

"Good, they make me a little nervous, ya know? They are like your daughters, right? Except you're way too young. If you don't mind me askin', how did you find them? Are they just boarders?"

"No, not exactly. They're all foster kids, or they were in the system until they were eighteen. Most of them were fending for themselves, pretty much, when I found them. First it was Jackobie—she's been with me the longest. I found her on a park bench. I'd go to walk my dog and there she was almost every day. I started taking her sandwiches and we'd just talk. She told me about her past; her present didn't look much better, and one day out of the blue she said, 'You wanna hear somethin' funny? I'm going to be a doctor someday. I don't know how, but I know that's what I'm here for.' I told her that it wasn't funny at all. I told her she should do it. And, well...one thing led to another and she moved in with me and I adopted her pretty much—unofficially, of course. It was the best thing I ever did."

"Med school—you paid for her school?"

"Yeah."

"At Yale? That's got to be..."

"Yes, it is," she confirmed.

"She's gonna pay you back, right?"

"Someday she will. And I don't mean monetarily. It never hurts to have a doctor out there on your side, right? No, that's one of the stipulations. They have to learn how to accept it as a free gift—they have to learn how to accept kindness freely—no strings. That's the only way they'll ever learn how to give kindness freely."

"You'd do all that for a stranger?" he said in awe.

"Well, before I did I seriously prayed about it and I felt that God wanted me to do it. And now, it's amazing, really. I mean she's not a stranger. She's my daughter, or my sister. Well, I don't know, they're just 'my girls.' They're my family now, at least as far as I'm concerned. Jackobie found most of the other girls, except Aurora. I heard her and fell in love with her voice before I even saw her. She was downtown on a street corner singing her heart out for dimes, pennies, dollar bills if she was lucky. I heard that kid's voice three blocks away, echoing through the brick buildings, and, I don't know how to explain it...I just fell in love with her—just like that. It took her a long time to warm up to me, a *really* long time, but I love that girl with my whole heart. I have since that day. She is so amazing when you get to know her."

"Yeah," he said, looking intently at her. "I think I know what you mean."

"And these girls are so helpful and appreciative. They cook, they clean, they garden—this place wouldn't look so good without them. That's the part I'm worried about. Pretty soon they'll all be gone. All of them—Jackobie's basically moved out, Kat's getting married this summer, Mia is graduating, and Aurora wants to study music abroad for a year."

"But she's coming back, right?"

"I don't know. But that's not what I'm doing this for, you know? They are totally free. I'm just here to help them for a while. If they keep in touch with me, that's just a bonus."

"They will. I can tell by the way they were hugging on you today. They love you. They won't forget about you. I can see that."

Then changing the subject a bit, he asked, "So what are you going to do for your year off?"

"I don't know," she said. "I guess look for somebody else who needs a temporary mother."

What if it's not temporary, he wanted so badly to ask, but he didn't.

chapter twelve

*T*HE NEXT MORNING, Jonathan was making his way to the kitchen to get a cup of coffee and happened upon Sienna and Katarina having an involved conversation at the breakfast bar. Kat noticed him enter and pulled her hand back from Sienna's, quickly trying to regain composure. She wiped her eyes with a tissue. Obviously she'd been crying for a while.

"Sorry," he said quietly. "I'll just go—"

"No, it's okay," Sienna interrupted him. "Come on in and I'll pour you a cup of coffee. There's some fruit and bagels, too, if you're hungry."

"Are you sure it's all right? I can come back."

"No, Jonathan, come on in. Make yourself at home," Kat insisted. "I'm sorry. I'm just a mess right now. No offense, but men—"

"Are jerks." He finished for her. "We are. I know."

Katarina looked to Sienna and back to him with an inquisitive look.

He continued, "We're insensitive and clueless, all of us. I know. I have a daughter—a little girl—and I don't want her to grow up because I can see what's coming. I think I'm just going to beat them all within an inch of their lives...right when they walk in the door."

Katarina started giggling through her tears and said to Sienna, "I like this guy. I do." She then left the room.

"Thank you," Sienna said to Jonathan. "She needed to laugh."

"Yeah, no problem. What's going on?" he asked.

"Bachelor party."

"Oh."

"Tomorrow night."

"Ah."

"Apparently his friends don't have standards, if you know what I mean. And her fiancé—Dillon's his name—isn't doing much to stop them."

"Not a wise move."

"Not so much, no."

"Where's the party?"

"At a club downtown."

"I could talk to him, if you think it might help," he offered.

"It couldn't hurt. I'd appreciate that and I think Kat would too."

"Then we'll have to time it right because I was going to ask you out on a date tomorrow night. Are there any nice places downtown?"

"I know a great place." She smiled.

They finished their breakfast slowly as the morning light lifted through the eastern sky. Shadows of girls passed now and again through the kitchen, their quiet intrusions blocking the warmth of the windows momentarily. Smirks and smiles remained cast toward the floor. Sienna didn't notice much of anyone but him. He was even better looking in the morning, she decided. She traced with her eyes the faintest mustache and goatee he'd left from his last shave. She wondered how many tattoos he had under that shirt. And she wondered how long it would be until she could see them.

"Let me show you something," she said.

She led him into the greenhouse which was much larger than it had appeared from the front of the house. It held miniature banana trees, orange trees, lemon trees, tomatoes, other vegetables, salad greens, and nearly every flower imaginable. She took his hand and they walked around a large circular fountain that contained several coy fish. She gave him a customary penny and he made a secret wish. On the far side of the fountain lay a large swimming pool and an inset hot tub designed to look like a natural pond.

"This is really nice," he said, "it's beautiful."

"Feel free to use it anytime. There's a shower and changing room just back there."

As the tour continued, she led him out French doors into a huge, landscaped backyard. Willow trees and apple trees and shrubs dotted the area, most just beginning to leaf out. A few robins were scattered about the lawn.

"This is all fenced in, so the dogs can come out here. The back porch is nice, it's good for creativity. I write out here a lot. Which reminds me—I owe you a guitar."

"I was going to talk to Aurora about that. Maybe I can borrow hers 'till we head back. If she's willing that would be fine. Hopefully Cheney hasn't smashed mine to bits yet."

"I hope she's doing okay."

"So do I," he said, and more quietly, "that's my favorite guitar."

They went back into the house, and she showed him the small gym room and the game room in the basement.

"This house is really exceptional. It's like a resort or something. Did you design it?"

"No, but I love how they did it—the previous owners. The only thing I added was the greenhouse and we just refurbished the pool last year."

"So, I overheard you telling Cheney that you write books—novels, I think you said?"

"I do. Let me show you my room."

They climbed the stairs still holding hands.

"My bedroom is a little unorthodox. It's actually a library which happens to have a bed in it. I don't really sleep regularly."

She opened the door to a great rectangular room with floor-to-ceiling mahogany shelves filled with volumes of books. The windows, perfectly centered on the far wall, were actually tall glass doors that led out to a quaint balcony overlooking the pool. They were framed by long silk olive-green curtains that spilled onto the dark wood floor like liquid. In the far corner was a big, red velvet chaise. The four-poster bed was casually layered in more olive silk and ivory linens, left unmade with several of the pillows scattered about it and the floor. The room was very elegant and was in fact an impressive library with a massive bed in its center. It was exquisitely luxurious but its layout simple. Hidden complexities resided in the intimidating, staggering number of books, all of which no one could possibly read—not in two lifetimes.

"You don't really sleep?" he repeated in a semi-question as his eyes scanned hundreds of leather-bound books.

"Sometimes, but most of the time I wake up dreaming in legends, colors, blood, sometimes light. I wake up in the middle of somebody's meadow—or their worst nightmare. I feel what they feel. See what they want me to see. Mostly I dream other peoples' lives, I guess. Their amazing love stories, and their tragedies—the gross injustices they've suffered and taken to the grave in silence...you know...secrets they now want to share with the world. And it's my job to turn them into...well, words that are hopefully true to their intention. I wake up in the middle of conversations I am having with people I've never met before, so I go to my computer and I'm up all night recording what happened, what they wanted to say. It's like I'm telling their stories, not mine. I generally have three or so books going at once."

"That must be exhausting."

"It can be, but it's mostly exhilarating to me. I'm very used to it. But I'm sure it would be hard on someone next to me."

"I'd get used to it," he said then quickly moved on. "So, what have you written?"

"The top shelf over here—this is me."

He started looking over the titles and the pseudonyms.

"Wait a minute!" he said hesitantly. "You're *him*?"

Sienna grinned, her eyes darting to the floor. "Don't tell anyone."

"But you're *him*," he repeated. "You've had movies done—you're talking A-list here."

"Well, I'm primarily on the B, C and D list—for some reason *that* series was deemed marketable. I've got to tell you, he's not my favorite version of myself."

"This whole shelf—all these writers are you?"

"Yeah—well, a reader ties certain expectations with a name. You change your style too much and you lose your following, ya know? I'm sure it's the same in music. Aurora, for instance, is a brilliant classical artist, but she's also in a punk band. She actually changes her hair more than anyone would think possible."

"Yeah—no, I get it. I do. I'm just...I mean you're...." he stammered.

"A lot to take in," she conceded.

"In a good way—in a very good way—but yes! I've got to admit, I'm a little intimidated. I feel like I'm out of my league here."

"I don't believe in leagues—just people. I'm the same person I was before we walked in here. I just have a writing obsession is all."

"Looks like I've got some reading to do."

"I've probably got a lot of listening to do, too. And I'm thinking you'll probably make me feel a little out of my league at that point."

He laughed and grabbed her in a whimsical hug, rocking her back and forth, "Are you kidding me, though? This is incredible—I just rented that movie like a month before I met you. And I gotta tell you, the reason I rented it. Bella's prayers—some of them seem to describe that character. It's...well, it's strange, a little. I mean for a five-year-old, isn't it? To pray about..."

"Vindication?"

"Yeah. I mean I don't let her watch anything questionable on TV, so I have no idea where she gets it."

"I think I might know," Sienna said quietly.

"You think it's that 'God-given gift' thing?"

"I do."

"But how could she know about things that awful?" he asked as he started to pace.

"How does anyone?" Sienna replied. "Children, in a lot of ways, are far wiser than adults, they can discern spiritual things so easily."

"Maybe you're right but... Oh, wait a minute!" he stopped his pacing mid-stride, instantly enthralled with something in the back corner of the room. "You have a baby grand. You have a baby grand *in your bedroom.*"

"Yeah, I do." She grinned. She followed him, watching him gravitate toward it. He touched it gently as if to ripple an introduction through its waters, and then he ran his hand over the pure black finish as if to dive into its layers of oil. The name whispered and read of gold script was barely audible as it dripped off his lips.

"May I?" he managed.

"Absolutely. Sit." *Before you melt*, she thought.

He found his place on the crushed velvet seat. On the piano's surface, a cast iron candelabrum held a triad of nearly burned down ivory candles.

"You spend a lot of time here," he said quietly. He looked to the opposite side, down to the floor, and came up with severely worn sheet music, "So you're studying..." and he hesitated when he saw the titles, his voice started to waver as he spoke them, "Beethoven, Sonata Fourteen, 'Moonlight' and Chopin, Ballade One."

He put the music on the piano with a slightly trembling hand. He sat very still and didn't attempt to touch the keys. He didn't look at her for a while, and then when he finally looked at her said, "You know I just officially, *completely,* fell in love with you, right?"

Sienna blushed and glanced toward the floor, but he reached for her hand.

"I have never been more serious," he said. "I *heard* you."

She finally looked at him. "What do you mean?"

"I heard you, *felt* you, playing. I know it sounds crazy, but I knew what you would sound like.

"I heard these two songs being played—I mean I'd wake up to it in the middle of the night, couldn't get them out of my head all day—six months ago, it started. And I could feel you—your breath, your skin, your warmth. But mostly...I could feel your heart. You were calling out to me and I had this unbelievable longing to find you, but I didn't know what it all meant, so I kept trying to force it out of my mind. I didn't realize...I mean, I didn't recognize that it was really you until just now. It's you, Sienna. I could hear you. I knew what you would sound like."

"Are you sure you're not..."

"Projecting? No, Sienna. I'm not. It's the same thing as when Bella told me what her name was before she could speak, remember?"

"Yes, I remember."

"I'm not a classical music sort of guy, Sienna. But I know these two songs by heart. I've never played them myself—ever. I never heard them before they started coming to me six months ago. I know these are the songs I heard. I know what they—what *you*, sound like."

Without saying a word, she walked around him and reached for some matches on a nearby shelf. She lit each candle as he watched her. She slowly walked across the room and drew the shades and the day got lost in the dark of night. She gestured toward the bed and he left the piano and lay amid silken down that smelled like her skin to listen and to watch while she played the most heartfelt version of the sad and epic music that seem to call out for love and light. She played mostly with her eyes closed. And, as times before, she played in a language that only her true love would understand. And his eyes, layered with color and with meaning, witnessed amidst the candlelight that he did.

chapter thirteen

"I'VE HEARD THAT all Irishmen can fish, build a wall out of stone, and ride horses. Is that true?"

"No, not at all," he said with a chuckle. "Most of us can find a pub without much problem, though."

"Well, there aren't any pubs where we're going. I'd like to take you riding."

"Thank God, I thought you were going to make me build a wall."

"No, that's later, after—"

"—the fishing," they both said together.

They smiled at each other for an inquisitive moment. He was wondering what he was in for. It had been a long time since he'd been around horses. She was trying her best to discern if the love of horses ran in Bella's family or if she was opening up an opportunity for disaster. People, in her experience, either loved horses or they didn't.

"Okay then," she said, becoming animated. "I have to go to town and get a few things first. I'll ask Aurora to lend you her guitar if you feel *inspired* or anything while I leave you alone. I have inspired you, haven't I?" she teased.

"Yes, you certainly have. Actually, you fascinate me. And if I don't write something about it soon, I might implode. I think I'll go to the back porch— your creative place, right? You'll be like an hour or so?"

"Around that, yeah. I'll ask Aurora to bring the guitar to you, cause I need to get going."

"Okay, I'll see you soon."

∞

Jonathan let the dogs into the back yard and played fetch with them until Aurora arrived on the porch, guitar in hand, hair spiked even higher than the last time he'd seen it. He wondered *how is that gravitationally possible?*

"Thank you, you're a life-saver," he gushed as he took the steps two at a time. She reluctantly handed it over to him, popped her gum and stared at him through an intense amount of eye makeup.

Finally she managed, "Scratch it and you're dead."

"Absolutely." he nodded. "Wouldn't think of it."

"That's the problem," she said.

"What is?" he inquired and took a seat on the top step. He glanced at her and all the metal on her face and ears caught the light and his eye. He silently counted the piercings on her eyebrows, lip, chin, and earlobes which all held tiny silver studs. He got up to seven on just her right side alone.

"People," she answered simply. "They don't think much. Not really. Not that I can see. Ya gotta tell 'em *everything*, ya know?"

"That's true," he agreed, growing more curious, and a bit more nervous, about where the conversation was headed.

"You're hot," she conceded. "In a good way. How old are you?"

"Uh...I'm thirty-three, actually. And thanks, I think."

"Welcome, *maybe*."

Her cool sarcasm hung in the air between them as she rolled her gum up in a wrapper and put it in her pocket.

"Smoke?" Her gesture was a peace offering, but her black-lined eyes were still glaring.

"No, I don't smoke."

"Tough crowd," she said under her breath as she pulled a pack and lighter from one of the many hiding places in her complicated outfit.

"I'm trying to quit—thus the gum. Problem is...I hate gum and I like to smoke."

"It's tough to quit bad habits—tough, but not impossible." He smiled encouragement up to her.

She sucked on her cigarette and got completely lost in it for a moment—like she was lying in a field between two tobacco rows, staring up at the sun and praying for a fireproof rope to pull it down. Finally, she came back.

"You were in a band then? Anybody, I'd know?" she asked.

"Maybe. Here..." and he played part of a couple of his hits, then some of the more popular songs he wrote recently that were recorded by other musicians.

"You...wrote those?" she scoffed.

"You don't believe me?" he asked, looking genuinely perplexed.

"Oh...I see, you're one of those sensitive types. Don't take it personal. Sienna says I have this wall up. I'm workin' on it, okay? So, sorry—you're real good—if that's really your stuff."

Jonathan stared at her for a moment. His mouth was open as if to speak but nothing would come out.

"Oh...see, I did it again. Sorry—I'm sure it's your stuff. Okay? We good? I've got what Sienna calls trust issues."

"I understand," he said.

"I don't think you do," said Aurora with a shrug and shake of her head, "So, I'm gonna help ya—Sienna? She's good people. Well, she's pretty much the only good person I know. So I don't want you to scratch her—like that guitar. I don't want you to hurt her. Understand?"

"Yeah, I do. I don't want to hurt her either—and I won't," he reassured her.

She appeared completely unaffected by his words, and she ground her cigarette out with her sneaker then flung it off. She took off her jacket and started unbuttoning her jeans and sliding them down.

"Hey!" Jonathan yelled as he jumped up and averted his eyes. "Don't do that—put your clothes back on!"

"Calm down, pretty boy. You're not my type," she retorted. "You didn't scratch my guitar jumpin' around like that did you?"

"No, I didn't scratch your guitar," he said with his back to her.

"You better not have," she warned.

He took a deep breath and tried to calm his mind. He softened his voice and finally asked over his shoulder, "What are you doing?"

"I'm showing you truth," she said. "If you can handle going to the beach—all the bikinis and what-not—you can handle my pink polka-dotted underwear. Turn around and look at me, I'm not gonna stand here like this all day—it's too cold."

"Why?" he asked.

"Why is a question without any answers," she said by rote, as if quoting something from an uninspiring AA meeting.

He slowly turned around and looked at her and suddenly it registered what he was seeing and he felt the wind knocked out of him. He nearly dropped to his knees.

"You'd better sit before you fall over."

He obeyed. And she quickly dressed herself to keep from shivering.

"Do you need my jacket?" he asked quietly, shaking a little himself.

"No," she said and went to sit next to him to put her sneakers back on. "I didn't show you my body for sympathy or to shock you. I showed you because people don't think abuse is real if they can't see it."

"What happened," he whispered, looking into her eyes. She coldly noted the tears starting up in his.

"I don't have the seventeen years it would take to tell you. Short version—and I don't tell people this—I mean, I don't want you to tell anybody about this, got it? Sienna already knows, but—short version—my step-father was sexually and physically abusive. There are also scars on the inside of me. Like Sienna, I can't ever have any kids of my own. My step found out I was pregnant by him and he tried to take care of it himself, if you know what I mean. Somebody found me dumped in a vacant lot and nearly dead. You all right? You look sick."

"Dear God..." he muttered. *Like Sienna?*

"Dear God! That's what I said. He didn't answer me. He didn't tell me why. But Sienna comes along—cuz I'm this freak-show street rat now. She comes along and starts throwing hundred dollar bills in my cup while I'm singing. She comes down there every night. I think she's stalking me, like she's crazy or something. But four thousand dollars later, I'm thinking she's crazy rich, so I let her take me home with her. And, well, I've been with her ever since. She's got me off the street, off drugs, she's getting me off cigarettes, alcohol and sheer hatred, she's showed me her God...and you know, I never would have let her if not for one thing."

"What?" he asked.

"She's an abuse survivor, too. Maybe not as bad as me, but bad. And you'd never know it. She'd never tell you. She'd say she's not her past. She'd say her future has nothing to do with Satan's plan because she's covered by the blood of Jesus. And I believe her. But you have no idea how hard that mountain is to climb. I don't want you to hurt her. Not now—not anymore. She's had enough for a lifetime, just believe me on that, okay? I'm just letting you know—and I want you to hear me on this—if God ain't movin' fast enough, she's got me and I'd die for her. In a heartbeat. You understand me? She's the only reason I'm alive. See these?"

She rolled up her jacket sleeves and took her wrist bands off revealing the obvious lines slashed across her wrists.

"These I actually did myself. I thought I couldn't go on, but Sienna taught me how to care about myself, especially when no one else does. And she's gotten me to start reading the Book. She says to me, 'Imagine how God feels going through a thousand different languages and hundreds of generations to answer you and you won't read what He wrote.' I guess you have to be a writer or something. So, anyway, I'm reading it. I'm getting there. I'm learning to do it myself, just me and God, but I'll never forget about Sienna—not as long as I live. So do we understand each other, Jonathan—is it?"

"Yeah…we do," he said and looked firmly into her dark chocolate eyes.

She held out her petite hand with silver rings on every finger and black polish on her fingernails. He reached for it and they shook hands.

"You can call me Aurora now."

"It's an honor to meet you, Aurora."

"Likewise. And you are definitely hot. I can help you with your music, though. Kidding—just kidding! You're a gifted songwriter for sure. See you around."

"See ya," he murmured, then caught her just before she closed the door. "Aurora?"

"What?"

"I won't hurt her," he said it softly, mostly making an oath with himself.

Left alone, Jonathan put the guitar down and blankly stared at it for some time before he realized he was holding his breath. He had to walk himself through the delicate art of breathing for a minute because it seemed he'd forgotten how. His knees were weak and he felt sick to his stomach. He reached into his jacket pocket for his phone and dialed home with a shaky hand.

"Hello?" his voice cracked and he tried again. "Mrs. Hopkins? Can I speak to Bella, please?"

The old woman replied that the child had just gone down for a nap.

"Mrs. Hopkins? Would you just put the phone beside her for a minute—so I can hear her breathe? Yes, I'm all right. Just do it, please? Thank you."

As he listened to his baby breathing, it seemed to become more acceptable for him too. A tear rolled down his cheek for Bella's life, her future, and how vulnerable he didn't know she was until today. He ran a trembling hand through his hair, infuriated at so-called men who give all other men unjust shame, unbearable burdens and, in general, a bad name.

"I love you, baby," he whispered. He listened to one more sweet breath release in peace just before Mrs. Hopkins picked up the receiver.

"Yeah, I'll be home in a couple days. Thank you, Mrs. Hopkins—and Mrs. Hopkins? Keep the doors locked okay? All right...take care...bye."

∞

To him it didn't feel like an hour, but an entire century that passed when Sienna finally found him on the back porch steps, shivering with cold, shocked and stagnant. She was feeling fine. He was feeling homeless like an orphan left behind, helpless like an alien standing ground on a lost planet spinning out of control. He was obviously paralyzed with thought and reason, with questions best reserved for God, coming to understand first-hand the sculpture of the man entrapped by his own thinking, missing the mark of an action so singular, so small and so incredibly significant...pivotal moments lost to time, notoriety stolen by indecision, fear immovable turns flesh to stone. She was obviously excited about their afternoon together, about the lighthearted plans she had made, and the stark contrast between their demeanors didn't register quite as quickly as it should have.

"Hey, Jonathan! How's the writing about me going?" she joked as she vigorously pet her dogs, each in turn. When she looked up from them, she sensed something was wrong—he hadn't turned around to greet her nor had he spoken. She immediately went to his side.

"Jonathan, what's wrong? Is everything okay? Is Bella okay?"

When he didn't respond she picked up the guitar, moved it aside and sat down beside him, searching his face. Finally, she touched his hand. It was ice cold.

"Jonathan?" she whispered, becoming increasingly concerned.

His eyes were red and he lifted a fist to hastily wipe a tear from his cheek before it fell in front of her. He felt awkward and embarrassed as he looked to the blank expanse of sky for personal help. He'd wanted to be more composed by the time she got there. He finally turned to her and forced a smile.

"Hey," he managed.

"Hey," she said softly. "What is it? Is Cheney...?"

"No, it's nothing like that...I'm sorry..."

He abruptly stopped talking when he realized he didn't know what he was sorry for. His words, *I'm sorry*, remained floating in the air around them as he looked at her, the color and pattern of her eyes, the black rays and white flecks layering through the softest steel gray that was mysterious like a misty day—illuminated from beneath like an incandescent fog. He reverently beheld her beauty—silently studied her face—the youthful way her black hair curled around her soft, porcelain skin; the natural plum tint of her lips, of her cheeks; the innocent sprinkling of freckles across her fine-featured nose. He was penetrating the layers, beyond the beautiful, angelic mask of her face, her body, in order to find the hidden monstrosities he perceived to be beneath its particular shape and innocent way of moving, breathing. He expected to find remnants of the unending years filled with ungodly people and the inescapable situations. He was scanning his imagination for her history book with its crooked spine and arduous cover; searching the seat of her soul for the decaying roots of her family tree, both its leaves of heaven and its branches of hell befallen.

Coming up from her surface with empty hands—he was finally able to speak. "Yeah...um...Bell's just fine. And I haven't called the hospital today, I'm sure Cheney's fine or—I don't know—I feel like I don't know anything anymore."

His gaze followed something evil off in the distance, and his eyes suddenly looked intensely angry, nearly murderous, but he could find no target to release the rage upon. Sienna noted how unfamiliar the expression seemed to his physical being—the muscles, the skin, the lines that defined him—didn't know how to portray his newly found vehemence. She also noted, with a sense of relief, that she felt no fear of him. None at all.

He cupped his face in his hands, his body rocked back and forth a bit, and when he came back to the world he said, "Where I come from, you have a clan, a family, a band of men who won't put up with it. They'll do whatever it takes to stop it..."

"Oh..." she gasped.

The utterance slipped through her lips as the situation suddenly dawned on her. She understood what he was talking about—what had brought this dark mood on.

"Aurora," was all she said and she saw his reply in the way the light hit his eyes.

And she let out a long, slow breath.

"I'm so sorry," she finally said, trying her best to comfort him. "I should have warned you, she can knock the wind right out of you. I've tried to get her to be more…well, less shocking when she decides to tell someone something. She hits you like a ton of bricks."

"It's not that," he said so quietly she almost didn't hear it.

"Oh," she said, suddenly feeling another kind of fear trying to creep up on her. This was something she didn't want to happen, not between Jonathan and her, and certainly not so soon, but she could feel it coming anyway. And he wasn't saying anything more, just looking off in the distance actively trying not to cry.

"She told you something about me, then," she whispered, mostly to herself.

He finally turned back toward her, looking directly into her eyes, and as he nodded and said, "Yeah," another tear escaped his control. He smiled weakly through it and he ran a hand nervously through his hair.

"I want to ask you one thing," he said gravely, glaring into the distant sky. "Is he alive?"

"No, he's not," she said quietly.

He bowed his head, brought his hands together then to his forehead as if in prayer and he whispered, "He's lucky then."

Silence settled in around them as the chill settled in around their bones. Finally she rose, slowly, reaching her hand out to him.

"Come on." She kindly encouraged him.

He grabbed the guitar, he got the door for her and the dogs followed them inside.

"Everybody's gone," she said. "So we can talk a bit. Do you want tea or coffee? Your hands are freezing."

"Whatever you're having."

She busied herself boiling water in the teakettle and getting two cups with teabags.

"Sugar?"

"No, just plain is fine for me, thanks."

"Me too." She smiled at him.

She sat opposite him at the breakfast bar. The only movement in the room was the rising of the steam from their two cups while they locked gazes. She reached her hand up to his face and gently ran her thumb over the worry lines that had unkindly erupted above his brow since she'd left him that morning.

"These," she said, "need to be erased."

He closed his eyes and quieted his mind in order to truly listen to her. When he opened them, she began.

"Aurora likes to hit people hard, right where they stand. She's done that to me, a lot, and I don't really blame her. It's just hard to move after that—literally. It's hard to take your next step. It's hard to take your next breath. And I should have warned you, I'm sorry.

"She's still discovering the difference between fact and truth, you know? I mean just the fact that something happened to you, doesn't necessarily make it part of the truth of *who you are*, or at least it doesn't if you understand who you are in Christ. I've been trying to explain to her that when you choose to bring all the evil of your past into your future, there will be no change.

"What I'm trying to say, Jonathan, is that it took me a long time to separate myself from the shame. It took me a long time to realize that I didn't do those things—the things that were done to me. Somebody else did. And they'll carry them all the way to Judgment Day. I'm free. It took a lot of lonely years with just me and God, but He did it, He completely healed me. It's not that I don't trust you with the information. I know you can handle it. It's that I see no reason for it to be here between us. Had we met earlier, I may have needed a lot more help like Cheney does or these girls did, but I don't. I'm not looking for that. I'm looking to love someone and to be with someone. I want us to be two people who are simply happy and relatively uncomplicated. I'm not looking for a savior—I've already found Him. I'm looking for a wonderful future...I mean...maybe you are my reward."

When that last statement resonated through him, he felt truly honored, and his entire countenance lifted.

"And as far as how you're feeling," she continued, "I apologize again. I am truly very sorry. When I taught school, I worked with kids who were abused, abandoned, just mistreated in the worst possible way. I remember one summer I did an internship at a residential psychiatric facility for teenage girls. I mean it was an intense place, lock down, similar to what a prison would be. When I read those charts, all the things that had happened to those girls, which had put them into that awful place, I cried for two days straight. It took me a year to get over the shock. To this day I haven't forgotten what was in those files. I haven't forgotten those girls. I still see their faces. And not a single one was crazy, Jonathan. Not one. They were all just love-starved. They were all abused—and society labeled them as the ones with the problem because they acted out in some way! Dear God, I still pray for those girls. All the time. Aurora represents those girls to me. See, I can't help them. I don't even know where they are now, but Aurora is so similar to those girls. She showed you her wrists?"

"Yeah...she did," he said quietly, absorbed in her life experiences.

"Upstairs bathroom." She pointed as he grimaced. "I almost didn't find her in time. But if you could see how far she's come. Just wait, Jonathan, just keep watching her. All it takes is love and time and God. Anyway, I guess that's why I can help girls like her, because I've been there myself. The hardest part is getting them to believe in God. I guess because He is love and they can't understand love. He's like a foreign language to them. But as long as they are breathing, there's hope. It's never too late to turn it all around."

He reached out for her hand and held it like he'd never seen anything so beautiful, and his gaze climbed up into her eyes and permeated her soul.

He'd never met anyone like Sienna. He didn't know people like her even existed.

"How did I find you?" he asked.

"Well, God...and your wife," she said.

"Ex—ex-wife," he clarified. "But yeah...I guess you're right."

"Saving a life is apparently a godly way to meet."

"Apparently it is," he agreed.

A quiet moment of contemplation passed between them, and finally he asked the questions weighing so heavily on his mind.

"Sienna?"

"Yeah?"

"Did you ever...I mean, were you ever in a place where you wanted to end your life?"

"Twice. Pills the first time, a gun the second time."

"A gun?"

"Thankfully I didn't pull the trigger."

"Jesus!"

"Exactly," Sienna said and lifted her eyes and an open hand toward the sky.

"Oh, I'm sorry for saying..."

"Well, He was there—saved my life. He's here right now. He doesn't miss a word. He doesn't miss a moment."

"Sorry, Sienna. And sorry, Lord. Thank you so much for saving this amazing woman. And please help me with what I say," he prayed aloud.

"He will." She smiled encouragement to him.

"One more question...but I don't...I don't know if I should...," he stammered, then forced the words out of his mouth most apologetically, "Aurora said you can't have kids."

Sienna's eyes darted down, and she started fidgeting with her tea bag. It was obvious she was trying her best to sound strong.

"Unfortunately that's true," her voice began to quake. "And that was something I had no idea how to tell you. So, I'm actually glad you asked."

"And you really wanted them, didn't you?" he asked remorsefully.

Tears welled up in his eyes as he gently squeezed her hand and for the first time in the conversation he saw her completely fold in on herself. He'd obviously touched upon something excruciatingly painful for her, and he could understand why.

"I'm sorry. I shouldn't have asked you that...it's just..."

"No, it's okay," she interrupted him, trying to sound brave. "It's just...that subject still gets to me, especially when I'm talking to someone who has children of their own. I don't know why that is..."

She got up from her seat for a tissue and as she stood wiping away some freshly fallen tears, she felt his hand at the small of her back.

"I'm so sorry," he repeated.

She turned to him, now the one embarrassed by her emotions. She attempted to smile and laughed a little.

"Sometimes helping Aurora backfires on me. Did she say why she was telling you all this?"

"Yeah, she did," he said, gently taking the tissue from her hand and wiping away the rest of her tears. "And her intentions were highly honorable, they really were. She made it very clear to me if I hurt you she'd—well I'm afraid to find out."

The both chuckled a bit.

"She said she'd die for you. 'In a heartbeat,' is how she put it. I don't think you have to worry about that one forgetting about you. She loves you, Sienna. She was doing her best to protect you."

"I figured it was something like that. Now you understand what I love about her—the girl's got some spirit, that's for sure."

"Kinda like you," he said sweetly as he kissed her forehead and held her in a hug for a time.

"The reason I was asking you about kids…" He hesitated because he was afraid she'd think it was too soon.

"The reason I was asking you is because I've got one…a daughter. Her name is Bella and she needs a mom." His tears started up again, but this time he didn't try to hide them. "And, I don't know how I found you, but I believe you are the only one in the world good enough for me to trust her to."

"That," he said, "and I love you."

He held her close, a sweet longing in his magnetic eyes that drew her in and told of his secret dreams. His mind unfurled before her, let go of all its defenses and revealed that it no longer held thoughts void of her. She felt that all-encompassing heart of his enveloping her. It was a feeling of warmth, safety, and of rest to her. He opened his entire being and handed it all to her, and she accepted the honor. His soul, to her, felt like home—a place of peace and grace, a place bound with every true goodness and possibility on earth that she'd come to imagine only existed in heaven.

God walks, with us, down here, she silently praised the Lord.

"I love you, Sienna. I can't help it. I can't hide it. I never want to be away from you—ever. That's the truth. That's how I feel and it's not ever going to change."

They stood cradled in each other's arms, neither of them embarrassed for the tears on their faces. They stood looking at each other for a long, silent moment. She, speechless, not finding even one word; and he, waiting both patiently and desperately for her reply. She stood there, stricken and amazed that he had finally found his way into the midst of her reality. That he wasn't just a ghost coming to her in the night to tell his story. He wasn't a character in a book. He was flesh and blood and breathing. And yet, here she was, being awakened and finding herself in the middle of his meadow.

Finally, she said, "Then we won't. We won't be away from each other—ever. We won't be apart, Jonathan. Because I love you, too."

He smiled fully—all lines of worry, gone—like someone who just won the lottery and knew all along that he would. Faith fulfilled amazed him. He'd waited for her, remained faithful to her, for years before her arrival. He'd dreamt of her, nights, long before she came. Their little family had finally found the most precious one, Sienna Jewel, to complete it.

When he'd finally come up for air, his whole being buried in that kiss, he whispered in her ear with the broadest of smiles.

"So, you can no longer say you can't have kids," he said.

He kissed her neck then pulled back just enough to look into her eyes and watched as she absorbed the knowledge that miracles do happen—the exact ones she'd prayed for so hard her pillow was too dampened with tears to sleep on. Suddenly, just like that, God's hand had moved across her cloudscape sky and delivered her rainbow—one of color and of light and of the sweetest sound. Now she would soon hear, off of the lips of youth, a kaleidoscopic word she'd nearly forgotten. Soon, she would hear a little girl call her "Mother."

chapter fourteen

*A*s THEY ARRIVED at the stables, Sienna introduced Jonathan to the trainer, Barbara. The woman was more rugged than feminine, but very warm-hearted. He instantly liked her.

"Jonathan, I'll have you take Peanut here," Barbara instructed. "Both horses have been on the walker and lunged, Sienna, but you might want to start with a warm-up in the arena just to be on the safe side. It's a little chilly, but it's a beautiful afternoon. Well, have fun you two. Glad you're back, Si. This old guy was starting to worry about you."

She patted Ira's shoulder and left them alone.

Peanut was huge. Jonathan stood next to him, stroking the horse's neck wondering how on earth he was supposed to get up there and look good doing it.

His concerns must have been obvious to Sienna because she quickly encouraged him, "We've got a mounting block—like stairs, to help with getting on. I'll show you. And, don't worry, he's a big teddy bear."

"*Big* being the key word in that comment," he said. "You didn't tell me how tall these horses were. What kind of horses are they?"

"Ira is an Appendix Quarter Horse which means he's half Quarter and half Thoroughbred. Peanut, who's for sale by the way, is a Paint but he's also got a lot of Thoroughbred in him."

"For sale by the way, means what exactly?" he looked at her with smiling eyes.

"Bella," she said. "I know this horse—he'd be perfect for her."

"That's a long way down, you sure?"

"Positive," she said. "He's a very conscientious guy. He'd take good care of her, and he needs somebody."

They went into the arena for a brief warm-up. Once he got up on the horse, Jonathan actually remembered the skill of riding very well. He seemed to be a natural. Sienna was relieved to see him relaxed and genuinely enjoying himself. Peanut seemed happy and ready to go.

"You're good at this," she said. "You ready?"

"Yep, I'll follow you."

Sienna jumped down and opened the gate for them. She grabbed a gear bag and tied it to Ira's saddle. She looked particularly small in relation to that big black horse, but she didn't show a trace of hesitation as she led him to the fence, climbed the fence, then mounted.

"All that might be easier if you'd gotten a shorter horse," he called out, teasing her.

"Just wait 'till you see this guy move; he's gorgeous to watch."

They headed out on a well-worn trail that wound through a beautifully wooded area. Everything was just beginning to turn green—the grasses, the trees—and it smelled heavenly. The air was crisp, but not too cold. Birds were flitting from tree to tree overhead. The sky was a brilliant blue, and there wasn't another person, car, or building in sight. The path grew steeper and the horses had to work a bit harder to climb it. Sienna's horse startled as three deer crossed the trail in front of them. She circled him around and gave him a pat on the neck and a soft, encouraging word. They rode on in relative silence, admiring God's design, and, for a time, all the abuses suffered in their world simply evaporated into the fresh, spring air.

Around a sharp turn, the woodland opened up into an expansive meadow that was already lush and a much brighter green than anything they'd seen that day. There was an old barn off in the distance and a faded wooden fence surrounded by poles with antiquated wiring draped between them, indicating that a riding arena had once been active there. As they dismounted, Sienna explained that Barbara's equine business had started back with her grandfather and that they were standing in the midst of where it all began.

"I'd forgotten how much I used to like going for rides as a kid," he said as he tied Peanut and loosened the gelding's saddle a bit. "This is refreshingly...simple. It's so quiet up here, it soothes the soul."

Sienna studied his countenance, the lightness around his eyes, and admitted to herself that he actually looked younger. It made her happy that she had helped him reconnect with the boy inside.

"It *is* beautiful here." She turned around, full-circle, and took it all in. The sky was so clear, she could see farther than usual so she studied the elusive horizon for a moment, guessing the miles. She smiled at Jonathan when she caught him staring at her.

"So...," she said to him, "welcome to my meadow. I come here to think and to pray and to basically go where no one can find me."

"I can understand that. It's perfect. Do you come here to write?" he asked.

"I don't, actually. I just come here to *be*, you know? I think it's good to set aside some time when you don't expect anything from yourself or anyone else. I just come here to breathe and connect with my Creator. That's it."

"I would love to come to a place like this to write songs with no interruptions. I haven't had that for...well, since I lived in Ireland. And I think my music has suffered for it. It sells...but it's not as authentic as it should be."

"You can come here anytime," she told him. "That's why I showed it to you. I was hoping you'd like it as much as I do. You should see it after it flowers; there are butterflies everywhere."

He spread out a woolen blanket in the sun. Then he helped her unpack her gear bag which contained a bottle of red wine and plastic glasses, gourmet pastries, including petits fours, and a thermos full of Mia's homemade soup with plastic bowls and spoons. They sat down and she served the soup while he poured the wine and said to her, "This is nice. Thank you for this, for this whole day."

Then he leaned in and kissed her sweetly.

After they'd finished eating and picked up, Jonathan laid down on the blanket and welcomed her next to him. It was so quiet and peaceful, the only sounds being a few birds, an occasional movement from the horses, and the sound of their own voices in turn and, sometimes, laughing together. They talked for hours about the course their lives would take, how their future together would unfold. He covered them both with the extra end of the blanket and they fell asleep in each other's arms.

Peaceful was their slumber, like rest found at the end of an impossible journey. Sweet solitude. When they awakened, it was pleasanter still for they found themselves covered in each other's warmth, underneath an iridescently peach and blush-pink sky streaked unabashedly with baby blues—colors she'd seldom let her eyes absorb before. She didn't permit herself to dream in these colors before—colors spread out so delicately before her, blanketing her meadow with their truth and telling of her joy-filled tomorrows. They whispered a promise that they would no longer be trapped in a dream or shackled upon a page on a shelf. No, from now on, they would be in her reality.

Her life was different now with him. Her book had finally been opened and out from among it would fly many brilliant butterflies...

∞

As they got ready to rejoin civilization, Sienna took Ira into the lower meadow for Jonathan to watch the horse's movement in what she called "Hunter Under Saddle." The horse's lean, black frame contrasted beautifully with the pastels of the sky behind him as he lowered his long neck, rounded his back, and swept the delicate blades of grass with each carefully contemplated stride. He covered a tremendous amount of ground, effortlessly. White puffs of breath escaped his nostrils into the chilled air. His black mane and tail danced with Sienna's long hair. She was a natural-born rider, and the two fit together seamlessly. As she asked the horse to transition into the canter he gazed forward with pointed ears, and a certain gentleness could be seen in his kind eye. It matched her gentle touch to the reins she held so delicately in her small hands. They both were looking for a fence to soar over, to jump from the earth and levitate in the air. As he witnessed the captivating display, he began to understand what she loved so much about that mesmerizing horse. Sienna was so thoroughly preoccupied with him that she had forgotten the fact that anyone was watching her. She'd completely forgotten about everything else in the world, and Jonathan wondered what it would feel like to be that free.

"Well," she said breathlessly as she rode up beside him, "now you know what he does for a living."

Her smile radiated through her entire being.

"He makes money at that?" Jonathan asked as he stroked the horse's soft nose and looked up at her.

"Yeah. Barbara and I take his earnings and apply them to horse rescue—that's Barbara's calling in life."

"You'd laugh if you knew his registered name," she said. "It's Move Your Moneymaker. And Peanut's real name is 'He's Got Legs'—like the song except, well, ya know...he's a boy."

He shook his head, chuckling at the names as they started back, but he knew in his heart that he'd never forget the vision of her riding in that meadow as long as he lived.

Night had completely fallen by the time they pulled into the driveway. Plans had been laid for the purchase of Peanut. The house was completely dark and empty except for the dogs, and neither could truthfully say they were disappointed.

"I need something to drink. You?" she offered.

"Just water would be great, thanks."

"You know what would feel good right now?" she asked.

"I'm thinkin' the hot tub myself," he said.

"That's what I was thinking," she agreed. "I'm gonna go shower and I'll meet you down there. If you didn't bring any, there are some guy's swimming trunks in the changing room by the pool. There's a shower in there, too. All the lights are on the left, in the greenhouse doorway."

She disappeared upstairs. And he easily beat her to the pool after a quick shower. He spent the time getting in a few laps. As his muscles started to relax, he found himself drawn to the architecture of the place—all the intricate details of the greenhouse windows, the massive glass ceiling with stained glass accents—the whole concept was breathtaking.

Then he saw her walk through the doors at the far end and slip off her robe.

Wow! You've got to be kidding me, he said to himself. He stood up in the water in order to watch her. He imagined her body to be beautiful, but he had no idea it would look as good as it did. He heard his favorite rock song get louder with every step she took. She was wearing a dark red two-piece. She had her long black hair pulled back, and she was smiling directly at him. When she dove into the pool—a graceful swan dive—he caught a glimpse of a large tattoo at the small of her back.

"I have won the lottery," he shouted. "Thank you, God. I will do anything You want from now on."

"What?" Sienna asked as she came up next to him.

He laughed and just looked at her. He didn't know what to say.

"What?" she asked again in a gentler tone.

"Seriously?"

"Yeah, tell me."

"I've never seen anyone look as good as you."

"Oh." She started to blush and then looked at him and said, "Thank you."

"No, thank you." He chuckled, though he was completely serious.

"I've thought that about you, too," she admitted with a grin.

"Yeah?"

"Yeah, like since the first time I saw you on your back porch? And the other night, when you came down the stairs? Yeah…"

"Yeah?" he said more softly and moved in to kiss her, and kiss her again. He took his time, looking at her face, into her eyes, while the warm water rocked around them, and he slowly said, "I remember watching you on the beach that day. You stopped to look out at the water and I wondered what you were thinking. I wondered what you were asking for. I thought to myself that if I were God, I'd give it to you—whatever it was—and just at that moment the clouds over you parted, they just opened up and this light came down on you and—that was it. I haven't stopped thinking about you since. And I never will."

She took in every word he said and tried to give her heart the time it needed to accept them, and to believe him.

"You're never going to stop telling me that, right?" she asked.

"I'll tell you that every night of our lives, if you want."

And he told her again, in Irish, and she drank in every word—swallowed them like honey and wished he would never stop. He began another set of unhurried kisses, then gently turned her around as if he were twirling her in a dance, so he could see her tattoo. It was a large cross with five butterflies in all different colors like those of a rainbow. Some of them were landed on the cross and some were flying out from it, toward the viewer. It was a beautiful work of art. He ran his fingers over the top of the cross tracing it into her wet skin.

"The butterflies," he said as he turned her back around, "they represent you five, don't they?"

"Yeah, me and my girls."

"That's beautiful," he said.

"What about yours?" she asked.

"Nothing that artistic, but I've got Bella's name, of course—here."

He had Bella Maura Driscoll, her birth date and the words *The day you were born I heard angels singing* inscribed on his chest, over his heart.

"And I've got some black razor thing on my arm which means nothing other than I have a tattoo. And I've got a compass rose on my back—here, to honor my family, mostly my dad and grandfather. They're fishermen. And a compass will always bring them home...at least that's the idea."

"That's nice," she said. "So three?"

"Yep, just three—that's it."

"I like them," she said. "Even the razor-wire one."

"Thanks."

"Let me show you something," she said as she swam over to the hot tub and climbed in.

"That wasn't it," she chuckled as she got settled.

"That looked pretty good to me," he smiled.

"Come here," she scolded playfully.

He climbed in next to her, and she opened a panel, concealed beside the tub. She pushed a button and the main lights went out. The room was lit only by white lights strung in the trees and plants surrounding them and the faint sub-lighting in the pool. It was beautiful.

"And," she continued, "if we're lucky enough to have a clear sky..."

She pushed a couple more buttons and all the outside lights, all the decorative lighting and pool lights went black and an array of stars above them was fully displayed. She pressed one final button and a surround sound system came on playing relaxing music.

"If Aurora's been in here, the thing is cranked and she's got her CDs in it. It about blows you out of the water."

He laughed at that then put his head back and looked at the stars for a while.

Finally he asked her, "What's your middle name?"

"Jewel."

"Sienna Jewel," he said thoughtfully. "That's a beautiful name."

Jonathan and Sienna cringed in startled surprise as deafening music began, most of the lights came on and they heard Aurora yelling, "Cannonball!!!" as she passed them running and jumped in the pool. When she came up, her hair was deflated but no less pink. She smiled at them both and splashed them with the cooler water. She was followed by an entire mob of squealing guests including her boyfriend, Collin, and a girl from her band named Jessica, Kat and her fiancé, Dillon, Mia and Josh, a friend from the restaurant where she worked, Jackobie and her boyfriend, Jamil.

"It is party time, people!" yelled Aurora. Jonathan and Sienna joined them in the pool.

The group swam and played water volleyball for nearly two hours. Then they had a late-night cookout of burgers and Mia's famous salads that she brought from the restaurant. Katarina made some fabulous non-alcoholic drinks, and they finished the evening by toasting marshmallows over a small fire for smores. They all begged Jonathan to sing, but he refused, insisting the first time Sienna heard him sing it would be a song he'd written about her, and he simply wasn't finished with it yet. So Aurora volunteered her voice, and it was astounding. It hit Jonathan with no less force than their previous conversation, but it swung the pendulum of his opinion about her in the opposite direction of purity, innocence, and warmth. Her voice was the one thing about her that had been left completely unmolested. When she sang, her strong soul was freed. Hearing her was an experience that no one would dare cross, interrupt, or touch. When she sang, it seemed the earth held its breath in order to listen. Jonathan surveyed the faces surrounding him, and they were all captivated, transported to her world, and he knew she had something universally special because they all looked like it was the first time they'd ever heard her, but he knew it wasn't. He knew the gift of music when he heard it and *she*, he thought, *she's definitely got it*. And, on that point, he'd never been wrong before.

chapter fifteen

$\mathcal{B}$EFORE SHE EVEN opened her eyes, in the familiar soft silk comforter around her skin, Sienna sensed it was late morning by the slant of the sun across her face. She guessed it to be about 10:00 a.m. and noted that the household seemed quiet and unmoving. She stretched her arms overhead and rolled into the light, smiling at the memory of the previous night.

When she finally did open her eyes, they rested on Jonathan's attentive presence. He was seated on the chaise lounge where he had spent the night and, apparently, he'd been watching her sleep for some time. His hands were folded peacefully, his forearms resting on his thighs, and his muscled shoulders were rounded—it was a thoughtful pose indicative of prayer and his forward gaze made it easy to deduce that she had been the primary focus. He was so intensely exquisite to her in the morning light, against that striking, red velvet backdrop, in his white tee with no sleeves, in his favorite blue jeans, in his bare feet. The colorless and angelic luminescence breathing just over his shoulder cast a fine glaze across the outline of his skin; it highlighted his black hair, his jaw line, and graced the tips of his boyish lashes like a silver lining—but his was a cloudless sky, one of purity and of simplicity and one of straight line. His eyes were soft and bright and unidentifiable in their color—they were not gray, they were not green, nor were they blue, rather they were layered with a mixture of all three. They seemed to change with the tide. *Something similar to the sea*, she finally decided, *where his fathers come from.*

He got up without saying anything and walked straight to her with serious intent. He climbed onto her bed and kissed her, gently touching her skin. He'd been entertaining certain things in his mind prior to her awakening and was not the least bit concerned with hiding that fact. It was after all natural in this paradise.

"Good morning, Butterfly," he said quietly as he looked into her eyes. His expression remained rather solemn. Between his fingers, he felt the softness of a loop of her hair, he thoughtfully got lost in the richness of color and how sharply it contrasted with her skin.

"I've been thinking," he said. "I apologize for my complete lack of manners and my inadequate self-control. But...I'm thinking we need to get married..."

He looked into her eyes and she thought she saw him beginning to blush as he grinned and then looked away.

"I'm thinking we need to get married before I compromise your morals," he said in a whisper. Now the words were out there, and he couldn't ever take them back. He released a warm breath against her skin. His eyes met hers expectantly.

"I'm askin' you to marry me, Sienna, because of everything that you are."

The words hung in the air, his intent open and vulnerable, and she thought she felt her heart skip a few beats, but she didn't answer. She sensed that there were more things he needed to say. And he was taking his time, going very slowly.

"I'm sorry if this seems crazy—too fast—I haven't even taken you out on a date yet. But this God of ours—He's got some instructions, some strong guidelines on how things ought to be done, and I don't think I'm strong enough to stay away from you anymore."

He touched her face, running his fingers over her soft skin, under her delicate jaw line. He kindly guided her toward him and kissed her again. It seemed nearly painful for him to release her. He lightly rested his forehead against hers for a moment, and then began again.

"My Dad married my Mum two weeks after he met her. That was more than forty years ago. We're an impulsive lot, but we stick with our decisions once they've been made. We're a little hot tempered, a little too kindhearted; some of us are really loud—especially after a couple pints..."

He chuckled and she smiled.

"We keep the promises we make," he continued. "We keep our word if it kills us."

He looked through her and into the mystic ghost of time to reach his family line. He recognized what was his, and he pulled it down and said these things to her as if they were in the midst of his father and his father's fathers as they dredged through seasons lived and the scarcities of death all the way back to God. He said these things to her as if they were surrounded by his children, his grandchildren and all the precious families his blood would inspire long after he'd fallen away unknown and forgotten all the way to the Second Coming of the Lord.

"We're very loyal," he said, summarizing his entire legacy in that final word. His eyes spread out oceans of shamelessness before her, oceans of time, oceans of connected journeys, in their wide open and rotating colors.

"I'll take care of you 'till I die." The oath he made to her was sealed, sacred and eternal, and his heart was hers forever no matter her answer. He kissed her hand, rolled his thumb over her finger where a ring should be. Its absence, to him, was intentional and a gesture of his respect for, his tortured experience with, his reverential fear of, something both abominable and glorious... something preordained by God to define the human condition... something simply called, freewill.

"Don't answer me now. I want to give you a chance to pray about it, because I know you want to, right?"

He smiled at her and she nodded her thanks.

"So," he said, "I am going to make you—and whoever else is here—some breakfast. Then I've got a song to finish. But we have a date tonight—around seven?"

"Yeah," she said.

"Yeah," he repeated softly and took a moment to get lost in his girl, in the tranquility of the morning, before the whole house erupted with young and boisterous people.

⚬⚬⚬

The blueberry pancakes were steaming and piled high on the center island; the glorious scent of perfectly brewed coffee wafted throughout the entire house. One by one people started to trickle down. Jonathan and Sienna were nearly done eating by the time the first one entered. Jonathan caught himself just before he asked, "Who's that?" And when he realized it was Aurora, he almost spewed his orange juice all over the white marble island. Sienna had been watching his reaction and laughed out loud.

"She's beautiful, isn't she?" she said.

"That's enough out of you two, this early in the morning. Give me some peace, will ya?"

It was Aurora all right. But if she hadn't spoken, Jonathan would've still been struggling to believe it. She was petite, and beautiful, with long, straight, dark brown hair. She was without the rings in her nose, lip, chin, eyebrow, and ears, and was dressed conservatively and sharply in a blazer and pencil skirt. Her makeup was modest and, well, pleasantly normal. She was so different and so uncomplicated. She poured herself some orange juice, and upon taking a swallow noticed Jonathan staring at her. She plunked down her glass.

"There's a picture of me in the upstairs hallway just like this," she said sarcastically as she spun around. "Keep staring at me and I'll change back right now."

"No...," he stammered. "It's just—well, you look really pretty."

"Great," she said flatly. "Just what I was goin' for."

"Aurora's got a symphony this afternoon," Sienna explained.

"Yeah, but I'll be punked out tonight. So...enjoy this while it lasts."

"She's playing downtown tonight," Sienna continued to explain. "Cello, right?"

"Yup. Or maybe just singing."

"Aurora performs downtown Saturday nights, and the money she earns goes to the Domestic Violence Shelter," Sienna said proudly.

Jonathan nodded acknowledgement and looked on in amazement at the many facets of Aurora. He could plainly recognize Sienna's hand in all of it, and it was truly something to see.

"Enough about me," Aurora spouted. "Are you two gettin' hitched or what? I mean, Sienna doesn't like 'bring home' guys. She must think you're pretty special for some reason."

She stared at Jonathan while chewing a huge mouthful of pancake.

"Well, I....." Jonathan looked to Sienna, his expression asking her direction. She grinned and shrugged her shoulders in reply.

"I knew it!" Aurora shouted and her fist hit the countertop. "Dang, I'm good."

"You knew what?" Jackobie asked nonchalantly as she entered the kitchen. She opened the stainless steel refrigerator and grabbed a carton of milk.

"These two are getting married," Aurora blurted.

"What!" Jackobie spun around, and milk splashed across the tiled floor.

"Who's getting married?" Kat asked as she and Mia strolled into the room, "Oh...blueberry pancakes!"

Mia slid into the barstool next to Jonathan's and winked at him. Jackobie remained locked in a frozen stupor, concern draped across her face, milk dripping down her hand and onto her blue, fuzzy house slipper.

Sienna leaned toward Jonathan and whispered, "Here it comes, let's see how well I raised them."

"Who's getting married?" Kat asked again, growing more impatient.

"These two, Sherlock," Aurora said, pointing her fork back and forth at Sienna and Jonathan.

Jackobie finally approached the bar and put the carton of milk down, seemingly in slow motion.

"Congratulations!" Katarina squealed with delight. A warm smile radiated out through her eyes as she made her way around the counter to give Sienna a hug. When she turned away from Sienna, she ran smack into Jackobie's glare. "What?"

Jackobie, being very reserved and responsible in nature, took the time to choose her words carefully. "Are you sure that's wise? I mean you barely know him—excuse me, Jonathan. Sienna—this is just crazy."

"Crazy talk!" Aurora chimed in, obviously enjoying the drama as she was grinning from ear to ear. "She's really just asking if you're a gold digger, Jonathan."

Jonathan choked a bit on his coffee in regard to that remark.

"Aurora...." Sienna quietly warned.

Meanwhile, Mia whispered to Jonathan, "I think it's great."

She gave him a warm smile which he returned, thankful for her subtlety.

Sienna placed a hand over Jackobie's and explained, "I haven't said yes yet...not exactly...," She turned and smiled at Jonathan before continuing, "...but I'll be all right. It'll all be all right and everything will work out the way it's supposed to. I understand this is sudden and a bit of a shock to you—all of you—and I really do appreciate your concern. I'm not getting married today. I mean, we've got some time to just kind of relax and take it all in, right?"

The heaviness on Jackobie's face lightened a bit, and she embraced Sienna. She didn't seem to want to let go. She wiped a tear from the corner of her eye.

"I just don't want to lose you," she admitted. "I don't want things to change. Sometimes I just want to stay in this house—the five of us—forever."

Jonathan witnessed their closeness as a family as they all gathered around

Jackobie and hugged her—even Aurora, which surprised him a little. Sienna reassured Jackobie that she would always be there for her, that she would never be "lost" to any of them. Soon after, Jackobie began to open up, talking about how she had lost a patient to cancer earlier in the week and how it had affected her. They all empathized with her, comforted her, and encouraged her in her abilities as a young doctor. Before long she was smiling and lighthearted and apologetic to both Jonathan and Sienna for her reaction to the immensely good news.

chapter sixteen

$\mathcal{A}$s Jonathan watched every minuscule move she made descending the stairs, he admitted to himself that although he had no earthly idea what women did for three hours by themselves in a bathroom, if this was what resulted from it, he'd never pressure her to hurry up or complain about being late for the rest of his days.

"Wow," he said. His eyes took in the scarlet hues of her dress as it flowed from the curve of her hips. She'd straightened her hair; it was beautiful and glistening and it seemed twice as long.

"Wow is good," she smiled warmly. "And you look very nice yourself."

And he did. He was sharply dressed in a crisp white shirt, black tie, and perfectly tailored trousers. She noticed he had very good taste in shoes; she believed them and his belt to be Italian made.

"Thanks," he said modestly.

He got the door for her, then the car door as well, and they headed downtown for the evening. They had reservations at Murray's, the upscale restaurant where Mia was one of the assistant chefs. On the way in, Sienna caught sight of Dillon's groomsmen herding him into a bar a block up the street. The notorious bachelor party was commencing. Dillon already looked disheveled and slightly tipsy. Jonathan followed Sienna's gaze, but his attention quickly made its way back to her. He read the feeling of helplessness in her expression as he silently studied her face. He thought he saw—or maybe he just sensed her apprehension. Her shoulders hunched ever so slightly, and he thought, as he held onto her hand, that he could feel her stomach muscles tighten as if somebody had just kicked her in the gut. She covered it all very well, but still he could see right through her and, in all honesty, his concern didn't lie with Dillon in the least. He considered Katarina and how Sienna felt about her. He asked himself how he would handle it if, twenty years from now, that were Bella's guy.

Feeling his anger rise, his jaw clenched and his eyes narrowed as he stared down the street. He moved his head to one side to shed some of the growing tension. He cleared his throat, forcing his voice to sound more innocent than the intentions beneath it.

"We're a little early. I could go talk to him," he offered lightly. "It'll only take a minute—it might help."

"Would you?" she asked with a sigh of relief.

"Yeah." He gently stroked her arm and attempted to reassure her with a slight smile. "I'll be right back."

She took a seat on a nearby bench and waited beneath a chokecherry tree that was just beginning to blossom. She picked up a stray petal that had fallen on her dress, folded her hands around it and placed them in her lap. The sunset was soft in its hue, and she released a breath beneath it that seemed to follow him as he walked away from her. She found herself thinking how odd it was, having someone to help her. She sat there alone on that bench, watching couples passing by in front of her, admitting she'd only known single parenting. This would be the first time—Jonathan would be the first one she ever trusted with any of her girls. To her it felt she stood on the surface of water, her heart hovering above and around the breathlessness of that first weak and shaky step, and the question she asked of herself was, "Will I walk?"

And then, closer to her truth, "Do I have any faith...in him?"

And the answer she heard back was, "I have faith in you, Mommy."

She turned to the right, then the left, scanning the sidewalks of strangers, swearing she had heard Bella's sweet voice. Of course Bella wasn't there, not physically. Sienna looked down at her left hand, she opened it and stared at her petal, then she closed her fingers around it slowly, softly, remembering what it felt like that day on the beach when that beautiful child grabbed her by the hand—free from inhibition, without question or reserve—putting all her young and untarnished faith *in her*. When she took the small hand that day she made a promise, a promise to never let go, and she didn't even realize it at the time. It was a promise as delicate as the petal in her hand, but its undertaking could not be denied. Its pledge had been whispered on the air between them; it spread out as angel's wings. *What are they for?* (If the answer be *to fly*...one would also reach the understanding that the notion is an utter impossibility without *faith*.) These secrets were now emerging, and they had all been spoken within that touch, with God their only witness.

Sienna watched a young family of five walk by. She saw herself, for the first time, as a completely acceptable, qualified adult. *I have the skills; I need to use them.* Suddenly, she started hearing an awful lot of "I" in her internal dialogue. She knew that to be a cautionary thing and stopped her pushing, random thoughts. She set aside her worldly ambitions and her bright ideas that did nothing more than blanket her own insecurities—simply put, she no longer had time for dead-end roads. She knew parenting wasn't supposed to be about the parent anyway. She quieted her soul and calmed her mind. She tried on some humility, a discipline which had earned her respect somewhere in her past, and turned her questions and desires to her Lord.

In the stillness, in her waiting, came His peace. More petals softly fell; something in her being started listening to His voice, and His divine plan seemed to open up before her eyes. And what she saw, in the light of Truth there, was a *chosen* mother, a mother hand-picked, not of her own design but of God's, after His sweet heart for a motherless child (for His was a child intricately known, a soon-to-be blessed child resting in His palm and in need of a mother who had been purified by worldly trial, proved by time and by fire). And what she heard was a blessing—echoed against her previous pain, against her hardened, cracked and weathered past. She heard the question Bella asked, truly and for the first time, she heard the intent behind Bella's prayer, "Are you somebody's mother?" She heard the essential part that she missed before which God illumined, "If not, would you be mine?"

The question resonated through her mind, filtering down through her soul until she held its answer in the deepest part of her heart like a jewel divinely cut. It radiated a most brilliant light.

And He said it to His chosen one upon her story called, *Today*:

> When you bleed for it no more, only then can your soul carry it,
>   and so then, only, it is given you—mysteriously handed, granted,
>   a prayer answered in Our Shared and Perfect Time together, I
>   openeth the door forever....
> How could one with decades lived dare hint there be no God;
> How could one with Scripture read turn from faith in front of Me,
>   question Me their enemy...?
> Don't you know, I am found in you..., and I do not hideth long in
>   lore.
> Don't I whisper the very breath of dawn upon your essence
>   evermore?

Don't you sing within My presence a new song on glory shore?
I smile out through you like the heavens shining new day down.
Don't you know that you are Mine; that I am handing you My
   Crown....

The umbrella tree shivered sweetly, blossoms shuddering with quaking joy, whispering with independent breeze a lilt no one else near recognized; its pink petals floated all around, blanketing Wisdom's floor.

And she smiled up at Him, "And it all started today..."

And God smiled His answer back, "A day is as a thousand years..."

And somehow she and He understood each other perfectly—a girl and her God.

And as she came back down, the part of Bella's question—the part Sienna had missed—now took her breath away as she heard it over and over in her mind.

"How could I have been so blind? That's what she meant. That's exactly what she was asking—if I would be her mom!"

Sienna slowly realized that she had been too wrapped up in her own past hurts to even recognize what the girl was saying to her. And children, Sienna had always believed, possess the wisdom of Eternity in each tiny step and offer the purity of God in every soft spoken word.

"Thank you, God, that I didn't miss it entirely."

She sat on that bench contemplating how the past and future sometimes violently collide, how—when they are brought together by an outside force, such as by an act of God—sometimes the "now" is just too much to handle. It was simply too much to process no matter how many years it had been hoped for, no matter how exact its visualization had been as it played upon a blank ceiling through those countless sleepless nights. And there was absolutely no proof of this except inside the one to whom it was happening. Miracles could be so solitary, as if designed to be a private matter, yet so unforgettable, as if meant to last a lifetime.

This was her miracle, one of her very own. And so to prevent the human blindness caused by looking directly into the face of God, she backed away from it and thought about Bella herself. The child so much resembled her father externally—in her mannerisms, in the way that she smiled, the color of her hair, her sense of humor, her warmth and kindness, her eyes. Sienna could plainly see it running deeper now; Jonathan and Bella matched each other perfectly in the way they looked for someone to love. As she reexamined her recent memories of them both, she was blown away by how similar their hearts and souls were, how brave they had been asking for someone to love them. Their words were lines cast out into a miserable, loveless sea—looking for true love from another person in this lonely world. How blessed was she to be floating in that current.

They simply weren't afraid like other people were. They weren't afraid to love, to put themselves out there, and that was proof that their foundation was strong and built on morals and on faith rather than on feeble insecurities and corrosive past hurts....

"Sienna? You look a million miles away," Kat observed as she sat down beside her. "You all right?"

"Oh, I'm fine—great, actually. I don't remember a time I've ever been better than this," she replied, her expression slowly catching up to her words with a genuine smile.

"Really? Wow...I wish I could say the same. I'm really bummed right now."

Sienna reached over and squeezed Kat's hand.

"I know, but keep up your faith," she encouraged, "we're workin' on it. It'll be okay—it will. Just remember you're not alone. And I don't care how old you get, Katarina, or how far away you get. As long as I'm alive, I'll always think of you as my girl; you'll always be my family. And family sticks together; we'll help each other through the hard times. And if you believe Dillon is the one, we'll all work with him, we'll all give him some time, and I believe he's going to get there—I do. Don't you?"

Kat smiled and nodded a teary-eyed "yes," hugging Sienna with one arm. They watched on in silence as the people passed by. After a few moments, Kat asked what Sienna was so happy about.

"I just discovered that one of the godliest traits anyone could develop is listening. I mean truly hearing what someone's heart is saying from behind their words. It's something I've missed in my life, and it can mean the difference in everything."

"Well, my heart is saying that I love you, Sienna. And if this Jonathan guy makes you this happy, you should definitely go for it."

"I should," Sienna agreed and they both started laughing.

∽∾

Jonathan entered the bar and headed toward the loudest patrons. They were not hard to find.

"Hey, Dillon—these your friends?" he asked, scanning the group; there were about twelve of them.

"Yeah, man. Hey everybody, this is—" Dillon snapped his fingers mid-air, trying to trigger recollection of his name, "—ah—Jonathan, right?"

"Right."

Jonathan shook hands with some of the friendlier young men, ignoring the others that mildly resented his intrusion.

"I'm afraid I need to take your friend away for a minute. There's something important I have to discuss with him. Won't take long."

Dillon obliged him. Jonathan stopped at the bar and got a coffee to go and soon the two were out in the fresh evening air. They walked in silence for a while before Dillon asked, "What's up, man...something wrong? Is it Kat?"

"Drink some of this," Jonathan handed him the coffee. They found themselves on a modest bridge overlooking a pond surrounded by a park area. It was a peaceful looking place. Three ducks floated quietly beneath them leaving a liquid "V" wake.

"I'm on a date with Sienna so I won't take much of your time," Jonathan said directly. "I just wanted to suggest to you, strongly, that you rethink your bachelor party."

"Oh no! You, too? I've already gone over this with Kat. These are my friends, nothin's gonna happen. It's only one night."

Jonathan looked at Dillon, at how young and inexperienced he was, then his gaze floated out over the water and hardened.

"Dillon, you might not know it, but you're taking advantage of the fact that Katarina doesn't have a father. So, I'm stepping in and telling you that from now on, that guy is me."

Dillon's eyes got a bit wider as Jonathan continued, "Let's not make this complicated. If you don't want to upset me, then don't upset her."

Jonathan's tone was forceful and firm, and his intent was serious enough to raise the hairs on the back of Dillon's neck. The young man certainly didn't see this coming. He swallowed hard, then suddenly became occupied with drinking his coffee.

Jonathan went on. "You've already upset her. You've made her cry over this and you've made it clear to her and everyone else that your friends and their lack of judgment mean more to you than she does."

Jonathan turned to him with a set jaw and steel in his eyes, "I'm suggesting you change that."

Dillon humbly met his look and accepted the suggestion. He was silent for a while, considering his own recent behavior and evaluating all the quarrels he'd been having with Kat. He couldn't deny that most of them had been his fault, nor could he deny the fact that the only reason he hadn't corrected the problem was because he didn't have to. He'd simply been getting away with it—until now.

Finally he quietly admitted, "You're right. I guess I just didn't think about it that way."

Jonathan's being relaxed, and he silently let out a sigh of relief. He looked up to the twilight sky and released his appreciation to the One holding the stars. He was new at this father thing in relation to the boyfriend thing. He secretly observed Dillon's demeanor as he stood there cowered like a whipped pup.

Jonathan softened his tone and said, "Don't be ashamed to love a woman, to take care of her. Those guys in there...if they're your real friends they'll get over it, and if not, it doesn't matter anymore. She comes first. That's just the way it is."

Dillon nodded, accepting the words and appreciating the fatherly direction he'd been sorely lacking, though he didn't say as much. They walked back to the bar in relative silence, and Jonathan waited outside while Dillon broke the news to his friends. There would be no massive intoxications or strip clubs, at least none that involved him. When he walked out of the bar, he appeared taller. He held a slight grin on his lips. His chest was puffed out a bit. Jonathan looked out into the street to hide his smile. Dillon's brother jogged up to them and put his arm around the soon-to-be groom, whispered something in his ear, and slapped him supportively on the back. Soon another friend was alongside as well. Jonathan thought to himself, *Now, those are your friends, kid.*

Sienna could see the four men approaching as if victors from a battle easily won. Kat rose to her feet slowly and mumbled, "I don't believe it..."

Sienna also stood and when she did, she smiled from ear to ear with pride.

117

It was a magnetic smile Jonathan could see from a distance, and he walked directly toward it without looking away as if no one else existed. He was reading something in that smile; there was something about her carriage and the light around that flowered tree. He could see that her soul had changed. And he couldn't wait to take her to Bella, to guide his child into Sienna's arms so he could love them together. As she wrapped herself around his neck to hug him and to thank him, he felt the motherhood inside her that he always longed to know. He couldn't put it into words—he'd never be able to describe it. He looked at her and *knew* he'd found the mother of his child.

⊗◎

The restaurant was beautifully decorated, yet elegantly simple. The food was amazing; the service, unparalleled; and the atmosphere was perfect, complete with candlelight and a medley of strings and piano playing softly in the background. Mia had prepared the dishes especially for them, and when they finished, she approached their table which was customary.

"Good evening. I'd like to introduce myself if I may, I'm Mia, Associate Chef at Murray's. I've prepared your food this evening. Was it to your liking?"

They both agreed that it was excellent. Mia then turned her attention to Jonathan.

"Sir, may I suggest that you accompany me to choose the final course for this evening for the lady?"

"Of course." He smiled at Mia and lifted a brow to Sienna.

"Right this way, Sir. Excuse us, Miss." She winked coyly at Sienna.

As they walked toward the elegant pastries, toward the in-house chocolaterie, Mia relaxed her professionalism a bit and became more like her sweet, down-to-earth self. She directed Jonathan into a secluded corner. She reached into her pocket as her smile broadened and her eyes began to twinkle with excitement and wonder. What she pulled out was undoubtedly a jewelry box, and what she was proposing was undoubtedly to his benefit.

"I thought I'd better move fast," she said in a heated whisper. "You don't have to do this tonight—I mean if you want to wait—we can do it some other night."

She was as excited as a kid on Christmas morning, and she opened the box for him as her eyes darted around making sure they wouldn't be discovered. She revealed a gorgeously designed ring with a fire opal at its center, surrounded by beautifully laid diamonds. She was beaming as brightly as the ring.

He said, "Sienna Jewel—it matches her name."

"Exactly. Sienna loves this ring. She even tried it on one day, but she said it was—and I quote—'the kind of ring a man should buy a woman'," Mia nearly squealed, but checked herself and scanned the kitchen area to make sure her coworkers weren't getting impatient with her.

She went on, "I should warn you—it's expensive. I know the jeweler, and he let me take it...we girls made the down payment."

She nodded toward a far table, and Jonathan followed her gesture, discovering all the girls were present plus Dillon and his two friends.

"And, by the way, we don't want to be paid back. But when I say it's expensive," she continued, "I mean it's kind of like buying a car."

She studied him with inquisitive eyes, her hand up in the air in the form of a question.

"Um...just so I know, are we talking a Ford or a Bentley?" he asked.

She thought for a moment then said, "A Lincoln? But, you know, a *used* Lincoln without the down payment."

He glanced over at the table full of young people. Dillon smiled and nodded and raised his coffee cup. Kat put her hands together and tapped her lips in a mixture of a plea and a prayer. Aurora flapped her arms and mouthed, "Chicken?" And Jackobie, still in her scrubs, watched him silently with her pale green eyes that were hard to read and at certain times—like now—a little spooky.

He looked down at Mia, and a sheepish grin came upon his lips and broadened into a full, warmhearted smile that came gloriously through his eyes.

"Yeah," he said. "Let's do it."

Mia threw her arms around his neck and kissed his cheek. He laughed and hugged her in return. Just then she caught sight of the Executive Chef beckoning her.

"I have to go. Thank you, Jonathan, she'll love it!" She squeezed his hand good-bye. "Oh...it'll be with the dessert."

Jonathan stepped out the side door of the restaurant. He took a deep breath and checked for confirmation from the sky. He was still smiling. He grasped the railing in front of him tightly, then relaxed his hold. He noticed a busboy on a cigarette break was staring at him.

"How you doin?'" Jonathan said with a nod.

The kid raised a hand in hello and continued to smoke.

"Dear God, please bless this union," Jonathan said out loud. "Like You, I want it to last forever. I want this love to be real."

The busboy stared, but Jonathan didn't care. He smiled at the kid. The kid looked away and privately rolled his eyes.

Jonathan bowed his head, then his entire upper body, still grasping the railing with both hands. He felt his earthly father's presence and for a moment was transported to the deck of the man's ship, which was also—more times than not—his church. The waters about them were still; the waters about them were peaceful. Father and son had always shared a special, silent code of honor that wouldn't diminish a half-world round. He felt his father's hand upon his shoulder, gently guiding him into his future.

"Okay, Dad," he said, then looking up into the stars which were his compass, "Okay, Father. Let's do this."

The smoking kid had become overtly anti-social, turning his back on the praying man entirely.

"You have yourself a nice night then," Jonathan called to him.

The young man lifted his cigarette and flicked some ashes to the ground in reply.

Jonathan rejoined Sienna at their table which was out on the veranda, positioned near the outdoor fireplace. It was a beautiful setting, but nothing looked as good as she did in the firelight and in the candlelight as they both played off her rich, red dress. He kissed her cheek before taking his place across from her. He smiled, doing his best to contain himself, concealing his plan, and for all intents and purposes it seemed to work. Mia hadn't arrived with the dessert, so he asked his love a question.

"What does your name mean to you?"

"Well...," she said thoughtfully. "I was raised by my grandmother—she gave it to me. I miss her terribly. She was...she *is* a big part of who I am. I credit her for the way I turned out. I only had her 'till I was thirteen, but she instilled nearly all of my values just by the way she lived. My name, mostly, reminds me of her. I never got the chance, before she died, to ask her why she picked that name. Sienna obviously is not my coloring," she said and slightly twirled a strand of her jet black hair, "but she always said I was her little jewel."

Mia was waiting in the wings thinking, *He's good.*

She could tell by Sienna's facial expressions that she was talking about her grandmother. She correctly assumed it was because Jonathan asked her about the origin of her name.

Jonathan thought that Mia was an extraordinarily intuitive host, because she was delivering the dessert at exactly the right time as if on cue. The rest of the gang, lead by Sienna's girls, slowly, silently, filtered into the space between the building and the veranda. Two of them were already crying and holding on to each other in anticipation.

Mia placed the tray of tiny and delectable desserts, chocolates and mousses and decorated artisanal works, in the middle of the table, directly between them. It took a moment for Sienna's eyes to land on that ring which was in the center them all. It took her breath away as it caught her eye. Mia politely bowed and exited the scene, with a huge smile and a little dance as she moved back toward her peers. The remaining patrons on the veranda abandoned their meals one by one to also witness the event.

"Sienna…," he started to say. He reached across the table for her hand and held it confidently and lovingly. He was not at all nervous. His hand didn't tremble, his mouth did not go dry, his words did not elude him. Not at all. This, to him, was as natural as his heartbeat. He forgot that anyone was present but her. "I know you prayed today. I hope I've given you enough time." His eyes indicated a hint of apology.

"I meant all the things I said to you before. When I say I am loyal, that's exactly what I mean. When I said that I will take care of you as long as I live, that's exactly what I'll do. And when I tell you that I love you, I mean I will love you forever. I will love you forever. I will love you forever…"

His eyes became misty as he spoke. He maintained his composure, though he barely contained his joy. He let go of her hand to take up the ring. He slid back his chair and moved in front of her bending down on one knee. He looked into her eyes and discovered astonished happiness there. He smiled at her, at her amazement, and they both giggled together. He wordlessly asked for her hand, and she willingly gave it.

"Sienna Jewel." He smiled at her, releasing all of the charms God gave him to use on her. "Will you honor me; will you make me the luckiest guy on earth, by becoming my wife?"

He waited as she said, "Yes," through tears of joy that she couldn't stop.

She said it again, "Yes…yes, I will." He slipped that ring that reminded her of her name, that reminded her of her grandmother, on her hand. And they embraced each other, laughing, and they stood together, kissing, until their family encircled them raining down tears, joy, and congratulations amid a restaurant full of people who stood up, clapped, and cheered.

Finally, most of the onlookers sat back down, but they were still watching with smiles. Most of Sienna's family had circled around her and had finished their hugging.

"If you don't mind," Jonathan boldly addressed the entire veranda, "I'd like to sing my girl a song."

The group clapped and nodded their encouragement, as they enjoyed the show. He took Sienna's hand and led her to the piano. The pianist was more than happy to relinquish it to them. Sienna sat next to Jonathan.

"This song is called, 'Butterfly,'" he said as began to play the song he'd written for her.

> Hushed through a dozen winters, desert dry a dozen souls,
> the years became a blanket hiding stories never told.
> Seasons cursed and ragged, drift by atop the snow,
> time threatening to bury young lives before they're old.
>
> Until you, my jeweled butterfly, painted blue the crystalline sky,
> caused us to look up with our dark and clouded eyes.
> You saw right through all our reasons why we could not live until we
>   died
> unto our past, all the hate, all the things to leave behind.
> And so we're free in a blessed, sweetened summer light
> and with you fly, my jeweled, Sienna butterfly.
>
> Your summer fields awaken me to a world of truth and knowing.
> Your meadow seems to me to be a place of love that's growing.
> Your wings, your breath, a mystic picture and a story
> of lives you changed from burial to glory.
>
> Your gentleness is evident through your stalwart power.
> Your holy force is felt beneath the slow and silent hour.
> His compass guides your heart through storm to lighted haven
>   towers.

You land, my dream, in fields of rainbow flowers.

You're delicate in strength while you flutter above.
Your beauty, it soars with peace on winged doves.
It's only you, Sienna Jewel, I will ever and always love.
For you, Butterfly, I will find all you've dreamed of.

The song was to Sienna, almost as beautiful as his eyes which truly *saw* her. With a voice, that was as pure as his heart. And his rare talent was to her as amazing as his presence before her.

He was, simply, the only man her grandmother would have approved of. And he was, amazingly, the father of her child and the answer to her most secret, spiritual prayers.

chapter seventeen

*L*IKE WHEN THE sweet weather surrounds a perfect growing day in baby blue haze. Like when an artist's sunset blends a most manic palate into peace. Like when an unencumbered moon drawn close on a night string kisses the trees with dripping silver light..., they all looked up. They wondered from where it came. Like magic traces memory for visions gone unseen, somehow it happens. And no one knows why.

> *Love—when it happens real—moves through shadow undetected; through phantom mist and vapor, steals. And what one would have thought, it matters not, our secure judgments then, it breaches. It's far above our unholy knowing, far beyond our selfish reaches. It can be taken, only, to give without bounds, and in its presence, only, is the absence of sin found.*

> *Love, therefore, defines (and is defined by) nothing but God.*

Autonomous wonderments and awakenings like these floated about their thoughts but never came down throughout their lighthearted conversation to land beneath an owner. They were too happy to question anything of love; too mesmerized by its aura to claim it, too drunk with it to think. They were chatty for a flitting time, then each was found suddenly, silently sitting with dreamy smiles upon their faces, wide-eyed and gazing at the night stars flying by and wishing upon them like a child would—not one of the many was wasted—not one was lost. As they all filtered in through Sienna's front door (*home*—the word experienced at its very best that evening), the segregate mood collected, gathered into an inexplicable joy that gained a fantastic roving energy. A union of spirit and hope moved them confidently toward their futures, both apart and intertwined together; a feeling of security and light came about them that graced them as a blessing, and they knew it was from Above. Everyone was blanketed in soft laughter, capped with homespun warmth, and tucked into the folds of time with gentleness as should a true family do for one another; though several stray tears were still being restfully shed and modestly pressed away from smiling eye corners, covered beneath someone else's strong shoulder, they simply didn't stay. It was a quiet, peaceful night and moving slowly; every being was glistening with an inner light; every heart was holding on to fleeting moments as if to draw them out, giving the mind enough of time to savor the bitter with the sweet.

And Jonathan watched it pass by like a hallmark Christmas Eve, one he wanted to remember always, one he wanted to replay in his mind should he ever find himself an old man running short of days. He was seated on one of the ivory sofas near the fireplace with the rest of the guys but was only partially listening to their conversation—rather, he was intently watching Sienna, and every so often, she glanced at him and gave him a rewarding smile. He watched her contentedly; genuinely proud of and impressed by how naturally she interacted with each of her girls—comfortably, openly, warmly, respectfully. He noted how many hugs passed between them, and he observed that even though their personalities were all strikingly different, there were no one-sided relationships here. Everyone seemed mutually *known* and accepted; there seemed to be no typical modern-day miscommunication, no misunderstanding, no withdrawal, no proximal social isolation. And upon this realization, he understood the immense amount of work it must have entailed—the time, effort, money, self-control, self-discipline, modeling, and sleepless nights—the sheer amount of herself she must have given to get this kind of result. *These things just don't happen by themselves*, he thought.

While watching these things unfold—full-well knowing their origin to be a precious rarity, and most unfortunately, these days, a youth's most coveted luxury—he became engrossed as he witnessed them. He considered himself blessed, truly honored to be the one breathing beside the stories as they transpired beautifully in front of him each like a singular, ivory flower opening brilliantly beneath the midnight haze on the moor. (Had he put the miracles he saw into flat spoken word as did the reverenced storytellers of old, had he put them into mere one-dimensional writing as the great scholars once transcribed upon paragon scrolls, no one in the common, present daylight would have believed him nor shared in their passing glory. They would have waved a rude and silencing hand of dismissal, disrespectfully turned their back, or spat on the rocky ground in front of him; they would have misused his beautiful name and called his wondrous angelic find rubbish—a waste of time when there was real work to be done, and this, both his lifelong annoyance and their deeply tragic loss, was the birthplace of his very first song. And this current enlightened experience, too, he'd be sure to be lifting back up to the heavens with acknowledging thankful sound, swirling its anointed message within the folds of music's non-confrontational, peacefully inviting magic, and with the heartwarming imaginings brought on by just the right soul-soothing melody, they'd be listening to him fully—with their whole hearts, they would—while at the helm, the plow, the grinding stone, the filleting knife, while kneeling in the garden, they'd be singing it out of their very own mouths like a uniting, universal prayer before they had the wicked chance to disbelieve it. Through his music, they'd not have the chance to waste a God-ordained miracle simply because it filtered into their hopeless world through one imperfect, mortal man.) And so like a vivid dream, it continued, quickly becoming his favorite of them all, and he heard again that familiar voice above sprinkling down around him like song dust off angels' wings, *Use your gift... it's God shining through.* The vision allowed him was exceptional, expansive like the sea; the view translucent, like a crystal, like a moonlit rainbow ring drifting softly through stilling sliver-charcoal cloud, and yet warm beneath as summer sand through his childhood toes as he awakened, and he stretched his soul, far beyond his skin, far beyond his reach, far beyond his beloved ocean, and he smiled with his childhood smile, accepting boyishly the wonder, the treasure in God's hand tossed to his endless shore. His heart was opened, and as an adult he'd never been so alive.

And this is what he saw.

He was being graced with sweet innocence regained and with glances from hope-filled, confident, and radiantly smiling eyes, eyes that once were hopeless, afraid and ignoble, possessed by pain grown nearly permanent, running deep. Had this pain stayed long (or for another mere moment in time), had it hardened there in soft soul, had Sienna not found a crack to creep in through, it would have been a travesty most dire, spackling beauty with ash; covering interesting authenticity with a dull sort of survivorship holding ignorantly to repetition; barely providing weak energy, like drudgery to be walked through endlessly, an energy only enough for horrors to be resurrected and secret sorrows to be relived. Yes, it would have been a travesty most dire, keeping generational abuse afloat and alive and rampantly, currently, actually happening. (*That's how it happens after the wreckage*, he thought to himself. *That's how the devastation carries on, and Sienna stopped it, she salvaged peace for many.*) And had their young, smooth shoulders not been unburdened or unscarred somehow, had someone special and aligned not come along by being humbly led—and then not audaciously, fearlessly acted—truth and destiny-bold would have been darkly cloaked with a coward-cringing stagnation waiting on death alone for a lifetime; mesmerizing irises many-a-shade around him now like butterflied fields of clover would have been injected with malignant deception to the point of a different jaundiced tint, all blended to sameness, to bland-ness, to erasure, and matched with the unnatural, the unlovely, the unfruitful, and the dead, ubiquitously multiplying with the color evil like lush pastures bleed down to shifting sand. And everyone around them starves...

But these dreadful things never happened to these girls or to their future daughters or their sons—at least, they didn't happen for long—because of one determined woman under God who reached out and made a better way.

And right then and there he wrote their family song and tucked it safely in memory, in a secret pocket nearest to his heart. And thinking he was doing all the giving here, he received from them a most precious gift in return.

Seeing this much wisdom lived out, being enveloped by this much love and selflessness, it helped him. It restored some of his own integral faith in humanity when God moves through it; faith he hadn't known he'd lost somewhere along his way. He hadn't realized, until that very moment, that something inside of him had gone missing, that somehow, something to do with the pressures of making money, something to do with too much unneces-sary pain, had caused him, too, to spit on the very Spirit moving through the unlovely to love all. And he repented to his Lord for slowly growing calloused and blind over time, for possibly doing to others that which he most despised, rejecting their sincere attempts to reach out to another, to him, from whatever angle they had tried; the hugs he didn't quite return, the conversations he cut short for no good reason or the words he didn't truly hear, the gazes he ignored rather than smiled back to, the gifts he rejected from fans, from an elderly neighbor, from a stranger's child; the random acts of kindness he met with haughty pride; the amazing singers and writers he denied entry into the business because of a jealous, competitive vein; his human judgments, any of them, that limited a limitless God. And he received God's mercy and covering in regard to all these things; he accepted His forgiveness instantly so that another moment wasn't lost on himself. And automatically, his own eyes shone out clearer toward the others in the room, in his life; his own soul emanated through him truer, more true to the color divinely given him from the start. And he could no longer take his eyes off of her in particular; he could no longer separate his soul from hers; there was no way he could live another day without her. She'd shown him the deepest part of who he was—someone he'd almost forgotten to be true to; she'd reminded him that the best part of him was the child within—the purest version of himself and that closest to what God created.

His thoughts were interrupted by Aurora, her prominent voice commanding everyone's attention. She wanted to offer up a toast with her bubbling cider. She passed around the filled glasses, then wished Sienna and Jonathan every happiness in the world, indicating that she felt they both deserved it. She appropriately left out any sarcastic remarks she may have been itching to let loose, and everyone politely drank to the newly engaged couple. Jonathan went to stand next to his lady and kissed her affectionately after the toast. The hour was getting late, and the group started saying their good-byes, except Katarina. She asked Dillon to wait for her, then she tapped Jonathan on the arm.

"Jonathan, can I speak with you for a minute—alone?"

She seemed a little nervous with him, so he gently took her by the arm and guided her toward the greenhouse. His steady touch and his self-assuredness noticeably calmed her as they walked. Once they were alone, she looked around at her beloved plants; the trees, with their delicate strings of light, that cast a warm glow over the fountain and she nearly burst into tears right then and there. She'd strung all those lights with Sienna, just the two of them. She disappeared for a moment inside the memory, its image trapped within a distorted timeline that, to her, felt just like yesterday.

"Hey," Jonathan said softly, trying to console her while bringing her back. He rubbed her arm and offered her a smile.

"It's been a pretty emotional night, hasn't it?"

"Yeah," she said, shaking her head. "I'm sorry, it's just... I'm really going to miss this place. I can't even begin to tell you how much."

"It'll still be here," he said, then added quietly, "but most importantly, so will Sienna. No matter where she's at, she'll always be there for you."

"Oh, I know. I'm sorry," she said as she pulled herself together, changing her focus from the greenhouse, and all the fond memories it held, to him.

She looked up at him with large, emerald green eyes. He noticed her light, freckled skin and how it contrasted with her deep red hair. He fell in love with her sweet disposition. She was such an open, honest person.

"I wanted to talk to you. It's nothing bad... it's just...," she stammered, shaking her hand by her face as if that helped her hold back the tears she desperately needed to cry.

Somehow she fell into the look he held in his eyes, and she began studying them; she seemed to get utterly lost in their depth and mystery and she didn't say anything for a long moment. She just stared at him; he simply waited and allowed her to observe whatever she thought she saw in him.

"Dillon told me what you said," she started, almost accusatorily. "He told me what you did—for me."

Jonathan could see her entire body starting to tremble; he noticed her hands were shaking so he reached out and held one of them tightly, and he quietly told her, "It's okay...."

Her defiant chin dropped a touch; her defenses seemed to be crumbling down around her ankles, and he watched as she silently made the choice to say what she needed to say. She took a deep breath and went on bravely, pushing her way through a faltering voice.

"He said...." She swallowed back some more fear. "He said that you told him he was taking advantage of the fact that I didn't have a father. He said you said that from now on...you'd be my dad. I've never had a father, Jonathan. Not ever. I always wanted one. I mean, I always felt I needed one—badly. Every time I needed him to be there, when I needed defending, or I needed protecting, or I just needed a hug, I'd turn around and no one was there— ever. No one was ever standing behind me, not when I was five, thirteen, or eighteen...not until tonight. For the first time in my life, I turned around and you were there. I've been waiting for you for so long..."

Her voice gave out and her eyes filled with tears, but she didn't look away from him; she didn't blink for fear that he'd disappear. She hesitated to ask him but finally got up the raw nerve, and she whispered, almost sacredly, through the cracks in her soul, "Did you really mean it—what you said?"

She stood there waiting for his answer, holding her breath, as if teetering on the brink of her childhood. Tears quietly trailing her skin fell into an abyss of her past, and she wondered if he would salvage it for her.

He was speechless for a moment. He didn't realize at the time how much his statements would mean to her, but he meant them then, and he meant them now.

"Yes, Katarina, I meant it—every word. If a father is what you need, then that's what I'll be."

She stood before him a minute more, letting it all sink in, weighing her pent-up rage against her inability to trust someone with something this huge, and it all came down to one question—could she trust *him*? This was the most tender part of her broken heart, and she was considering handing it over to him while it was still bleeding, allowing him to do with it whatever he would. And she didn't know if she could let it go; she'd held onto it for so long as if the pain and the emptiness *were* her dad, but she also knew that if she didn't let it go, she'd die slowly from its disease, and all the life would eventually be drained from her. So, in the stagnant midst of this indecision, she stared him down some more; she found the look in his eyes to be sincere, and she could find no reason to question his honesty or his integrity. Her mind scanned backward, racing over two decades without a father, retracing all the miserable memories she had tried her best to neatly compartmentalize and hide. This continued until all her thoughts consummated at one point—him. *Jonathan.* When she spoke his name inside her mind, it was like a light had been shifted from the cursed, unanswerable word *why* to the wonderful, possibility-laden words *why not*. It was a brilliant illumination that highlighted this man's beautiful face which commenced to tell her exactly who he was—his skin was shining like a silver cloud and rather angelic, like a boy's; his expression was unbelievably kind, and yet it held to a powerful force earned through private horrors and endless experiences endured; his jaw was strong, set, determined and seemed to define his essence as unflinching toward fear, unyielding of the good. And then he smiled...and all these traits came together in such an ethereal way, they made no room for lies—there wasn't a single falsehood to be found within him. His look, his being, his willingness, and his readiness to give seemed to evaporate all the emptiness her memory sought to cling to. She retraced his countenance with her eyes as if she were creating his everlasting portrait—she wanted to remember this moment in time forever. She didn't touch his skin, but she colored it in layered brushstrokes within her mind. She painted him beneath a fatherhood crown of jewels, drew him above all others to a lofty tower over her life—an elevated place of favor, of instant reverence and honor, and it was rare like art perfectly preserved and graced, found still hanging above a charred mantle in a beloved home of cinder and ash.

"So this is what you look like," she whispered, utterly mystified.

She threw her arms around him and buried her face in his chest, started sobbing and saying she was sorry at the same time. He stroked her hair and held onto her tightly, whispering, "It's okay, sweetheart. You don't have anything to be sorry for. Understand that, please. You don't have anything to be sorry for..."

He shook his head, momentarily cursing all absentee fathers as he gently rocked her in his arms. He looked into the main house, and Sienna and Dillon were watching them. Sienna smiled and nodded, placing a hand over her heart and mouthing, "Thank you." Dillon just stared at them blankly, wondering what it was going to mean for him to have this Jonathan guy around permanently. Sienna took Dillon by the arm and led him into the kitchen to offer them more privacy.

Katarina eventually quit crying and looked up at Jonathan. He offered her a handkerchief from his pocket. She habitually apologized again, this time for getting mascara on his white shirt, and he immediately tilted her chin up and looked her in the eye.

"You don't have anything to be sorry for. Please promise me you'll think about that, okay?" he asked gently then added, "I haven't seen you do one thing wrong yet."

And they smiled sweetly at each other.

"I don't really know how to act around guys—any of them," she admitted to him.

"Well, I can tell you one thing. Never apologize unless you've truly done something wrong, which I would guess will be next to never," he instructed. "From what I can see you look like a princess, like a queen—you're beautiful, you're kind, you're obviously patient with that one out there..."

He pointed out toward Dillon, and she smiled.

"And you have the most amazing smile and heart I've ever seen. You're an amazing person. Don't ever apologize for being who you are. You're beautiful. You're valuable, precious, and most definitely loved. It's your father's loss that he was missing, not yours. Don't carry it with you, not anymore. You've carried it long enough. It's over. And you—look at you, at your life—you've turned out beautifully. I'm proud of you."

Katarina looked at him, speechless, wondering how he could know so much about her, so soon. She'd never been able to get the help she needed before. For some reason, she needed help from a man—someone kind, decent, someone worthy of the title, Father.

"I don't have to carry it anymore . . . ," she finally said, searching his face.

"No. It's over. You've officially got a father in me. You are no longer fatherless."

He winked at her kindly, and as his words resonated within her, she smiled back a more permanent, a more confident, smile. It was one that showed the immense relief she felt from hearing those powerful healing words.

"I don't know what to say except thank you," she said. "Thank you for what you did for me tonight with Dillon. I just kept thinking all last week, 'If I only had a dad,' and then you showed up and, well, you amaze me. You are the first prayer I've had answered *exactly*.

"And I didn't know how much I needed to hear someone say that I'm no longer fatherless. I mean those things you just said to me . . . thank you . . . thank you so much."

As she dabbed at her eyes, he considered the weight of *her* words. To be the answer to somebody's prayer was astounding—uplifting and intimidating at the same time. It made him stand deathly still as if on a pedestal perched upon holy ground. *How did I get here? Where do I go from here?* It dared him to mentally retrace the path he'd been walking, and it forced him to admit he'd been walking it blind. He wasn't the one in control. Timing was everything, and tonight the timing had been perfect—a product of grace. And hers was an answered prayer that left him breathless, as if someone greater than he had taken the air from his lungs in order to speak to her the solution. He heard the words, *My steps are ordered by the Lord*, as if whispered off one of Bella's prayers, and he got chills along his spine.

He was truly humbled when he finally replied, "I mean what I'm saying to you, Kat, every word. And if you ever need anything else from me—anything at all—you let me know unapologetically. Do we have a deal?"

"Deal." She smiled, taking a moment to acknowledge the seriousness in his tone. "You know . . . you're a little young to be my dad but I'm used to it . . . with Sienna and all. To me you are perfect."

"Well, I can assure you I'm not that." He chuckled, blushed a bit, and said, "But thanks for tellin' me that I am."

She looked at him again with those big eyes of hers, "Jonathan?"

"Yes, sweetheart."

"Would you...." She hesitated for a moment. She had always believed she'd have no one to ask. "...would you walk me down the aisle at my wedding?"

He was amazed by her. He was truly touched that this young woman could be so accepting and loving toward him so soon—she made him feel like part of Sienna's family, and for that he was overwhelmingly thankful.

"I'd be honored to," he said quietly.

He kissed her hand and held onto it until he returned her to her fiancé.

One last trip to the stables the following morning, and Jonathan and Sienna were on the road again, six hours in the car, each taking their turn at the wheel. Intermittent conversations occurred between them as did smiles and laughter and affectionate touches. She liked the way her ring reflected the light, but it didn't hold a candle to his eyes. They were full of peace, hope, and wonder, especially when he looked at her and asked himself how he got so lucky.

The conversations were these...

"Explain to me your God."

"He is lovely. He is beautiful. Nothing is wasted, and He knows everything about us. He knows us better than we know ourselves. We just need to trust Him, follow Him, be patient with Him as He is with us, and He will take care of it all—everything. We truly do not need to worry once we get to know Him. I didn't know what love was; I didn't know peace or joy. I didn't know what it felt like to feel right about anything until I got to know Him. He means everything to me."

And...

"You don't have to tell me, you don't have to talk about it if you don't want to, but you were married before?"

"I was."

"If you don't mind me askin', what happened?"

"To be honest—it was a mess from the beginning. He'd been abused, I'd been abused, and when we got together our intentions were good, but we just ended up abusing each other. It was the most horrible experience of my life because we were actually trying to do it right, but we just lacked the skills; we lacked God. So, everything fell apart. We lost money, friends, and our reputations. We lost everything, but then God intervened."

"How do you mean?"

"It got so bad, I turned it all over to God, and He took it. I got saved. Eventually, so did my husband. We actually turned it all around, with God's help. Everything changed. Nobody around us believed it—you know, the 'everyone would rather watch you fall' thing, but we knew. And then, he was gone."

"He left you?"

"He left his life here. He was a foreman for a road construction crew. They were working on a bridge and a crane gave out."

"I'm sorry," he said, studying her with compassion then staring down the road. "I guess nobody knows what's coming."

"That's true. But the good thing is—I know where he's at."

"Heaven," he said and gently squeezed her hand.

"Heaven," she agreed. "You'd be amazed how much strength that has given me over the years."

And also...

"Why Connecticut?"

"Barbara. Nice horses. Distance. Change of scenery. Mostly, I have no earthly idea. But once I got here, it just felt like I belonged here." She looked at the countryside passing by outside the window—at the green, the trees, and she smiled. "Secretly, I've been steadily working my way back to the Motherland."

"Ireland?"

"Ireland, Scotland, and England, primarily. And I'm a little German and Native American, and my Grandpa said something about Gypsies, but I'm not sure he was being serious."

"So you're a Heinz 57, then," he teased her.

"I'm an American, then," she answered with a genteel pride. "I'm more like ketchup."

∞

They pulled onto Jonathan's street mid-afternoon and the neighborhood seemed extraordinarily quiet. He was scanning his yard, the windows, whatever he could glimpse of the back porch, for his daughter. He was so anxious to get out of the car that he switched off the ignition before putting it in park.

Upon realization of his mistake, he laughed and said, "Thank God we're here! I've missed her so much."

"Let's just leave the bags; we can get them later," she suggested and they both started jogging toward the house with smiles on their faces. Jonathan took the stairs two at a time, fully expecting to see the happy and beautiful little girl he'd left a few days prior. But upon entering the house, he quickly realized something didn't feel right. He instantly realized something had gone terribly wrong. The old dog—typically silent and apathetic—was standing at attention in the corner, barking incessantly into thin air.

Mrs. Hopkins was roaming mindlessly about the kitchen, obviously exhausted and grumpy. She started toward them complaining and running off at the mouth about everything the girl had done wrong, but neither Jonathan nor Sienna were intent on listening. Bella was crying on the floor of her playroom, and her dad pushed past the old woman and ran to her. He picked her up and held her close to him, telling her everything would be all right now, that he was home now, but she seemed inconsolable. Mrs. Hopkins was still talking, directing her efforts on Sienna as she picked up some of her things to go.

"That child is out of control. She's started up her stories again. She should be in school. That's what's wrong with her. She's got too much time on her hands if you ask me. I'm out of chocolate mix, and I wasn't going to run to the store to get more. She's mad at me." She paused for the first time since they'd entered the door, and she looked directly at Sienna and said, "I'm sorry, but there's something wrong with that girl."

With that the woman abruptly closed the door and was gone. Sienna ran to Jonathan's side. The concern was weighing on his face as if he felt guilt-sick all the way down through his bones.

"I shouldn't have left her," he whispered into the sobbing girl's hair.

"Bella?" Sienna asked gently. "I can go to the store. Would you like some chocolate milk?"

The child quieted her sobs and slowly looked up from her father's soaked shoulder. She stared into Sienna's eyes and seemed to Sienna to be a different soul altogether. *Dear God . . .*

"What happened, baby?" Sienna inquired, glancing toward Jonathan with a fervently growing concern.

"Mommy," Bella whispered and reached a hand down to Sienna's face.

"Mommy," she said again, this time with more urgency in her voice.

She started crying again and pointed at the floor behind her dad. Sienna immediately went down to her knees reaching out to them, nearly a dozen pictures colored in blood-red crayon, all of them indicating a motherly figure surrounded by what looked like violent slashes and blood. She started picking them up, one by one, studying each of them while Bella whimpered.

Jonathan looked on and said, "She's never drawn anything like that before."

He put the little girl down and, kneeling in front of his child, tenderly wiped her eyes with the tail of his shirt.

"Bella," his tone was gravely serious, "I want you to tell Dad what these pictures are about, okay? Tell me what happened here, while I was gone."

The girl walked around him to Sienna and put her arms around her neck. Sienna hugged her and told her everything was going to be all right. She handed Jonathan the pictures and he looked at a couple of them, shaking his head in confusion.

"Let's get some hot chocolate. Let's eat something and take a nap, okay? We'll all feel better and then we can talk. How does that sound?"

Bella nodded her head in acceptance but would not let go of Sienna. The child seemed terrified.

"I'm going over to talk to that woman," Jonathan muttered angrily. "I'll run to the store quick. You'll be all right here?"

Sienna nodded and carried the child to the sofa where they reclined together. Bella's little body was exhausted. Sienna held the child close to her until the last of the sobs ceased and she fell asleep. When Jonathan returned Sienna left Bella's side to discuss what he'd found out.

"She said Bella started one of her stories—one of her Irish prayers—and in this story, Bella prayed for a mother, which isn't unusual. But then, Mrs. Hopkins said she just started screaming in Irish, and I asked the old woman to repeat what she said. Well, Mrs. Hopkins doesn't know the language, but she did say that Bella said some things in English."

He took a deep breath and looked empathetically at Sienna, wondering if he should continue.

"What did she say?" Sienna encouraged.

"Mrs. Hopkins says Bella said you were going to die. She kept saying, 'Mommy's gonna die,' and she kept saying your name over and over again, apparently she was hysterical. And I believe Mrs. Hopkins is telling the truth. I mean, she's been around Bella for years, I don't think it was anything the old woman did. I just...I hate this...ya know? What father can handle his daughter being that upset, let alone the things she was saying about you?"

Jonathan started pacing, nervously running his hand through his hair, "I shouldn't have left her this long."

"We'll figure it out," Sienna reassured him. "We will."

"I'm sorry if this scares you," he said to her. "Honestly, it scares me...more than a little. She's never said anything this specific before. It's like she's warning us. She's never done that before."

The two of them walked over to the sofa and stared down at the sleeping girl.

"Jonathan," Sienna finally whispered.

"Yeah?"

"Does this town have a decent library?"

"Yeah, I guess," he said absentmindedly.

"As soon as she wakes up, I want to go. I have to show you something."

chapter eighteen

$\mathcal{B}$ELLA FELT MUCH better after a long nap and a cup of strong hot chocolate. She ate half of a grilled cheese sandwich and some grapes, then they were off to the library, wasting no time. The little girl was quiet but much more like the Bella they both knew. They found her several books, and she snuggled into a pillow in the children's section of the old, yet charming, building. Sienna claimed a nearby table and asked Jonathan to wait for her there. She returned shortly thereafter with a huge stack of books and a Bible.

"What is all this?" Jonathan asked. He noticed one of the books was the novel she had written, the movie he had recently watched. It was the story about the vindicator.

She didn't answer him, but she flipped through the Bible and read several passages about the gift of prophesy—supernatural revelation of the will of God. She read passages about intercession and the interpretation of dreams. She read passages about speaking in unknown tongues—a supernatural fluency in other languages from around the world as well as a heavenly prayer language of the Holy Spirit. She found the passages with shocking speed and read them with a sense of urgency as if she didn't have much time. She then flew to the stack of books written on the subjects—some of them fictional novels, and others, factual accounts written by experts. She voraciously read excerpts to him and, one by one, the pieces started to come together into the mysterious puzzle named Bella.

"Wait," he said, putting a hand over the page she was consumed with. He looked over at his daughter then directly back to Sienna. She closed the book.

"What are you saying?"

The tone in his voice was as near to a threat as she had ever heard coming from him. She could smell the spirit of fear standing next to him, could almost feel it breathing, contaminating the air between them.

"Let's go for a walk," she said calmly, trying to reassure him with a forced smile. She offered him her hand, but he didn't take it.

The three of them rode home in complete silence—not a single word was spoken. Bella put her books in the house and pulled on her rubber boots. They headed for the beach, which was cooling in the slant of the late afternoon sun. Jonathan sat on a large piece of driftwood, the dog curled up in the sand at his feet. Bella started drawing pictures with a stick, and Sienna stood looking out at the water which was still asking its timeless questions and taking with it all the answers. She silently begged it to speak. When his voice broke through, she jumped a bit, startled by the reality of it. He sounded colder than she ever hoped he would.

"Are you going to tell me what's going on with my little girl?"

She turned to him but didn't come any closer. She didn't say anything; she just looked at his face that seemed hard and cold and defiant. She didn't like seeing him like that, but she understood it.

"Go on," he dared her, "tell me about my daughter. Tell me what you think is wrong with her."

"Nothing's wrong with her, Jonathan..."

He looked past her into the gray water and his jaw quivered a bit. He was trying not to cry.

"Tell me!"

He raised his voice as if shouting at the demons of the sea instead of her. Bella looked up at him for a moment, before she continued her drawing.

"I believe...," she began, a little shakily, "that Bella is special. I believe she has been given a spiritual gift. I know this might sound crazy to you, that's why I wanted to show you the books. I guess they are some proof so you don't think all this is just in a writer's head."

She glanced at him, and he finally looked at her with tenderness, almost an outright guilt. She accepted his apology and continued, talking to him but also to the sea and to God.

"Somehow, over the centuries, people have become afraid of certain parts of the Bible. They dismiss those parts because they can't understand them. They can't understand them because they are rare. Bella is beautiful and she is rare. The Holy Spirit has blessed her with a gift to interpret stories and events, to speak prophetic prayers on the earth in order for God to summon leagues of angels in which to act on His behalf. And He entrusted her to you. You are her father. Your job is to protect her."

She turned to him and stared him down as if from an apocalyptic pulpit.

"Jonathan, if you are not a fierce protector of this child the world will crucify her. The burden of her gift alone will be almost impossibly heavy."

The sun broke from beyond a cloud behind his shoulder and cast a fiery light across her face.

"Don't ask me how I know this, but her demons will be alcohol or drugs to drown out the voices she hears if she can't discern which is from God and which is from Satan. Her enemies will be child psychologists and psychiatrists and counselors and teachers at school. Social workers will question you and watch you constantly until she is grown. Do not ever let those people get her alone."

The look on his face was something close to terror. He stared at Bella who was listening to the whole thing calmly, as if accepting it all as a truth she'd known since she was born. She looked at her father and said nothing, but he thought he heard, *Listen to her, Daddy*. He blinked back tears of frustration and rubbed at the headache forming just above his brow.

"What you can do," she went on, "and I will help if you would like, is teach her to accept her gift and use it carefully for God. It is a true gift from God, but sometimes others in the family line may have experienced something similar. If you can look back—they are usually social outcasts, as all greats generally are; they are typically shunned by the family and ostracized by the community and especially, ironically, the church. You can teach her how to operate in it appropriately, like when to use it and when not to, when to speak, when to stay quiet. A person's gift is generally their curse—like your music, like my writing. You just can't do it all the time, it'd kill you.

"But the beauty of all this, Jonathan, is that she has the power to change lives for the better. I don't think I'd be here now if someone hadn't prayed my way here."

Jonathan swore he saw a hint of pride graze across Bella's face in regard to that statement.

Sienna went on, "The power of prayer is the most amazing force on earth, and she has a direct link to the will of God."

Sienna turned to face the sea and stretched out her arms. Her body formed the shape of a cross, perfectly.

"She's in good company," she said. "Jesus is interceding for us right now."

She seemed to offer thanks to the sky and her arms slowly descended. She turned back toward him, and Bella walked up to her side and clung to her as if finally finding a place to rest. He looked at them in wonder, feeling as if he was trapped inside a warped dream.

"Are you scared?" he finally asked.

"No," Sienna answered matter-of-factly.

"Why not? I mean you saw those pictures..."

"Because God trusts us with her, or we wouldn't be here right now."

She turned to Bella and got down on her knees. She smiled at her and gently brushed the hair out of her eyes.

"Bella, will you do something for me?"

The girl nodded.

"Every time you get to the end of your stories, when you finish your prayer?"

The child nodded again, indicating she understood.

"I want you to say, 'God's will be done.' Can you remember that?"

"God's will be done."

Bella rehearsed it while locking eyes with the soul of her mother. She meant it with all the power she was endowed; and she prayed it over the life kneeling before her. And Sienna was well aware of that fact.

"Yep, just like that. If you say that, everything will be okay."

"Promise?"

"I promise."

The three of them walked home slowly, hand-in-hand, with Bella between them. Sienna looked peaceful. Bella looked tired but content and no longer afraid. Jonathan just looked at Sienna.

⬿⬾

"When did you know this about her?" he asked after they'd read Bella a story and she'd fallen asleep.

"The first day I spent with her, on the beach. I knew those were prayers she couldn't possibly have come up with on her own."

"And you tried to tell me the best way you could," he conceded, reaching over and gently squeezing her hand.

He studied her face silently; he visually traced over her lips and recalled her voice, taking the time to remember and truly hear everything she'd said to him earlier that day.

"Sienna, I'm sorry," he said, ashamed of how he had treated her. "You were trying to help us—you did help us—and I just...I shouldn't have acted that way and I'm sorry."

"It's okay," she said, "I understand. I'm actually impressed that you are even listening to me. Most people would just assume I'm crazy."

"I know you're not crazy. I know...." His voice broke with the weight of admitting it. "I know you're right. What I don't know is how to handle it. I don't know what I'm supposed to do. I've kept her out of school and she's nearly six years old. I never really would admit it to myself—the real reason why I kept her home. I guess I was afraid for her."

A moment of silence passed between them as they stared down at the sleeping child. Jonathan put his face in his hands and rocked back and forth a few times.

"Sienna," he finally whispered. "I don't know what to do."

She took his hand and said, "We'll figure it out. As long as we accept her just the way she is, she will be fine. She will. God knows what He is doing. We just need to have a little faith—and absolutely no fear."

She smiled encouragement toward him, and some relief settled in through his eyes as he started to trust her. She had, after all, single-handedly helped four young women overcome terrible odds to become amazing, successful, and outrageously kind, adults.

"Thank God you are here," he said to her. "I would be lost without you—you know that? We both would. Thank you, Sienna. Thank you for being here with us. And thank you for your wisdom."

He lay down on the bed and so did she. He covered her with a spare blanket then closed his eyes, sliding his arm around Bella. His face was buried in her hair, and Sienna knew a few tears were falling.

"Let me tell you a story," Sienna said, staring at the ceiling. "More like an idea, I guess. You know how, when you are standing on that shore out there and your heart becomes a compass and, just naturally, automatically, you are perfectly lined up to face your home country? You know how far away it is...but you swear...if you just close your eyes, you can reach out and touch it with your fingertips? That's what this little girl will be like to raise. Because she's greater than we are. The gift she has is real, so God will carry her and He'll guide us. Like the ocean, sometimes you might feel like you are drowning in the middle of it, but if you just keep going, keep following your heart, eventually the depth of it will fade, the waters will get warmer, and the current will grow softer, and she'll just flow. And then, when you open your eyes—you'll be there. You will be home, Jonathan. And you got there on nothing but a prayer."

She ended her story and looked over to two people whose eyes were intently watching her, completely absorbed in her story.

Jonathan leaned up on his elbow, suddenly gaining the energy of revelation, and he asked her, "How do you know that? How do you know that's how I feel when I look out at that water? How do you possibly know that?"

"I *don't*," Sienna answered him laughing. "Do you get how amazing that is? I *don't* know that about you, only God does. I think He just sent you a message through me. I think He's showing you how close He really is. That's a detail I'd have no way of knowing, but He knows. And He cares about the smallest of things concerning you. I have no doubt He'll take care of the biggest things, too."

Bella looked up at her mystified dad and said, "I knew she was one of us. She's like us, Daddy. This is my real mommy, the one I asked God for."

chapter nineteen

$\mathcal{E}$VENING CAME UPON them, and Bella had fallen into a deep, restful sleep. The two adults quietly made their way downstairs. Jonathan fixed them both a cup of tea. He slid hers across the counter but didn't let go of the handle. He just stared down at its spiraling steam for a moment before he looked into her eyes.

"I am really, very sorry for the way that I acted. I have a bad temper, but it blows over like the wind. I'm used to it, but I know you're not. I just want to make sure you're okay."

"I am," she said quietly. "Jonathan, I don't expect to become her mom overnight. It's going to take some time for all of us to adjust, and that's okay."

He looked relieved, thankful that she was so patient and understanding.

Honestly," she said, "I'd be more concerned if you weren't upset. That's your little girl I'm talking about. Your anger is a good sign."

"Thanks," he said in a way that indicated he wasn't totally convinced.

"You're welcome. And thank you for not writing me off as a crazy person."

They went to the sofa and sat in the relative quiet. The only sound was the dog snoring, and it was comforting. Their minds were both revolving around the events of the day. They were both tired, but neither would be able to sleep for some time. Sienna thought of a line from her favorite poem by Robert Frost, "Miles to go before I sleep."

"I haven't been completely honest with you," Jonathan said, breaking the silence. "Truthfully, I haven't been completely honest with myself."

She didn't say anything. She just listened, allowing him the time to process his thoughts and his feelings.

"I've been wishing for a mother for Bell since the day she was born. I don't know, I just think a girl should have a woman to look up to. But that's not all. I know Bella is...well, she's different. She's beautiful, she's got an amazing sense of humor, she's kind, but she's also got what I always thought of as a wild imagination. The things that she says...they're vivid, and violent, and they don't seem to go away. In other words, she's not growing out of it as I hoped. She's actually growing *into* it. And I was praying for a mother for her, but not just for her...for me as well. I was praying for someone who understood her and could help me with her. And here you are..."

He turned to her and forced a smile.

"You're everything I've ever wanted, everything I've ever asked for. And I can't believe I'm put off about you coming in and reading her like a book. Maybe I'm jealous, because you seem to know her better than I do. I don't know. Maybe I'm just scared. I don't understand most of what it is you're talking about, and those pictures she drew of you...Sienna, I don't want anything to happen to you. I think that would kill me.

"I guess I just feel pretty helpless right now. I feel really pathetic, actually."

The dog woke up and lifted his heavy head, checking on his people. They seemed sane. He went back to sleep.

"Jonathan?" Sienna said softly.

"Yeah."

"I don't believe God would have given that girl to just anyone."

"What do you mean?"

"I mean..." She took his hand and looked him square in the eye. "You were chosen by God to protect one of His angels. And if God can put that much faith in you, we certainly can."

He considered her words, and his confidence slowly but surely began to filter back into his being. He sat up a little taller, his chest was a bit more inflated, and the worry lines across his forehead eased their torturous grip. He smiled a sideways smile and shook his head, "Where did you come from?"

"You prayed for me, remember?"

She playfully bumped her shoulder to his, prompting him toward the positive.

"I guess I did," he put his arm around her and kissed her cheek.

They rested together another moment before he began again, "I have some questions."

"Okay."

"In your movie—the one about the vindicator—the children that are praying him down and creating a path for his vengeance...that's what you think Bella does?"

"I do. Though I'm pretty sure her prayers are not just about God's avenging

145

angels. The ones I heard her describe were peaceful, and, well, they were beautiful."

"But why does it have to be a child?"

"Because, and I mean no offense by this, look at the way you reacted to just the idea of it—it was a typical, adult reaction. Adults have more of the stains of the world smeared across their eyes; the way they see things is distorted. They live amid deception, and most of them are so deluded about spiritual matters, they'll fight the truth themselves; they'll fight the very thing that can set them free. They are not pure anymore. If there isn't a way to prove it, touch it, if they cannot see it, they don't believe it. They believe lies easier than the truth because truth is often stranger than fiction. They would get scared. They would run to a psychiatrist to get drugs to quiet the voices in their head, they would loose themselves in alcohol, they would jump off a bridge, they simply couldn't handle being that different. That's why the Bible says we need to become like a child to enter the kingdom of God; it takes a certain purity and humility to realize we are here for His use, not the other way around. And children…well, they just arrived here, and they have a special relationship with the Holy Spirit. No internal complications."

"And," she added, "you might want to read the book. The movie only covers about a tenth of it. And you'll want to be reading the Bible, specifically what the Apostle Paul wrote."

He sat still for a moment as if stopping time, letting all her words sink in through his skin, letting them find their way into the internal workings of his mind.

"How do you know all this stuff?" he finally asked her.

"*I* don't," she said, thinking for a minute. "It is a gift given to me by God for the sake of other people. I guess it is closest to interpretation or teaching. I have no idea why these things seem so evident to me and not everyone else. I very rarely talk to anyone about it, that's why I write fiction novels. People will accept it in that form. I guess they feel safer that way. It is hard to explain, but this stuff doesn't come from me—it comes through me. I am not intelligent enough to come up with it on my own. The two things I have going for me are one, I know God, and two, I'm humble enough to let Him use me. And that's what I hope to teach your daughter, if I'm given the chance."

"You've got the chance," he said, then asked her, "Will she be all right? I mean, you were saying her demons would be alcohol and drugs—the thought of that makes me sick. Why did you say that?"

"I meant, if we *don't* protect her, if we *don't* teach her how to operate in her gift, it—or the world—will eat her alive. But I believe we can protect her and teach her, and I think she will be just fine. I'm sorry if I was out of line when I said that. But it's readily available—I mean, it got Cheney, it got Aurora, it sounds like it got you, for a time. We just need to be careful that she stays close to God, because gifts are a burden and her gift is huge, so the burden will be greater. You struggled with your music; I'm sure coming from generations of fishermen, I'm betting that it wasn't easy to change your course. They probably didn't understand, and you didn't understand, but you did it anyway, because it's what you were called to do. It's your God-given gift. And you almost got lost in alcohol, drugs, and worldly things, which would have, ultimately, destroyed it—your gift and you. Now just imagine if your gift wasn't music. Imagine if your gift was saving lives by praying. The forces working against that child will be fierce. But I believe she can do it."

"How can you be so sure?"

"Because God doesn't ask us to do something that He won't lead us through. She'll make it. And if we stay diligent and teach her the spiritual things she needs to know, she will probably live one of the most blessed lives on the face of the earth."

"Dear God, I hope so." He whispered a prayer to God, then spoke to Sienna, "I think I'm starting to understand what you are saying. I'm beginning to see the things I've been missing. Believe it or not, this is starting to make sense to me."

"Good, just keep an open mind." She smiled. "There are a few more things I need to talk to you about."

"Lay it on me."

"I believe that I have some 'proof' that may help solidify this for you."

"Like what."

"Bella—some of the prayers she's prayed in the past. Think back...now, I'm kind of reaching here....Was one of them about a bird with a voice of an angel that was struck down somehow; was there a rainbow with blood on it, an open field with yellow flowers and stones?"

Jonathan's mouth went dry, and he nearly started to hyperventilate. He swallowed, forced himself to take a deep breath, and as he leaned forward, he nodded confirmation. Sienna smiled, because she realized Bella had prayed for them all.

"That was Aurora. The day she was left for dead, she had on a white T-shirt with a rainbow on it. It is covered with blood stains. She said that was always her favorite shirt, and she forced the orderly at the hospital to dig it out of a garbage bin and return it to her. She still has it. Aurora says she was dumped in a vacant lot with dandelions and stones all around her. She says she saw angels descending from the sky telling her to breathe and to sing. She says she would take a breath and let it out in a song. She did that over and over again until somebody found her. She thinks that is what kept her alive.

"And it wouldn't have happened, Jonathan, unless somebody prayed."

She went on.

"Was there another prayer about a healer who couldn't walk because her legs and arms were bound?"

"Yes," he whispered, turning to look at her.

"Jackobie. She's almost completely recovered from a childhood disease. Her parents abandoned her because they couldn't afford the treatments."

"Dear God," Jonathan whispered.

"She wouldn't have made it without those treatments, Jonathan, unless somebody prayed."

He nodded his head, beginning to realize the expansive scope, the immense gravity, of the situation.

"Mia is a chef, she will probably travel the world. She was found nearly starved, locked inside a trash bin when she was a baby. She spent years in foster homes. No one ever adopted her. She's always been a free spirit."

"I remember that prayer. It was about a baby in a bag that couldn't see, couldn't breathe. Bella kept saying, 'The baby's hungry—she's lost, she's cold.' I had no idea what she was talking about. Then a few days later she said, 'The baby's been fed—she's found, she's warm.' She said she was beautiful, she said, 'She speaks Irish, Daddy'."

Jonathan admitted to himself that this all seemed impossible, but he knew, somehow, its disjointed illusions formed the truth.

"What about Kat?" he asked. "Was she the sister in the fire?"

Sienna nodded.

"Her dad was an alcoholic. He'd fallen asleep in the recliner still smoking a cigarette. The cigarette caught the chair on fire, burned the whole house down. Katarina was just a baby; her father died in the hospital from the burns and the smoke. Her mother saved Katarina, but then she just left her at the hospital and never came back."

"Bella said a prayer about her sister with hair like fire. She said that one just a few months ago. She was talking about fire and smoke and a long journey from a country house of ash. But I still don't understand. I mean these things happened before Bella was even born."

"Not all the things. It takes a lot of intercession to save a life, Jonathan. There were a lot of corrections that needed to be made to compensate for those horrible events. I've only had Aurora for three years, Mia for three and a half, Katarina for four. Jackobie is the only one that's been with me for seven and she didn't start medical school—you know, to become a healer herself—until three years ago. And all the girls took about a year to adjust, I mean it took them a while to believe in God and to start seeing Him work in their own lives. Does that sort of fit?"

"It does."

"And listen to the words she is choosing, like *a long journey from a country house of ash*.... She's speaking about spiritual things, not just practical. She's being figurative and literal at the same time. And from a writer's standpoint, the only book I know that's written like that is the Bible. And it did take Kat a heck of a long journey from that house of ash to where she is now. 'I will give you beauty for ashes...,' that's a Bible verse. Kat asked you to be her father, didn't she?"

"Yeah, she did."

"So there, you see? She is Bella's sister. Amazing, isn't it."

"Sienna?"

"Yeah."

"Do you think she'll be able to change actual events, that she'll be able to operate in real time?"

"I don't know. My guess is that she's already operating on God's time. So far, it seems they've done a perfect job."

Another blanket of silence enveloped their thinking. She listened to Jonathan breathe in unnatural segments indicative of immense mental pressure. He certainly let out his share of heavy sighs.

"Another question," he said, "why do you think psychologists and psychiatrists will be her enemies?"

"It's classic—voices in your head? I'm sure there are some experts that are excellent, but the general trend doesn't seem to be good for children. In my experience working with kids, it just doesn't take much these days...an over-worked, single parent, the kid ate too many sugar-coated chocolate bombs for breakfast, he blinked too many times. They seem to pick almost any reason to stick a kid on meds. You need to be very careful who you let talk to her."

"You make it sound like a war."

"It can certainly get that way—but it's mostly a spiritual one. If her spirit is well, she'll be protected in the natural."

She stared blankly at the dog, getting lost in a memory she didn't know if she should share, but she finally decided to.

"Jonathan, do you remember when I told you about those girls in that psychiatric facility?"

"I do."

"Well, I've got a story to tell you that I've never told anyone. I've never written about it, I've never even prayed about it to tell you the truth. It is the one thing I don't have any of my own words for, so I will just tell it like it was."

"Okay," he said quietly.

"Many of those girls had been raped, molested; many of them were victims of incest and violence. I mean...the files." She shook her head and let out a long sigh of her own. "Anyway, you get the idea."

"I do."

"Well, part of their 'treatment,' part of *my job*, was to do what is called a take-down. A take-down can result from anything, like they are slitting their wrists with a pop-can, or they are in a fight with their roommate. But, from what I saw, a take-down resulted from a bad attitude, a personality conflict between a girl and a social worker, a change in the weather. They seemed to happen often, for no good reason. At least that's how I saw it. And a take-down went like this. Six of us were called in to surround that girl. None of us spoke or were to look her in the eye. We each grabbed a limb, somebody grabbed her head from behind her and stuffed a towel in her mouth to keep her from screaming or biting or breathing. Another of us got the door opened to the padded cell. We drug her in there. We stripped off all her clothes—to make sure that she didn't have a cigarette lighter to start the place on fire, or that she didn't hang herself with her jeans or saw on her veins with the zipper.

And, anyway, when she was lying there on the floor, we covered her with a sheet, but held her down until she stopped fighting. Then we each got up and locked her in that room for hours."

She stopped talking for a moment.

"I am not a doctor of psychology. I am not a professor of psychiatry. I am just a woman who was once a girl who was once raped and molested myself. Maybe I don't know everything, but I do know that if that was supposed to help that girl overcome her past, we must have all been a special kind of stupid."

She got up and walked in front of the window and looked out.

"Of all the things I have done, Jonathan—and believe me when I say I was no saint—that is the one thing I have never been able to justify or make peace with or ask forgiveness for. I simply do not understand it—it paralyses me to this day."

She turned to him, the silver outline of the moon resting on her shoulders, and said, "The only thing I know, Jonathan, is that you do not want your little girl falling into their hands. You do not want your daughter to walk through any door that is closed to God."

He got up and walked toward her, taking her in his arms. He hugged her and, without saying a word, expressed how thankful he was to have her on his side. She held so much wisdom, so many experiences. He admitted to himself that without her, he'd be completely lost on these matters.

"One last question," he said, pulling back from her to see her face. "What about school?"

"To be honest, if she were mine..."

"She is yours, honestly," he interrupted.

"I'd home school her. Or I'd find a truly Christian school, but I'd watch them like a hawk... or I'd take her somewhere else..."

"Like?"

"Like another country, someplace quiet, someplace less complicated."

"Ireland," he said.

"Yes," she answered. "But I'm not sure. I mean, maybe she's supposed to be here, right in the middle of the chaos, right in the middle of difficulty, and if we took her someplace quiet, she wouldn't be... I don't know, as *inspired*."

"I understand. Her place of inspiration might be different from ours. It might be different than say a writer, or a musician, hers might be more... intense."

151

"Maybe . . . I'm not sure."

"Well, she's done plenty of praying here. She's rather secluded. She likes the water . . . in fact, the sea seems to be her source. And you know when you said she probably received the call of God just like others in my family line? I have a great aunt, on my father's side. She's still alive. And I need to go see her."

They were both getting exhausted. Sienna yawned and tried to get the kinks out of her neck. He rubbed her shoulders a moment and said, "I don't want you to go over there," indicating the house next door. "It doesn't feel right anymore."

"Okay, but I've got to get a few things I left there."

"I'll go with you."

He grabbed one of Cheney's house keys off the wall. The night air was brisk as they walked.

He said, "I'm selling it. As soon as I can."

"Cheney's house?"

"I need the money to pay for her rehab. And her hospital bills. I'll probably give her whatever's left over. Hopefully she'll go somewhere and make a new start. I haven't told her yet."

He reached for the doorknob and realized the door was wide open. He stood still for a second listening for noises, but there weren't any. He scanned the driveway, the neighbor's yard—it was all empty and still.

"Let's go," he said, taking her by the arm. "I'm callin' the cops."

"No," she said, "Don't do that."

"Why not?"

"In my experience, they tend to make things worse."

"You've had some interesting experiences then, haven't ya?" he said in passing. "Stay behind me, love."

He stepped into the house and switched on the lights. The place had been ransacked. There was overturned furniture, random papers, and broken glass strewn all over the floor. An end table was upright in the middle of it all and on it, neatly placed, was Sienna's book about the vindicator. It stood out like the Holy Grail.

"What's goin' on around here?" he asked. "You don't have a stalker or anything like that, do ya?"

"Not the kind you're thinking of."

He swore under his breath. "What do you mean?"

"First of all, you need to quit inviting it in, please," she said coolly as she picked up her book—no inscriptions, no library jacket.

"Inviting what in?"

"Evil. Stop swearing and start saying something like *what in the name of God is going on here*—at this point, that might help. I'm not being trite, I'm being serious. You have to start being very careful what you say."

She tapped her book against her palm trying to think. He stood in the middle of the mess and stared at her with his mouth open.

"Yeah," she said, absentmindedly, "...just don't say anything at all until you get the hang of it."

"The hang of what?"

She looked at him for the first time since entering the house; she looked at him like he was an alien—they were not at all on the same page.

She tried to take a moment to explain spiritual warfare, "The power of life and death is in the tongue. Speak to the mountain and it shall be moved. Man does not live by bread alone but by every word that comes forth out of the mouth of the Lord. Just...trust me, Jonathan, be very careful what you say."

"Why?"

"Because hell has started its bidding," she said in a tone near that of exasperation.

"Bidding for what? I don't know what you are talking about. Try speaking bloody English...."

"Jonathan, there is a war going on here if you want to see it or not. Hell has started bidding for our souls—or for someone's soul....I've been through it all before. I've seen it all before—you get to where you can feel it breathing down your neck."

"Explain to me why you think this?" he said as he set the recliner back upright.

"Because now we know what Satan has been trying so hard to hide. We just blew his plan wide open, and he knows it. If you were a fallen angel trying to steal souls, would you want that little girl to have two God-fearing allies?"

He stopped straightening furniture and looked at her again.

"It's starting," she said simply. "I don't have any other words for it. I don't know how else to explain it, but you'd best get ready for the fight of your life."

She passed by him and thrust the novel into his hands.

"Read it," she commanded. "This stuff is comin' at you fast, my friend."

"Where are you going?"

"To check the rest of the house."

He cursed under his breath. "Why are the good-lookin' ones always mental?"

And he ran after her, struggling to keep up.

chapter twenty

$\mathcal{D}$AWN BROKE OUT over the waters slowly, peacefully, as if in a treaty. She shed her revelation and light on the two of them like brother and sister not really speaking, like kindred spirits in a deadlock, like soul mates caught in a twisted struggle of wills. He noticed her first, a half mile down the shoreline curled up in his blanket beneath the driftwood. The sun gently kissed and illuminated his face, his eyes, as he silently studied her, watching from a distance as she made peace with his ocean—its power, its secrets, and the bizarre stories it hurled up mercilessly. Over half of the men in his family were buried somewhere beneath it, to him still floating unfound in their fishermen sweaters of the Driscoll Family pattern, woven with the sorrow of sooner or later, worn in an all-out defiance of fate, swamped through with mold and time, and left unread like dog tags lost in a hundred-year war.

She felt his presence, but she didn't acknowledge it. She'd been there all night writing novels in her head, and he hadn't even known she'd left her room. He glanced back at the house, wondering if Bella was still asleep. He looked behind him surveying Cheney's house and saw nothing noteworthy but he still felt exposed and invaded and angry. He looked back at her, and she had started walking towards him. He rose and jogged out to meet her. She didn't really look at his face; she didn't say anything to him except, "I think we're on the wrong side of this ocean." He couldn't say he disagreed. He walked beside her in silence as they made their way back inside his house.

"Coffee?" he offered.

"No, thank you," she muttered. She was completely exhausted.

"Can I get you anything?" he asked.

"A dark room and time. My laptop—where did I put it? I'm sorry, but my work is kicking in; this is the writer part coming through. Remember when I told you I don't really sleep at night and that it would be hard on someone next to me?"

"I remember."

She nodded, indicating relation to the current circumstance, then explained, "I won't be around much today or tomorrow. And I really wanted to help with Cheney—I'm sorry."

"I understand."

She grabbed her computer case, the crumpled papers she'd gathered from the mess the night before, and started for the stairs. She stopped abruptly, as if just remembering something, and turned back around. She walked toward him, digging in her jacket pocket. She handed him her cell phone.

"Aurora," she said. "Call her, talk to her—she can help explain about me." She reached up to touch his face, and she kissed him and left.

He made himself some coffee and scrambled a couple eggs. He texted Aurora, *A this is J—call me on this phone, when you have time.* He checked on Bella who had turned over since he last looked. She was sound asleep with the dog stretched out next to her—taking up most of the bed. He took a picture on Sienna's phone and smiled, thinking she'd like it when she found it later. He walked by Sienna's door and heard the keys of her laptop clicking. He stood there for a while and listened. He thought she had a poetic rhythm.

Back downstairs, he saw Sienna's book on the coffee table. He picked it up and thumbed through the four hundred thirty-four pages of fine print. He recalled asking her the night before if the book was hers, and had she left it there. She said it wasn't, and she hadn't. His mind started reeling a bit because, if the book wasn't hers, that would mean that whoever broke into Cheney's house knew who Sienna was. They were familiar with her work beyond her pseudonyms; they knew where she had been staying.

Jonathan walked to the window and stared at Cheney's house with an intensity so vehement the thing could have caught fire. *What is going on here?*

He tapped the window pane relentlessly with his fingers, then he slammed his fist against it. The room that had been ransacked painted a portrait, she had said. That's why she wasn't scared that anyone would still be there, she'd said. They left her this message for a reason, she told him. After they'd checked the entire house—nothing else appeared to have been touched—they returned to the living room. Someone had taken the pages of the new novel she had been working on and crumpled them, one by one, and strewn them on the floor in a twelve foot oval. They overturned the furniture and knifed some of it so that the stuffing was coming out. They then took glass from the kitchen, from the coffee table, from the fireplace panes and smashed it, also in an oval, overtop the pages. They then took an end table, placing it neatly in the center of the mess, and laid her book on it, face down.

"Someone is apparently trying to send you a message," he had said. "Do you have any idea who?"

"No."

"I don't get it," he'd said, bewildered, staring blankly at what they'd done.

"This new book is called *Stained Glass*. At least they are symbolic...you know...the broken glass. Looks like they don't want me to finish it, I guess," she'd observed.

"But who would know you wrote that book, the one about the vindicator? Who would know that it was you? And how would they know you were here, in this house?"

"I don't know; a lot of people know I wrote this. I mean, I met the actors and their assistants; I met the music people, the screenwriters, the producer, of course. Probably close to five hundred people." She thought for a moment. "And all of my girls know what I write, and they've probably let it slip to some of their friends or their boyfriends—they all know a lot of people. But I don't think any of them would know that I'd been here."

"Do you know anyone who would want to hurt you?"

"No. Whoever it is—they're just a tool, anyway."

"A tool?"

"Of the devil. The best thing I can do is pray."

He recalled watching her in amazement as she calmly walked out into the night and didn't seem frightened or unsettled at all. He'd switched off the lights, locked the door, and ran up next to her.

"Why don't you seem...scared?"

"Fear not," was all she said.

He now stood by his window rubbing his forehead, feebly trying to stave off a massive headache. He walked over to a cabinet and started rummaging through it. He found the Bible his mother had given him years ago. It was dusty. He wiped it off and opened the first few pages to the family tree she had completed for him. He traced its branches with his finger until his eyes landed on a particular name—*Brigh Driscoll*. It seemed to jump off the page and levitate toward him.

"Brigh means high, it means power. And Driscoll means interpreter, or messenger," he said aloud, considering his great aunt's name. *High interpreter, powerful messenger.* He picked up the phone, changed his mind, and hung it back up. He picked up the receiver again, thumbing through the phone book, and he booked three tickets to Ireland.

Sienna's phone started playing bagpipes—Amazing Grace. He smiled as he answered it, "Yeah."

"It's typically 'Hello' or 'Hi' so, whatever... *Yeah* to you, too, I guess. What's up, J?"

He heard her chuckling at her own sense of humor, and he chuckled right along with her. Something about Aurora's persona was so authentic... it was comforting to him.

"Hey, thanks for callin' me back."

"No prob. Seriously, what's up?"

"Well, first I need to ask ya when Katarina's wedding is."

"Three weeks. Saturday."

"Oh, that's great. We'll be back by then."

"Goin' somewhere?"

"Yeah, family business."

"Cool, cool, I got ya...."

Her voice trailed off into silence. He stood there holding the phone, not knowing where to begin.

"One thing you oughta know by now, pretty boy, I ain't shy. So there's no point in you bein'. You got somethin' to say, why don't you just say it? I'm roaming here and my minutes suck."

"Yeah... sorry," he said. "It's Sienna. Somebody trashed the house she was staying in here. They made it look pretty personal, like they were stalking her or something. They knew about her fake name..."

"Let me guess, the vindicator book?" she interrupted.

"Yeah," he replied.

"She brought the eccentrics out of the woodwork with that one, struck some kinda nerve runnin' through society. She must be onto somethin', huh?"

"Must be...," he said. "Anyway, she started talking about heaven and hell stuff, and the devil, and how this guy is a tool and... well..."

"So you're freakin' out, and she's straight as an arrow," she interrupted again.

He let out a sigh.

"Exactly," he said, his body starting to relax.

"Let me guess again—you have never heard anyone talk like she does your entire life. Am I right?"

"Yes."

"And it has crossed your mind that she's loco. Right?"

"Um..."

"I'll take that as a yes. Listen to me, Jonathan. Sienna is the sanest person I know, and I've known some crazy people, so believe me when I say I know the difference. But she's intense—extremely intense—about these spiritual matters, I mean. She can see things that nobody else can. She can sense things that nobody else can. All's I know is this—if there is a spiritual demon that needs to be exorcised—I ain't callin' no pasty priest. I'm standing behind that woman."

"It's just that this is all so strange."

"Yeah, I will agree with you there. But take a turn through some of the Old Testament, why don't you? You can trust her, Jonathan. I don't know how she does it, but she can pull you through fire you didn't even know you were standing in."

"I'm starting to get that feeling."

"I bet she was up all night and she's holed up somewhere taking it out on her computer?"

"She is."

"Well, she's not just writing a bestseller. That's how she prays. She'll come out in a couple days her typical, low-key self. And, Jonathan?"

"Yeah."

"You're working from a disadvantage, my friend. I know, I've been there. She can scare you—she's not trying to, she can't help it. When I cut my wrists?"

"Yes...?"

"I let the fear get to me. She was my last hope, and I freaked out completely because of some of the stuff she was saying to me. But I lived, and I lived to find out that everything she said—everything—it was the God's honest truth. So don't get scared and run off. In her defense, there is no gentle way to fight a spiritual war. Just hang in there. And, if anything, thank your lucky stars she showed up in your life. I know, beyond a doubt, that without her, I'd be dead right now and I'd have landed smack in the middle of hell! Well, keep your chin up and be a man. Gotta go."

"Aurora?"

"Yo."

"Thanks."

"No problem. And, remember, you promised you wouldn't hurt her—so let the woman do what she do, ya got it?"

"I will."

"Good. Bye-Bye, now."

He pressed the end-call button and stared at the phone like she was still inside it. He looked out the back door and watched the calm water rocking its way toward his shore, calling him out. He felt settled inside, and he felt strong. He felt a warmth—a sense of peace and of power—filter in though his chest, his heart, his entire being. And he made up his mind. He'd prayed for her—it was a miracle in itself that she even showed up, that she even agreed to love him and to accept his child as her own. Who was he to deny the answer to his own prayer? So he made a decision, at that very moment, to accept her, to accept his fate, to put on that sweater knowing he might not make it back. His gaze fell back from the sea, and he looked around him, seeing, for the first time, certain objects and the vast meaning behind them. His mind became absorbed in the blankets and pillows woven in that familiar pattern. His heart entered into the Holy Bible, its pages open to the significance of that tree. And he felt, for the first time, complete and whole and lined up to his purpose— he felt like a true Driscoll, no longer an impostor to the name... *Interpreter, Messenger.*

He sat down on the sofa, he opened her book, and he began to read—no longer claiming ignorance as an excuse to float downstream.

chapter twenty-one

PAGE SEVENTY-TWO AND Bella had made her way down the stairs. It was nearly noon. She seemed happy and peaceful, and her father was more than just a little relieved. He made her something to eat and then laid out her clothes while she sang loudly in the bathtub.

"You are actually getting clean in there, aren't ya, Bell?"

She quit singing. He grinned at her answer of silence while finding her a pair of flowered sneakers and some pink socks that actually matched each other.

"Dad needs to go see a friend in the city, and we need some groceries. Anything you want to do?"

"Chocolate ice cream."

"Besides that..."

"I want to ride the ponies at the park."

"If they're there today, we'll swing by. I thought about taking you to a museum—we can go look at art. Would you like that?"

"Okay."

He walked down the hall and stopped to listen at Sienna's door. She was still typing away almost manically. He wrote her a note and put it on the floor.

> *Went to make sure Cheney is headed to rehab. We'll be gettin' some better food. Get some sleep. I love you.*
>
> *Oh—all the doors are locked. I've got one of my buddies keeping an eye on the place 'till I get back. His name is Alex. He's the big, ugly, excessively tattooed brute roamin' around like a guard dog.*
>
> *Did I say I love you? I do. More than anything else in the world.*

∞

Vengeance is Mine, thus sayeth the Lord.

At the museum, this was scrawled in old calligraphy on a scarlet banner crown, arched above a gold-leaf frame encasing a painting Jonathan would not be able to forget. Ever. Bella was standing directly in front of him, locked eye-to-eye with the shock of it, absorbing its meaning and depth as if soaking its liquid colors in through her skin. It did indeed, and permanently, permeate every inch of her small being with its pigmentation and stain. It did indeed saturate every corner of her developing mind with its swirling earthen oil, and it stayed as it dripped but it was never washed away, not for the duration of all her days.

Because she did not fear it, she understood it...felt it and she owned it...like no one since the artist had.

She did not cringe in the face of evil. Holiness is nothing if not bold. She didn't look away nor, like many adults, ask herself *How much room is left in my soul?* Selectivity does not always intelligence find—narrower the path, broader the mind.

Jonathan had his hand on her tiny shoulder, and as he turned to step away from it, he found his daughter wouldn't budge. He glanced back up at the painting and stared it down with a look of contention in his eyes. It was one of those original works most mysterious, almost wet and still warm, reaching out from the very hand of an old master long since dead, breathing with a collective sense of spirit donned "The Enlightenment Age" and entrapped in time with such a skill and such a style as no modern man could ever hope to recreate or capture. And though impossible, the black eyes of its characters followed the movement of the observer's down through all their sorted fears to the farthest reaches of their very soul and laid it open. (It was as if these unparalleled people, who came together through pure anointing at the appointed age, with their unduplicated artworks; stained glass cathedrals of pillar gold and arched stone; inventions ahead of their time; their beautifully written word and massive expansion of knowledge—it was as if they had something prevalent to say.) This rapturous thing, in its infinite wisdom of centuries told, with its dreadful blacks, swollen flesh and its slashes of red near freshly bled, seemed to be moaning out a warning from beyond a thousand graves—graves strewn throughout a hundred distant lands. The thing was wicked down to its core and defined true sorrow (the kind vacant of Goodness buffering); the suffering it entailed was immense and, at least to Jonathan's child, it was revealing its message bold, and its slit tongue was still telling these horrible things to be true—that hell was very much real and alive and filled with such evil to the point of no other earthly expression.

Jonathan let loose an unsettling breath over Bella's head and on into the mystic art center where he felt the heart of it to be. As he studied it, he found primarily the blinding fact that he didn't want to be looking at it. But there he was. He could no longer honestly say that he hadn't been warned about the summation of consequences. That painting literally made him sick to his stomach and weak in the knees.

Almost autonomously, he heard himself asking his daughter, "What do you see in that, sweetheart?"

"Fallen angels," she said in her young, innocent voice. "With broken wings. See the serpent, Daddy?"

"I do."

"That's Satan. The rotten fruit...? Those are all his lies."

The men, the fallen angels in the painting, each looked to be, in all aspects, starving with no impending, relieving death; they were as destitute and forlorn as any creatures Jonathan had ever seen portrayed.

"They lost their faith," Bella whispered. "They didn't believe and they stopped praying."

Jonathan bent down and lifted her into his arms.

"We won't, baby girl," he said. "We won't ever stop praying."

He scanned the room for a lighter, more heavenly pastel piece and started heading toward it. He could have sworn he felt a physical hold on his body; he had to rip himself and his daughter away from the clutches of that God-forsaken picture that seemed to frame the actual Gates of Gehenna. They toured the rest of the gallery uneventfully—actually, it was rather dull in comparison—and when they walked out of it, they both glanced back to that miserable painting as if paying last respects to a dead body at a funeral of someone who, it could be deemed fairly certain, was presently burning in hell as they peered over the cold edge of the casket.

"The artist certainly did his job with that one, didn't he, Bell? Puts the fear of God in you."

"Fear not," she said, "For I am with you."

She skipped a couple steps and twirled, flaring out the hem of her skirt.

"You just keep praying," he said to her, as if defying the wicked forces at his back.

He grabbed onto his daughter's tiny hand and they kept on walking into the light.

∞

He slipped a second note under her door after he realized the first one had gone unnoticed.

I know you don't sleep, but do ya eat, love?

The keyboard went silent. He heard her footsteps approach then stop.

"I do. But I'll be terrible company," she said through the closed door.

"You could never be that," he said with his hand resting upon the door. "I'll let you know when it's ready, then?"

"Yes...thank you," she said.

She ate silently, in a trance of sorts, locked inside her own world of riddled words, lofty ideas, temporal people, and God's divinity and will. They called it fiction; she called it a scale model. When she got up from the table, she gave both Bella and her dad a hug, thanking Alex with her first and only words spoken that evening. (He later asked, "Hey, Johnny...is she on somethin', man? Cuz I don't need to remind you what number one was like.") Then she quietly shuffled up the stairs, disappearing into that room for the entire night, the whole next day, and the remainder of that night, too. She slept off and on throughout, but then slept heavily on the third day.

She was showered, wide awake, and cheerful when she finally came back down the stairs, emerging as her typical pleasant and lovable self—just as Aurora had predicted. He'd just finished reading her book and was sitting on the sofa letting it percolate through his mind—there were layers and layers to that thing. He stared up at the ceiling with his arms flung wide open at his sides.

"So you're alive," he finally said, looking over at her and smiling as if it had been weeks since he last laid eyes on her.

"I am, I think," she said and smiled back. "What day is this?"

"Wednesday."

"What time is it?"

"Ten o'clock at night."

"Bella's asleep?"

"She is. Come here and give me a hug—I've missed you."

After she did, she went to the kitchen to get a drink of water. She grabbed a banana off the counter and started peeling it.

"So, what's it like living with a writer?" she asked him.

He thought for a brief moment and said, "Excessively quiet."

She laughed, walking over to sit next to him, and she said, "That's to balance out the times that I'm too intense for ya."

"Well, it worked very well. I was really starting to miss *you*—you know, *all of you*. I missed hearing your voice and seeing you smile."

They looked at each other for a while. He took hold of her hand and studied it, becoming lost to his own thoughts for a time.

"I read your book," he said quietly, still pondering it. "Just finished it, actually."

"Okay...what do you think?"

"About you? You're amazing. The way you write is unbelievable. And your storyline...well...it's like the movie. It's very heavy. Incredibly intense. I'll probably be getting things out of it for a year or more. When I was reading it, I looked some verses up in the Bible—just certain stories it reminded me of. I wanted to check them out again for myself."

"Good. I am always relieved when I hear people say that. This is just a novel, Jonathan," she picked up her book, quickly leafed through it, and tossed it back down on the table. "It's just an attempt to get people to discover God for themselves, to discover the power of prayer, and to trust Him enough to let Him be their Vindicator."

"And it does get that point across very well—especially when it warns that vengeance can easily turn the victim into the very thing they're fighting against; the thing they hate the most is suddenly staring back at them in the mirror. That's one of Satan's plans, right?"

She nodded confirmation and added, "Probably one of the most despicable ploys He uses, yes."

"But I've still got a few questions."

"Sure."

"The vindicator is an angel of God, right?"

"Right."

"Angels are so powerful that it only takes one to kill, say, two-hundred thousand people in one night."

"That is biblically true, yes. Actually, it is like one-hundred eighty-five thousand men, I think is the record, but yes."

"And these are God's angels, not fallen angels."

"Correct."

"And in this book, you have these children praying a way for this angel to descend. They pray, because they are pure and an avenue easily traversed by God and because they witness these horrible crimes against men, women and other children on the earth. They pray, then this angel descends and takes the perpetrator through various levels of hell—almost exactly what the guy did to the victim. Then the angel simply leaves without saying a word. And in your book, all these criminals, if they're still alive after that experience, they instantly change."

"Not just because of their suffering, but because they know they've been touched by God through one of His angels," she explained.

"And once you've been touched by God, you can see the spirit world and you can understand a whole other realm of existence."

"Exactly."

"So, in this book, Bella would be one of the children that pray this vindicator down. You think she witnesses crimes that have actually been committed, even if she wasn't there?"

"I think she can see them in the spirit, yes, as God allows her to. And as she prays, she opens a door on the earth for God to move in whatever way He deems fit. That's why I told her to say, 'God's will be done.' Because Satan's lies could get involved and deceive her mind, or her flesh could get involved...."

Jonathan looked somewhat confused with that term.

"The flesh is or our fallen nature—we all have one," she tried to explain. "And it gets in the way of the spirit. In other words, we not only get in the way of ourselves, we inhibit God's use of us. It generally happens because of some form of selfishness. So if our prayer is outside of the will of God, He simply won't heed it or He'll help us to realign it so He can. But as soon as we cross the line entirely and try to serve or avenge ourselves, we will be destroyed by our own hand in some way or another because that's not the reason we were created—we were created for others. Like Jesus' example."

"That's why in the novel one of the older children gets killed?" he asked intently.

"Right...that character tried to operate outside the will of God. He tried to use his gift for his own sake rather than for the good of others. And he simply took it too far because he was out of balance in other spiritual areas. He didn't humble himself under the hand of God because he didn't know all of Him. In my development of his character, I wanted to show how partial knowledge mixed with selfish pride can destroy; how not loving God, not respecting His design when He is love—well, anything attempted in that vein cannot possibly work. One has to know God's complete character in order to know how to effectively pray or act on a perceived calling. Only God Himself can determine how far a prayer will go, no matter who on earth utters it, because He, ultimately, holds all the power—both in the beginning and in the end."

"So, in other words, a spiritual gift is basically a life-long calling and God will take care of its development if the person is open to knowing all of God."

"Beautifully put, yes. If the person truly loves God, does their best to understand all the balancing facets of God, and then obeys Him to the best of their ability, then, and only then, will He be able to use their gift completely and prosper it."

She let him think about it for a moment before she continued.

"Personally, Jonathan? I think He just wants to be known and loved back. I mean He knows the number of hairs on your head—but did you ever wonder why He uses that as an example? I think it's because we don't even know that number from day to day ourselves. That's how well He knows us; that's how closely He pays attention to us. And I think He wants us to pray; He wants His children to talk to Him, to start a dialogue with Him, to tell Him what they want and what they need so He can act and show Himself as real to them. He can still act without us—I mean, He *is* God—but I think there is something about Him, about His heart and His character. He's a gentleman who simply wants His kids to talk to Him and trust Him. He wants to know how much we need and love Him. And, truth be told, it's for our own good anyway. We are actually the ones who need to know how much we need and love Him. He's a good Daddy—it's all about relationship, not religion. He's brilliant...people just need to give Him a personal chance and He's there— just like that. We just don't get it sometimes, do we? That He *created* us. I mean we run around thinking we need to understand everything. We're just not going to, Jonathan. Not down here, the Bible even says that. That's what faith is—not knowing all the answers and trusting Him because He does.

"I guess what I'm really saying to you is that whatever gift He's given your daughter, as long as she loves God and she desires to know Him, she'll be okay. In fact, I think she'll be way more than okay. I think she'll become a great woman of God."

"I think that, too," he said thoughtfully. "And it's Bella's choice. I mean, she's the one who'll have to ultimately decide, but as for right now, she's seeing things in the spirit—some of them are obviously terrifying and evil—and she automatically knows she is supposed to open her mouth and pray."

He shook his head in wonderment.

"Yes, God's already taught her very well. And she's such a sweet, loving child. I think she's already made her choice to follow Him, no matter where that leads," said Sienna.

Jonathan grinned and released a sigh of thankfulness as he agreed, "That's good."

Then reflecting upon himself, he asked, "So my job, like the man in the book, is to protect her from Satan working though deceived people on the earth?"

"Yes, that's the reason why I wanted you to read the book. Unfortunately, that man isn't portrayed in the movie, but without him, none of those children would have lasted very long."

"I can see that, and I'm starting to truly believe that not just about myself, but of all fathers. As I was going through this book, I started to see how greatly they are missed in the real world; it's like our families are running off the track just a little, and that's causing the whole society to become derailed."

"It's kind of a disaster to miss the mark, isn't it," she said remorsefully. "I wrote something about that in there, about how it's like the adults are slowly seeping out of the lines of God's carefully drawn design, and society's children are sliding entirely off His page. We've got to do whatever we can to get the lost ones back. I mean children are suffering out there every day, unnecessarily."

"I know," he said, consoling her by gently squeezing her hand.

"And as far as here, in our little family," she continued, "my primary job with Bella—like the woman in the book—is to teach her what I can about God and about her gift so she'll understand what's happening to her, or through her, and she'll be better able to handle it. At least that's what I hope to do."

"I have no doubt in my mind you will—you'll be amazing with her. You already are," he reassured her. "All of this stuff is coming together in my mind, it is. But I can't help but wonder why God just doesn't prevent all the bad things from happening in the first place—it'd be a whole lot easier. Don't you ever wonder that?"

"Absolutely, I do."

"How do you answer that for yourself?" he pressed her.

"Oh, boy, that's a tough one," she stammered, then took a deep breath. "Well...He's trying to work through His people on the earth and on some personal or collective level we're just not getting that. We're just not getting that meeting basic needs is a precursor to the luxury of thought. But besides that, Billy Graham once prayed to make peace with the fact that this is how Jesus left the world. It can get overwhelming sometimes, but that's not an excuse to do nothing while evil prevails. We've got to stand against it wherever we see it. Unnecessary evil needs to be met with necessary holiness, and it's a fine line to walk and, in fact, impossible without holy discernment.

"But primarily the way I see it, is that life is a test. Jesus Himself admitted it when He said, 'I set before you life and death; choose life that you and your descendants might live.' Life...*and* death. Good...*and* evil. It is impossible to understand or even desire the good unless we've experienced evil. Jesus came to renew, repair, and restore...not entirely to prevent. This is a sinful world, and it is temporal; our time here is like a drop in the ocean and, ultimately, all of these things He will take care of in the end—or the beginning—depending on how you look at it. But we have to make a choice between good and evil, between life or death while we are here, while we still have that opportunity. Seeing the bad, seeing the good...it helps us make that choice. That's what I think," she finished.

"That helps...it does," he said quietly. "So that's why you write these books, isn't it? You sacrifice all that time...you take whole slices out of your own life in order to help people see and make the choice?"

"Yeah," she said, grinning at him—so few people in her everyday life really *got* her. "Well that and, personally, it helps me vent. This particular book represents my wrath, my rage against abuse. I get really angry about the prevalent mistreatment of people and sometimes, as a single woman, you feel powerless to fight it, and you do wish you could send down an avenger in certain situations. I know the abusers will eventually get what's coming to them—if they don't repent—and I know God is ultimately in charge of these things, but writing this book was sort of therapeutic for me. Yet it was nothing compared to discovering Bella—what a *force* she is, bless her little heart. Her prayers all seem to be answered directly. And this book...well, it was mostly just hopeful thinking that someone could pray and these horrible things—child trafficking, starvation, genocide, abuse—would be instantly stopped. Then here I find, in one little girl, the proof that God has already created ones like these—sensitive souls that really *pray*. It's humbled me greatly. Who was I to assume God isn't working? He's working all the time in the most amazing ways! Sometimes we're just completely blind to what He *is* doing, you know?

"But God placed a different kind of gift in me—apparently I'm supposed to write about spiritual things in fiction—then it's up to the readers to pull them back out and apply them to their own lives and situations. That's what I'm here to do. Because like I told you before, people understand it better that way, it's less intimidating in a fictional storyline. If I tried to tell you all this directly you wouldn't get it because first of all, I can't communicate that way very well, and second of all, you would definitely think I was crazy. But you read the book, and you were open to it because it was a different medium. I wasn't even in the room, and now we automatically understand each other and pretty much agree on everything that is going on here."

"That's exactly what my music is like. It breaks down barriers like they're not there at all" he said, shaking his head in awe. "God is amazing. So you wrote this what—two years ago?"

"Published two years ago, so I was working on it three years ago."

"When Bella started praying for a mom who would understand her."

Sienna smiled. "Yes. God is most definitely amazing."

"Now, the last question is this, how am I supposed to protect Bella and you without letting you out of my sight?"

"Pray."

"Pray," he repeated.

"Absolutely. All the time. All day long, everyday, no matter what you are doing. And when you feel what is called a 'check in your spirit,' instantly heed it. Change your plans, stop what you are doing, or make me stop what I'm doing or whatever. When you sense an impression in your soul, that is the Holy Spirit moving. I have a feeling He probably used the nature of the sea to teach it to you, but that check is subtle, calm, and very quiet because He's a gentleman. And if you obey it and have faith, we will be fine."

She moved to sit on the coffee table in front of him, meeting him head-on.

"I have faith in you, Jonathan. And I have faith in God working through you. And, if you make a mistake, God will cover you. And if it all falls through, then it was just my time to go. It's that simple. I know where I'm going, and I'm very okay with it, and I will be waiting for you there, no matter how long. And I want you to understand...."

He looked down and to the side—he didn't want to hear any more. But she said it anyway.

"I want you to understand that if that should ever happen, no matter what the circumstances or the cause, you'll have absolutely no reason to feel sorry for me at all."

He looked back into her eyes—his were misty with a saddened fear, hers were filled with a radiant light near joy.

He wiped a single tear away, somewhat embarrassed of it as he whispered, "How can you be that sure?"

"I'm more sure of that than the fact that I'm sitting here with you right now. Facts change, Jonathan, but truth doesn't."

They stared at one another, and in the light of her ethereal patience and her complete eternal assurance, his countenance gradually lightened a touch, traversing the minute gradations toward absolute belief.

Finally he said, "But the fact of the matter is, you seem to have a highly intelligent stalker, and that shouldn't be coming into play."

"Well, then let's start this battle by praying."

They bowed their heads and prayed together about their future, their safety, and their divinely significant daughter.

⸙

Cheney was four days into rehab when they visited her. Jonathan spoke to the director, warning him about some of the things they were going to tell her that day. He didn't want to sabotage her recovery, but he was not willing to be controlled by her erratic behavior or to fund her bad habits. He felt he'd been part of the problem, enabling her like he did. She never had to get clean to hold a job. He'd been paying for everything, and it was time to let her go for the second time.

"I'm selling the house to a friend."

"Let me guess—you're selling it to Roger."

"Yes. I need the money, Cheney."

"Yeah right, you need the money. Just sell a song or whatever it is you do these days. I mean, what am I supposed to do, Jonathan? You come in here and tell me that when I get out I have no place to go?"

"He's buying the house as is; he's always had his eye on that place. I'll get enough money from it to pay your hospital bills, pay for you to stay here for up to three months, and there should be enough left over to help you get started somewhere else. And don't think you're moving in with Roger. I've already talked to him about that.

"Cheney," he said and rubbed his face with both hands, completely exasperated with her, "you need to go someplace new and start over. If I could do it for you, I would. But I can't. Just go somewhere and get some new friends— clean friends. Get a job. Just live—I don't know—*normally* for a while. Just be glad you're alive and that you've got a second chance. Can ya just do that for yourself, please?"

"You sound just like Sienna," she said cynically. "She's gettin' in your head, isn't she? Tell me the truth, Jonathan, tell me you never want to get wasted anymore, tell me you never want a joint, tell me you never want to snort a line. I know you...you used to be a hog—so don't you dare judge me. You want it just as bad as I do, if not more."

He felt like swearing, but he bit his lip instead, staring at her coldly until the air returned to his lungs and his blood backed down.

"You had better stay here a while, Cheney. You have a long road ahead of you," he said as he stood up. "And I won't be on it with ya anymore."

He paced a bit, back and forth across the room. He stopped and looked out the window for a moment, then went to stand directly in front of her.

He looked her in the eye and said, "You just don't get it, do ya? I felt responsible," he emphasized, putting his fist to his chest, "I feel like I'm the one that got you into this mess—it was my band—it was the people I let in. I was messed up myself, Cheney, for a long time, and now I can't get you out. And I'm sorry, okay? I'm sorry, I'm sorry, I'm sorry....I am so sorry for whatever I did to get you started on this terrible road you're on. But I can't do anything else for ya. I've tried everything I can. You have to quit on your own. If I could do it for you, God knows that I would. I have to get rid of all this stinking guilt that I've carried around with me every single day for five years. I'm layin' it down today—all of it, because I just can't take it anymore. I'm sorry, Cheney, but I have to go for good this time. It's over...it's time we both moved on. So whatever you do from this point on...it's all yours, not mine."

He picked up his guitar case and Sienna's Bible and walked out, turning to her one last time, "I hope nothin' but the best for you," and with that, he let the door gently swing shut behind him.

As he walked down the corridor, he felt taller and lighter with every step he took. He felt sweetly unburdened and was nearly joy-filled by the time he got to them. Sienna was lying on the waiting room floor playing checkers with Bella. The two of them were laughing together, and he stood at a distance for a moment to truly listen and to absorb that uncomplicated, freeing sound.

"I don't know if you should go in there right now," he said as he approached her. "It's up to you, but she's a little messed up...her typical self, in other words."

"When does our plane leave?" she asked.

"Tomorrow, six a.m." He put his things down and helped her to her feet.

"And we'll be gone for..."

"Seven beautiful days," he smiled.

"After which I've got to go home and help Kat with her wedding, so...I guess I had better see her now."

Jonathan started to run his hand through his hair, as he always did when he felt pressure, but he stopped the gesture mid-motion and he hugged her tightly instead. She noticed that he felt different to her somehow—more authentically himself. And it was nice. It made him even easier to love.

"Don't let her get to ya, baby," he whispered into her ear, "She's pretty thirsty, she's cravin' things pretty bad, I think. And she just found out she's lost her house. But don't let her talk bad to ya. Just walk out on her if you have to...promise me."

"I will."

"Good. We'll be waiting for you."

He watched her walk away from him, down the hallway toward that sick person he never really trusted. He didn't feel good about letting her go.

"Hi, Cheney." Sienna knocked softly as she opened the door.

"Sienna." Cheney's voice was hard.

"This is a nice room," Sienna scanned it quickly. "This seems like a nice place...decent people. How have you been?"

"How have *you* been, that's the question. Movin' in on my poor abandoned little family, aren't ya?" Cheney glared at her then whispered under her breath, "Don't waste much time..."

Sienna slowly took a deep breath and held it in for a moment. She felt like she deserved that.

"I guess you are getting a lot of news all at once, but you have some time here. At the end of two or three months you'll probably have a lot of new plans. You probably won't want to go back to that house anyway."

"That would be convenient for you, wouldn't it?" she snapped.

"Cheney, I thought we were okay with this—you and I, but I understand why you would feel..." She was going to say "betrayed" but decided against it. "I'm sorry...I guess I don't really know what to say."

"Well, there's the door—nobody asked you to come in the first place."

They sat there in the quiet for a time. Sienna began to shift nervously in her chair. The light caught the ring on her finger and drew Cheney's complete angry attention.

"Spend money, much?" she said, and then it dawned on her. "Don't tell me you're engaged. Already?"

"Yeah, we are," Sienna nearly cringed.

Cheney swore under her breath.

"He always did move kinda fast...but you guys really should consider that I'm a junkie in recovery here. You know, before you come back again and give me anything else to deal with?"

"Well, hopefully this should be about it," Sienna said, feeling remorseful.

She twisted again in her chair, and her face was scrunched up in an expression that indicated physical pain. Cheney watched her squirm for a moment then completely broke mood by laughing at her.

"Oh, calm down, Sienna, you look like you've got a massive case of hemorrhoids over there. Just sit still and relax. I'm not upset about you and Jonathan...really, I'm not. I'm just peeved at the whole stinking world right now. I guess I should be happy for ya. If I could just get a cigarette, my whole attitude would probably change. I'm just in a perpetually bad mood, Si. You'll have to excuse me."

Sienna let out a slow breath and managed a slight smile.

"Sienna, seriously...are you all right? You don't look like you're feelin' so good."

"Sorry. It's hospitals...sometimes they get to me."

"Well, this isn't a hospital—it's rehab. I mean look at it, it's a resort for cryin' out loud, and they waste it on people like me that couldn't care less."

"I just didn't know what to do, Cheney, about the ring. I guess I didn't see the point in hiding anything from you. But it is a little awkward for both of us. I'm sorry."

"Yeah...there are a lot of sorry people comin' through here today. And I'm sure you are reconsidering being friends with me and all. I mean, that's my ex and my kid you're after and I'm a—well...you know what I am—I've never made it a secret. And you, being the goody-two-shoes that you are, which I find *unbelievably* annoying by the way, will probably want to do what is best for your new little family." Her countenance suddenly changed back to hatred. "I'm sure you'll want to cut me out of the picture entirely, won't you? And that's okay, Sienna. Cuz I actually figured as much from you."

Another mood swing landed heavily between them while Sienna stared at the wall, feeling just as blank and dry and generic as the overpriced décor. She felt completely uninspired, and she really was starting to get sick to her stomach. She could feel the blood slowly draining from her face.

"I don't know about all that, Cheney. Honestly, I just want you to be well."

Cheney glared at her again, with more force than when Sienna had first entered the room.

She spewed her words out vengefully, "Sienna. I have a newsflash for you. I've never been well, not a day in my life."

Sienna doubled over in her chair, holding her stomach.

Cheney blurted, "What's the matter with you...don't tell me you're already pregnant!"

The two of them momentarily locked eyes. And Cheney's darted down in regret as Sienna ran into the bathroom.

∞

After they had returned home and she had somewhat recovered, Jonathan took the teacup from her hands, and she reclined on his couch, her body heavy with utter exhaustion. He covered her with a blanket, kissed her forehead, and gently moved the hair back from her face. He spoke to her reassuringly, his caring voice guiding her into a deep and peaceful sleep.

"She has a way of making you guilt-sick, I know. That's how I used to feel everyday until I met you. Somehow you made me believe I didn't deserve to feel that way anymore. And I just want you to know that I'm thankful for how

175

you've treated me. You've been nothing but good to me. And I also want you to know, I didn't put all that bondage off so that you could take it on. You've done nothing wrong here, sweetheart. You've done nothing wrong at all."

chapter twenty-two

$\mathcal{T}$HEY HAD A long flight ahead of them. They were up over the ocean with its blues and with its poignant solar reflections. Jonathan leaned across Sienna, his gaze diving down to the infinite water below. He had the look of a boy casting his first fishing line. She'd never seen an adult so excited to be going back home.

"What made you decide to leave it?" she asked.

"Well." He sat back, remembering. "Like you said, I was a musician, and they were all fishermen. I was young, wanted my independence. America seemed like the next step for my band—everybody in Ireland thinks you go there to make money, and well, I guess I didn't prove them wrong. That's what I did. I live there for the money. That sounds awful, but it's true. I mean, before I met you, of course. Now I live there because of you."

He winked at her and grinned, then glanced at his daughter.

"Bella, put your feet down, love. That guy can probably feel that."

She took her feet off the seat ahead of her. He helped her get her iPod going.

"If she wants to switch, let me know," Sienna offered, indicating the window seat.

"I'm sure she will. She'll probably want to switch with everybody on here by the time we land....What?" he asked, catching her staring at him a certain way.

"Your eyes," she said.

"What about 'em?" he asked, blushing like a youth.

"I just like seeing you this happy, that's all."

He looked at her, then he kissed her, a little too passionately for a public place. Then they both started laughing.

They heard, from the row directly behind them, the voice of a middle-aged man with an Irish accent as he muttered with derision, "Newlyweds."

They both laughed harder. When they became more sober, Jonathan said to her, "I'm only this happy because you're here, you do know that." But he could see she didn't entirely buy it. "I'm serious. I'm that proud of you. I get to show you off. That's why I'm this happy, it's because of you. Believe me, normally, I'd be dreading this—you'll understand when you meet my father. He's ... formidable, that's what he is."

"But you seem to respect him so much."

"Oh, I do. I love me dad."

He looked out the window, watching a few clouds drift over the wing.

"They're beautiful up here, aren't they," he pointed.

"They are."

"You know, I never told you why I quit—the drinking and the partyin' and the drugs and the whole insane music scene. It was because of him—and Bella. When I found out she was on the way, I just let go of everything I knew—I just dropped it all and picked her up instead. Ever since then it's just been me and her against the whole bloody world.

"But, without my dad, I probably would have missed it. Anyway, I had no idea he was coming, but he flew all the way over here from Ireland just to knock me in the jaw. That was just before I found out about Bell. To this day, I still have no earthly idea how he found me—he must have read one too many articles about the band and all the parties, and he just walked through the house we were in, and he found me, and right there in front of everybody, he punched me square in the jaw—hard. He knocked me on my—well, you know—and he said to me, 'You straighten up—you understand me, lad?' And he turned around and he left—flew straight back to Ireland."

He had a twinkle in his eye as he told the story, a certain type of pride reserved only for his father. He turned to look at her, studying her expression.

"You must think that's terrible. But it got me to wake up—you see, my old man isn't the type to hit anybody. People are generally intimidated enough by how he looks. He never laid a hand on me before that day, and I was an absolute nightmare to raise. And I'll never forget what he did for me. I'm actually very indebted to him. I think he saved my miserable hide."

He gazed out at the clouds for a while more, and she just stared at him. She was completely in love with him.

"So," he said, meeting her eyes again with a smile in his own, "how did you do it? How did you convince Aurora to quit?"

Sienna grimaced a bit and resituated herself in her chair.

"You'll probably think this is terrible." She paused for a moment, recalling the confrontation; she checked to make sure Bella was still listening to her music before she began.

"She came home one night, and she was high, which was typical for her, but she was still quite cognizant. She was pushing me—you know, testing me to see what I'd do about it. All I could think of to say was, 'You're poisoning your own life.' She scoffed at me like that was weak, and lame, and then she rolled her eyes back in her head like only she can...and I don't know why I said this but I did—I got in her face and said, 'Picture the person you hate the most on the face of the earth.' I could almost see him in her eyes. Then I said, 'Picture the person who has taken the most from you. Picture the person who has abused you the worst.' This sounds strange, but I could have sworn he was standing there with us. Then I said, 'Picture him pouring your booze. Picture him putting the drugs in your hand.' I said, 'Take them. Drink it. Go on, do whatever he wants you to do.'"

"Wow," he said quietly.

"Yeah, it was pretty intense. She got violently angry, and she thoroughly trashed her room—and I mean she really trashed it. I had to have someone come in and hang new drywall and repaint. She broke her wrist hitting the wall, but she hasn't touched the stuff since, not that I know of, anyway. And since then she's seemed at peace like her demons left her."

"Wow," he said again.

"Then later, I think it was like two weeks after that, she came up and asked me out of the blue, 'That guy, the one you had me picture? That man is mostly Satan, isn't it?' And that's the last we've ever spoken about it. That was quite a while ago," she mused as she gazed out the window.

"Daddy?" Bella interjected.

"What, sweetheart?"

"Can Sienna read me a book?"

"I don't know, you'll have to ask her."

"Sienna, would you read me a book?"

"You know what? I'd love to read with you, thanks for asking me."

Jonathan traded seats with his little girl, and he watched the two of them interacting together. He listened as the pair of them exchanged ideas both lofty and common. He noted the great imagination employed around the simplest of children's stories, and he concluded that they just seamlessly *went* together, like they were woven from the same cloth. Bella already loved Sienna—he was fully aware of that. She touched Sienna's hand and her arm and her cheek whenever opportunity allowed. She leaned against her and listened to her voice, her breath. She absorbed her new mother's warmth, nestling against her as she read. The child's being absorbed hers like liquid, hanging on her every word and intonation. Bella was already beginning to mimic Sienna's mannerisms—how she moved, how she sounded, and how she acted like a lady.

Hours passed and he watched them sleep. Their outlines were drawn together against the colossal red-orange clouds. He looked at Bella's sweet face and found peace and timeless grace. They were drifting closer to the gates of heaven—a place to feel weightless, completely safe, and abundantly blessed. And he fell asleep a happier man than he could ever recall himself being before; and as a father, he found rest.

His hometown was a good distance from Dublin. They'd rented a car for the drive, and once they'd arrived, it was late to them and early to everyone else. They said some exhausted hellos. Sienna hugged a lot of people. She even got kissed pretty hard on the mouth by one man who feigned it to get in a mock fight with Jonathan. She went to bed not having the foggiest idea who any of them were, but she knew she liked them. She shared a bed with Bella and slept for another three hours. She woke before Bella did but stayed snuggled next to her, listening to the child softly breathe and following the melodic, beautiful voices of her dad and his family like a song which was coming from the main room of the house. He was right—they were loud. But Bella didn't notice at all.

When the girl finally did wake up, Sienna was there to reassure her with a smile and a soft word. She rubbed her tummy, and the child laughed. Sienna was glad she didn't let the girl wake up alone in a strange house in a distant land.

"We're at Daddy's house?" she asked groggily with a yawn.

"Yep. With your grandma and grandpa. Probably some uncles and aunts and cousins, too. Maybe we can find some kids for you to play with, how would that be?"

"Good," she said eagerly.

Sienna combed Bella's hair and braided it through the crown. She attempted to fix her own hair, but decided just to pull it back in a pony tail. They were as presentable as they were going to get for the time being. She took a deep breath hoping they'd all like her, as they made their entrance.

"There she is!"

A woman immediately came toward Bella with outstretched arms, kneeling before her.

"Hi, honey. It's Grandma. I just can't get over how good it is to see you. I can't believe you are really here! Look at how pretty you are. I thought I'd only get to talk to you on the telephone, but here you are! Give me a hug, sweetheart."

She looked up at Sienna, "Ciara is my name, Sienna."

She smiled and held out her hand, and Sienna took it, helping her up off the floor.

"These knees of mine—they're gettin' a little stiff," she explained. "Thank you, dear."

"You're very welcome."

"Here, sit, sit. Coffee?"

"Coffee might help, yes. Thank you very much."

"Sienna, this is Jude, Jonathan's father."

"Sienna."

He nodded his greeting but didn't smile at her. Rather, his eyes tore through her flesh down to her bones as if he held a skeleton key with no time for the living doors. He had Jonathan's eyes, but his were ghostly and darker and akin to what one would call wicked rather than soulless. His soul was there behind their shadow, vast and threatening like storm clouds rolling up the banks; it reflected a lifetime of his shoreline visions—months of monotonous steely gray; seasons of dampness and bitter cold; and decades of death and the blood of his brothers dripping through his hands. Those eyes of his held unapologetically to the emphatic curses of water and of time; they revealed the perpetual pattern of a hard life—it had worn them smooth, defenseless, and unmoving like a maritime stone. Her eyes trailed down his arms to his hands. His skin was cracked and raw. Her gaze crept back up into his weathered face, and his intense stare had not departed from her, nor had it softened.

Sienna shivered. His eyes were like silver blades. *They pierce right through you*, she thought to herself.

"I told ya," Jonathan winked his understanding toward her as if reading her mind, and he offered a substitute smile on behalf of his father, "formidable."

He reached under the table and put his hand on her thigh (his hand was warm; she was ice cold). He stroked her reassuringly and then left it there.

"That's Kegan over there cowered in the corner. He's an antisocial good-for-nothin'."

"Shut up, Driscoll!" he yelled, then waved a hand at Sienna, "Hey. Nice ta meet ya. Though I got ta warn ya, you got your work cut out," he pointed the knife he was sharpening toward Jonathan. "Oh...and, I'm sorry about the kiss—I couldn't help it."

He winked at her, and Sienna turned red.

"Do it again and I'll kill ya," Jonathan warned, staring straight at him.

Sienna wasn't sure if he was serious or joking. She felt like she was standing in an open field between two angry bulls. No one was saying anything, so finally she whispered, "He's got a knife, Jonathan."

Slowly, quiet chuckling sprung up around them, then it burst into an all out, collective laughter. Even Jude eventually grinned, and smile lines sprung out around his eyes, softening them a hundred-fold like somebody flipped a switch and his light came on.

Kegan said, "Smart girl. And she's beautiful."

"Yeah," Jonathan remarked to Sienna, "What he's not tellin' ya, sweetheart, is that he can't gut a fish without stabbin' himself at least twice."

Then he turned to Kegan, "Isn't that right?"

"Shut up, Driscoll—" Kegan said again with a growl, "—that was only the one time. So what part of America is she from, and are there any more like her?" He winked at Sienna again.

"He's a great best friend, isn't he? His wife's name is Lilly. I don't know how the woman puts up with it—he's a mess, a big overgrown bully, actually. She must be a saint," Jonathan declared, "Saint Lilly."

"Here's your cocoa, Bella dear," Ciara interjected. "Never mind them, Sienna. They've been like this since they were old enough to talk. Every once in a while, they like to brawl with each other, so don't be alarmed when that happens."

Kegan smiled to himself, sharpening that knife like he was preparing for battle.

"Don't think I don't see you over there, Kegan," Jonathan said. "I know what you're thinkin.' You can't wait to see if I still got it. But not in front of my little girl, you hear me?"

"Wouldn't think of it," he replied with a twinkle in his eye. "I'm gonna get ya in yer sleep."

"Anyway," Jonathan rolled his eyes and continued, "this here is Grandpa Driscoll. He's the one responsible for this whole clan, so if ya have any complaints, see him—he's the one who started it."

"They call me Brody," the old man said quietly. He seemed sweet.

"It's good to meet you, Brody." Sienna smiled warmly at him and he smiled back, lifting his coffee mug toward her.

Ciara added, "Michael and Nessa are coming over tonight—that's Jonathan's older brother and his wife, Sienna. They have a little baby boy. And Shay—Jonathan's younger brother—well, where did he go? He was here a minute ago.... Why can I never find that boy?"

"He's gettin' the ships tended," Jude answered gruffly. "Are you goin' out?"

"Yeah, I'll go out, Dad. Just not today," Jonathan said. "I was wondering..."

Just then a rather large young man walked through the door and started pouring coffee in a thermos. "You ready," he asked, seemingly to everyone in general.

"This is Killian, my cousin. Killian, I'd like you to meet Sienna, and this is Bella, my daughter."

The man stretched out a hand to Sienna. He had friendly eyes well emphasized by smile lines. "Honored to meet you. And you, little girl, you're as pretty as a rose, aren't ya?"

Bella giggled.

"All right, let's go," Jude said as he stood up. He grabbed some gear and headed toward the door with all the men trailing him, with Jonathan the exception.

"See ya later," Jonathan called to them, and then he asked his mother, "Mum?"

"Yes, dear."

"Aunt Brigh—she's still alive and kickin' isn't she?"

"Why do you ask?"

"I need to talk to her, if she's able."

"Why, she's never talked a day in her life, son. But, yes, she's at the elderly home—Ferguson's, up the main road—if you want to see her. You'd best be sayin' your good-byes to her, if ya have any. She's not doin' well, last I heard."

Ciara picked up a bowl and started wiping it fervently with a towel. She turned to look at Jonathan, then to Bella. Whatever it was she was thinking, she sure seemed to be talking it out on that bowl.

∞

Sienna and Bella stood in the doorway of the tiny, suffocating room. It smelled like old people, fish, and something Sienna couldn't quite describe; she guessed it was the lingering stench of the perpetual "waiting for death" trapped inside the walls. The place desperately needed airing out; the whole house felt closed off like a collapsed lung. The atmosphere within was fearfully riddled with backward, meaningless messages and the voices emanating through its stillness. As with every hundred-year structure, it announced that time was unraveling at a terrible pace and that tomorrow they would all be old.

Bella whispered, "Tick-tock."

They watched as Jonathan went ahead of them, kneeling before an old woman in an antiquated wheelchair with a high, woven back. The woman was Brody's older sister, Jonathan's great aunt.

"How ya doin', Brigh? Holdin' up, I see," he said weakly, wishing he'd spent more time—any time at all—getting to know her before.

He continued, "I'm Jude's boy. My name is Jonathan. I haven't seen ya much—I've been living in America."

He glanced back at Sienna; uncertainty was written in his eyes. She nodded her head, encouraging him to go on, but from where she was standing, it didn't appear very promising.

"Bella," he whispered, waving her into the room.

The girl bravely entered and looked into the old woman's eyes. Brigh seemed to light up. She straightened herself in her chair.

"Brigh, this is Bella, my daughter."

"I know who she is," she breathed with a crackling voice that was seldom used. "Come here, child."

She extended a nearly skeletal hand. It hung in mid-air, waiting, trembling, as if daring the laws of physics and defying the decrepit trickery of time. It fell to the girl's shoulder and clung on with a fierce grip. The two locked eyes, but

184

only for that singular, fleeting moment. She slowly let go and her arm dropped back into her lap.

"Thank you," she said, gasping for breath, as if she'd just run a marathon. "Now, I can die."

"What?" Jonathan stammered. "No, I...we need to talk to you. She has this...gift, I guess. She can see things. She prays. Did you live with it? Do you have the same thing?"

Sienna had entered the room, quietly moving closer, immersing herself into the scene as if it were a pool of rippling water. She reverenced the infinite effects it might release. Brigh looked up at her. She stopped moving.

"You," she said. "You're her mother."

"Yes," Sienna said, standing very still.

"Let me see you," the old woman said.

Jonathan moved aside to make room while Sienna got down on her knees, seemingly in slow motion, as if trying not to awaken any giants or provoke any evil forces. Again, Brigh looked into her eyes, and time seemed to hold its breath.

"You are going to teach her well," she said with a glint of white fire in her coal black eyes.

"Yes," Sienna whispered, as if asking her permission.

"Good." She collapsed back against her chair. "That'll do..." She took a breath and said, "...just fine."

"Brigh, would you like some water? Would you like me to open a window?" Sienna offered softly.

"Yes," she said with a nod. "Both."

Jonathan worked on the window which hadn't been opened since they'd painted the sills. It took some doing, but he finally got it open. Sienna helped the feeble woman hold the glass while she sipped from it.

"My pills," she finally said, pointing to the dresser.

"Just one?" Sienna asked, and Brigh slightly nodded agreement.

They gave her some time to breathe in the fresh air. They gave her some time to let that little pill do whatever it did. It took about ten minutes, and then the woman lifted her head. She talked steadily and quietly, and none of them interrupted.

"It's a gift our family shares, but never has any one of us met the other until today. I was getting tired of waiting. I should have died a long time ago. I was beginning to think you wouldn't come.

"You are the first I have ever told..."

She rested a moment then went on, "When I was a little girl, about her age, I spoke my stories. Back then, we were under the rule of the church rather than our own. My mother was terrified of the horrible things I was saying. She took me to a priest. He told her I was possessed with a demon and that he would get it out."

She stopped talking, and a tear leaked out of the corner of her eye. Jonathan reached up and gently pressed it away, into the back of his hand. His face was deeply creased with empathy, his shoulders heavily laden with his family's shame. He couldn't believe that they'd all so grossly misjudged her.

"After that, I never spoke to anyone again. I would say my prayers, but only when I was alone."

She pulled herself up with great effort and looked at Jonathan.

"Had they let me be what I was," she said to him, "I could have saved most of the men in our family from drowning. I could have saved my own brother from going down with that fishing boat. I could have stopped the storm from swallowing him."

She leaned back against her chair and closed her eyes.

"They all thought I was a lunatic, a monster—something to be afraid of. I've been in and out of institutions all of my life. I never got married, never had any children. I didn't get the chance to really live. Listen to me, she hasn't inherited insanity; she's been blessed with the gift of intercession. She's a go-between.

"And you," she laboriously picked her head up to address Sienna, "you know all about it, don't you."

"Yes, I do."

"Thank God...now I can die," she said again, "In peace. I knew she was out there, I just didn't know where. And now that I know she'll be understood, I can go...I'm so very tired."

Bella instinctively reached for her hand, and the old woman squeezed it and started mumbling something no one else could understand, but they felt it—it was the unmistakable presence of the Lord. Then there was an exchange of sorts...there was no denying it.

When she was finished Bella said again, simply, "Tick-tock."

The old woman laughed with a glimmer in her eye. She reached up and touched the girl's cheek and said, "Yes, child. Ask Him to stop it...ask Him to silence my clock."

∞

Word reached the Driscoll family the next morning. Brigh Driscoll had passed away in her sleep.

The antique clock on the old woman's dresser had stopped of its own accord at twelve o'clock midnight.

Exactly.

chapter twenty-three

ELLA WAS GETTING ready to go into town with her grandmother. Ciara said she needed the girl's help running errands, but everyone knew the real reason Bella was invited—Ciara wanted to spend as much time as possible getting to know her granddaughter. Sienna stood in the doorway, watching the two of them leave. Jonathan noticed a certain expression on Sienna's face, and it held his attention. There was something in her eyes that he'd never seen before—anxiety—and he didn't like it at all. She was almost on the verge of tears, and he didn't know why.

He scanned the empty house behind them, thankful they were finally alone. It'd been the first time since they'd arrived.

"Hey," he said, gently moving a strand of hair from her cheek and tucking it over her shoulder as a tear fell.

She looked, to him, like a little girl who had just watched her mother drive away knowing she'd never come back again. If he had to watch her like that for much longer, it would break his heart completely in two.

"Hey, Butterfly," he said again, "I know my family is a disaster, but somehow they've managed to make it this far—they'll be all right."

She slowly smiled, then chuckled a little bit at his sense of humor. She wiped her cheek with her sleeve.

"It's not that," she told him, looking up into his kind eyes—he was home to her.

"I know." He held her in his arms and rubbed her back, thinking about the place he always used to go when he felt like escaping. "Come with me."

"Where?"

"I'll show you, just...here, put these boots on, and I'll find you a real sweater. You've looked cold ever since we got here."

He came back with a couple of wool sweaters for them. They were home-knit, incredibly heavy, and Sienna was grateful. He had an old guitar, "My first one," he said as he held it up to her. It was scratched and beaten up, and something about it was sweetly endearing. He put it on the table, gently, as if it held a biblical quality.

"An old man," he explained as he put on his sweater and laced his boots, "...still don't know who he was. I was passin' him in the street when I was about nine, I think. And he just handed it to me without sayin' a word—never seen him before or since."

They'd walked together for about a mile and a half, but the trail was smooth and well-worn, and the misty air hovering above it made it easier to breathe. He slung his guitar across his back and took her by the hand. They climbed up a hill with a circle of fire stones at its peak then descended down through a lush emerald valley, crossing somebody's fence that was bordering a herd of contentedly grazing cattle. On its far end stood an abandoned dark-stone church. It was as solemn as it was beautiful. The fibers of Sienna's very heart and being went out to it immediately, fully, and stayed. Layers of her essence settled within its ancient secrets and mortar, enraptured, and were entrapped there forever. She felt it drawing her soul into it like all true churches should. It spoke to her in living words floating in front of her eyes like stoical clouds, propelled by the sweet breeze of beating angels' wings from angels who had long been awaiting her arrival there, whispered her name and greetings that flowed forth like liquid to soothe her dry and tired spirit, things like *Holy...Mystique...Sanctuary...Peace...*

The corner edge had caved in, but the arches still seemed strong and stable. Those who had dearly reverenced this temple of the Lord when they built it had taken the time to collect contrasting light ivory stones to accent every window and each door, paying homage to light and the permeation of soul. She ran her hand over one of them. It was cool and porous, with its tiny holes filled in with moss, and she could feel the masons' hands as strong—reaching out to her from another century to offer her the understanding that this very moment was one reason they'd built it to last.

"This must have taken them years," she said in awe, withdrawing her hand and looking at it; she clenched it closed and then opened it again, lightly shaking the strange tingling feeling out of it.

"Depends on how many were working on it," he answered her back as he sat down on the front steps, giving her time to explore inside.

There was still a wooden cross hanging on the altar wall. She saw the remnants of a book—a hymnal or Bible, she couldn't be sure—on the floor nestled underneath the rubble. The window frames were arched like the doorway he was sitting in. She became aware that he was watching her.

"This is beautiful," she whispered as she looked up at the ceiling.

Many birds had nested in its beamed rafters over the years. The beams appeared to have been each hand-carved from a singular and massive piece of wood that arched in the same upward formation as the windows and the door. Eventually, Sienna came out and sat beside Jonathan. The view looking out from the steps was equally spectacular with its grazing cattle and green rolling hills all enveloped in a charming Irish mist. She took a deep breath—she'd never inhaled air as refreshing as this. She felt renewed in nearly every aspect.

"Welcome to my meadow—to my inspirational place." He beamed as he formally introduced her, looking out over the valley haze so dear to him in his youth. It was so woven through his very essence and physicality that it was part of him still.

It was an integral part, this breathtaking creative source—she could easily see that, like drawing water up from his well. Now joined together with his beloved land, he looked different, *lighter* to her somehow. His ivory skin seemed to glow with the air-dew and come alive. He looked so fresh and so young, so much more at ease with who he was that she found herself instantly convinced beyond a shadow of doubt, *This is where he really belongs...*

"I wrote my first song here," he said, interrupting her thoughts, "and all our band's hits and my favorite songs that I've never played for anyone."

"You have songs you've never let anyone hear?" she said, almost shocked.

"A lot," he nodded as he tried to explain, "I guess I've always thought of them as between me and God, or me and myself, anyway—they're private. Maybe I'll leave 'em for Bella, and after I'm dead she can get the royalties, but, I don't know...while I'm alive, I just feel that they need to stay silent. You don't have any books like that?"

"Besides my first one which sort of leaked out before I was entirely ready? No, not really," she said thoughtfully, trying to interpret the hidden artist in him.

"I guess I always had too many plans for the money," she said. "When I started, I was flat broke. Then when some money finally did start coming in, I always had somebody who needed help—horse, human, or hound..."

He grinned at her, and she smiled back.

"So, I've always sold everything as long as there was a market for it of some kind. I'm pretty shameless that way. And I blew my personal reputation a long time ago—you know, with the people from my youth. My only cover is my pseudonyms, and those are for professional reasons. People can probably Google their way through those, anyway. So, no, nothing with my career is private. I find it just gets too complicated, trying to hide parts of who you really are.

"But I can definitely see your point...and I compliment your ability on being able to separate. I'm just not very good at that, or I probably would, too."

They were silent for a moment.

"I just can't imagine you blowing your reputation. Are you tellin' me you were a bad girl?" he teased her.

"Maybe not bad, just disappointing to some people," she said.

"Then those people were bloody blind," he said and he defiantly tossed out a pebble he'd picked up.

"It always felt like I was under a lot of pressure to be perfect, a farm girl from the outskirts of a perfect little town. And I just never was *perfect* and, truth be told, neither were they. I tried to cover it all up for years, all the mistreatment—but one day the dam just broke, and let me tell you, it flooded right down Main Street. So, I just decided a long time ago that I'd rather be wrong and be authentically myself than be what everybody else thinks is right. To me, conformity just always seemed like I was selling out. Actually, it seemed like I was cheating God, robbing Him of what He created me to be. I never understood it—the social expectation to be something you're not. That attitude denies God's individual artistic design for each of us."

"So you blew your reputation on purpose, then."

"Looking back, it sure seems that way. And now I'm so glad I did, Jonathan," she admitted. "'To thine own self be true' and all that? I'm just the way God made me, so I got over feeling self-conscious about being transparent a long time ago. I am what I am—all the many different facets of me. And if God hasn't stuck me down, and I'm still breathin', I must be who I am for a reason."

He took a moment to think about what she had said, realizing a lot of it struck a chord within himself. He had a ways to go—he still wasn't ready to be totally transparent. Not yet.

"You and I sort of have the same history," he said with a smile. "In my social circles being perfect means fishing, like all the *real* men around here. I was 'wrong' and authentically myself with this..." and he strummed a couple chords.

"Michael," he continued, "now there is a fishing boat captain. He lives, eats, and breathes it, and he always has. But my father...," Jonathan said and looked up with his father's eyes and shook his head, "...somehow, he has always been obsessed with turning it all over to me. He's always tried to pressure me to be something I'm not. And Michael hates me for it. Maybe I should draw them a map."

"Have Bella draw them a picture," Sienna kidded.

"Yeah..." He thought for a moment. "The whole problem is that they're exactly alike. Oh, I'm the one who looks like Dad all right, but only on the outside. Michael looks like my mum's dad, but he's my old man on the inside one hundred percent. And they've just never gotten along with each other. It really doesn't have anything to do with me, but they're both stubborn. And poor Shay, he just tries to stay quiet and invisible. He just does whatever he's told by whoever's screamin' at him the loudest that day."

"So, in all this struggle, it's been hard to find the space to be yourself," she said.

"Exactly."

He looked her in the eye, thankful that another human being actually understood something about him, after all these isolated years.

"So," she said, "as a young man, you really rebelled. You were probably pretty frustrated."

"Yeah, I was a holy terror, and everybody knew about it."

"Especially the church people."

"Most definitely them. 'That Driscoll Boy' is what they call me—still to this day. I'm a heathen if there ever was one," he smiled. "They've got the tabloids to prove it...internationally."

She could tell that what he was recalling was beginning to weigh on him again, so she changed the subject.

"Would you play me something?"

"I'd be honored to," he said humbly, quietly bringing to his own recollection the first few lines before presenting them officially to her. He chose one of the many songs he'd held in his heart and reserved from the public, sharing with her one of his most private experiences with his God.

When he finished, she looked at him with amazement in her eyes, "That was unbelievable."

"Thanks," he said, and shrugged his shoulders as if uncertain about it.

"Jonathan...I have *never* heard anything like that before! It is so original. This is what people need to hear," she said, obviously stirred up with an absolute conviction. "It is just my opinion, but please reconsider—don't wait until you die—get that stuff out there now. The world needs all the help it can get."

Then, with a slightly mischievous twinkle in her eye, she added, "And if you really want to ruffle this town's feathers, let 'That Driscoll Boy' become a well-known *Christian* artist. The judgmental folks won't know what to do with that—must mean there actually is a God somewhere and that He's doing something without their permission."

He laughed and nodded, completely understanding what she meant. Then his eyes gazed out over the resplendent pasture right as the sun made its way through the clouds to greet them, their contrasting hues becoming cleaner, their intenseness growing sharper, and their rotating colors appearing richer, truer, and refilling with their ultimate source of light. Those beautiful eyes simply matched his diverse and haunting country, and they were illuminated with the power of the One who created them both.

"I wrote that song right here, on these steps—it's one of the authentic ones I was telling you about. There's a very old cemetery in a clearing in the woods behind this church about two hundred yards back," he said to her, "...someday I'll take you and translate the messages I can still read from the stones...but it's mostly the feeling when you're standing there that you have to experience. I can hardly describe it except in that song."

And then, almost as a passing thought, Jonathan added, "I just can't seem to write as well in America—my songs are here. And they always will be."

His face took on a nostalgic expression. He reached across his guitar to hold her hand. He didn't take his eyes off her for a long moment.

"What is it?" she finally asked softly.

"I can't believe you're here," he said. "You are really sitting here, with me, in my boyhood place. It's like you've always belonged here. This is the place where I used to dream all of my dreams. This is where my soul grew into me."

He looked out over the hills, reminiscing, then he brought his focus solely back to her.

"I always wanted you. God only knows how much... I'd actually sit here and talk to you out loud for hours, for years...," he looked down, shaking his head with regard to the memory. "It's just that I never thought that you'd really be here. Over the years, I guess I gave up the hope that you even existed. I started thinking that even if you did, the odds of actually finding you...."

His words trailed off, and he looked away from her, swallowing some raw emotion down.

"He always said to me, 'Have faith, Jonathan,' or 'Wait,' that was a big one, *wait*...I heard His voice coming from behind me, from inside this church." He pointed a thumb over his shoulder. "I just should have listened...I know that now. I got myself into so much trouble runnin' the other way. Did I tell you I almost died? They had to take me to the emergency room, at least three different times. It was like I didn't care...just because you weren't there—that's how much I needed you. And I always have."

They both listened to the surrounding birds for a moment which brought with them peace as they'd come nearer, soaking into glistening feather what little sun they could find before it passed them by and disappeared.

"But out of all that trouble," she reminded him gently, "came Bella. And you survived—you're beautiful to me. 'All things work together for good for those who love God and are called according to His purpose.' Amen?"

She smiled at him. He smiled back his amen, and it was true, genuine, and it seemed to cover all the years he'd been alive. But hers still had some of her own sadness coming through, and he could feel it.

"Are ya gonna tell me what's the matter, love?" he said softly, touching the arm of her sweater with a guitar pick. He then put it between his lips like a thoughtful habit, and he chewed on it as he waited.

"It's just...it's silly, I know. But it's just that you have a family. I don't. I have no one alive. And the ones who are...well..."

She needed a bit to think. She watched the cows for a moment—they were moving in one long cooperative line toward their water tank. *Why*, she thought to herself, *are people so complicated?*

"I just want them to like me," she said to simplify, "your mom and your dad, your brothers, even Kegan."

She smirked at herself with a hint of internal confusion about that last one, then she went on, "I'd like to have them as...I'd like your family to be my family. And I'm feeling a little, well a lot insecure, actually. I didn't think I'd be such a mess about it, frankly. I'm kind of embarrassed."

He silently thought about what she'd said. He took the guitar pick from his lips and leaned forward to get a better look at her face.

"Are you homesick, by any chance?" he asked her.

She thought for a moment even though she already knew the answer.

"No," she said, turning to look at him. She saw a wonderment, something near disbelief, in his eyes, and a soft and gentle grin on his lips.

"You'd want to stay here," he said, pointing his guitar pick toward the ground and his beloved country.

"Yeah, I would," she said definitively.

"It's slow and quiet...," he stammered, attempting to be the voice of reason, "and you eat fish 'till you gag. We've got bad things runnin' through this family, but the good generally outweighs the bad...generally," he repeated, checking to make sure he really wanted to stay himself. "It's a hard life—you can see that on their faces, can't ya?"

Silence filtered in between them like a fluttering dove descending to the earth. Neither turned around, but both could feel ancestral beings standing behind them like a choir of angels robed and belted and lifting up their hands. She sensed they were not all of his family line. She thought about her grandfather, himself from this very island.

"You want to live here, with me?" he asked, checking reality again.

"Yes."

"You're sure?"

"Yes," she said, starting to smile.

"What about your girls?"

"A lot of plane tickets," she answered simply.

"What about your house?"

"I'll keep it...or give it to Dillon and Kat. You know, as a wedding gift, maybe. Or I'll sell it—I mean, it's just a house, Jonathan, soon to be empty anyway. But what about your house?" she asked him.

"I don't know. I'll probably keep it for a while...in case these people start driving you crazy and you want to be alone. If you want a place to write, or a place we can be alone—you, me, and Bell." He thought about it for a moment. "Yeah, I'll probably keep it and, ya know, see how much we use it."

They looked at each other and grinned. He laughed to himself and shook his head.

"What about your horse and Peanut?" he inquired.

"I'll fly them over when we get a place here—people do it all the time."

"You're serious, aren't you," he said, lightly bumping the side of her knee with his.

"I love it here," she said. "It looks exactly like I pictured it in my head, and I've been picturing it since I was five years old. It just feels like home to me."

"Butterfly," he said, taking the guitar strap down from around his neck. He leaned his old guitar against the stone wall. "Come here, sweetheart, and sit with me."

She sat directly in front of him, and he put his arms around her. They rested together looking out over the countryside as it flowed out into the timeless sea.

He kissed the back of her head and talked into her hair, "I love you, Sienna. And they'll love you, too—if they don't already. But ya don't have to move here for that. It doesn't matter to me what side of the world we're on. I just want you to be happy—then I will be.

"And the reason my dad seems cold is because he's the captain of the family and some of our closest friends. He feels responsible for keeping everyone alive out there. He's had to play the role of God ever since I can remember. He's a good man...he's just constantly worried. I think the man sleeps worried. And it's just made him hard over the years. He's lost his uncle, his grandfather, and the worst was his best friend—a man who needed the work because his family was starvin', went out and got 'imself killed the third run. He left a wife and three kids behind. My father's never been a rich man and couldn't do much for 'em. I think that about killed him, but he won't talk about it—any of it. He just gets up the next day and does it again.

"And my mother already likes you—I can see it on her face. I think she's relieved that I actually did something with some sense this time. I think I surprised her by landing you." He laughed with a heart full of pride regarding the girl in his arms.

"And Kegan's a good guy, he'd do anything for ya. Lilly, his wife, she's a very sweet girl—well, she'd about have ta be, wouldn't she? But Kegan, he likes to drink a few too many beers and pick a fight with me. It's nothin' more than a full-body arm wrestling match neither one of us can win. We'll probably be fightin' with our canes if we live to be old men, so don't pay any attention to us. Don't let it bother ya at all."

"An' as far as old Brody—he's sweet on ya, I can tell. So, I'm pretty sure they all like you, Sienna. And if they don't, I'll beat it into their thick heads eventually. I mean, if they can't love you, there's somethin' seriously wrong with them. They're not much, but they're all I have—so if it's a family you want, they're all yours, sweetheart."

He couldn't see her face, but he knew there were tears streaming down.

"That means everything to me," she said. "I've waited all my life to belong somewhere."

"Well, you'll always belong here." He gently squeezed her, indicating that he meant she belonged in his arms.

They sat on the steps of that dilapidated church for an hour more, each focused on their own God-given imagination. He wrote songs in his head as authentic as the ones he'd written on those very steps years prior, but this time they were light and filled with joy. She wrote novels off the energy of the sea air; its pages came in layers that seemed to filter in off distant waves that told of great enduring love. The chapters became solidified in her mind, stone by precious stone; the frame, the spine, was to her reality, built; and arching upward unto heaven for any of those that should ever follow—no matter how long after, no matter how far.

"Well, we'd better get back," he said reluctantly, helping her up. "I have to talk to old man Kearney about some land."

"What land?"

"This pasture," he said with a twinkle in his eye as he jumped down off the steps. "I always wanted to rebuild this church. The land goes down through that valley, and up over those hills. We could put the house right over there against those trees."

He turned back toward her, "What do you think about that?"

She was standing there speechless, her hands cupped over her mouth like a prayer. She scanned the countryside again, this time with fresh and wide eyes—to wake up to this everyday of her life would be her heaven. Suddenly she ran toward him, leaping off the steps into his arms and kissed him with everything she had. As she slid back down her eyes were filled with joy. She skipped away from him a step and jumped up and down a couple times, taking in the view once more.

"So that's a yes, I take it?" he said breathlessly, regaining his composure.

She threw her head back, laughing out loud as if she recognized the humor of God. She extended her arms toward the sky to embrace it. She started walking, doing a happy little jig out to the side for a bit, her arms outstretched as she twirled an ecstatic little circle.

He watched her for a while (wishing they were already married because if they were...) then, looking up to the sky pitifully, he jogged after her, "This is killin' me, God," was all he could think of to say to Him.

chapter twenty-four

*T*HAT NIGHT, THE Driscoll family held a fish fry in honor of Jonathan's visit. There were well over forty people in attendance.

"Wanna beer?" asked Kegan.

"No, thanks," said Jonathan.

Kegan's brow raised in response to Jonathan's refusal of alcohol because to him, this was definitely a first.

"I was gettin' to where I couldn't find the bottom of the glass, so I quit," Jonathan explained. "I only drink on rare occasions, and then it's the stuff I don't really like, okay? Now get your bloody jaw up off the ground before you start droolin' all over. I don't want you to embarrass yourself."

"What the blazes goes on in that country?" Kegan asked, as if in a private quarrel with the state of the world.

"What do you mean?" Jonathan asked, and he couldn't wait to hear the reply.

"You go over there, get into all kinds of trouble... make all kinds of crazy money, then you burn through it like it's kindlin'. Okay, that's the Jonathan I know. And then your old man goes over there and whips your behind and gets himself plastered in all the tabloids down at the market—I get that. And you're married to some dysfunctional drug addict—that's the Jonathan I know. But you show up here, out of the blue, completely changed with a beautiful woman and a daughter. And you, Jonathan Driscoll! You don't drink? What goes on *in that country*?" he asked, taking a hefty swig of his own.

Jonathan smiled, but he didn't say a word. He was watching Sienna get Bella's plate filled. Kegan easily followed his eye.

"So, tell me about this girl," he said. "I mean, what's she doin' with an idiot like you?"

"Well, first of all," Jonathan started, "you can keep your bloody hands off of her. And I'm being serious—this isn't part of the twisted game that we play, you got me? She's a good-natured girl, she's got a sense of humor, but men and her past...well, that's all I'm gonna say. Just, take it easy with her."

"Yeah, man. Hey...I didn't know, I'm sorry."

"I told her that you and I kid around a lot; she didn't say anything about it to me. I'm just tellin' you this from me to you. Just, pick another way if you're jokin' with her."

"I will," Kegan said, looking humbled.

"But, Sienna." Jonathan's eyes became warm and peaceful. "She's amazing. I mean, look at her—she's beautiful. She's this amazing writer. They've made movies of some of her books. And she's great with Bella, it's like she's her real mother. I don't know how to explain it, but she's everything to me...everything."

Kegan studied the newness in his old friend and was relieved on the inside. He'd always worried about the kid. Jonathan had been reckless ever since he could walk. He'd always lived as fast and as hard as he could, like he was trying to outrun something. And everyone around him could see he was headed straight for a brick wall at two hundred miles an hour, yet he refused to listen to anyone, refused to slow down. All the while they were growing up, Jonathan's was the first name that came to everyone's mind at the initial news that there had been an accident of some kind. For years, everyone seemed to be holding their breath and crossing their fingers and saying extra prayers at night—maybe they had worked. Kegan felt appreciative to the forces that be. It finally appeared that his friend was going to make it after all—and he didn't mind if he took a drink to that.

Jonathan continued, oblivious to anything but Sienna. "But it's more than that. You should see what she does for people...she takes her money and puts homeless girls through college at Yale. They live with her—she's adopted them as her own. I mean, who does that?"

"Apparently she does," Kegan said, lifting his bottle toward her.

Jonathan was about to go on, but Kegan interrupted him, "I get it, man. I do. And I'm happy for ya. I've never seen you this, well, determined to stay alive. She must be good for you."

"She is."

"So how long have ya known this girl?"

"About a month."

The swig of ale in Kegan's mouth spewed all over the ground. He sputtered the words out between coughs, "And there he is—there's the Jonathan I know."

Jonathan slapped him on the back a couple times. "Are ya all right, man? I'm tellin' ya that stuff will kill ya one way or the other—you should think about quitting, too."

They laughed together, but Kegan was still stuck on the initial point that caused his reaction. Jonathan simply shrugged his shoulders in regard to the brief timeline.

"So when ya gonna marry her, then...or have ya already?" Kegan asked.

"No, unfortunately I haven't...and there's no date yet," Jonathan answered. "So, is this interrogation about over?"

"I only have one more question," Kegan said, his face finally returning to a more normal shade than cherry red.

"What's that."

"If you're not gonna get drunken and disorderly, how am I supposed ta fight ya then?"

∞

Jonathan and a few of his friends (one was a former band member that had moved back home) played songs while others danced, including Bella. Bella quickly made friends with some of the other kids there, and, clearly, she was having a good time. It was difficult for Jonathan and Sienna to get her to go to bed, but she finally did at eleven o'clock at night.

Over the course of the evening, Sienna had met Shay, Jonathan's younger brother; he was quiet and calm with a kind disposition, and he could have easily been mistaken for Jonathan's twin except he didn't have the same eyes and he was taller. He asked Sienna to dance for a couple of songs. He asked her about America, about her life there, and revealed very little about himself, but Sienna knew she liked him. She also noticed the cluster of young women eyeing him and giggling. He'd smile their way on occasion but didn't really talk to any of them in particular. Sienna also met Michael, Nessa, and their six-month-old baby boy. Nessa was preoccupied with the baby and didn't visit with anyone much, so at one point Sienna sat down beside her to see the baby. They called him "J.J.," but his given name was Jonathan Jude. She let Sienna hold him, which caught Jonathan's eye from across the yard. He watched Sienna's expression transform into something angelic as she looked into the child's face—talking to him, brushing his cheeks with her finger—it was a scene Jonathan would never forget. It literally made him ache inside over things that would never be. Nessa seemed thankful someone had taken the time to visit with her. As Sienna carefully handed her baby back to her, Nessa's smile indicated that she completely approved of Jonathan's choice. Michael was the coldest of the three brothers and didn't seem happy that Jonathan was back at all, but Sienna regarded him kindly thinking—and rightfully so—that the man would've never named his son after a brother he hated.

Sienna did make good friends with Lilly. Everything Jonathan had said about her was true. And, somewhat surprisingly, Kegan and Lilly appeared to be very happily married. Toward the end of the evening (and there had been one other actual fight that had nothing to do with the Driscoll boys) Kegan did get Jonathan to rumble with him. The men stood around and put down their bets.

Ciara was standing next to Sienna when it started, and she said, almost whimsically, "I don't think they'll ever change. Neither of them ever wins. They just stay at each other 'till they call a truce."

And she continued folding up chairs and stacking them together, completely unconcerned with the situation at hand. Sienna didn't want to watch it, but she did—from between her fingers as they partially covered her eyes. When Kegan threw a wicked punch against Jonathan's face, she swore she actually felt it land with the cracking sound it made—she winced and grabbed onto Lilly's arm for support.

"Oh my gosh—they aren't pretending!" she exclaimed just as Jonathan forcefully tackled Kegan to the ground, his body hit the rocky ground with a dull thud.

"No, they knock the stuffing out of each other. I never have understood it. And that's a brand-new shirt," Lilly commented nonchalantly. "Don't worry— they do have an agreement to try to leave each other's teeth in their heads."

Somehow, Sienna didn't find that very comforting.

Toward the end, the two were sprawled out on the ground, moaning and squirming around. Eventually they both started laughing. An old man waved his hand at them in disgust and left, apparently no richer than when he'd came (but at least the fish had been good). He toddled up the hill and disappeared. Jude stepped in between, pulling them both up by their collars. He told Kegan to go home and sleep it off, shoving him in that general direction.

Kegan was holding his stomach and still smiling though there was a trickle of blood running down his arm, his shirt was completely ruined, and Sienna swore his entire nose was a bit off to the side. Lilly rolled her eyes and followed after her husband. Sienna stood aside and watched as Jude gently put his arm around Jonathan's waist and helped him into the house.

When she entered, Jonathan was bent over the sink, spitting blood into it. He was still laughing and so was his dad—or at least it was as close to a laugh as his dad ever got. Jude's eyes met Sienna's as Jonathan splashed cold water on his face—the white porcelain sink was pink; the water running through his hands was twirling with thick ribbons of his blood. Her knees went a little weak.

"He deserves it," Jude said simply in regard to her worry. "Don't use the brains he was born with."

Jonathan snapped him with a towel and said, "Get me some ice, will ya, Dad?" And he dried his face. He looked up at Sienna, and he was still a mess, but he looked happy.

"I'm sorry, sweetheart," he said. "I know it doesn't make any sense, but I had to find out if I still got it."

"Well, do you?" she asked rather flatly.

"I'm happy ta say that I do," he answered, and he plopped himself down in a chair.

Jude tossed a bag of ice in his lap. Jonathan brought it up to his right cheekbone. Jude continued to ramble around the kitchen, finding some rubbing alcohol in a cabinet. He located some clean towels, then placed everything on the table.

"I'm goin' to bed," he said, turning to leave Jonathan and Sienna alone.

He stopped in the far hallway and then came back in. He looked at his disaster of a son, and he looked at the woman he'd brought with him.

Finally he said, "It's good to have you home—both of you." And he left again.

"See," Jonathan said to her, "I think you two have bonded over my bloody face."

She smiled, opening the bottle of alcohol. She winced with empathy for him, saying, "This is really gonna sting."

"That's all right. Like he said, I deserve it. It is pretty idiotic, I'll admit that."

She poured some on a towel and stood up.

"You don't have to do that," he said. "I can get it."

She took care of him anyway, and he let her. He had a cut above his eyebrow—it was bleeding the worst. He'd cut the corner of his lip, and his cheek was starting to swell in spite of the ice. The knuckles on his right hand were raw.

"Nothing needs stitches," she observed.

"Thank God for that," he said. "The doctor here is…well, let's just say more than likely I wouldn't make it back."

"From stitches?"

"Yeah…well he was the gray-haired tipsy guy—the one who fell out of his chair? Did you see him?"

Sienna laughed, "I did. I did."

"He's all right before noon. If it's after that, you may as well just suffer through 'till the next mornin' or just give it up and die."

She shook her head and looked at him. It seemed she had to peer deeper to find him in his eyes. She could tell he was starting to ache.

"Go ahead," he said. "Give me a lecture, I have it comin', love."

"I'm not going to lecture you," she said, holding the cloth to his brow.

"Where's the fun in that?"

"Eventually you two will figure this thing out and just start arm-wrestling each other."

"You know, that's a grand idea—why didn't I think of that?" he chuckled then he grabbed his side, "Ouch. Laughing's not gonna be good for a couple days."

"You know," she said thoughtfully, "somewhere in the middle? Like after you broke his nose…"

"I broke his nose, did I?" he mused proudly.

"I think so…just a little bit. But anyway, somewhere in the middle I began thinking that it was a lot like the teenagers I used to work with—the ones who cut themselves in that psych ward?"

"We look that bad, huh?"

"Sort of, yeah," she said. "I mean I get that you are trying to see which one of you is stronger, and I understand that the old men like to place their bets and you sort of put on a show for them, but…," she stepped back and pondered for a while, "this is a lot of pain to go through for a bunch of two dollar bets."

"Yeah, it is," he admitted.

"Are you frustrated about something?" she inquired of him.

"Very," he admitted.

"What?"

He looked at her for a while then he said, "You really want to know the truth?"

She nodded her head, indicating she did.

"We need to set a wedding date," he said straightforwardly.

She didn't really know what to say back. He slowly took her hand, and the towel in it, down off his face. He tossed the ice pack on the table and leaned back against his chair, staring up at the ceiling.

"I've been waiting for you for more than six years." He looked at her. "*Six years*," he repeated, searching her face, "and I truly mean that I have *waited*. And it's driving me out of my ever livin' mind! I mean, you're finally here and you are *so beautiful* and, well...I can't help it. I think this is slowly killing me. And I'm tellin' you the truth...that *this* (he made a gesture toward his beaten body) actually feels better. And I'm sorry if that was more than you needed to know, but that's the truth—that's how I feel."

She put the ice pack back on his cheek as she straddled him, sitting on his lap.

"I love you, Jonathan Driscoll. I'll marry you whenever you want," she said, with complete sincerity and regard for his feelings.

"Tomorrow?" he asked.

"Yeah," she said. "I'll marry you tomorrow."

"Just like that?" he asked.

"Yeah, just like that—you know I would."

"What about your family—your girls?" he asked.

"You're my family now," she kissed him on the face in a place that appeared uninjured. "That doesn't mean I don't love everybody else...but you come first. You're going to be my husband, and I'm going to be your wife. That's just the way it is," she explained, intently smiling into his eyes.

"You decide when you want to get married, and I'll be there," she said simply, and then she started to leave him, thinking there wasn't anything more she could do, but he grabbed her hand, his pleading gesture asking her not to go.

"That's not everything...," he said, warning her through his dark eyes. "You wanted me to tell you the truth, and that's not all of it."

He hugged her tenderly then held on to her more tightly and for a longer while. He obviously didn't want to let go of her; he didn't know how to say what he needed to tell her.

Finally she encouraged him. "Just tell me. Whatever it is, it'll be all right."

He pulled back from her, and he looked absolutely miserable down to the core. He opened his mouth, but nothing came out of it. His torn fist hit the table, and his bruising jaw clenched in against itself.

"What's wrong, Jonathan?" she asked, growing more concerned by the moment.

He looked up at her, and he finally said, "I don't know if I should be tellin' you this...I probably need more time to think it through, but I just can't seem to get my head around it. Tonight, when you were holding that baby, it just suddenly hit me for the first time—that will never be us. And I can't describe it, but it just about took me to my knees; it just about killed me deep down on the inside. And I don't know what to do about it, and I don't know who to blame. I mean if anyone deserves to be a mother, Sienna, it's you! I saw the way you were lookin' at him, and I've never seen that before, not in anyone's eyes. And it broke my heart that I can't ever give that to you..."

He had to quit talking or he would break down completely. The look in her eyes told him she was hurt by some of the things he was saying, which only made him feel worse.

"Maybe I shouldn't have told you that, sweetheart. I'm so sorry if I'm out of line here," he immediately apologized. "I'm probably not thinking very clearly, maybe I got hit a little too hard on the head."

"No," she replied to his attempts to soften it, "don't ever be sorry for telling me the truth about how you feel or what you're going through. I don't care what it is, I want you to tell me everything. I'm not afraid of pain, Jonathan. It's generally where we learn and can start to grow."

The cut above his eye started to bleed again, and she lifted the towel back up to it and pressed—he didn't even feel it. He brought his hand up to kindly cover hers.

"Believe me," she whispered, "I know it's painful. It's something that's very hard to deal with, but it does get better with time."

She tried to console him through her lonely experiences, through her hard lessons learned in the classroom of isolation.

"It does...it gets better," she repeated, sounding a bit more sure of herself this time. "I just feel bad that you'll have to sacrifice something that huge to be with me..."

"Oh, no...no, that's not what I meant at all, Butterfly," he interrupted her. "Please don't ever say that. I'd give up anything to be with you and not think twice about it all of my days. No, I'm not trying to make anything harder on you, I'm trying to express to you—and obviously doing a deplorable job of it. I'm trying to tell you that I'll be carrying this burden with you from now on. You're not alone with it anymore. I truly understand your pain and how very strong you are."

There was nothing more to say. What more could be said in a situation like this? It was best to give and get a hug, and go to sleep praying for the strength for another day, and being thankful for the blessings already tucked beneath your arm. And that's what they did, because the night gave them no other answer to cling to.

chapter twenty-five

ОТН HIS CHEEKBONE and his eye had turned from a wicked blood-red to a ghostly ink-cloud of blue somewhere during the night. The pain wasn't bad; it was already fading into nothing. But it was a strange memory because the pieces this time just didn't fit—that was his first and last unnecessary fight as a father. He certainly looked better than Sienna thought he would, considering. He'd put one of Bella's cartoon bandages over the worst cut—it softened the shock for the little girl as she scanned her daddy's face with worried eyes. As he knelt down before her and bent a knee to her innocence, he was embarrassed to such an extreme degree he was physically uncomfortable, more so by the moral dilemma he'd created than by his bodily wounds. He didn't have to say it—Sienna knew he regretted his actions. He was nervously fidgeting again like he had done so often, back in America.

Bella asked him what had happened, her soft hand resting atop a bruise— the concern evident in her expression as she took it all in and recorded it for life, he was fairly certain.

"Dad got in a stupid fight with Kegan, but we made up. Right, Kegan?" Jonathan called over his shoulder for backup. Kegan entered the bedroom behind him, and Jonathan said, "See, sweetheart, we are still friends. Aren't we, Kegan?"

"Oh, yeah, we're definitely friends," he agreed, kneeling down in front of Bella, wincing and holding his stomach; his nose was taped to his face and he sounded like he had a cold.

He looked absolutely terrible—his entire nose and both of his eyes were black and blue and swollen. This was the first time he had seen Kegan since last night, and Jonathan was horrified. His appearance would do nothing but add to Bella's trauma, but it was too late to do anything about it.

"It was all my fault, lamb," Kegan graciously continued. "Your dad was just trying to calm me down, and he got in my way is all. He showed me that fighting is bad. It's very, very bad, and I won't ever do it again. It's very, very bad—I don't recommend it."

Jonathan eyeballed him, signaling that that was enough of an explanation, and Kegan humbly exited the room.

"Daddy," Bella said.

"Yes, love."

"Don't go out on the trawler."

"Now how on earth do you know what a trawler is?" he chuckled. "We aren't takin' the trawler, we're goin' on the big vessel today...but why shouldn't Dad go with Grandpa Jude and Uncle Michael?"

"Because I don't want you to die, Daddy," she answered straightforwardly.

Jonathan released a heavy sigh, rubbing out the creases that had gripped his forehead as he recognized the burden again in his sweet child. She was too young for this.... He looked up at Sienna, uncertain what he should do or what to say next, but she didn't have any answers for him.

"Listen to me, sweetheart. I am not going to die. Neither is Sienna. We'll be just fine. And if you need to, pray. You go ahead and do whatever it is that you do—and don't let anybody stop you," he looked straight into her eyes, checking to make sure she understood. "And do you remember what Sienna told you to say when you get to the end?"

She nodded and whispered, "God's will be done."

"That's right, angel. And please remember that ya can't pray very well if you're worried all the time—okay? So don't worry, your hands are too tiny to carry all that. God will carry it for us both...see, His hands are bigger..."

It was an endearing sight for Sienna to see as they held up their hands, together, palm to palm, father and daughter—it was like she was witnessing God's Spirit in him shining right through to grace his child, the words he spoke flowing from the very lips of Jesus Christ Himself. *Do not worry about tomorrow; neither be ye anxious...I have conquered this world.*

"Now come here and give your ol' dad a hug 'cuz he already misses ya."

He cradled her in his arms affectionately, and he kissed and stroked her hair. Jude hollered an unkindly, "Let's go," from the other room. Jonathan reacted with a visible jerk that struck his back and through his shoulders as if somebody had cracked a whip against his spine. The old man's order obviously triggered deep-seated memories from somewhere inside him. Jonathan addressed Sienna's face again, finding that she seemed to be more concerned about him and the sea's mood than little Bella was.

"Nothin's gonna happen to me, you two...okay?" he said to both of them. "My dad's too mean to let me die out there—you heard it in his voice, didn't ya? He'd stick a hook in me back if he had to, an' fish me out. So how about some smiles instead of these long faces—both of you? You're gonna break my heart lookin' at me that way!"

He kissed Bella good-bye then took Sienna in his arms. "I'll be just fine," he whispered to her. His breath felt warm against her face. He'd never admit to it, but he did have some doubts.

"It's for my dad." He attempted to explain the tradition with a hint of his own uncertainty. "It means a lot to the old man, and it's just a short run—I'll be back tonight—I will.

And about last night," he said, looking into her eyes, "as soon as possible, I want ta marry you, but I want your girls to be there for you. I know they'd never forgive me if they weren't."

She nodded and forced a smile. "That's better...," he said and touched her cheek, then he was gone.

Her fingers were still spread out in mid-air, lingering long after the dissipating warmth of his final touch. Bella looked up at Sienna, and the two of them firmly held hands, getting lost in another mystical world they shared together.

"Pray, baby girl. I can feel it, too," Sienna said as she gazed out at the closed door he'd just walked through. She'd watched him grab one of those Driscoll Family sweaters off the hook just before it swung shut behind him.

"Pray...," she said again, squeezing the little girl's hand.

"I don't know what to say, I've not gotten a story," Bella said in a tiny voice that indicated her soul was drowning.

Sienna knelt down in front of her. The child's face read something borderline to terror. Sienna quickly evaluated and checked the amount of responsibility the child could handle. It was an impossible estimation, its only assurance being God uses what's broken to pass to the multitudes. She took a deep breath. *This is just a little child,* and she offered up a silent prayer, *Help me, please.* With lightened voice, Sienna attempted to sound confident and calm though she was trembling inside.

"Don't worry, Bella. If God doesn't give you any stories to tell, then it's just not the right time. And that's okay. I just want you to listen for them, listen quietly. And if you find the words, say them out loud no matter who is listening, no matter where you are. That's all you can do—the rest is out of your hands. Okay, sweetheart?"

"Okay, Mommy."

They seemed to have nothing further to say to each other, so Sienna made her some cocoa and started putting dishes away that had dried overnight on the counter. When she was done with that, she folded the laundry and started another load. Afterwards, she stood next to Bella, lightly tapping her fingers on the table. Then she started pacing back and forth, stopping at the door to look out the window on regular intervals, though she couldn't see the dock from there anyway.

Bella asked for some paper and crayons. The picture she was drawing was nondescript. She simply covered the entire sheet of paper with solid color, but Sienna quickly noticed the shades she chose were blues, grays, and greens—the color of the ocean that was holding their loved one upon it. Sienna visualized ocean waves on the night shore, and they pulled her under with doubt. Its true intentions and stoical loyalties freely taunted her. Would it be evil or good, or would it be mixed on this particular day? It wouldn't tell her. It simply infiltrated the water in her very body like blood to her veins, became one with her thoughts and allowed only this for her to discover: *When things are endlessly stolen from me, life treasures in the deep I be holding, slowly suffocated with air . . . someone, somehow, will have to equally pay for my pearls taken . . . life for life, breath for breath, cruelty for cruelty, matched; and fair, like a bartered exchange. I am the sea, and its souls I do trade in. You best pray to your God of land for a fog to be rollin' in late . . . a stormy haze to cover my angry face—it'll mean warmer water, for his fortunate sake. What's about to happen, the others' eyes will be blinded to. Forces are bein' kind to you, but that all can change . . . as the spirits drifting by beneath my surface so often do. I never know what's inside of me, what terror is lurkin'—what I'll be forced to swallow, what'll be torn out.*

Just then Ciara entered the room, "Why, you look a million miles away, my dear . . . Oh, and thank you much for doing the laundry for me, Sienna. I don't know a woman in the world who doesn't get sick and tired of doing it. You know, I actually have dreams, and all I'm doing in them is more laundry— sometimes in piles up to the very sky, if you could imagine.

"Coloring I see. And what do we have there, Bella dear?"

She peered at the pictures, and though they were far from what one would call beautiful, that's what she said anyway, kissing her granddaughter squarely on the head.

Bella smiled up at her.

"You are such a warmhearted child," she mused almost to herself. "Sienna, I have to go to town to get some things for Brigh's funeral tomorrow. And I need to run by the market to check on the flowers. Would you like to come along?"

Sienna silently gazed out the window.

"Something wrong today, dear?"

"Oh, no, I'm sorry. I think I'll just stay here if that's all right. I have some writing to catch up on; I'm way behind."

"Sure, that's fine, dear. You don't mind if I take Bella, then?"

"No, not at all. Would you like that, Bell?"

The child nodded, and there seemed to be no evident change to her drawings—indicative of surface waters still and silent, not abnegating to her their sunken secrets either.

⟨⟩

As soon as they left, Sienna opened her laptop and began working on her book, *Stained Glass*. The first several chapters of it were on paper—crumpled, wrinkled, and torn by whoever had tried to frighten her back at Cheney's house. She picked up the pages and ran her hand over them, pressing her palm into their secretive center, asking the Lord for some sort of spiritual connection to the person's intent or identity. All she got was an empty void, a massive black hole, a stagnant vortex...and she put them back down; she got the distinct impression that that was the state of their soul.

"Nature abhors a vacuum, stagnant water rots. Declivity...it will prevail unless you take a stand against it," she spoke her thoughts aloud, picking up a pen that said *Killybegs Fishermen's Organization Ltd.* on it. She tapped it repetitively against her knee then paraphrased a scripture that came to mind, "...and when the demon returns, the state of that person is seven times worse than the first."

"We have to do something, lest we do nothing." She looked at the words on the pen again and smiled.

She gazed out the window, considering the message the intruder meant to send her and evaluating the spiritual answer. She prayed for them, whoever and wherever they were. *Reveal it to them. God, show them that You're the only One great enough to fill their cavernous soul.* Slanted drops of rain began spitting against the glass....*A single soul is bigger than the universe. We have to fill it with something of a similar vastness and wonder, or it will swallow us whole just like that sea out there, which I'm asking you to appease with something besides my Jonathan—please.*

She continued to pray receptively and got a quote commonly attributed to Edmund Burke in return, and she repeated it out loud, "The only thing necessary for evil to prevail is for good men to do nothing."

Good men... she pondered the phrase as if calling them forth.

Regardless of who had initially spoken the words, she asked that God would show her what needed to be done and give her the courage to do it...*because we each need to do something...the first obviously being that we believe in God's goodness and become aligned with His goodness.*

She refocused her thoughts on her work. She'd reached a section in the book where it was time to describe her take on stained glass. She thought about all the risk involved in fulfilling an office, all the hazards surrounding a singular occupation. She mused at how people are so driven to do what God places them on the planet to do that they will stop at nothing. Through her mind passed images of fishermen on boats, fishermen with families and dreams of their own, as they head out into a sea that may decide to avenge itself on them that particular day. These men pushed their lives out into the middle of its mercies, full well knowing the swings of its mood; the unsuspecting power of its surf; the jaws of jagged rock it splayed wide open, hiding its promises of just how deep. They plead with it silently in the morning knowing it may decide to erase them from the time of day, remove them from the hope of solid ground and the arms of a woman at shore...but for what reason should they do this every day? Sienna could think of only two things greater than the immediate desire to stay alive: one, the love of a woman, or man, or a son or daughter...so love, in general; and two, the desire to fulfill God-given purpose. For men's hearts are brave when they love and when they accept their God-given calling.

She determined that the latter reason of fulfilling God-given purpose delivered a lot of heft toward a solitary soul moving across the earth; a good deal of responsibility pressed down and shaken together; and an exponential list of requirements strapped to a being whose only flaw was being born. But she also realized she was dually describing the very nature of faith—its cause, its core, its entire essence and culture. God knew the man He'd created would need a solid reason to reach out, to reach up. A dogged weight around his ankle would be necessary to get him to ask for the Help he needed, to make it through all the drudgery and toil. Only the weariest of eyes would dare to look for and believe in a side with no struggle, no tears; and each of these chosen created ones would sacrifice anything and everything to fulfill their God-given purpose—so long as they came to understand what it was.

People who never find their calling, she figured, become somewhat suicidal, or at the very least, self-abusive, dry, ungiving, and destructive. But there are others who spend their youth and all their energy in a rampant race against time to find it, and then once they do, they'll spend every day from that point to the grave doing it, cultivating it, giving it to others even if they have to give it away for free. (And sometimes they'll even pay someone else to take what their soul bled out, drop by painful drop. They'll look at a stranger like he's their brother...if he'd only take it with him for just a little while.)

Wisdom, she considered, *is bought with a steep price and is meant to be handed out for free.*

"Pick up your cross and follow Me," she spoke into the center of her glowing screen; the "cross" in her current vein of thinking represented the call on a person's life—what they were born to do, what they are meant to do. And carrying a cross...well, it isn't easy—it's a burden one drags across their back across the earth all the way to their own death. It becomes a part of them, and they love it and hate it, both. It is what they do while they are retracing the footsteps of their Lord, and it is their greatest gift to give and, equally, their most debilitating curse to try and restrain.

She considered her writing, for the closest example to her. She loved it—it was automatic like her breathing. It was also lonely. She'd literally spent years to create a parallel world, all for the sake of helping someone else with her words—words that were bottled up inside like a dammed river threatening to break if she didn't release them, little by little, and throughout the entire course of her allotted time. Words that may very well end up on a dusty shelf unnoticed, unrecognized for what they once were, somebody's life—the dash in between the numbers on their tombstone. No one would ever know that they were bartered for unborn children, a spouse, a day of fresh air and sunshine and blessed uncomplication, or simply a walk with a favorite dog down the country lane. No one would ever think that they were traded as would be filthy money for a friend who never got to be one.

The Great Exchange, the Great Commission...oh, how the soul does bleed its life-blood..., but she could sit on that thinking stone for the rest of her life and turn into it before finding anything else she'd rather do, and so there she had it, and she tried to capture it for somebody's chapter twenty-five.

And she thought about Jonathan's music, how he'd traveled halfway around the world to sell a piece of his soul to the devil, in order to do what God had created him to do. She thought about Jude, taking his father, his sons, and his friends out on a dare in order to clothe them, shelter them, to do his best to take care of them while they fed hungry people all over their land. Then she thought of Bella... *What on earth will that child have to sacrifice to this greedy world just to be able to have the freedom to pray?*

And so her thoughts wound back down around her story, wound back down to a solitary piece of clear glass in the glassmaker's hand. One slip, one fraction of a moment in a lifetime that he wasn't diligent, and that glass would slide..., slowly, deeply, and then deeper still, into the very skin that had formed it. Cruelly slicing through the flesh and muscle, severing the tendons and sinews that had bound together unto its movement and fire, lovingly, for to create it. It cut right through, mercilessly, and seemingly without thanks for the time which could have been spent elsewhere, the expenditure of breath that could have been released upon someone else's soft graces. It called for the price of his blood and he let it, but was it against his will? Looking down at his work, did he curse it? No and never..., because upon those lips came forth a smile. A wonderment filtered in through the clear sun, and he upheld it there in the glistening light. His colorless glass was now colored and dripping with a part of himself, and God had glorified his efforts with a brilliant crimson red. And in the enlightenment, the Lord God whispered to his ear alone, *You'll tell My story. It'll be the first of its kind. You are an original son, and you are the father of the Stained Glass window—go and help build all of My Churches, fill them with Illumination and with Light.* And that is exactly what the glassmaker did, one-handed, for the rest of his days.

"Pain," she typed the word as she prayed its ink, "is what spurs us on. It'll kill us if we ever stop moving; swallow us whole if we ever stop giving. It is

215

inescapable, and it forces us to run straight along our Destiny Road. We must endure it in whatever form it comes—we simply have no other choice—we must carry its load, for without the resistance of its weight, we would simply grow old. We would perish."

Her fingers rested atop the keys as she stared coldly into the gray light. The rain was falling harder outside now.

She said aloud, "Jesus, help us endure. Help us to trust You to take us to the other side of it. Help us to believe that the other side holds the sweet rest of God. And then we start again, a more brilliant chapter."

Suddenly the door flew open, and she heard the wind scatter in disarray Bella's drawings from the table to the floor in the next room. Chills went down her spine, and she slammed her laptop closed, tossing it on the bed. She set her jaw and raced straight into the possibility of a pain so colossal, she couldn't acknowledge the depth of it.

chapter twenty-six

*C*IARA BURST INTO the house, screaming at the top of her lungs, "Sienna, where are you?...Sienna!"

Their eyes met, and Ciara's were full of fear as she clutched both of Sienna's arms and continued, "It's Bella...the girl is acting so strangely. I don't know what to do....quickly! Quickly, Sienna! She's at the edge of the sea. I couldn't get her to move! I tried to lift her, and I...I couldn't get her to move—it's like she is a statue!"

The women ran outside together, and Ciara both pointed and pushed Sienna in the direction of a cliff overlooking the sea—a sea which had momentarily bound and stolen the whole of Sienna's attention, breath, energy, and sanity. It was all in an instant...but the message it revealed ran so deep, she'd never really be able to express it in words or capture it on paper, no matter how hard she tried.

It reintroduced itself to her as a dreadful body of deception and liquid death, entirely violent in scope and strength with its wilderness of white-capped waves thrown upwards as if grinding, arctic mountains from an evil, bottomless land. Its bluff was in the hiding of its true and stolen power...a swarming undercurrent churning out chaotic, unnatural rhythms which, as with a slow suffocation, held no sound. No proof. And, as with departure, no soul. It was never held accountable, no matter how many years imprisoned. And it never saw the sun, no matter how many dawns its cold skin reflected, no matter how many ships it carried out across its back each morning.

And so it told its story to only her, saying that from time to time, the violence it rendered soothed and temporarily appeased its wretched nature down to its silent core where, indeed, rested the beginning of time, the dawning of all the ages. And what it held up for her, in its cold, immeasurable hand, was a bitterness offer—all the cards of her game...her heart and its love flowing out, flowing in; her fortunate status and comfort and material plunder; her king, and herself the queen, and a princess that is her ace. It told her, in cruel sideways winks and horrible ghastly stares, that in one sick hand she could lose it all, that on this beautiful and miserable island every day it licked closer to its own starving throat, the sea would smile—she could be clubbed to death, be buried with a rusty shovel—and, in the rain…all the rain, the rain, rain…no one would ever know she'd been there like MacSweeney Bannagh's poor thirteen hundred.

To this sea a thousand years was but a drop of rain, a thousand souls nothing but charlatans to charter.

Sienna blinked her eyes, turning from the vacant sorrow of it (though there's always something about looking at a sea that invites its liquid, its molecules, its memory, its vapor, into the very essence of the anatomy and amazing composition of the eyes as they watch it, they *become* it, and vice versa, in equated measure and form), but still, she was completely and inerasably absorbed by it, and would always be. She'd never tasted of such bitterness and endless unrest, such loneliness and bravery that would force one to cross its liquid gates. Her mind's eye she could not close, so she weakly rejected its massive power and sickening threat of death while her being and body welcomed it to her life. All the while, amidst her slow-motion reaction, she was still swallowing its colors down as if tasting a salt that goes directly from the tongue into the bloodstream, never to part. She forced her legs to move out as she started, sprinting with all her might against the cold, unyielding rain and her own warm, emerging tears; she fought against the absence of air to get to her girl with a colossal strength, but little Bella was disappearing over the jagged edge like a sunset that could never be touched ('twas up to God, should it ever rise again). It was a sight illustrated and read like the worst kind of beautiful misfortune, like the absolute end of all time and the final countdown of numberless second chances. Just as there will be a reckoning, there will be emptiness in the spaces once so filled, and that cliff seemed to Sienna to be the beginning of solid truth. And it hit her—the believing—hard between the eyes; rows of teeth and jaw swallowing her future as easily as one crystalline fish swallows another—commonly, beneath each still surface of every cryptic pool of peace.

She was already crying out, "Why?" and, "Why now?" as it was showing her her true identity—who she was without the title of Motherhood draped across her chest, what she was with and without the dictatorship of Control (for what she was really asking, was why *me?*). It was offering her a warning, wisdom to heed and to reap from, that the Two Titles were nowhere near synonymous. It was telling her with as much delicacy as an omnipotent Power can rend, *If you want something so badly that you cannot be happy without it, you cannot possibly be resting upon nor operating in the will of God.* It, in the form of a little girl willing to die in order to skirt the slippery rocks of a single, solitary prayer, was opening the door between the lies of her reality and the truth of her fiction. Before her eyes fluttered the loosed pages of all of her books—those written, those to be written still—and upon those pages, revealed to her in blotted ink and blood and wasted time and choices and the guts of a faith put into actual play with the risk of all the blame...upon those pages were words written by the same quill monitoring the Lamb's Book of Life, holy and reverential words that described her forward-living life.

Put simply, through droplets of clear and uncomplicated rain, it was time to move. It was time to battle circumstance with the weight of a dream, to test its true origination. Would it be from the laughable recesses of a delusional mind, or was it given from the beginning, from the Creator in hopes He'd found a willing and competent person to oblige. She was willing to find out, as well as stand alone. She was brave enough to walk and wield that invisible two-edged sword. She just hadn't been aware that God's perfect timing was in its keeping. She didn't know when that sweet day would come, but here it was happening now—this very day and running wide open. No sun, nor star to guide her...or to stop her.

She was now a true mother; her *me* turned into *she*, in an instant.

From this day forward, everything could end up being her fault.

People could end up getting hurt for generations because of the things she did or didn't do.

She wasn't weaving the story inside the blanket of a book any longer. She was no longer covered. She was completely exposed in the light of awesome responsibility. She was now the author of the story of their lives. The books themselves had only been a means to an end. Their experience was being brought to life, proving she'd been blatantly misguided with the direct opposition of logic that reality turned. Her characters, no longer falsified, nor coincidental, were filtering slowly forth as pieces of one or each of the Three. Her career—her expansive and impressive body of work—to her, had become as useless as kindling save one thing, it was a manual for the actual job at hand...this child, her little family, following after the footsteps of the Triune God.

And no, this was not at all inflated to the spiritual eye, not while looking through the eyes of God where not one is disrespected, where every one is counted a Grand Master of their granted and regal domain—He's the King of all kings, and Sienna understood this well...

"Bella...Bell!" Sienna called out desperately, not recognizing her own voice as it separated from her body and became absorbed by the mocking sea. She was slipping repeatedly in the saturated sod, struggling with everything she had to continue toward the cliff with an increasing sense of panic. She saw her own fingers reaching out into the gray abyss before her, grabbing nothing but empty sky. *Dear God...*

She skidded toward the ledge, nearly going over herself. She slid across the muck and landed on her hind end, both her feet dangling over the edge. She gasped for breath, peering down between her knees. The mud was falling from her boots in chunks, floating down twenty, thirty feet or more. The child was descending large, slippery boulders, stopping and shielding her face against incoming surf, and then starting again.

And, yes, to a spiritually daft onlooker, the child seemed possessed and possibly, to a set of ill-educated eyes (those holding earthly intelligence without morals), she even seemed committable.

"Bella!" Sienna screamed with everything she was made of, clutching her stomach where an unborn baby would be.

"Bella, stop!"

She openly sobbed the words as her other hand clawed through the sod and rock beside her, squeezing it as if for an answer, or a rope.

But the child couldn't hear, nor could she heed, her mother's plea. For she was completely consumed with obeying Another.

And a loving voice, not of the sea, but rolling in off of it with greater force and in quieter tones, came to Sienna and said, "Be careful, Mother, what you ask of your child. Take care that your request not conflict with Mine."

Sienna's soul fell silent against the smile she perceived upon the lips of her kind Lord. Slowly, It was moving in, and she felt comfort and a significant release. Her breath returned to her and expanded within her, and outside her, and back again. And she watched her daughter climb betwixt hard rock and soft death, and she let her go through it, biting her own tongue until it bled down the back of her throat. Her tears mingled with the salty rain on her heated cheeks stung her eyes—what a wicked body of water.

She was a futile opponent. All she could do was wait.

Ciara ran up behind her, regaining her breath as she evaluated the dire situation, "Father, Son, and the Holy Ghost," she said and crossed herself, momentarily rolling her eyes back in her head.

"Mother Mary and all the saints," she whispered her conclusion as she watched the child continue scaling the rocks. Her focus swiftly shifted down toward earthen vessels, and she addressed Sienna angrily, "Aren't you going to do anything? Aren't you going down after her?"

"No," Sienna said softly, suddenly feeling nauseous and slightly faint, taking in the seriousness of it all.

Ciara started calling Bella's name, persevering until her voice cracked with wear.

"She can't hear you," Sienna finally said simply, calmly.

"What on earth do ya mean she won't hear me? She's a stubborn child, she is, half-crazy, if ya ask me—just like her father was."

"Ciara," Sienna continued, "I didn't say she *won't* hear you, I said she *can't* hear you. There is a difference. Here...sit down."

"Not there. Move back, Sienna. That ledge could give way and be the death of you as well."

Sienna slid back far enough to be safe, but she didn't take her eyes off Bella for a moment.

"What do you mean by sayin' she *can't* hear me, then?" Ciara inquired again, having nothing of use to offer but conversation. She knelt down beside Sienna, her stiff knees sinking down into the dampness and cold.

"You already know, don't you, Ciara?" Sienna's eyes were hard, and their gray seemed cold and icy, illuminated with a hallowed sharpness that was nearly unnatural for a living person.

Ciara shivered at the ghostly sight of them, although they were amazingly beautiful, they also seemed wicked somehow—certainly intimidating. She pulled her woolen scarf up against the rain, but mostly to shield herself from those unholy eyes. She fell silent for a moment, staring out over her beloved grandchild and the sea she both admired and despised. She did know some things, or she thought she knew, anyway. Her intuition had told her Bella was a special child who had picked up the Driscoll family curse, otherwise

Jonathan wouldn't have brought her back without warning or reason, wouldn't have been asking after Brigh like he did, and just before the old woman died, too. But the curse was nothing to talk about out loud, if it be helped—it was never mentioned lightly, never spoken of unless it came knocking at the door. And it seemed to her to be knocking, it did...with both sets of its knuckles.

"She's got the Driscoll curse, hasn't she?" Ciara whispered with a superstitious terror, so low and so quietly it was nearly inaudible.

"Not a curse, Ciara, a gift..."

"Posh," Ciara scoffed at the notion, "A gift! How's loosin' yer bloody head a gift, I'd like to know?"

"It's a gift from God. Just watch her. Just sit here and watch. And if you are going to say anything, I would suggest it be a prayer," Sienna concluded, and went back to watching over her child from a distance, biting her swollen tongue, and glancing toward heaven intermittently with a hint of motherly threat mixed in with complete Fatherly dependence. *Isn't that how we all survive, anyway?* she thought of the latter.

⚭

The organized chaos which ensued on deck upon the storm's arrival had reached a momentary, yet deceptive, lull. Jude was still barking orders over the loudspeaker, though his crew seemed to be collectively dumbstruck or deaf. But more than likely they were just frozen and sick to death of Michael's mouth, he figured. Brody was sitting quietly by Jude's side in the cabin; his only job was keeping the coffee contained and out of the controls. Thankfully, they'd had good luck—the holding tank was topped off so there was little threat of capsizing. Jude checked the weather radar screen, still irritated that there hadn't been a single warning to announce the storm. He tapped it with his fist, concluding that it must be acting up again. *Worthless piece of...*

"Jonathan, where's your vest?" he shouted into the mike, just before he saw it coming.

"Hold on!" he shouted to everyone just as a huge wall of water splashed in against the deck. *That lean was about fifty degrees*, he thought to himself as the boat set itself aright. His neck muscles tensed up. The sea was actin' strange. His well-versed eyes scanned and counted heads for what seemed to be the hundredth time that day. He quickly checked the state of his beloved vessel. He couldn't afford to damage or lose any more equipment. If he did, they'd all be starvin'. He gave more orders to secure stray equipment, latches, netting, and gear, ending with, "If you don't move, I'm comin' down there and kickin' every single one of your arses."

Michael was second in command, typically giving orders to Shay, Killian, and Kegan on deck, and this day had been no different. He was running his mouth, shouting at them to do this task, to tie off that rope, until he caught sight of something that silenced him completely. All the deckhands followed his gaze which could have meant death for any one of them. Jude saw it, too...he'd miscounted. He'd overlooked it. And he never overlooked anything.

It was, simply and monumentally, an empty space.

"Hold on!" came his cry over the loudspeaker, an atypical desperation apparent in his voice. The deckhands automatically grabbed for something secure without thinking about it, riding another wave back down. All eyes were blank with shock; all bodies were filling slowly with a filtering terror as they started toward an empty railing—a railing where Jonathan had been just a moment before.

"Man overboard! Man overboard! Cut the engine!" Michael yelled and signaled to his father. He leaned over and listened, but there was no human noise to be heard. His eyes scanned the quaking sea, but there was nowhere to throw a preserver. He cursed a long line that didn't make any sense then started calling out for his brother.

"Jonathan! Jon-a-than!" he cried it out so slowly—a most desolate, drawn, soul-tearing sound—as if pushing the blood and the life of the name down a battle-swollen rill, forcing the stain onto God's hand. He was actually keening a floating islet call, straining against the wicked storm and the isolation of the death of a young man in his care. He was singing a coarse song with every fiber that bound him together before the truth of it pulled him completely apart.

(He called his brother's name as if drawing closed the ends of the earth within himself, sealing their borders with a knot tied of his own sinews for to haul his brother up in a net woven and borne by the singular strength of his own arm—if it be severed—fine, if *only he be alive*).

As he screamed, still wishing it a nightmare soon over, his entire body was turning a circle as a compass, with his lungs and his heart and his mouth wide open, his eyes pressed shut against reality and rain, his mind closed tight against the gravity and the weight of it—against the pain. Anyone watching would have truly and permanently witnessed how deep the love of a brother actually goes. He finally opened his eyes in the middle of some sort of hope for a miracle but was met only with pity or astonishment in the expressions of those still on deck. He grabbed one of them angrily by the collar. He had no idea which one; he couldn't see his face. "What are ya doin' just standin' there? Circle that boat! *Find* him!"

The men scurried like rats. They looked in every direction. They peered behind, beneath, and around every rain-droplet wave. Shay fought back stinging tears and saltwater. He couldn't see anything either. He couldn't see anything at all.

"Hold on!" Jude cried as another wave washed the deck with spray. He felt like somebody cut his heart out with a knife and handed it to him, still beating, the blood leaking from its severed valves warm and running between his cooling, stiffening fingers—but that would have been better than this.

∞

Bella had reached the lowest rock, the largest rock, the one closest to the sea, and she stood with her arms stretched over the water as if she were getting ready to part it. She was speaking in Gaeilge. She was saying a lot of things. And somehow, just before every crashing wave, she'd lie down and hug that rock like a seal and place her tiny hands into its crevices, and the water would swallow her little spread-eagle body—and Sienna's breath—whole. But each time, as the white foam left her outline, her little dark coat would emerge and she'd stand again and resume her speaking.

"What's she saying?" Sienna asked, shaking violently from the cold.

Ciara's face was white as a ghost. Her lips were quivering. Sienna knew it must be something dreadful.

"It's an old, old dialect...from what I can hear she's asking God for breath, for air. She's telling her father's lips to open, to smile, to kiss the bubbles so that they can enter into his lungs. She's asking God to bring warmth from the undercurrent for his body's blood to keep circling. She's asking for a legion of angels to swim below his lifeless body..."

She stopped and gasped, clasping her hands to her trembling lips. Large tears dropped from her beautiful brown eyes. She swallowed hard and continued.

"She's asking for the angels to drag his body up by the threads of his sweater unraveling...unraveling and weaving into a net for them to carry. She's asking for time to stand still under the ocean. She's telling the fishes to stop swimming. She's telling the sand to stop shifting. She's telling the reefs to stop growing..., seaweed to stop its swaying. She's commanding everything to stop counting so that her father can have that time. She says his time is going backwards now—I don't know what that means—what does that mean, Sienna?"

Sienna wasn't crying anymore, she was praying so hard in her heart it felt like it would burst. She stood up at once and started babbling in the spirit, talking in tongues, and pacing back and forth. She opened her eyes for a moment and glanced at Ciara who looked nothing short of horrified.

"Get up, woman!" Sienna commanded. "Or stay on your knees...whatever....Dear God...just please start praying in whatever prayers or languages you've got."

Ciara obeyed.

chapter twenty-seven

*J*ONATHAN, DO YOU love Me?"

"Yes, Lord."

"Jonathan, do you love Me?"

"Yes, Lord, I love You."

"Jonathan, do you *really* love Me?"

"Yes, Lord, You know that I do."

Space and distance and water drifted by, before the Lord replied.

"Then get out of the boat."

Jonathan looked around him and laughed as he answered, "Looks like You've already taken care of that one, Lord."

And to his most pleasant surprise, the Lord laughed with him. And the sea held His Voice in its belly. In the ironic humor of death—or whatever state he was in now—Jonathan and his Lord understood one another without words, Jonathan full well knowing that Jesus talked literally and figuratively at the same time, in Living Words. The *boat* had to do with a normal, safe life. It was time to expect a change, to do things differently, to follow Him. Christians can't walk on water without trusting Him fully and, truthfully, Jonathan had never done that. Not completely. And so he was ready, for the first time, to truly claim the title, understanding that to call oneself a Christian, the name of Christ and all He represents must come *first*.

They smiled at one another, Jonathan and his Lord. Somehow Jonathan knew he would not die that day. So he relaxed, he completely let go. He twirled onto his back and looked up at the choppy surface of the water—its stinging cold—its salty white foam. Its anger, its chaos, lifted further and further away from him as he descended into the serene warmth, the blues, the grays, the greens of this underwater place, this peace...Time disappeared with the surface noise as he went deeper still. He heard the sweet voice of his daughter all around him, and he smiled. He blew her a kiss through the water, and his lungs filled with bubbles of air that swiftly went back into him—air he hadn't realized that he needed.

Deeper still and he heard angels singing, an old, old Irish chant he'd never heard before, with deep men's voices, warm and strong and telling of safe havens in secret places they'd found; with women's melodies surrounding them and woven through their silent spaces like the mothers of heaven on wings of sound; and with baby's breath like the clouds floating against their porcelain skin, playing it like sweet violins. Cellos. Bagpipes. And drum, and heartbeat, and boots fallen down of traveling foot soldiers always marching. And there went a flute as well. But above all was the collective voice filled with collective souls having one thing only in common with him—a love of the Lord. They formed a liquid band of a peace and of a harmony he'd never felt before, and should the sea water not have been in his eyes, he could have cried it in drops one at a time 'till it was found just as full, and he would not have grown tired of hearing it—a musician's heaven tucked inside a place with no sound.

It's all on the inside...

Just as he found himself wondering how much time had actually passed, he saw a brigade of corpses—though not grotesque—rising beneath him, ghostly shadows and spirits gaining flesh and warmth and light and animation, eventually forming an endless line of men all wearing the Driscoll family pattern. They pieced themselves back into complete being from the reefs, and their skin was as rainbows of the brightest coral colors so when they'd move with an act of kindness—a nod, a smile toward him—they would shimmer and shine like a most beautiful and priceless creature.

As he swam above them in a wake of pure bliss, he felt the infiltration of their strength to the point of reaching pain. They gave him their unused strength in exact measure—the strength each would have needed to live out the days stolen from them by the very sea they all floated in now, together. And so as they left him, he thanked them, and they wordlessly indicated they'd carry the thanks and the praises back to the Lord from where they first came.

So, it could be said, that in those mystic waters he would never tell of, Jonathan Driscoll gained the spiritual strength of forty men. And he wouldn't have gained it unless the Lord deemed he would surely be in need of it.

Nothing is wasted...

◦∞◦

Sienna quit pacing just as the rain stopped. Ciara looked up from her one-sided litany. As the clouds parted, they both peered down at the child as she touched the waters and instantly stilled them. They looked to each other, recording the miracle witnessed within one another's eyes so as to hold each other accountable for never forgetting or dismissing it, for never explaining it away. They stood beneath a hastily clearing sky. Bella looked up to the sun and offered her thanks, "Buiochas le Dia!" which her grandmother quietly repeated.

Then, as the little girl turned to smile up at her mother, she shouted to her with complete joy, "God's will be done!"

Sienna nodded her approval and smiled, thanking God while fervidly waving the child to come up. She gave Ciara a hug and said, "I think every-thing will be all right." Both of them silently lifted up another prayer for Jonathan.

◦∞◦

Brody squinted against the sun and took a sip of lukewarm coffee. He noncha-lantly commented to the Captain, "Crew's coming undone."

Jude looked all but dead, like an old battered fish come up from the deep and floating on its side in the setting sun. His skin was sallow but for beneath his eyes where clung slashes of ashen black upon sagging and rifts—that, and he wasn't moving. Brody gave thought to poking him, but then thought better of it. Truth beneath was, Jude couldn't care less if the whole world caught on fire. He stared blankly at the four idiots he had left, and he didn't care. He'd lost his Jonathan. He'd lost his son.

On deck, Shay was bawlin' like a baby and had a busted lip—he had blood all over his face, and it was runnin' down his neck and smeared across the back of his hand. Kegan had slipped on that blasted green-painted wood that was not only unlucky, it was dang slick. He'd cracked the back of his head trying to stop those hot-headed brothers from killin' each other over the one that was apparently dead. He was dizzy and starting to see stars and other mysterious apparitions. He slunk down in a corner and stayed. He didn't feel too good, didn't look too good either. Michael was throwin' crates and rope and his fists around like a madman. Killian was still runnin' around the rail cryin' out for Jonathan to resurface. It was a pathetic sight, really...because he'd been under water way too long.

∞

As he broke the surface, he brought the peace beneath with him, and upon his emergence the waves became smooth like a sheet of liquid glass. The sun was warm on his face, and he closed his smiling eyes for a moment. He floated there on his back, watching the beautiful heavens—their colossal clouds parting, lifting and rising up with brilliant colors much like the skin of his risen ancestors. His body was completely relaxed as if he were resting on a feather bed.

Slowly, their voices filtered in and penetrated his ethereal shell.

Killian swore at Michael in an attempt to get him to shut his mouth and look where he pointed. "See, I told you I wasn't seein' things."

The life preserver slapped Jonathan hard across his nose and smack in the center of his privates—the most painful thing that had happened to him that day. The moment he grabbed onto it was the first moment of fear he'd experienced that day. His body was suddenly cold, extremely cold, and he started to panic a little before remembering that today wasn't his day to die. He relaxed and let them pull him in. Collectively, they looked like a bloody, angry mob that was ready to kill him once they got him to safety.

"Welcome back, Driscoll," he said to himself through chattering teeth.

∞

He didn't remember a thing any of them said to him, didn't remember changing clothes, couldn't recall who brought the coffee or who sat with him while his body regained circulation and slowly heated back up. He didn't remember anything remarkable about coming into dock. But once they stood on floating planks that promised land, he would never forget what his father said to him or the way it made him feel.

Jude moved up beside him with his uneven stride and grabbed his rebel son by the scruff of the neck. His voice was gruff, weary, and full of pride. It cracked as he spoke, in a most endearing way, "As long as I live, you'll never set foot on one of my boats again. You're bad luck if I ever saw it."

Jonathan smiled as his father roughly rocked him back and forth and

229

finally let go—there was more love in the letting go than in all the holding on. And after half a lifetime of struggling, of trying everything imaginable on his own, Jonathan had just gotten his father's full blessing and eternal permission to be a musician—and nothing—or anything else. All he could think about was something that made him simply happy. It made his essence shine with a purity of self and soul combined. He thought, *Well, hallelujah! That didn't take long, did it?* He watched with respect in his eyes as his father walked out ahead of him, older, wiser, closer than he to death. He watched his father walking ahead of him, alone, and for once he didn't feel guilty about it. He didn't try to catch up or bridge that gap, instead, he measured clearly the distance between them and reverenced it as something necessary and good, something that could not be manipulated any further—a useless endeavor from the start.

As they reached the end of the pier, his eyes were immediately drawn to Sienna—her body, her clothes, her skin, her hair, the shape of her lovely face. She brought tears to his eyes, instantly, as he realized how close he'd come to leaving her. Bella was running behind her as they moved toward him with open arms. He embraced them tightly, for they were, simply, his sweet gravity and all the noble reasons to his why. He breathed in the smell of Sienna's hair. He stroked her soft skin, her cheek, her neck, absorbing all the warmth she had to offer into his ice-cold hands, then he kissed her deeply as if her body were his land, and her breath, all the air he'd ever need. He looked into her holy-impressed eyes and could tell by the wondrous illumination she held in them, the outright belief that she had been a witness to whatever Bella had prayed. His little girl had stirred up and called down a miracle. She was clinging to his leg, her face buried in his jeans, her being, her will, and her strength as close to her father's as she could get it to be. He scooped the little girl up in his arms and he rocked her.

He whispered into her ear, "I know what you did for me today, Bell. You prayed my way back to you. You listened to God, and He listened to you. Thank you, baby girl, thank you for being who you are."

He stood there together with his blessed daughter breathing in her air and holding on to her body as if she were his only anchor. He didn't care who was watching them or what they might be thinking. He just clung to his little girl like she was his private shore in a world that had drifted out and disappeared like a nameless ship in a moonlit fog. Sienna silently watched them, so thankful they were both alive. When she glanced around, she saw the unspoken words written on the deep and haggard lines of the other men's faces. She understood and felt their eternal hell from this single day—it nearly rolled off of them like burnt flesh. She could tell just by looking that all their human skill, all their virile confidence, had been pirated from them. The ghosts of their essences had been permanently inked, impressed forever with the fear stamped by Jonathan's loss—not knowing its full and wicked sorrow 'till he be gone from this place. The pain was unspeakable. They were tattooed with the guilt, with his white blood upon their hands, the souls of each branded with the shame of nearly losing their friend, their son, their brother, their grandson to the sea and cutting short the dear life of this eminent soul (and for no good reason—they all knew he was no seaman). They carried a hollowness in their chest that left barely room for their own breath, and a horror was draped and heavily stacked across their backs as they looked at him—timid eyes glancing, obsessively checking, to make sure, once and again and once more, to know for certain that he was really there with them still.

"Let's go home," she said to all of them, but she took a moment to tilt Shay's chin gently towards her so she could get a better look at his injury. He looked so young and so innocent, like a little boy. "Come back with us, I'll fix that lip up for you."

Shay tried to hide beneath a masculinity that just didn't fit him; he tried to shrug her off, but it was useless. His eyes softened with relief; he needed someone as gentle as he was to care for him on that day. Sienna was glad she'd been there to recognize it. And just as Kegan was about to give him grief, she addressed him with a directness not to be trifled with, "And I can help you clean up the back of your head, Kegan—you don't look so good."

And Kegan's lips went back together, swallowing whatever cruel words he had planned, knowing what she meant was, *And not another word from you against this kind young man.*

They walked on a good distance before her, nobody saying a word to anyone else (although Shay was still slightly grinning from beneath a downturned head). She watched the line of them move forward slowly from the clutches of the sea, her daughter the only one looking back to her as she balanced on her father's hip, her small hands imbedded across his broad back as if holding on to him for righteousness sake, opposing the force of certain harbingers unkind, and pressing him down toward the safety of the inland earth with all her summoning, holy power. They were all several paces ahead as Sienna thought she heard *I'm sorry* floating in off of the sea in waves, its sad story pulling her heart back in. She turned back to glance at it, to give it another chance to redeem itself, and as she did she remembered Lot's wife at the same time Brody touched her shoulder. She gasped and spun forward, looking into the old man's eyes. He stared at her for a long and wordless moment—a family trait she'd learned to wait out—then he quietly told her, "Don't talk to it like it's a bloody person, girl. That'll only make things worse."

They walked on together, and she didn't look back again, no matter what voices she thought she heard.

But what she didn't know was that the old man walking quietly beside her heard them, too. Every word. And he always had.

chapter twenty-eight

$\mathcal{I}$T WAS AN all-out oddity for the house to be so full and yet so silent. Exhaustion came into play, of course, but mostly it was the wonderment of it all. The miracles found and witnessed all around didn't fit in with the common workings of the mind. This certainly would take everyone some time to process so long as they weren't in such a hurry to forget it. Jonathan was soaking in a hot bath. Jude and Ciara had prematurely retired to their room. Bella went to sleep without any supper or her cocoa. Killian had decided to go straight to the pub with Michael.

"Ouch," Kegan winced the word.

"Sorry," Sienna said, "but it's really deep. I think you need stitches."

"Not 'till tomorrow," he said. "Doc's got to sleep it off."

"But you'll go," Sienna half-asked, half-warned as she taped on a bandage and gently pressed on it.

"I will," he promised, squirming away from the pain.

"Hold pressure on it or it's gonna bleed all night. Do you want me to call Lilly?"

"Good Lord, no. I've got a splitting headache as it is."

"You could have a concussion. Are you sleepy?"

Kegan looked up at her and smiled, "Don't you know by now, sweetheart? I'm too hard-headed for anything to get to my brain."

Sienna laughed with him. He stood up and kissed her cheek sweetly, "Thank you, my dear."

"You're welcome," she smiled up at him. "Take care of yourself."

And he was out the door, more than likely on his way to the pub as well, leaving her with Shay and Brody.

"You're next." She smiled at Shay, which he bashfully returned.

As she cleaned up dried blood and disinfected and taped his lip, she felt how gentle and sweet his mannerisms were. She instantly felt protective of him. Finally she asked him softly, "How did this happen?"

233

His eyes insecurely shot over toward Brody then crept slowly back up to meet hers. He confessed to her, "Michael and I don't get along."

"I see," she said, with as much sympathy as she could extend. She sat down in a chair and wiped the blood off his hand as she continued, "People, complete strangers, have sat down and talked to me and told me, 'I don't see how anyone could not get along with you.' I never really understood how they could say that about me after five minutes, but I think I do now."

She stopped cleaning his skin and let go, looking into his soft eyes as she confided in him, "I used to have bruises and cuts, and I just looked generally beaten down. But I had no idea what to do about it. It seemed no matter what I tried, it wouldn't stop."

"What did you do?" he asked a little too eagerly, glancing again at his grandfather as if apologizing for the question.

"I let it get so bad it almost killed me."

The gaze in his eyes revealed his secret years of loneliness and drawn-out fear... it was a sentiment truly felt but not so much for her, as for himself.

"And then I left," she finished, standing up and gently squeezing his shoulder.

She went to the sink to rinse out the bloody cloth. Soon she felt him breathing quietly beside her. She waited.

"Can I go with you?" he asked timidly and sacredly as if those words would break the stone tablets on which his future was chiseled.

She turned to him and said, "You can do whatever you want to do, Shay. Sometimes the best thing to do is the exact thing you'd tell someone else in your situation."

He looked down, and slowly a smile spread across his swollen lip. He put a finger to the bandage to keep it from popping free.

"I want to go with you—to America." This time his voice held a hint of confidence in it.

"I'll get another ticket, then."

He walked out the door a taller man and Sienna's satisfaction met with Brody's silent stare and cooled like spilt blood on ice.

"I'm sorry, Brody," she said, not knowing what else to.

The old man looked into the bottom of his coffee cup, and to Sienna's amazement he started talking.

"My sister is dead. Most everyone I grew up with is dead. I'm next," he observed all of this matter-of-factly as Sienna pulled up a chair and sat beside him.

He went on, "I know what happened out there today. I know what happened back here. You see," he said and looked into her eyes, "I have it, too. Same thing as my sister had, same thing as that dear little child has."

He lifted his cup in the general direction of Bella's room.

"I have only one thing I can tell ya. It'll drive you crazy, that curse, or gift—'tis the same thing. Don't matter what anyone else thinks. Ain't nobody can get inside yer head, now can they? Matters what she thinks. Does *she* believe in herself, ya see. You can't make her, can't do it for her. She's got to do the believin' for herself. It's a lonely existence. That's why I never open me mouth. Afraid of what's gonna come out of it next. 'Tis lonely, lonely, lonely. But that's the way it is when it's just you an' God. My sister, Brigh, she got the bad end of it, she did. But it ain't childhood that's the problem—God's grace is on that. It's the middle of the road. The place where there's forks, and you have to accept yourself the way you are even if you don't like it, even if you'd never choose it fer yourself. You go down that road anyway. That's the place where nobody can help you. That's the place the devil starts talkin' louder than the angels. That's the place where the sea starts takin' over your own mind an' ye drown in it."

He paused for a moment and looked at her blankly, with just the slightest touch of empathy she perceived coming through him. "Only one thing I can tell ya. If it fails...t'wasn't yer fault. If the sea drowns her, it ain't yer fault. And if ya let it be, might as well slit yer own throat right then and there, you won't be worth the air you're breathin' in. If she becomes an angel, if she holds to herself and don't reject herself—who she is, what she is down here for—that's not to your credit, either. It's to hers. You look out for her...you don't become her. If God created her, He'll reveal everything to her in time. You've got listenin' of your own ta do, you got a life all yer own. You don't ever put down your pen, you hear me, lass? Don't you dare burn your paper—that is how you become an angel, not her. You mind what I say...

"That's the only thing I can tell ya. Good intentions get in the way. Lovin' a child has a lot of freedom to it. The closer ya get, the less ya can see her," he said and then went silent, as if permanently.

She did something surprising, to herself and to him...she grabbed his hand

and looked him in the eye, "Why did you feel the need to tell me that?" she asked forwardly.

"T'was what killed me own mother, child."

They sat together; she continued holding his hand as she absorbed from him as much wisdom as spiritual osmosis would allow.

Finally she said, "Sometimes the good thing isn't always the best thing."

His eyes sparkled a bit, and he lifted his cup, "To Saint Paul," he said.

When she got up she kissed his cheek, "Thank you for telling me, Brody. I will mind what you say. I was on the verge of making that very mistake, trading in my call to foster hers... and you are right. I don't know why I didn't see it. As much as I love and respect God, I was trying to step into His place as her parent. It was a trap, wasn't it?"

He felt her gracious warmth surrounding him as she left the room. He sat alone in the dark for nearly an hour, on the outside looking like a blank and useless old man, but on the inside, he was silently praying with the angels, soaring above, beneath, and between all the seas upon this great earth. And, oh, the things he could see...

∞

"Shay's coming with us," Sienna told Jonathan quietly.

She heard him chuckling to himself. Her eyes were closed, but she could still see the beautiful smile she knew he held on his face.

Finally he said, "You can't adopt him, Sienna. That would make my brother my son. I've got to draw the line somewhere."

They were in bed together, Bella in the middle with her arms around her mom. Jonathan was stroking Sienna's hair, rubbing her back... he didn't want to let go of her... not for a single moment ever again. She pulled the blanket up around his shoulders and she felt his skin—he finally felt warm enough, safe enough, so that she could sleep.

∞

Brigh's funeral achieved quite a turn out—more people in one room at one time than the woman had seen her whole life. They came to watch the drama unfold, to get a glimpse of the Driscolls since they'd been the most gossiped about family in all of County Donegal for the last three centuries.

236

Jonathan walked up to the pulpit—an act which in itself was near heresy, but as easy as paying off the priest with a handsome donation. He couldn't help any of it; he had something he needed to say. He looked out at the faces staring up at him. Shay and Kegan looked dreadful as did he with a black eye still healing and now a bruised nose from the life preserver yesterday. And with the tabloids burned in everyone's heads of his own father whacking him in the jaw over in America and these splattered all about the produce section, the checkout counter, the booze aisle, and primarily displayed in the pharmacy window on the main street running through town—well, it couldn't be said that people weren't widely informed and equally interested. And so, it was with these thoughts that he began.

"As you can see, we've had a typical Driscoll Family reunion."

Nobody laughed. It was, after all, a funeral.

He bowed his head nearly down to his shoes and certainly behind the pulpit, completely disappearing from view for a moment. He thought he might hurl, but he ended up taking a deep breath before reemerging. He nervously drummed the pulpit with his fingers, then realized the microphone was picking it up. The priest was glaring at him. Jonathan ran his fingers through his hair, offering an expression of apology to everyone in general. His mother was looking just as perplexed as the time she caught Jude attempting to do a load of laundry. The uppity townsfolk began squirming with delight— a squiggly wave crawling across the back of the church, they were barely able to keep their tongues in their mouths for all the storytelling that was about to commence after this. Brody was sitting patiently, waiting for the boy to say something—anything. Sienna smiled and sweetly nodded her encouragement. Bella waved.

"Sorry...I'm not used to this sort of thing," he started again, "but there's something I need to set straight. First of all, Brigh Driscoll was as far from insane as a person could get. She was amazing, intelligent, warm, and caring far beyond what most of us could comprehend. She had a God-given gift called intercession. And because that gift is rare, people don't understand it. And what they don't understand, they become afraid of—but it is a gift that could literally save their lives. I know, because that very thing happened to me yesterday."

He waved back at Bella and gave her a wink.

"And I ask you, my family, my friends, that if anything should ever happen

237

to me or that beautiful woman I was lucky enough to show up here with (as if on cue, the entire congregation turned to stare at Sienna, so she smiled her hello to all of Killybegs), please remember the life of Brigh Driscoll and how the people around her, probably with the best of intentions, decided what was best for her instead of realizing that God already had. And please understand that my beautiful little girl, Bella Maura Driscoll, also has this same gift. And I've never been more proud.

"And, I'll close my little speech with this…the name Brigh means 'high power.' The name Driscoll means 'messenger or interpreter.' And I am here to say that the woman in that box is, and will always be, a gifted intercessor, a high-power, a messenger of the angels and an interpreter of the divine will of God. She is a special creation and a beautiful child of God.

"And, Brigh Driscoll, you are now in heaven where you will forever be free to pray. And thank you. Thank you. Thank you. For whatever prayers you did offer up for all of us here today."

After the service, there was a party which started out solemnly proper and transpired into something emotionally untamed. Brody hugged Jonathan and patted him appreciatively on the back, but didn't say anything.

Kegan commented again, "What the blazes goes on in that country?" in regard to Jonathan's speech, while sipping on another beer. But rather than sticking around for a senseless fight of one kind or another, Jonathan took his little family for a walk, the three of them trekking to the old church to give Bella some time to get acquainted with her future home. Jonathan held Sienna in their favorite spot on the front steps. The two of them watched quietly while Bella explored, asking random questions of the grasses, the stones, and of the God who made them. They listened reverentially as she looked out into her dad's meadow to pray a few holy stories through it.

"I'm going to publish the songs," he said to Sienna while leaning in over her shoulder. She smiled as she rested against his chest, and he softly sang one of them to her, accompanied only by the night birds and the magic of the twilight breeze.

LONELY
by Jonathan Driscoll

Lonely, I traveled the world in search of love
Got to the end and learned it was all above
While we are lost down here, it's up to us
To create for ourselves that risen from the dust

I went to the Lord and begged Him for a crumb
Whatever was left from the body of His Son
He broke through the clouds and met me with bolder tones
Death, saying Him, was Home for the lonely ones

He said, I created you to walk along the long road
It's up to you the stories you will have told
And no matter where you are or what you do
I couldn't have made a more beautiful you

You are loved, you are loved
You are love, you are love
You are Mine
A day doesn't pass that I don't look you in the eye

And His love filled me from above
I turned from the edge of earth to walk it all alone
I will wait, I will wait on the story to unfold
Of how He created me to release it from my soul

You are loved, you are loved
You are love, you are love
You are Mine
A day hasn't passed I haven't looked out through your eyes

Here's My light, here's your light
You are love, you give love
Because you're Mine
A day will not pass that I won't put love in your eyes

For I created you to walk along the long road
It's up to you the stories you will have told

And no matter where you go or who's around you
I couldn't have made a more beautiful you
I couldn't have made a more loveable you

chapter twenty-nine

$\mathcal{S}$HAY FOLLOWED THEM to America quietly, taking it—her mystic and tragic young secrets, her blatancy, and her blazon—all in. One thing was for certain, he was at peace. And it was a peace of distance that mattered little the coastal shroud it wore. They'd stopped at Jonathan's to rest, to check in on Mrs. Hopkins and the dog she'd been babysitting with better luck than she seemed to have with Bella, as of late. While Bella and Sienna slept, Jonathan and Shay dropped in on Roger next door. He was covered with flecks of dried paint and a huge smile, and what surrounded him already had the appearance of a brand new house—shiny and clean and actually cared for. Roger handed Jonathan a sizable check (Shay hadn't meant to look, but his eyes were immediately drawn into the long line of zeros written on it as they paraded past him) which they took directly to the bank.

Later that afternoon, the four of them drove out to the rehab center to check up on Cheney's physical, mental, and financial condition. Bella stayed with Jonathan as he took care of all the bills and paperwork, while Sienna went off toward Cheney's room. Without being asked, Shay silently followed a step behind her, then he stood with a solid stance in the doorway as if to protect Sienna. He could tell she'd been unsettled regarding Jonathan's ex-wife, and he didn't like it because, secretly, he'd adopted Sienna as his own personal angel and, in return, had taken it upon his own shoulders to ensure that no harm came to her in his brother's absence.

But this time, Cheney was completely contained and civil, except toward Shay when she said rudely, "Who is that, Sienna?" and then to him, "Don't you talk?" to which he coldly stared down at her without reply. At one point in their conversation, she even attempted to be thankful for Sienna's concern, for her help and her friendship. And, although it sounded rote like something learned and rehearsed in a group meeting, Sienna got up and hugged her, sincerely.

As Sienna and Shay walked away, she commented to him that she thought

Cheney seemed to be "gaining...bored...but gaining," in the sense that she hadn't backslidden, at least.

He didn't say it, but he thought it to himself as he looked over his shoulder, back toward that woman's room, *If that's gaining, I'm glad I didn't meet her before...* And he didn't do it, but he felt like putting his arm around Sienna to shield her from something he could have sworn was hunting them down, stalking them like a shadow in the dark. It was something indescribable creeping along, and it was mean-spirited—of that he was sure.

Back at the house, Sienna and Jonathan wasted little time as they repacked their things, rearranged the vehicle, and loaded up the dog, his snuggly-bear toy, and his favorite blanket, along with a new stack of books, games, and educational worksheets for Bell. They were heading directly for New Haven. With each mile, Sienna felt an increasing weight of responsibility upon the base of her neck. Her thoughts raced with upcoming events and the people involved in them with their many expectations. Her muscles were tense, and she mindlessly tapped the armrest like someone running late and stuck in a traffic jam. There was Kat's wedding in the final stages, with its tuxedo and dress fittings, and with its bridal nerves to calm. There was the rehearsal party at her house. And there was the all-important reason—Sienna wanted everyone to meet Bella. And she wanted Bella to meet everyone else. All this, and she had a deadline to meet on her half-written book, and she *hated* to rush her writing; forcing art, to her, was like leaving gold dust on the mission floor...scattered, trampled, and wasted beneath those it did hunger for.

She'd simply have to ask for an extension. Hopefully, they'd understand.

As if reading her thoughts, Jonathan put his hand on her thigh and interrupted them, "I'm going as fast as I can...legally."

He looked around for any state patrol and decided to pass another car before continuing, "Everything will be fine. Kat has a wedding planner—I'm sure everything's okay. I'm sure they've cleaned the house, gotten everything ready. Mia's taking care of the food, right?"

Sienna nodded.

"All they want you to do is show up happy and rested, I guarantee it. If you have a good time, that will help them more than anything. Aurora called me earlier..."

"What did she say?"

"She wanted me to tell you not to worry; people get married every day. And if they don't know how to do it by now…how did she say it? Oh! She said if they are too stupid to walk down the aisle, stand at the end of it, and say two one-syllable words, then there isn't much you can do for them anyway."

He smiled over at her as she giggled a bit, then looked in the rearview mirror at the triad of sleeping beings lumped in a pile in the backseat.

"Maybe you should get some rest while you can." He winked at her kindly and went to pass a pickup pulling a horse trailer. "I know you've got a horse that misses you, and Aurora also told me that you have a deadline coming up on your book. She said someone from the publishing company's been calling the house. But I will help you, okay? With anything you need. I will fill in with this wedding or do whatever else you want me to do so you can spend some time with Ira and catch up on your novel. It's my fault you're running behind on it, anyway. I've been distracting you…flying you to other lands and handing you a child and all that."

Something he said seemed to have worked because she relaxed and closed her eyes. And shortly thereafter, he watched her fall completely asleep. What he couldn't see were her dreams, bleeding out the energy fields and weaving the elaborate finishing strings that tied together the loose ends of her imagination and of her story.

∞

Shay's eyes were rather big when he asked, "This is your house?"

"It's yours, too, for as long as you need it to be," she answered, rifling through her bag for a house key. "Oh…and I'm sorry about all the women."

Jonathan chuckled, but then finished his light-hearted thought looking a little worried as he grabbed some luggage and jogged to catch up.

Upon entering, the dogs nearly knocked Sienna down then changed their focus to the new, older dog. They took to him instantly, and the old fellow seemed to exude a new energy with his tail-wagging and his friendly play. Bella happily helped her dog get acquainted with them.

Just then Aurora's distinct voice rippled through the air, "Who the crap *is* that?"

She said it with a brazenness that would stun any other stranger, but it didn't seem to phase Shay. He was looking straight at her, not her catastrophic outfit, not Sienna's grand home…but *her*.

Sienna was taken aback by what she initially perceived as Aurora's rudeness, so she quickly attempted to explain, "Aurora, this is..."

"Shut up," Aurora interrupted with her typical light-hearted phrase, though she was not kidding this time. She was deathly serious in her commandment for there to be nothing but absolute quiet. She walked by all the dogs and a little stranger looking up at her unnoticed. She walked through the middle of Sienna and Jonathan as if they didn't even exist. She walked a straight line directly to Shay with her punk attire and her unbelievably tall and pink hair, she grabbed both sides of his face with her black painted nails and with her silver rings so thick she barely had any visible fingers, and she kissed him. Hard. And long.

Sienna looked at Jonathan, utterly speechless. He looked back at her with his jaw dropped, shaking his head, *I don't know*... Eventually, he picked Bella up and took Sienna's hand, quietly leading them into the kitchen where they waited for what seemed to be a half-hour. The two never came in.

Nor did they part a single day for the rest of their lives.

∞

All of Sienna's girls met and fell in love with Bella, but none of them with as much permanency and avocation as Aurora did. Aurora and Bella quickly formed a bond closer than natural born sisters. They understood each other on a level removed from anyone else's comprehension and the two of them spent nearly every waking hour together as Shay quietly and lovingly watched over them both. It could have been narrowed down to the fact that Aurora knew, regardless of proof or possibility, that Bella's voice was the one she heard on that day—the day she was lying beside the dumpster and about be put in it. That was Bella's angel voice she heard that told her, *Sing*. And so became the second person Aurora solemnly vowed she'd die for *in a heartbeat*.

Bella's birthday party became Shay and Aurora's pet project while Sienna spent her time between *Stained Glass* and Ira. Jonathan began running errands with Kat and Bella, and in-between, started working deals with his contacts in Los Angeles and in New York City, sending in songs he'd already written and introducing the seeds of his next project—a series of songs God inspired in the heart of a teenaged boy.

"Are you ever going to tell me what happened?" Sienna asked one evening, as Jonathan and she rested in each other's arms in her library, in the sweet midst of her cool, dark, and quiet sanctuary, far removed from any pressing needs.

"No, sweetheart," he said and began to think about his direct encounter with the Lord as he gazed up at the mahogany paneled ceiling, its intricate design reflecting the simplicity of the moon. "I don't think I could."

"Something reserved, then, to be reverenced as a sacred bond between you and God."

"Alone..." he said, then, "Yeah...that's exactly it," and he kissed the back of her delicate writer's hand, his mind floated like liquid through the stream of words she could draw together like stars to a Milky Way. She could create a bridge with them to anywhere, and over anything he'd follow them through like a siren's call. "It might come through in my music—in sounds that have never come through me before, but I don't think I could ever put it into words," he said "All I can say is that it changed me."

"Yes it did," she agreed. "I can see it."

∞

"Finally, your face is healing," Aurora quipped to Jonathan as he was eating his breakfast, "At least now you'll be presentable enough for Kat's precious wedding."

"I hope so...I've never walked anyone down the aisle before."

"Just don't trip it all up in that twenty-gee dress of hers and you'll be good." She smiled at Jonathan, and he smiled in return. "Maybe it's just me," she continued, "but aren't there starving children in the world? I mean she could fit like five of them under that dress of hers..."

Jonathan didn't want to take sides, but he could certainly see her point.

"By the way," she said and changed gears while studying his face, "what goes on in that country?"

He laughed a little, swearing he could hear Kegan's voice coming through her.

"I mean...do they line you up when you get off the plane and beat you within an inch of your lives?"

"Not quite," he answered, "but close."

"Can't wait," she rolled her eyes.

"Shay taking you?" Jonathan wondered out loud.

"Not your business, big brother. Not your business, my friend. I'm the only one steppin' on these toes." She pointed down toward her fuzzy socks.

Jonathan smiled and shook his head, envisioning his family meeting Aurora for the first time—all the clash and the culture shock that would take place. He hoped he'd be there to see it. He hoped she'd keep her clothes on, at least. Then, being the protective brother he was, he couldn't stop himself from asking the next question.

"Aurora?"

"What up?"

"You're not like... *with* Collin anymore, right?"

"Good Lord, man. What kind of a woman do you take me for?" She slammed the refrigerator door and strode out, winking at him and shaking her head *no* just as she rounded the corner and disappeared from sight.

He heard voices—Aurora and Sienna's—but he couldn't make out what they were saying. Eventually, Sienna entered the kitchen in a zombie-like state. She gave him a big hug, resting her head on his shoulder for a moment before managing to say, "I need some coffee."

"Here... sit down." He offered her his chair. "I'll get it for you."

"Thank you, baby," she muttered.

"You've been hitting that book pretty hard. Sugar?"

"No, thanks—just black is fine. I was up most of the night, I'm just about finished."

"Don't work yourself too hard... promise me," he said as he kissed her forehead. She nodded her promise, not sure what "too hard" meant, exactly since she was used to working until she could barely function.

"Something occurred to me last night," she said and took a sip of the coffee. "I mean, it just came to me... not really my idea, maybe something from God."

"What?"

"This book is good enough for a movie, if I don't completely screw up this last bit anyway—it's got to hit pretty hard for the message to get across. But anyway, I've got a screenplay starting to narrow itself down in the back of my mind, and I think I can get some people on board. So, if it gets that far, would you want to do the music for it?"

He looked at her for a while, reaching up to sweep back the strand of hair that had fallen across her amazingly beautiful, visionary-pumped, and physically exhausted eyes.

"Or...," she proposed, "I could write a novel around your Christian collection, when you get it ready. What do you think?"

"I think I would love to work with you on anything," he said, with genuine warmth, a hopeful sparkle, in his eyes. "I'm honored that you would even ask me."

A new level of ambition seemed to rise up in him as he looked ahead, envisioning their lives together—he'd never really thought about *creatively* joining forces. And when he moved closer toward their future, he felt nothing short of amazement.

"Thank you," she said smiling at him, then down at her hands that were wrapped around the warm mug. "Secretly, I just want to spend more time with you. And I want to get to know you better—you know—your *soul*. The only way we can really do that is to bring our gifts together. I think we could accomplish some great things for God."

He picked up her hand and held it, laced his fingers between hers and told her, "There's a verse...where two come together in harmony, there I am with them. For the first time, I really have a deep desire to help the world with what I do, not just entertain them, not just make money, but to use what I have to *help* them."

"Exactly," she said, "to tell you the truth, I wouldn't have the energy to keep going without that desire in me. It's like fuel, isn't it?"

"It's amazing...the energy and the passion I seem to have now. I haven't felt this way...well, in a long time, if ever."

"There's another verse," she said, "about your eye being the lamp of your soul. I think a body not fulfilling its office will be filled with darkness, and that a body that is fulfilling its office will be flooded with light, and that light comes through your eyes—it *is* life, it's a spark, it's passion, it's your purpose—it's the reason He put you here. I love that phrase, *fulfilling your office*, and I thank God everyday that I actually found mine after thirty years of wandering around aimlessly. I *love* what I do now, and I am so happy that you do, too. I can see it in your eyes—they are so bright now. Just since I've known you, there has been such a change in you. I'm proud of you, Jonathan. And I admire you. So many people seem to miss it—they take the wrong turn at the fork in the road."

"Forks in the road...," Jonathan mused. "You must have been talking to old Brody. But thank you, Sienna. I don't think I could have done any of this without you."

He leaned in to kiss her but was interrupted by Aurora, Shay, and Bella as they entered the kitchen.

"Minors in tow, here. Let's clean it up, people, at least to PG," Aurora announced.

Shay smiled at Aurora's sense of humor which he obviously loved, and he kissed Bell's cheek as he set her down on the counter, helping her tie her shoes.

"Hi, Mommy," Bella said sweetly, her father's charm, warmth, and open love coming through her big eyes to greet her.

"Hi, birthday girl!" Sienna reached up and stroked the girl's soft and rosy cheek. "You've got a pretty special day in store—you ready for it?"

"Yeah," she said simply, with eyes full of anticipation.

"Everybody else ready?" she asked in general, then looking to Jonathan, "Are you ready for this, Dad?"

"Yeah, I'm ready. Let's go and do this thing," he said as he lifted Bella off the counter and twirled her in a big circle.

That child's laugh has got to be the most healing sound in the world, Sienna thought.

So they took a drive which ended at Barbara's stable.

Bella whispered, "Where are we, Daddy?"

"Just keep your eyes closed...don't open them yet, love."

And when she did, the surprise nearly knocked her to her little knees. Jonathan reached down to steady her, and she swiftly turned and buried her face in his jeans. It was a reaction no one expected. He knelt down to look into her face, and she had tears streaming down her cheeks.

He wiped them away with the tail of his shirt like he'd done for years while he told her, "We love you, Bella. You know how you always tell me that you want a pony? We found one for you—he's all yours."

Her lip quivered a bit, and she finally managed, "My very own?"

"Yes, sweetheart," he answered softly, "Happy birthday."

She slowly turned back around and stared up at the huge horse with a bow around his neck. The horse lowered his head and reached his nose toward her kindly, as if knowing exactly which person was to be his. Sienna knelt down beside Bella.

"This is Peanut. He is tall, but he's very sweet. Just put your hand out like this, and he'll get to know you a little bit."

She held Bella's hand from underneath until she felt it—the connection between the little girl and her horse—and she let go.

Barbara watched with the others as Sienna helped Bella brush and saddle Peanut. They watched on as Sienna lunged the horse then got on and warmed him up. Aurora seldom watched Sienna ride, but she stood there quietly enamored, thinking to herself, *That's her voice...*

Shay reached up and patted Jonathan on the back, noticing he was getting a little tense, "She'll be fine."

"I know," Jonathan said, "It's just a long way down."

"Sienna knows what she's doing," Aurora said.

"That she does," Barbara agreed.

Bella was standing out in the middle of the arena looking smaller than the mounting block when Sienna rode up next to her and slid down.

"Do you want to ride him? You don't have to if you don't want to," Sienna looked into the child's face, trying to read her. Bella looked nothing short of determined to get up there and try; she'd been watching Sienna's every move and was hooked. She reminded Sienna of herself nearly twenty-five years ago.

"How do I get on?" she asked.

"Climb on here, to the top. Wait just a minute—let me shorten these stirrups. Okay, hold this stirrup, like this... and put your foot in. Grab this. Now pull yourself all the way up."

Sienna gave her a supportive lift and held onto her tightly, making sure she didn't slide down the opposite side.

"Hold the reins like this... that's it. Now cluck, like this." Sienna made a clicking sound and Bella tried to copy her. "Squeeze just a little with your legs."

The horse started to walk forward, and Sienna walked at Bella's side.

"Now tell him whoa, sit back a little, and pull back with both hands."

The horse stopped.

"Now release your hands a bit and pet him. Very good, Bella! I think you are a natural."

The smile that spread across the child's face was duplicated on her father's.

He watched as his daughter's confidence grew by leaps and bounds in just a few minutes. She quickly learned how to stop, back, walk, and turn the horse in both directions. And before she helped her down, Sienna showed Bella how to pull the horse's head around to her knee if he ever acted naughty.

"You won't be naughty, will you, Peanut?" she asked already in love with him. Barbara joined them, giving a carrot to Bella and showing her how to feed it to Peanut.

She turned to Jonathan and said quietly, "I was running out of the money to keep this horse—thank you so much for this. I raised him, he was born here, fell into the wrong hands somewhere down the line. It was a miracle I even found him again. I just couldn't bear to let him go to strangers. This is a Godsend to me. I can't thank you enough."

Jonathan saw the tears in the woman's eyes, and he told her, "He will be taken care of forever. We won't sell him—I don't think Sienna would ever speak to me again if I did something like that. And, I don't think Bella would ever give him up."

"People do some strange things when circumstances change. Horses are expensive, and if there is divorce, or the kids go off to college, these beautiful animals seem to pay for all that dearly."

"Not this one, Barbara," and he said it with a conviction that she didn't question. "He won't go through that ever again, not as long as I'm alive. You have my word on that."

He looked her square in the eye, solidifying his promise. She felt relieved for more than just the welfare of the horse, for up to that very moment, she didn't think she'd be able to let Sienna go, either.

Back at home, there was a pony-themed party with cake and ice cream, streamers and party hats, and Bella was an ecstatic little girl in the midst of torn paper, wonderful presents, and a whole family of people who all seemed to adore her. This was followed by an afternoon of swimming and an evening barbeque. Jonathan couldn't remember when his daughter ever looked happier.

He said to Shay as they watched her, "I'm so glad you are here, my brother. I've felt like an island for so long—it's always been just the two of us—little Bell and me. So, thanks. Thanks for being here for my kid's birthday."

He raised his plastic pony glass of green punch to tap his brother's.

"Thanks for havin' me," Shay answered. "Thanks for goin' before me...for having the guts to come over here by yourself. I really needed someplace else to go, man."

"I know. Believe me...I know," was all he said.

Late that evening, Jonathan, Sienna, and Bella were on the back porch swing looking at the stars as they glistened in the night sky. Bella's eyes were getting heavy, but she seemed to have something burdening her youthful soul. She seemed to have something to say, while at the same time not wanting to.

"Say what ya need to say, baby girl," her dad encouraged, finally opening the door.

She held her mother's hand most tenderly and said, "Nature abhors a vacuum."

Sienna looked to Jonathan, both of them knowing the words were not those of a six-year-old girl. They said nothing, just listened, waiting for whatever might follow.

After a moment she continued, "Stagnant water rots. The furniture has been rearranged. And it will be seven times worse than the first."

She looked up at her mother's face reaching a tiny hand to her chin. She felt Sienna's soft skin with her fingertips, her large eyes wide open.

"You will not want to go back to the house from which you came, Mommy."

The child's hand returned to her side, and she whispered, "God's will be done," just before she fell asleep.

chapter thirty

SIENNA PULLED BACK the covers on her bed, and Jonathan put his exhausted daughter down for the night, kissing her forehead tenderly. He counted to himself the years she'd been his—*six*...The house was quiet though entirely occupied with all of Sienna's girls, and it gave her a feeling of comfort. She didn't mind a full house. She'd sleep in a chair, or on the floor, or on the front lawn if she had to. It made her feel safe—the *knowing* where everyone else was. And another thing she knew, this would be one of the last nights they'd all be under the same roof.

Jonathan came up behind her and cradled her in his arms. She'd been peering out her chamber window, looking into the mysterious moon as if it held all the answers to how she could get things to stay the same. But it just wasn't telling her. Because it was somewhat cruel, somewhat shifty, with its knowledge of time. There simply was no key to unlock its secrets. Time was completely its own, the only thing that touched every living creature, while itself escaping touch.

He moved her hair away and kissed the back of her neck—the start of another night he'd have to fight his desires. So he stopped. He looked at the suspended, heavenly being she was silently speaking to and he asked her.

"What do you think it meant?"

"Bella?" she whispered.

"Yeah." He kissed her again, and suddenly pulling his arms away from her body, announced, "I'm going to go sit over there."

"Don't follow me, please," he added, holding up a hand as he sat on the chaise and rubbed his face, letting out a miserable sigh as he whispered, *Lord have mercy on me, I am only a man...*

"I think...well, I'm almost certain," she started, turning toward him and reflecting the light beautifully, "it's about Cheney."

"I thought so, too," he admitted.

"I didn't say anything, but the last time we were there, when I went to visit her? Something wasn't right."

"Shay told me."

"What did he say?"

"He said I should keep you two apart."

"Why?"

"He didn't tell me that, but the way he said it gave me chills. What happened, anyway?"

"Between Cheney and me? Nothing. Not really...she just seemed like a black hole. She seemed...empty. But like she was trying to cover it up by putting on a mask."

"So when you drive a demon out, in this case alcohol, drugs, and her associations, and you rearrange the furniture—clean it up, in other words, and send it to rehab, and you decorate it—she's putting on a mask that everything is fine, but then the demon comes back and finds the house empty, and it goes and gets seven more."

"And the state of that person is seven times worse than the first," Sienna finished, then added, "Jonathan, we are failing her."

Bella shot straight up in bed and started speaking a long string of words, "No, My child, she is failing herself. For the size of a soul is greater than the universe. The size of a single soul is bigger than this world. There is only one thing big enough to fill it, and that is God. There is only one thing fit to match its borders and its spaces, and that is God. There is only one thing that moves with the correct rhythms and flows as it changes, as it grows, and that is God's gift. No purpose can be found lest the man first find God, who creates all reasons and all purposes to answer them, under heaven, on the earth, below the earth, in the center of the creation of the world. She knows not her Creator, she who doesn't create. Only God will lead a vacant soul to her lot. She must be content with it, and she cannot be content with nothing. And so she answers it, herself, with sin and idle hands left ever unfulfilled."

Bella fell back against her pillow, her skin dripping with sweat, for she had spoken what came through her with the voice of a holy leader. Jonathan and Sienna had both moved beside her. He whispered, "This is really getting strange..."

"Are you all right, sweetheart?" Sienna asked her, wiping the sweat away with her hands, moving the child's hair back from her face; Bella grabbed

Sienna's hand and repeated what she had said earlier, this time with more fervor.

"You will not want to go back to the house from which you came, Mommy."

"Sienna," Jonathan's voice quaked with a sound that summoned instant fear in her.

"What?" Sienna answered.

"Where is your Bible? The one you lent to Cheney?"

"I think it's over here somewhere," she said as she walked toward a shelf. She found it and turned to take it back to him, finding him directly on her heels. He grabbed the book from her hands and laid it out on the piano.

"Light a candle…or turn on a light, please."

She turned on a small lamp, and he slid himself and the Good Book toward it.

"What are you looking for?"

"Is there anything in here that would give a reference to your Vindicator book?"

"I don't think so…," she said, trying her best to recall as he ripped through it like a madman.

"Then what's this?" he pointed to the page titled "Births" and looked up at Sienna, "That horrible witch!"

His fist hit the top of the piano and one of the candlesticks fell out of its holder and rolled to the floor.

"I am seriously going to kill her this time."

"No…don't," Sienna scrambled for words, "We don't know for sure…"

He looked at her in such a way that she fell silent. She sat down and pulled her Bible closer to her. She looked at the names listed, her fingers carefully tracing over each one.

"I went through a really horrible time…," she started to remember out loud, "it went on for about four or five years. I was trying so hard to have a baby. I went through fertility treatments, everyone I knew had a baby or was telling me about their kids. Everyone, I mean everyone, wherever I went, whether it was the library, grocery store, doctor's office, hairstylist, *everyone* would ask me, 'So, do you have kids?' And when I'd tell them no, they'd keep going, telling me I should, telling me parenthood was great. It was awful. I ended up telling everyone from the gas station attendant to my banker, 'No, I don't have kids and I can never have kids, so please don't ask me.'"

She looked up at Jonathan who had softened at her story a bit, but Sienna could still see his rage.

"I was praying to God every day and every night. I was believing God so hard, I couldn't accept His answer. These were the names I had picked out for my children. I was going to have as many as I could. I put a lot of thought into these names. I could see their faces, Jonathan. But years passed and so did my husband... I was lying over there in that bed when God told me to use the names of my children for the characters in the Vindicator book."

She ran her finger down to the bottom of the list of names where she had written a couple years prior, *Vindicator—the children who pray Him down*, and had circled it in red and had long since forgotten she had done either. She looked again at Jonathan who was actively trying not to speak for the hate that would come out of him. He didn't want Sienna or his daughter to have to hear it.

"I'm going for a walk," he finally managed to say, "Just around the pool. I promise I won't leave or do anything stupid... at least not tonight. So don't worry... get some rest. I love you, Sienna."

And he left the room, shutting the door hard enough to reawaken Bella.

"It's okay, honey. Go back to sleep. You must be so tired."

Sienna sat there in the dark at her silent piano staring at her Bible. Eventually a sleepy Bella came over and quietly stood by her.

"You wanna sit?"

Sienna pulled her up next to her, and the child stayed nestled beneath her arm, leaning heavily against her side.

"Bella," Sienna said, looking over the names on that page, "I never thought I'd have the chance to be somebody's mom. I prayed for you and I prayed for you. I thought you'd be a little baby in my arms, but you know what? This is even better. I'm so glad it's you."

"I could hear you praying sometimes," Bella said.

"You could?"

"I could hear the prayers you used to say—the ones when you were crying. I could see the things you were looking at, a sea of green plants with furry things on their heads."

"Cornfields," Sienna laughed.

"God heard you," Bella said, "He didn't tell you no."

Sienna searched back to those days, finding what the girl said to be true.

"No, I guess He didn't. He never told me no."

"He tried to tell you to wait, but you were too sad."

"That is true. I was so sad, I couldn't hear Him."

"I don't know what that's like," Bella said, striking a piano key.

"What?"

"What it is like not to hear God."

"It is a dreadful silence, Bella. Especially when you can't feel Him, either. I hope you never get to the point that you cannot hear Him, but if that happens, just wait until you can again, no matter how long that takes. Now, let's get some sleep, okay?"

Sienna turned out the light and settled into bed next to Bell. She prayed for Jonathan to get some relief from his anger. And she prayed for Cheney, finding that none of her behavior surprised her, not really. Cheney must have found the names in the front of the Bible and linked it to the movie and book. She must have gotten one of her friends to do the damage in her old house in order to scare Sienna off, or at least get back at her. Cheney had had access to the *Stained Glass* manuscript from when Sienna had first arrived. Sienna had made no secret about what she was working on, or where she kept it. Sienna recalled the look of that trashed room, the broken glass, her book overturned in the center, and she felt she deserved it, stepping in and taking her friend's ex-husband and daughter as her own. Cheney probably felt horribly betrayed and angry and vengeful. Sienna went to sleep hoping it was all over but was awakened by her writer's call shortly thereafter.

∞

Jonathan was walking around the pool room, pacing back and forth in front of the delicately lit plants. He stopped by the fountain, but the tranquility of it did nothing to calm his body or cool his anger, rather it seemed to entice him into a murderous trance. He wondered where his brother was and hadn't finished the thought before he saw him walking through the door as if answering his silent call.

"You can't sleep either, huh?" Shay asked lightheartedly.

"No."

"What's the matter?" Shay asked, immediately noticing something was wrong.

"I think Cheney is messing with Sienna."

"How?" Shay's tone was alert and defensive, it indicated that he was automatically ready to protect Sienna from anything that other woman even hinted at doing.

"She had somebody vandalize the house—the one Roger's in now. Sienna had been staying there before...so whoever it was broke glass everywhere and trashed the place and then put Sienna's book in the center of it like some kind of message or something. I didn't say anything to Sienna—but I can't handle that stuff. Stalkers following my girl—it drives me out of my mind! I mean, they're cowards. And you don't know who to fight against to protect the one you love. You know?"

"I do. That would be hard."

"I mean, I'm not paranoid—I'm furious!" He ran his fingers through his hair and started pacing again.

"And now," he said, "everything seems to point to Cheney and that—" Jonathan swallowed his curse word into silence, "—she's the one who called Sienna and asked her to come and help her in the first place. Sienna drove six hours and dropped everything she was doing to try to help Cheney get off drugs. And that's how she repays her.

"And the thing that bothers me the most? Why did I ever marry that woman? What did I ever see in her? I must have been way more messed up than I thought."

"That's what I heard." Shay said quietly. "Back home, that's what they all said about you. You had everybody sick with worry for a long, long time. But you made it. I mean, you're all right now, and that's what matters. And you got Bella out of the deal—right?"

Jonathan looked at his little brother who was now a full-grown man.

"Will you help me?" Jonathan asked him.

"You know I will."

"Don't let me go after her. I don't really feel like going to prison."

Shay looked at his older brother with more respect than he ever had before. The love of a woman was something Shay was an expert on, not wo*men*, but *the* woman. "The one and only love of a man's life" had always been his soul's music...the ideal of her and her sweet mystery had always enraptured his

257

heart. A hopeful romantic, he'd waited to find his and would have 'till the day he died because she had to be the *right* one, not just any one. And he was proud of his brother because he'd found his girl...and on that level felt more connected to him than he thought he ever would.

But he'd never say anything of this, ever.

"You want to know what I think?" Shay asked in another vein.

"Please...tell me somethin' that makes some sense," Jonathan pleaded.

"I think that woman, Cheney? I think she's going to kill herself pretty soon anyway."

Jonathan stared at the tiny white lights about them until they became a blurry haze.

Finally he said, "You took one look at her and that's what you got from it?"

"Yeah," Shay answered him, pulling a tiny leaf off the tree they were standing by, "She's so ready to die, you can smell it."

And sadness, with the cold weight of a boulder, rounded itself between them and stayed as, together, they shared the burden. Jonathan had tried, for years, to keep Cheney alive, and the simple act of him stepping back from the edge of her cliff meant there was nothing there to stop her from jumping.

And he hated being that man.

chapter thirty-one

MIA, JACKOBIE, AND Aurora, with the help of Jonathan and Shay, pulled off every detail of Katarina's rehearsal dinner without a hitch. Sienna's house was packed with well-dressed guests. The backyard and porch, the pool area and greenhouse, the living area and even the kitchen, seemed to be running over with people Sienna had never seen before. The main bathroom was like Grand Central Station. But Kat was happy, and that made Sienna happy. More than just a rehearsal dinner, it was an all-out party, giving Dillon's mother a chance to show everyone how well her son was marrying. A lot of people who would have thrown the invitation immediately in the recycling bin not only kept it displayed on their refrigerators for a month, but bought brand new outfits and matching shoes in order to attend and see the home of the area's most exclusive, and alluringly reclusive, author.

When the last guest left, Sienna's designer shoes got kicked across the floor.

"Man, my feet hurt." She sighed, trying to walk on them normally as she waddled to Kat and put her arms around her neck.

"I love you, my Katarina. I remember the first day I met you. I thought to myself, 'This girl is amazing.' I did...You seemed so strong and sure of yourself, and you have been every day of your life. And tomorrow you are going to walk down the aisle with the best looking guy in the world and he's going to give you away to the second-best looking guy in the world."

They both giggled for a while.

"And you are going to start a new chapter in your life. It will have challenges...lots of good times and some bad ones, but I'm not worried about you at all. I release you with complete peace because I know you'll always be amazing. I know you can handle whatever happens with a great attitude. I am so proud of you."

Kat wiped a tear off of her cheek.

"And I don't mean because you're getting married," Sienna said, "I'm proud of you because of who you are."

∞

Jonathan looked rather model-like in his tailored tux and tie—he knew how to wear a suit that was for sure. The men were ready well before the ladies, of course, but eventually they started descending the staircase in all their feminine glory, and he watched them as they came down in a long breathtaking line. Aurora and Bella held hands and leaded them all. Bella looked absolutely beautiful with her elegant dress, little patent leather shoes, and her hair done up to match all the other women, but mostly to him, it was her smile that was priceless. As his eyes traced the line back, they fell on Sienna as she followed the bride, carefully gathering the excess of that white bridal gown in her arms. That dress, although amazingly exquisite, could have qualified for its own zip code. She was completely engrossed in mastering its many layers in order to ensure that Katarina navigated the stairs safely. Sienna was completely stunning to him in her silk dress, in her perfect make-up, and in her motherly glow, and he had to admit that he barely noticed the bride.

Meanwhile, Shay was standing beside him taking in the transformation of Aurora for the first time. She was just as captivating to him either way, and he said to her simply, "You are as beautiful as you always are to me," which instantly became her favorite response to the change yet.

They made it to the church (which was more like a cathedral) with everyone in good spirits, and Jonathan was proud to be a part of the grand ceremony. As he and Kat made it down the long marbled aisle, and up to the altar, he was asked the question, "Who gives this bride's hand in marriage?"

He smiled up at Sienna, who was also the Maid of Honor. He winked at her and said, "Sienna and I do." Then he kissed Kat's cheek, holding her a moment while he whispered, "If you ever need any help keeping him in line, you don't hesitate to call me."

"Thank you, Jonathan." She beamed up at him.

The reception was amazing, albeit a tad bit overdone, with its gourmet food and drink, abundant flowers, subtle candlelight, and reflective copper fountains everywhere, not to mention the swan ice sculptures, the string quartet, the parfait bar, the seven-tiered cake, and the live coy fish in the central fountain. The chance to advertise to high-end future clientele certainly wasn't wasted on Dillon's mother, who seemed to be showcasing all her wedding planner skill at once to the hundreds she'd invited. But she was obviously very good at what she did. Sienna couldn't have been more pleased with how everything turned out.

Over the course of the evening, Sienna asked several times, "Have you seen Aurora and Shay?"

No one ever seemed to have an answer.

The minister was a big man, a strong, heavily muscled man. And, should he announce to his congregation one morning that he moonlighted as a club bouncer or a bounty hunter or perhaps even a military sniper, it would not be surprising to them in the least. Jonathan felt a bit squeamish as he watched this man walking directly toward him. He saw, as if in slow motion, the man's arm coming up around him and pressing into his back.

"Let's take a walk, shall we, brother," the man said, not really asking at all.

They made their way to a secluded corner, and this is what he said.

"Jonathan, is it?"

Jonathan nodded.

"Jonathan, I'm going to tell you a story. It's about a beautiful, vivacious, wholesome woman..."

Jonathan was counting the adjectives which he assumed were describing his fiancée.

"And this woman makes it her call in life to take in other young women who are less fortunate than herself."

He paused dramatically.

"And all of the sudden, this woman, this gorgeous, amazing, kindhearted, warm, loving woman, shows up with this male-model type, musician, is it?"

Jonathan nodded and swallowed.

"And this 'musician' slash 'model' decides to take her away... make her his own, should we say, which makes it impossible for this sensational, resplendent, dignified woman in her sweet prime to help anyone but him."

Jonathan was starting to sweat.

And this preacher went on for a long cruel moment before slapping him on the back and saying, "I'm just messin' with ya, man! I'm just messin'!"

Jonathan mocked a little laugh and loosened his tie.

"You need to lighten up, son," the minister said. "I'm Bishop Jacobs."

He extended his huge hand for Jonathan to shake.

"Friends just call me Bishop. Are you my friend, Jonathan?"

"No, not really," Jonathan said, grabbing a glass of water off a passing tray.

"Not really," the man pondered Jonathan's answer. "Not very definitive are you? Seriously, Jonathan, I've known Sienna since she moved here. I love her to pieces. We've spent countless hours in my office talking about how to save people's souls. She is an amazing person—but you know that, right? Sure you do."

He smiled down at Jonathan before going on.

"I just want you to think long and hard about the changes you are going to make in her life. She's doing a lot of good on her own. And I'm not saying you shouldn't get married. I mean, obviously she sees somethin' in ya that I don't. But I trust her. I just don't trust you yet."

Jonathan looked him straight in the eye, quickly realizing he was locking eyes with a man who was just looking out for Sienna the best way he knew how. And that made Jonathan respect him.

"Thank you, Bishop," he finally said, to which the man raised a brow. "Anybody who looks out for the love of my life is a friend of mine. And I know what she's done with these girls, and from what I know of her, she's a force, and she's not gonna quit. There's no way I could stop God from using her if I tried—I'm smart enough to stay out of the way of that, at least. And I don't want to stop her anyway, I want to join her."

"Well said, well said, brother," Bishop replied, somewhat stunned. "She's found herself a pretty boy with some depth to him, good for her!" and he smiled and walked away, shaking his head.

Jonathan's gaze followed him with a smile emerging just underneath it. He hoped it wasn't the last time he'd get the chance to talk to Bishop Jacobs.

∞

Jonathan and Sienna returned home before anyone else. Bella was asleep in the backseat of the car. Jonathan lifted her up into his arms—she didn't wake at all—and carried her to the door, following Sienna into the dark house. She absentmindedly kicked off her shoes as she switched on the light.

"What the—" Jonathan didn't finish his phrase, he was too shocked.

Sienna looked around, her wide eyes taking in a panoramic view of her ransacked house. The glass coffee table was broken, the sofas ripped to shreds and overturned, and spray-painted across the wall were the words *Stop Writing Lies*.

Sienna started running up the stairs, yelling for the dogs. They were scratching at the backdoor. She ran back down and let them in, checking to make sure they were okay. They took off up the stairs, toward her room. Sienna frantically sprinted past them.

Jonathan jogged up after her, still carrying Bella who had awakened in the commotion. He stumbled upon one of the most dreadful sights he'd ever witnessed. Sienna was on the floor, sobbing. He knew, he could feel it himself...she was completely brokenhearted.

Someone had destroyed her library.

She was doubled over, grabbing crumpled sheets in her fist and holding them to her stomach. She was down on her knees in the midst of torn books and ripped pages. The devastation was overwhelming, the damage, irreparable, and her beloved works—her own, someone else's—were irreplaceable.

For her, the room started spinning at a sinister speed. She felt sick, but she heard footsteps running to her in a straight line that cut definitively between her past and her future. And like Brody's sea, there could be no looking back.

That'll only make things worse, he had said.

"Mommy, Mommy, Mommy!" two little arms wrapped around her and then stronger ones from behind. They held onto each other in the midst of the mess because their togetherness was all that they had or truly needed.

∞

This time Jonathan called the police, he gave them Cheney's information, but he couldn't think of anything or anyone else. Neither could Sienna. The two officers said they'd check it out. They disappeared upstairs for a while, took some pictures of the damage, and then they left. Couple by young couple filtered in through the door, and Sienna experienced the incident all over again through their eyes. Together they pulled an all-nighter and cleaned up everything they could, looking for any evidence the police may have missed. They found nothing.

The next day, the sofas and three-quarters of Sienna's library—including her collectable editions and her baby grand piano—ended up in the back of

263

a dump truck. Mia and her friend found new furniture while Jackobie and Jamil painted the wall. Amazingly, Sienna found that her laptop still worked even though it had a cracked screen and was banged up a bit. Her book was still there. She copied it to five different CDs before she fell asleep with her computer in her arms, clutching it like it was her infant.

Jonathan watched her sleep while Shay watched him get an ulcer.

"I'll take Bella for the day. You need to get some sleep, Johnny," he whispered, to which Jonathan absentmindedly nodded, not hearing a word his brother said.

When the phone rang, he sprinted for it. The police department said that according to the staff Cheney had been in the rehab center and had had no visitors or connections with the outside world. There were no other leads.

chapter thirty-two

WHAT'S YOUR NOVEL about, sweetheart?" he asked her, tenderly stroking her hair as she lay across his chest.

"Brokenness."

He looked out the window; he felt like crying. He remembered back to when he was a little kid . . . he'd found a butterfly whose wing had fallen away from its body. It couldn't fly. He'd taken the thing carefully home to his father, hoping he could fix it. He said that he couldn't. And that was the first time Jonathan ever cried because of sadness.

"You know," she continued explaining, "I read those stories, the ones where Jesus broke the bread, and a few loaves ended up feeding multitudes of people. I read those stories and thought that they were a description of one of the miracles He worked. I took them at face value, but they mean more than that. The remnants of the broken bread, what was left over after feeding the people, was more than what they started with. God's not interested in the loaf. He's interested in what's left over after the loaf has been broken. Because that's the good stuff—that's the stuff He's had a hand in, and it's so much better than the first."

She looked up at him, and he down at her. Their eyes met and held each other's gaze steadily.

"I'm not worried, Jonathan. And I don't want you to be either. This is just a stage of brokenness—it's barely worth noticing because something amazing is about to happen. I can feel it."

She put her head back down on his chest, and it felt softer somehow. He let the tears roll silently down his face as he stared out the window again, hoping he could have half of her faith, wishing he could have all of her trust so he could know what absolute fearlessness felt like, but above all, he was praying that this time his Father could fix it.

∞

"Thank you, Jesus!" Sienna exclaimed loudly with a smile as she strolled through the kitchen unaware everyone else was in it.

"Oh, sorry," she offered. "Good morning, everybody."

"That's what I like to see," Jonathan winked at her, "A happy girl. I take it you are done."

"Yep. And deadline's this afternoon. I just have to email it."

She poured some orange juice and kissed Bella's cheek. Her eyes went to Aurora and Shay and she immediately noted Aurora's odd silence.

"Everything okay over there?" she asked Aurora.

Aurora's eyes darted to Shay, to the ceiling, to the table, then out the window. A speechless Aurora didn't exist before this moment. Sienna looked to Jonathan who shook his head that he didn't know.

Finally Aurora said, "Most people would want to say this sort of thing in private, which I never understood, because that just makes people more curious, and curious people are, quite frankly, idiots. Isn't that how gossip starts?"

"Aurora," Sienna said, "Just say it, then."

Aurora looked at Shay, and so did Jonathan, with an expression indicating that he'd kill him if he messed anything up. She slowly held up her hand. She had a small diamond on one of her rings. Sienna's eyes lit up, and her mouth opened, but Aurora stopped whatever was about to come out of it with a silencing palm.

"It's not an engagement ring, Sienna."

Sienna's joy dropped to the floor.

"It's a wedding ring. We got married—alone—in the church—right after Kat's wedding. Bishop said we're good in the eyes of God, but probably not in the eyes of Uncle Sam...citizenship and paperwork and whatnot. But I don't really want to stay here anyway."

Sienna's eyes went rather big, and she wasn't saying anything. Actually, she wasn't really breathing either.

"There's more...," Aurora sucked in a heavy dose of air that landed across her man like the end of a whip. "Judas Priest and all the crime in Italy, Shay, can't you take the hard part?"

Sienna stared the boy down, and he started to squirm. Jonathan glared at him and kicked his shin under the table. Hard.

"Oh... never mind, I'll say it. I'm pregnant."

Sienna's glass slid out of her hand and crashed to the floor. She instantly started weeping, her hand still in the air, fingers curved around the juice that wasn't there. Huge tears ran down her face, and she looked like she would fall over. Aurora sprung up and went to her, and Sienna clung tightly to her. Jonathan watched, waiting, not knowing what to do until it quickly became clear that they were tears of joy. It slowly filtered in through his memory, *Aurora can't have kids...*

"But I thought..." Sienna stammered.

"I *know*," Aurora pulled back and nodded, pointing to her stomach, "This is a miracle, right?"

"Yes!" Sienna squealed, and Aurora threw her head back thanking God in the ceiling that Sienna was reacting this way instead of the other way.

"But we have to get you to a specialist," Sienna ordered, "You are going to have to be extra careful, Aurora."

"Got it handled, Grandma. Jackobie has me on with one of her Einstein buddies. I've already been checked out, so we're good to go."

"Vitamins?"

"On 'em," she said looking down and lightly patting her belly, "even though Junior's smaller than the vitamin."

Sienna hugged her again while Jonathan did the math in his head behind an inquisitive brow.

"Don't waste any time, do ya, Shay?" he half-whispered to his brother.

"Sorry," he grinned and Jonathan slowly returned it.

"Congratulations," he offered warmly.

"Thanks."

∞

The next few days were as perfect and uncomplicated as days can be. Having handed her book over, with the utmost care, into her publisher's hands, Sienna felt free to relax and to recreate, to move unhurriedly through the warm, soothing flow of a less demanding season. On a sunny Thursday, she and Mia went to a yoga class downtown followed by a day spa visit. They later met Aurora, Shay, Jonathan, and Bella for an evening meal. Aurora discussed some of the happenings at the Domestic Abuse Shelter. They needed new beds, a new nursery wing, and a new heating system. Her eyes lit up with stories of women and children they had successfully helped and how one woman had decided to come back to volunteer herself. At the end of the meal, Shay carried her cello case, and they headed downtown to play and to raise money. The rest of the group followed along to listen.

And what they heard, as it echoed and blossomed down through the cobbled avenues of the historic district, was beautiful. The sounds she made with that single cello were large, warm, and ran deep as the veins through somebody's heart. Jonathan sat on the ledge of a nearby fountain, listening and watching the people gather and disperse and toss spare change onto the red velvet lining which clothed the instrument's home. He watched as Sienna and Bella departed for a carriage ride, then returned and settled in next to him. He watched his brother as he watched his new wife play with amazing depth, soul, and artistic transportation while carrying their unborn child behind that massive piece of carved wood and strings. Jonathan simply watched all the reasons why he was the luckiest man alive.

Since it was nearly dark, they soon departed. But not before Jonathan took a wad of cash and tossed it in her case. Her hand stopped, the music stopped, as she looked down at it then back up into his eyes. He'd never seen her more vulnerable or feminine or innocent than in that one moment. She picked up the cash and shoved it in her jacket, the ex-street rat in her scanning the area, making sure nobody else had seen it. She didn't even count it. Just took it to the director's house and tossed it on her table. But it was enough...enough to cover everything she had mentioned over dinner.

The next day was a perfect riding day for Sienna and Bell, full of instruction, learning, beautiful weather, fresh air, and fun. Jonathan stayed behind to play fetch with the dogs and to make a few phone calls. The first was to his family in Ireland.

"Dad? Are ya there?"

"Yeah, son..."

"Dad, has Shay called ya yet?"

"No."

"Ah..., I'll tell him to."

"What has he done?" the gruff voice asked nonchalantly.

"Nothin' bad...don't worry, not at all. Okay? He just needs ta talk to ya. And Dad?"

"Yeah."

"I need you to do somethin' for me...a favor."

"What is it, son...?"

And the second phone call was to his producer to discuss business. And the third was to Roger, to ask him to keep an eye on the house and to check in on Mrs. Hopkins, but no one was home. He called Alex instead.

"Hey, buddy? How are things?"

"Good, man. Good. Pretty quiet."

"Hey, have ya checked in on my house...is everything okay?"

"With your house...? Yeah, looks tight, man."

"What about Mrs. Hopkins?"

"As brassy as ever. She's holdin' up good."

"Good."

"But there is somethin'...." Alex's voice trailed off like he was distracted.

"What?"

"Well, man. I'm lookin' out the window, and I can see Roger's house...."

"Yeah?"

"Well, you ain't gonna like this..., but Cheney's back."

Silence.

"Jonathan? You there, man?"

"I am."

"Looks like you just wasted a boat-load a' cash on that rehab, man."

"Looks like."

"You need me to do anything else?"

"Mow my yard, would ya?"

"Cash money, my friend."

"Alex, I'll make you an offer...you sell my house for me, and you can have twenty percent."

"You're not comin' back?"

"No."

"All right, man. If that's what you want..."

"It is. Thanks, Alex."

"Later, man."

"And, Alex?"

"Yeah."

"Do not touch my music stuff... or my computer. I'll be comin' by to get that. I don't care about anything else. Anything you want, just take it."

He hung up the phone feeling incredibly unburdened. He was glad to get away from that house next-door and from Cheney. He spent the entire day happy, out on the back porch, writing one new song then rediscovering the ones of his youth that he'd nearly forgotten. Her wrote the lyrics down, taped the melodies, and sketched out a record sequence. He had enough material for two or three separate releases. And he prayed that God would make a way for them into this world.

chapter thirty-three

G'LL SEE YOU in a couple days, baby." He kissed his daughter good-bye, then did the same with Sienna, and he was off, leaving them in the hands of his baby brother. He had to go pack up his things, he told them, but it was more than that—secretly, he needed to confront a certain someone.

Once there, he stopped at Alex's house first. He needed his help packing, but, primarily, he wanted someone there in case he needed restraining. He was determined to get the truth out of her, one way or the other.

They walked directly to Roger's house and rang the bell. Nobody was home.

"Alex?"

"Yeah."

"What I'm about to do never happened, all right?"

"Sure, man. You know me—I can't remember my own name, most days."

Jonathan rummaged around on his key chain, hopeful that Roger hadn't yet changed the locks. He put the key in...it worked and the door opened.

"It's not *breaking* and entering anyway," Alex observed.

The house looked nice, quiet...but nice. The furnishings were impeccable. Everything was clean, neat, and tidy. They separated and checked the entire house, making sure it was empty. When they came back together Alex asked him what he was looking for.

"I don't know," Jonathan said, "it's just a feeling I have."

Upon saying this, he opened the door to the last room to be searched. They walked into something that looked like the office of a madman, and it gave Jonathan the chills. The walls were covered with crucifixes of the Christ and press releases of various Christian literature and movies, but had become most recently dominated by an obsession—pictures of Sienna and photocopied pages of Sienna's books. On the desk was an interrupted and apparently extensive Bible study in direct relation to the Vindicator book. He had scribbled random, pharisaical notes, circled text in angry red, and highlighted sections to which he labeled, "Biblically incorrect!" or "Unscriptural!" or "Blasphemy...."

"This is really weird, man," Alex whispered just as the front door slammed shut.

Cheney rounded the corner and gasped a bit when she saw them, drawn mostly into the look on Jonathan's face.

"I can ex—" she couldn't get the words out before Jonathan's fingers closed around her throat.

"Easy, man," Alex said, grabbing Jonathan's arm.

He let go, still locked in a dead-on glare with her.

"You're gonna tell me what is going on, and you're gonna do it now," he said seething. "You tell me what you know."

She didn't say anything.

"Now!" he shouted.

She jumped and then put a hand to her throat, rubbing it. "Okay! okay..."

She leaned against the doorframe, looking just as skinny, frail and weak as she always had.

"You know Roger always wanted this house," she began. "He heard you kicked me out, so he came to the hospital..."

"When?" Jonathan interrupted.

"When I first got there. Anyway, he asked me about the house, and I brushed him off, because back then, I thought the house was still mine."

She looked down at her shoes.

"So, he must have driven by and saw the lights on sometime, I don't know. He asked me who was staying there. So I told him. And he just went nuts, saying, 'You mean the writer? The novelist?' and I said yeah. I mean what's the big deal, right?

"Then I didn't hear from him for a while, and he came back, out of the blue, when I was in rehab. They let me outside one day, and he talked to me over the fence. He said he'd work a deal with me...he'd give me a place to stay if I helped him."

"Helped him do what?" Jonathan screamed.

"Just give him information on her."

"Like what?"

"Like...I didn't know she was the one who wrote those Vindicator books—the ones from that movie—until I saw it written in her Bible."

"What else?" he demanded.

"There was a wedding invitation in there...and some stuff about a rehearsal dinner party. It had her address on it. And I gave it to him. And that's it, I swear."

"That's it," he mocked, "Why would he need to know that stuff, Cheney?"

"I don't know..." she stammered.

He stepped up and got directly in her face.

"He gives you drugs, doesn't he? And for that, you don't care what he does to her. She tried to help you, Cheney. What is wrong with you?"

He felt like hitting her, but had been taught to never hit a woman. He hit the wall beside her head instead, then he took a deep breath.

"Where is he?" he said coldly, an inch from her face.

"Where he's always at," she replied, defiantly glaring back at him.

"Where's that?" he yelled it so loudly, he blew the hair back from her forehead.

"New Haven, Connecticut," she said with a twisted smile.

Jonathan sprinted out the door with Alex on his heels.

"I'll drive you, man," he offered.

"No," Jonathan said as he slammed his car door, "Stay here in case he comes back."

He peeled out into the street, laying rubber down behind him. Alex turned a bewildered circle and saw Mrs. Hopkins shaking her head in their direction as she closed her mailbox and headed back towards her front door. He looked back at Roger's house and saw Cheney walking out towards him like a zombie with an empty syringe falling out of her hand, it bounced and rolled to a stop in the drive. A needle still stuck in her vein was slowly leaking thick, burgundy drops. He watched as she said, "I'm sorry...." to no one and fell face first on the concrete and died.

He simply left her there, walked back into his house, and quietly closed the door.

✌

How he managed to get all the way to the gas station he chose, unnoticed, was a miracle. He did it without gaining a single cop's attention, without rousing the brigade of squad cars he probably deserved. By the grace of God, he kept it on the road, barely between the lines, and he did not blow the engine nor did he endanger anyone else while driving like that. It was as if he were the only man in the universe, lost and invisible, and traveling at a speed immeasurable, headed for a destination that had since evaporated. Everything was standing still as he passed it by. Everything else was void of motion, but for the endless miles he couldn't get ahead of. His mind raced with enough fear to drive himself clean out of it.

So he did what anyone would do—he took it out on his phone.

His cell phone battery had died from his ceaseless dialing and endless message leaving. He'd gotten a hold of no one before it did. He'd thrown it against the passenger window in a fit of rage and was now feeling on the floorboards for it, cursing at it. His fingers finally found it, but they were shaking, and he fumbled it, dropping it twice before he had it. As he came up strangling it, he noticed the police car across the parking lot. He wondered if he should ask for help or if it would be a waste of valuable time. He searched the console for a battery charger and plugged it in. He got some change together for the pay phone.

As he stood up, he realized he was dizzy. He forced himself to take a few deep breaths. *Get a hold of yourself, Driscoll. You're being pathetic...*

But he still felt sick to his stomach. There was no way around the feeling in the pit of it—*Something's wrong—something's very, very wrong!* He just couldn't shake it. It was too heavy like an unavoidable truth hanging just outside himself with no one left to carry the weight of it but him. He pressed on toward the pay phone, dialing a number he was certain no one would answer. He was right. He looked around the station's parking lot, witnessing for a long liquid moment the flow of mindless living uninterrupted, jealously watching as the people took for granted a much better day than his. He tried to steal, with his sheer will, their comfort, and to thieve their frivolity through his eyes alone. For a breath, or two, he actually felt better. He dialed Sienna's home number again, nervously tapping on the hazy phone booth glass. This time someone did answer.

"New Haven Police Department. Caller, identify yourself."

Jonathan let out a groan, but couldn't speak. He was trying to keep his knees from buckling beneath him.

"Sir, this is a crime scene. Please, state your name," the woman said.

Jonathan heard shuffling and some muted voices. He heard someone snapping their fingers, once...twice...

"Sir, this call is being traced. Please, state your name and location."

Jonathan's knuckles were white. He opened his hand and let the receiver fall and bang against the glass. He stared at it with disbelief until all the blood drained from his face. He grabbed the door to hold himself up, puking his guts out just as he slid it open. He took several erratic steps, stumbled and fell across the hood of his car, landing on the asphalt with his back against the warm tire. He grabbed his chest because he couldn't breathe. He thought he was having a heart attack.

"Sir, have you been drinking?"

The officer was pulling out a pad about to follow the mundane routine pertaining to public drunks when Jonathan grabbed his pant leg, causing the man to take a step back and reach for his firearm.

"Help me!" Jonathan pleaded. "I'm not drunk. I'm in shock. I just called home...my fiancé, my little girl...there's a crime scene. I don't know what happened. I can't think straight. I'm still three hours away."

Jonathan pulled himself up, looking the man in the eye.

"I know it's not your problem, but I'm begging you to treat me like it is. What would you do if it was your family?"

The officer was an older man with blue eyes that still held a touch of kindness in their hardened wisdom. He radioed his unit for help, but didn't take his eyes off Jonathan for a second.

"Turn around, son. This is just a precaution."

He patted him down.

"You don't smell like booze...Come sit in the back of my car. I'm Sheriff Jonas. I need to see your driver's license, and give me the phone numbers to your house, your fiancée's cell...any information you can think of. Then I'm going to make a few calls...see what I can do, okay?"

"Thank you," Jonathan looked into his eyes as he handed him his license. He wrote everything else down with a shaky hand. The officer took the information and walked to another squad car to investigate it.

Five minutes had passed, then ten. It felt like an hour. Jonathan decided to pray, and he prayed like he never had in his entire life. Out loud and unashamed. Sheriff Jonas had entered the car and turned over the ignition, but didn't interrupt Jonathan or raise an eyebrow. He simply added his "Amen" of agreement at the end. They pulled out of the parking lot and once on the main road, he looked Jonathan in the eye via the rearview mirror.

"One of my deputies is taking your car to the station. It'll be well taken care of and available anytime you want to come back and pick it up. We are going to give you a police escort to New Haven. You just sit tight, okay?"

Jonathan nodded, blankly watching out the window as another squad car passed them and picked up speed. They had lights and sirens going and were well up to eighty-five and creeping beyond it when Jonathan quietly said, "What do you know?"

The officer didn't have to say a word or move a muscle for Jonathan to feel it. The news wasn't good.

"Please," Jonathan tried again, "if it were your wife and daughter, you'd want to know."

His hands gripped the steering wheel tightly then relaxed. He opened his mouth to speak...and even after thirty-five years on the job couldn't think of where to start.

chapter thirty-four

*A*URORA HAD GOTTEN a phone call earlier in the day. She was upset, visibly shaken, when she told Sienna she had to go down to the shelter to help out. There had been a tragedy with one of the women. Sienna had insisted that Shay go with her.

"We'll be fine," she had said, "won't we, Bell? We'll probably go swimming and watch a movie later. How does that sound?"

"Good," Bella smiled, and Shay reluctantly left them behind.

At the shelter, everyone was devastated—clients and staff alike. A regular, a beautiful young woman named Shelby, had finally been hit by her alcoholic husband too hard to ever recover. She'd been in and out of the shelter, typically once per month, for the last year. Everyone thought things had been getting better between the two. She'd told Aurora that her husband had been going to AA meetings and had quit drinking—she couldn't stop saying how proud she was of him. Aurora was sickened to learn that he'd fallen off the wagon and that his demon had returned with a unparalleled vengeance. She was certain he hadn't meant to do it, but he did it just the same. He was soon to be in the big house for life where not a drop of alcohol be served. But that was too little, too late, for them both.

Shelby was dead.

Over the course of an afternoon so sad and so heavy it nearly couldn't be lived through, somehow, by some grace befallen of the Lord that had stumbled down and across the wicked earth, Aurora overheard something most prevalent and most profound. She heard something that sounded like footsteps, like the Angel of Life walking, coming close and then closer still, coming straight toward her and finally stopping, offering promises on possibility, holding up time with something sacred in her arms.

"What did you just say?" she demanded loudly of the startled social worker and somehow, in reference to what the woman was saying, slowly, unequivocally, there came a smile that spread across Aurora's lips and stayed.

She grabbed Shay by the arm, "I'll be right back."

"Where are you going?"

"Just wait for me, I'll be right back," and she was gone.

∞

"You ready for a movie?"

"Ice cream."

"Ice cream," Sienna teased her, "Ice cream?"

She tickled the girl's belly while she giggled.

"Okay, but just a little bit. We can't spoil our supper, right?"

Bella had just finished her treat when Sienna heard someone knocking at the door. Her first instinct was not to answer it. In hindsight, she'd have no idea why she did. It was a young man selling products for a fundraiser. She purchased some sort of useless gadget from him which she wouldn't receive for another six to eight weeks and upon which would go directly into the garbage bin. She shut the door, glad that he was gone.

She said to Bella, as she put her wallet back in her handbag, "If you ever have school fundraisers, please suggest something useful, like running errands or mowing yards. Now that would be something worth donating to, don't you think? It's a little early for fundraisers, anyway."

She no more than got her last words out, when she felt something dark was creeping in behind her like a circling sin-cloud. She read Bella's face as if it were a mirror, and beneath the child's wide eyes an outright fear was burning, reflecting in its dancing light the very hounds of hell drooling at her back. She didn't turn to look, but lunged for the knives on the kitchen counter in front of her, twisting, hefting her purse at him with one hand and wickedly slashing him with the other—the blade slid down cleanly across his face, opening flesh eyebrow to chin. She didn't know the man grabbing her wrist and punching her in the gut—hard. She didn't recognize his face, leaking both blood and warm vengeance down—he wasn't anyone to her but a strange attacker.

"Bella!" Sienna screamed, though she'd had the wind knocked out of her.

He backhanded her across the face so ruthlessly that he struck her down, the knife dislodging from her hand and sliding just out of her reach, trailing a thin line of his blood across the marble floor in little splatters.

"Go to the secret place!" she yelled against the echoing tiles.

She watched Bella obey, watched her daughter round the corner at a run as

278

the man kicked her repeatedly in the ribs. She both heard and felt something snap inside her.

He hauled her limp body up. She was starting to go into shock, so he held her head back harshly with a fist full of her hair, glaring down into her fluttering eyes.

"I told you, but you wouldn't listen," he seethed, shoving her across the room then holding her against the white counter with his entire body.

"It's people like you," he whispered against her face, her ear, her neck, "that give us a bad name."

His evil breath was almost burning her skin as she tried to make sense of it. Her mind whirled a lifetime circle, but she couldn't place him anywhere inside it. She didn't know what he was talking about, couldn't think what to say to him, so she prayed from a place deep inside, *Please God, not like this…*

"People like you think you can take God's word and make a dime off of it." He was nearly choking on his hatred, kneeing her hard in the gut, again, and pulling her limp body back up to him, again—it wouldn't take much more of this…

She was close to passing out—everything was shrouded in a white heated haze—when she saw her Angel of Rescue—her Angel of Vindication, come through it, entering the death room and dispelling its suffocating walls and bringing with her, breath. She knew Bella was in her secret hiding place, praying her Angel's way there, out into the open light of day. There simply was no other answer, no other excuse, no other reason for the timing—it was perfectly orchestrated, down to the very last beat of a brave and battered heart. It was as if this miraculous timing was God's very own, and if it could be thought to have a rhythmic voice behind it, it surely said to her, *Hold on, just another beat more…*

"Batta, batta, swing," Aurora said it with absolute fearlessness, absolute confidence and resolve, and with her own brand of humor stamped on it. She almost *sang* it, skipping two sideways strides and hopping into a meticulous swing she'd physically memorized for survival as a very young girl—it was the only thing of usefulness her stepdad taught her, and she learned it well. She'd intended to use it on him, but she never got the chance. So, as far as she was concerned, here it was—today was the day. Finally.

His skull cracked open and his head caved in; his eyes rolled in on themselves and stayed. Sticky crimson liquid sprung out off the end of that aluminum baseball bat in wicked waves and splattered across Sienna's distorted face and the white marble tile; it clung stubbornly and then slowly dripped warm from the cool stainless steel surrounding. Sienna fell in a heap on the floor beside the dead body and everything, for her, went black.

Aurora dove down beside her, "Stay alive, Sienna. Stay alive. Come on, stay with me!"

She sprinted to the phone to dial 911. The bat was still rolling back and forth on the floor where she'd tossed it. As she paced, snapped her fingers, and nervously hopped around, she raised her eyes to the heavens, thankful they'd kept that bat in the hall closet, because one second more... They picked up, and she gave her name and address.

"I've killed an intruder. Self-defense, got it? Don't screw that part up. I need an ambulance. Now. He almost killed my mother. Hurry up or so help me I will personally hunt down anyone who didn't hustle, you hear me? Move!"

She hung up the receiver and checked on Sienna again. She was breathing steadily, but not responsive.

Aurora looked around at the bloody mess, bewildered and thinking out loud, "What is this? What's this about?"

She focused in on the crime until it dawned on her—*Bella's gone!*

"Bella!" she yelled, running up the stairs two at a time. She checked all the rooms and ran back down to the pool room. It was empty, but she saw right away where he had gotten in. A panel of greenhouse glass was leaning against the wall, having been removed carefully from the pane. She quickly deduced he'd used and concealed that entrance during his vandalism attack, as well. They'd just overlooked it.

"Bella!" she called again, her eyes falling on the elevator. Then she remembered. Sienna and Bella had been riding it earlier like they were playing a game.

She pressed the button. After a long moment, the gold-plated doors separated her worried image and revealed the child. Bella was feverishly praying, trance-like, saying over and over, "You will not want to go back to the house from which you came, Mommy," that and, "God's will be done."

Aurora picked the girl up. "It's okay, Baby Bell. Everything's going to be all right. You're safe now."

chapter thirty-five

SHERIFF JONAS LOOKED in the rearview again, sank his empathy down deep into those desperate eyes, swallowed, and said, "Apparently it happened a little over an hour ago, so I don't have a lot of the details. There's a little girl, I assume your daughter. She's okay. She's shaken—a little upset, but no evident physical harm. The perpetrator, a man, fits the description of this Roger fellow you know—he was killed on the scene. The young woman who killed him is in for questioning. Now, that's just standard procedure, sounds pretty cut and dried to me—Aurora? Pink hair?"

Jonathan confirmed the name with a nod through teary eyes.

"And the victim, your fiancé, she's in the hospital..."

He suddenly quit talking, his throat cracked a bit. Jonathan's tears were streaming down his face now, the whites of his eyes turning red as he stared blankly out the window at a horrible, blurry, messed-up world.

The officer glanced into the mirror again, his gut sinking hollow and low within him. He'd never seen a sadness run as deep and as evident as the one he read on Jonathan's face. He tried to offer sincerity and comfort in his voice, as much as ninety-miles-an-hour would allow him, "She's alive...but she's been beat up pretty bad, son. I'm sorry. I truly am."

They got there in less than two hours. They took Jonathan directly to the hospital, helped him locate Sienna's room, and offered New Haven P.D. information on Roger's home for evidence.

Jonathan wasn't allowed to see her yet. He sat on a bench just outside her room; he wasn't nervously fidgeting, he was nearly comatose, stricken still with graven fright. Staff rushed in; staff rushed out, all breezing by him with their white coats flaring out at the hem, squeaking by in their hospital shoes without so much as a single word. So he talked to God instead, praying Him a new song.

JUSTICE
by Jonathan Driscoll

Your saints are tired, Lord, and Lord.
Your soldiers battled, scarred and haggard.
Your sheeps be slaughter-led, Father, and Lord.
Your flock, Good Shepherd, she's scattered.

The woolen loom is silent and shorn.
Our cleansed blood, it be splattered.
Our minds be darted, Spirit, heart and muscle torn.
Too many fragments, our souls be shattered.

You see me drop, my will, it's tattered.
My knees and knuckle bleed unto Your ground.
Justice, come down, my plea is, Justice, come down.
For Your earth, still, she matter.

And he actually heard back, "God's answer cometh, son...wait."

Then Jackobie finally emerged from the forbidden room. She was Sienna's primary doctor, and for that Jonathan was grateful. She was very professional, but he noticed both her hands were shaking when she checked Sienna's chart. She glanced up and caught the desperate look hanging on his pitiful face. She opened Sienna's door and gestured him on in.

He gravitated toward her soul hovering in the middle of the room, her crumpled body lying on the bed and deathly still. When he saw her face, it didn't register as hers. He almost didn't recognize her, and as his heart and his mind slowly did, he couldn't think, couldn't move, and certainly couldn't speak.

Jackobie waited for him to get his air back.

"She's got a concussion," she stated. "It's severe and we are monitoring that closely. She's got some broken ribs, some are just cracked, but one has been dislocated. Other than that, she's got some nasty contusions. She's sedated. And she's on pain medication.

"Jonathan...," she finally addressed him directly with her translucent green eyes, "it's going to take her some time...six to eight weeks, minimum, but I think she's going to be all right. Eventually."

"Thank God," he whispered, letting out the breath he was holding in against the pit of his stomach like a prayer or, rather, a merciless dare, a wager with an exchange of souls on the balance because he, like Aurora, would die for her. In a heartbeat, he'd summon fate for a trade and carry all her temporal pain upon his back for eternity.

He pulled a chair up beside Sienna and gently held her hand. He cradled it kindly, brought the back of it to his lips and kissed it thankfully, and he let her pulse comfort him and soothe away the most dreadful of all fears—a life in which she was no longer. He couldn't even ask himself the question, *What if...?* He could not even imagine in the farthest recesses of his mind a future with her removed. Because the only thing he knew for sure in this moment was that a life, a world, a place, an existence in which she was no longer... for him, could not be lived, bartered, secured, or experienced at all. It would be worthless. For in his place, passively filling an entity that once was him, there would be a space, a void, a soul, empty and sullen; muscle with no forward movement; and a mind capable of no thought but memory. And as he pondered these things, full-well knowing they be true to their base, he rested his forehead against her weak and all-powerful hand as it safely hid him from the emptiness "everything she was" prevented. She had so permeated him, mind, body, and soul, that as he looked upon her sleeping face, he could no longer recall any of the days he lived before her.

Jackobie checked the I.V. bag and stared at a monitor for a moment. She jotted some notes on Sienna's chart as she absentmindedly said to him, "Bella's watching television with Mia. I think Kat's with her as well. It's down the hall, third door on the left if you want to see her."

"Thank you," Jonathan said, looking up at her. She was distant, cold, and dismissive, barely acknowledging that he was still in the room. He tried to get her attention, personally. "Jackobie... are you okay?"

Her pen stopped, and she stood motionless for a long while.

"No," she finally answered flatly, looking irritated as she went back to work, scanning Sienna's battered face and body. She ran her fingertips over Sienna's forearm, circling a bump and bruise and jotting another note.

"I see a lot of things in here, Jonathan. But nothing has prepared me for this."

She clicked the pen shut and put it in her pocket; she placed the chart in its holder at the foot of the bed. She glanced out at the empty hallway as if checking to make sure no one could hear her when she said, "When they wheeled her in...I couldn't move. One of the nurses had to take me aside and tell me to breathe again."

"This woman...," she choked on the words and looked at Sienna's unresponsive face. "This woman is my hero, Jonathan. This isn't supposed to happen to people like her."

Jonathan stood up and hugged her, feeling her rigid body slowly let itself melt against his kindness. She leaned on his shoulder for a moment before pulling herself back into her job.

"Just wait," he told her.

"Just keep watching her," he said.

"She'll take this and make something amazing out of it," he promised. "Just wait."

Jackobie studied him aloofly with her scientific eyes as if he were a specimen in a jar.

At last she said, "Faith. Is that what you are talking about?"

"I think so, yes."

"That's a hard sell on me, Jonathan. Sienna's spiritualism never rubbed off on me quite the way she had hoped. I like exact science. I like clear-cut answers that have proof to back them up. Even so, I believe you may be right. I don't see how anyone could pull a silver lining down from something as ugly as this, but I'm sure Sienna will. And I'm glad she has someone like you to believe in her, someone to help her do that. Because this time, Jonathan, I think she's going to need some human help. She was thinking God had made her bullet-proof. And to tell you the truth, so was I. I can't even explain God, but I know I don't want her to be disappointed in Him. This one's out of my league, Jonathan. If her faith slips, I don't think all the medicine in the world will heal her this time."

"It won't slip. This isn't out of God's league," Jonathan said with holy determination. "Just keep watching her. She'll be a hundred times better than before. She'll be stronger and wiser. This is just a time of brokenness...she'll make it through. Her life will be better than it was before."

Jackobie nodded, realizing he was talking more to himself than to her, and she quietly exited the room, leaving him alone with the love of his life as she was tattered and torn, misused and beaten down under his failure to watch. He thought she looked much like his boyhood butterfly with a lost wing, with no sky to be set free in. And so help him and his beloved God, he'd find her a new wing and a clearer sky with softer breezes and bluer tones in which to see her fly. And both her wings would grow back stronger than before, they'd take her higher than before. And as for him—he'd never leave her, not again, not for a moment, not for any reason beneath the sun, not for any of his remaining days. She was his purpose; she was his light.

And so he sang to her a more beautiful song of vastness in hope, of forward and colossal movement, and of God's grace for all, all, all the days ahead, trying with everything he had left in his soul to start rebuilding her sky while the Lord, kindly and at her lover's request, reached in and healed her from within, bone to sacred bone, keeping Potter's ashes delicately separated from finite ashes, keeping Creator's dust from mingling with inevitable ending dust.

Because it simply wasn't her time.

It was His...

And He understood its unfolding beautifully, for its counting started with and will end in Him.

And as she slept, she slept with a soul contented only with knowing the One Who Knows, His name, The Great I Am, within Whom there is found the only Rest that exists in this life, true Power called forth only with this soft and tiny breath.

∞

Katarina switched with Jonathan as per his request that Sienna not be left alone, not at all, not for a single moment. When he saw Bella, he directly and effortlessly read the exact extent of the damage done to her, to the heart, mind, and soul of his little girl. Before she caught sight of him in the corner of her eye, he tried to shift his sorrows into a smile to comfort her with, but could not. She ran into his arms, and he held her close, and he cried silently into her hair. He pressed his quivering lips shut because he didn't want to ask her anything she wasn't ready to tell. By the memorized feel of her he knew she had been changed. Forever. And he could not erase it. He understood, through the inherent messages and silent screams her beating heart sent into his, that in a single day she had aged exponentially. And he could not get that time back.

When she pulled back from him, she did so in order to look at her dad's face. She put a tiny hand to his cheek and held it there as she silently studied his eyes as if questioning them in regards to the thoughts of all men. She studied him, his skin, his eye lashes, his lips, for traces and signs of a murderer, searching, for what seemed to her to be a beast hidden within the hearts of all men. And he found that he had nothing to tell her. He was stunned and amazed with the inadequacy he found within himself when he couldn't think of a single thing to say to her. Not a solitary word of explanation came to his lips. Nothing salvageable or noteworthy came through his being at all. He had nothing useful to offer his daughter, no means to restore what had been stolen. He simply could not pay.

Finally she told him, as if she were reading his thoughts, "That's okay, Daddy. That's what Jesus did on the cross."

"What, love? What did Jesus do?"

"Paid the debt for all men because we cannot pay."

"We cannot pay," Jonathan repeated softly, almost in a question.

"For the sins of others, for the sins of our own, we cannot pay," she said with tired eyes that showed too much age and not enough innocence, not anymore. It was gone.

Mia came up beside them and said, "I have a small apartment downtown. It's right across from the restaurant. There's only one bed and a pull-out sofa, but you are welcome to it."

"Thank you," Jonathan said. He brought her in under his arm and kissed the top of her head, "I appreciate that, but I can't leave Sienna."

"I understand," Mia said. "I can take Bella. She needs some rest. I have time off work—they all know what happened."

"That would be great. Can you have dogs?"

"We already took care of that. Barbara has all of them out at the stables."

"I better go back to the house and check on things sometime... maybe after Shay gets here. I'll swing by then to check in on Bella, I'll bring her some clothes. It'll probably be later tonight?"

"That's fine. It's apartment 211, third floor. I'll be watching for you."

Jonathan said his goodbye to Bella, finding it nearly impossible to let her go.

"She'll be fine," Mia quietly reassured him as they left.

He walked into the hallway, heading back to Sienna's room when he saw Shay bursting through the doors at the far end. He started jogging towards him, securing a baby against his chest, a light green baby bag slung over his shoulder.

"I went to the house...." Shay panted, out of breath. "They had the whole thing taped off. There are cops everywhere. They told me to come here. What happened?"

"It's okay," Jonathan tried to reassure him, finding it useless. "Everyone's alive. Sienna got the worst of it, but she'll be okay. Aurora killed the guy—it was Roger, the one who bought the house."

Shay's eyes shifted down into a steely coldness.

"Yeah...," Jonathan said remorsefully. "She's downtown at the police station for routine questioning—you should go to her."

"I will...," Shay agreed, pealing off the diaper bag.

"You have a ride?"

"A taxi is waiting outside."

"Okay...hey."

"Yeah?"

"Aurora saved Sienna's life. She stood up and protected them. And Bella's okay. You tell her that. You tell her thank you, from the bottom of my heart, for whatever she did. Tell her I'll see her soon. Tell her Sienna is going to be fine. Will you tell her all that?"

"Yeah, yeah, I'll tell her. Here...."

Shay handed Jonathan the baby.

"Who is this?" Jonathan asked, taking the little guy in his arms.

Shay smiled in spite of everything happening around them and said, "Well, I'd like you to meet your son."

The brothers' eyes met. Jonathan didn't know if he heard Shay correctly.

"What?"

"You heard me. I'll explain later!" And he turned to run on to find Aurora.

Jonathan called down the hall after him, "Wait! What's his name?"

Shay turned back as he got to the doors and said, "Justice. Justice Quinn soon-to-be Driscoll. He even looks like you...but he's got Sienna's smile."

Jonathan held the baby up to the light and looked into his face. His brother was right, the little guy looked shockingly like a Driscoll.

And Jonathan asked him, "So what on earth is your story, little man? You need a dad, do ya?"

And then it happened, Justice smiled. And Jonathan could see Sienna's future held softly inside it.

chapter thirty-six

*G*T WAS THE most beautiful thing she had ever seen. It was more beautiful to her than anything she'd ever see again. And it happened at a moment so pivotal and so perfect, it dispelled any trace of doubt in her soul that there wasn't a God in heaven looking down, searching for children to bless. But before this, there was a darkness so thick, so dreadful and so heavy, she couldn't see a way out.

Over the course of her healing, she'd like to say she never took on a spirit of depression or sadness, but she did. And it was so deep and internal, her lungs seemed to wheeze and burn as if filled with water instead of air. She visualized herself sinking to the bottom of a placid lake never to resurface again. She felt cool nothingness surrounding, swallowing what once was her, and she heard the silence of her own absence wafting above her and dissipating forever into gray…into black. She tasted the peace that came with vanishing from the world; she barely discerned that it was a peace that would prove false—a cruel hoax she should not follow—for she was put in the world, in her body, by Another. So she slept instead with a weight of exhaustion so heavy it nearly suffocated her, but when she finally awakened from it, not knowing the day, the time, or even the month for sure, and not knowing if she cared…she exempted herself from the violence, the wrongness, the selfishness, and the terrible sound of a bullet shot into her own brain—the other course thoroughly considered. These were just passing things, eerie like a ghost ship emerging from and descending into the fog at will; they were just random attacks of the mind, satanic flashes if truth be told. And they were as grotesque as they were serious; superficial, yet if acted upon, the final decision one could ever make. They were passing, flighty, wretched things brought about by the mood, in the midnight with no moon, easily starved to death when not fed with pondering and study, simply exposed and obliterated when seen for what they really were. But she experienced them still, primarily because she was too physically, mentally, emotionally, and spiritually exhausted to dispel them entirely on her own.

So she waited on God.

And she'd like to say the senselessness of the abuses befallen her didn't set her traveling down the distant, broken trails of her younger days, but it did. And it drew them nearer to her than they ever were, bringing their desolation into her now and their wickedness into her future days, pulling a demon up from her past and multiplying it a hundred-fold, accusing her of the law of attraction as if she were the magnet and the sinner, her steel, and therefore, the blame solely hers just because (and how lame a reason) she was there. It was the aftermath she did calculate as a test against her godly mind. Satan told her only lies, and it was up to her only to resist them and cast everything over.

And so for longer lengths of time, she waited on God.

And she'd like to say she didn't get angry, but she certainly, most definitely, was that. And that, most unfortunately, nearly led to her demise. Not the act itself, but the injustices reeling inside her, sharp and pressing, ragged and banging against the inside of her chest—they did not make sense to her mind; she could find no place inside her to fit them. It made her sick to carry them around like that, but she could not heave them up. Her desired revenge was reeking and rotting her core, causing an unstable balance to hold. Her heart, a bridge between herself and the world, seemed to be impassable, and it was burning in such a way she doubted it would be repairable. It simply could not span her soul the way it used to, and she didn't know who had started the fire or why. And so, it was her anger—its fierceness and its justification—that nearly undid her, and it was a force all her own, if she wanted to admit it or not. And it would have gotten its evil way with her—its evil way being to turn her into her attacker—had it not been for the most beautiful thing she'd ever seen come walking through her door.

It was human help appropriate and well-timed. It was God working through man. She simply saw Jesus in them both—His kindness, His grace, and His love. And it brought her back, two hundred-fold.

And the wait was over.

For this is what she saw of Him....

It was Jonathan's secret. And it was a mighty secret to hold, but he did. He waited for just the right time. He made everybody swear they would not reveal it, because he was waiting for just the right time to tell her. He'd prayed for guidance for that perfect moment in time, and when he received confirmation of it, he walked in through her bedroom door, the afternoon sunlight falling brighter against his skin than it should have naturally been. And what he was carrying in his arms, and the way he looked down into the bundle of life, then over to her as he brought it nearer—well, it changed everything. She winced with pain as she pulled herself up in bed. He sat down next to her and held a baby up for her to see, then without a word he placed him in her arms and moved in beside her, kissing her cheek tenderly with the offering of the most precious gift he could have ever given her.

She looked down at her beautiful son, knowing full well who he was to her. Instantly, his personality joined her heart and pulled it back into the loving side of life. She looked into her man's sweet eyes, taking time back under her power as she memorized them and the meaning in the moment they were sharing.

How simply. How suddenly. How quietly, and without pretense, the Lord God answers a prayer.

"Who is this?" Sienna asked quietly as she touched the little guy's dark hair, gently brushing it to the side.

Jonathan was beaming, about to erupt from within.

"His name is Justice. Quinn is his middle name. Driscoll will be his last name as soon as we sign the adoption papers." He looked at her face and watched hope slowly returning, and he smiled sweetly as he witnessed the light filtering back into her glorious eyes.

"How...?" she started to ask, not knowing how to finish.

"You have a baby of your own, Sienna. God answered your prayer...again."

She stroked the baby's cheek. He smiled up at her. She said his name out loud, "Justice," and it rippled through the room almost with a rumbling sound of thunder following.

Then to Jonathan she said, "Did you feel that?"

She turned to Jonathan with a smile of wonderment just starting, it spread into the first true smile he'd seen on her face since the attack.

"I think this little one's got some holy verve in him, too. And he's a little angel man. He hasn't cried yet. Not once. He's been here the whole time...since you came back from the hospital. He's been in the next room...and he's just so quiet, and he's happy all the time. And Bella adores him."

"How did He do it? I mean, where did you get him?" she asked.

"Well...," Jonathan said slowly, treading delicately. "This little guy is why Aurora came home when she did that day. He's the reason she got here in time to save your life. His natural parents have a tragic story. But his won't be. He will have a great story. He's only seven months old, and he's already helped save a life. That's a pretty good record, I'd say."

Jonathan smiled down at the baby, obviously thrilled with being a father a second time.

Sienna looked into Justice's eyes, completely amazed. She cried some tears of joy, and she thanked God for the miracle in her arms until finally she said, "He's got your eyes, Jonathan. I mean, they're brown, but the way they look right into your soul..."

"And he's got your smile. Everybody says so."

She placed a hand on Jonathan's and took a moment to treasure him. She meditated on the events of the last month, being confined to her room that used to be a wonderful library but, recently, had been filled with so much more—life and love and servitude in living words such that Jesus would have spoken, and they all came through him. She'd been through times of pain and trial before, she'd been through atrocious abuses before, but this time she had a partner—in Jonathan. He experienced all her suffering and all her confusion right along with her. He never left her side unless she asked him to, and then he did so with regret, rounded shoulders, nervous hands, and watchful eyes. He was there when she'd awaken, no matter the hour, from the night sweats, the nightmares, the broken dreams of lightning fallen down, striking hard three times against the very heart of her and circumventing its holy, peaceable rhythms. He was the one who felt every sideways beat and told her, *Hold on until it's over...* or, *I'm here with you...* He held her hand, talked to her in Irish songs, poems, and prayers, in sweet and soothing tones for endless hours—if she needed his voice he'd lend it, without question or reserve. He brought her countless glasses of water, each one with an empathetic kiss upon her forehead, a gentle hand to her hair and then, more softly, against her face which held fear, confusion, anger, and pain in it. He'd look at her honestly, and he'd tell her everything would be okay. He'd tell her not to worry. He'd tell her she was loved, brave, beautiful, and strong.

She followed him in her thankful mind, remembering all of his blessed, kind actions up to the point of the present, when she was beginning to question her faith, and he told her, "I have something that will help you, it's a message from God telling you He hasn't forgotten about you. Not at all..." And he left her, going to another room to bring her back the jewel he'd found in it. He'd placed their son ever so reverently in the center of her lap, and she'd found herself experiencing a solid reason for believing in answered prayer. She found herself holding onto the robe of God through one man's gentle hand and a tiny baby's fist full of power—it is Love that is a promise left unbroken. She was amazed at the evanescence of her stain and tarnish as it lifted and was gone from the space between the three. For what she held in her arms, and looking up at her as if it always was, was something colossally made and named in the presence of the outcome yet to witness. Something sweet and stronger than all the rest, someone called Justice. And in his eyes he held a whisper, an ancient story yet untold. The words, *there will be a reckoning,* floating up from his loving soul.

A spirit of light hovered all around them, and it was gentle, free, and full of everything worth considering.

"Where have all the good men gone?" she asked quietly as if from off the restless tongues that cry through the unsettled dreams of a million other women still looking to the sky for just one. And she studied her son, the deepness in his eyes so like his father's beside her. "I have found two of them, the very best that God has." She looked at Jonathan, and he smiled back at her as she said with the wonderment found fully in truth, "How fortunate am I? I will never forget how blessed I am, Jonathan, for God to give me you. And Bell. And you, baby...I don't think I could find more to live for."

For the first time in over a month, Jonathan let out a sigh of relief. His girl was back. He secretly thanked God, and God secretly thanked him for his part in it. He watched Sienna's face, noting how it finally looked like her again, as she took the time to understand the difference between looking at the world with human eyes and looking at the world through the Holy Spirit's eyes. The difference was night and day, darkness and light, and she prayed she would never be without His eyes again. She straightened Justice's tiny blue shirt with a tiny blue puppy appliqué in the center. He pushed against her stomach with his feet, trying to work his legs and smiling the entire time like he had a one-person party going on constantly. She laughed with him and didn't seem to mind the discomfort he was causing her healing ribs; in fact, she barely noticed.

Jonathan had leaned back and closed his eyes for a moment of peace, but he didn't care that she interrupted him. He was happy she did.

"Jonathan?"

"Yeah, sweetheart," he smiled.

"Is Jackobie here?"

"She'll be here in a few minutes," he answered, checking his watch, "Why?"

"I'm getting out of this bed. I have a baby to take care of."

chapter thirty-seven

$\mathcal{S}$IENNA WAS DOING her physical therapy in the pool when Jonathan and Bella walked in. They'd just returned from the stables where Bella had been taking lessons on Peanut.

"Can we swim, too?" Bella asked.

"Absolutely. I would love some company, sweetie," Sienna answered.

Jonathan and Bella changed into their suits and joined her. Soon Aurora and Shay did as well, bringing Justice in with some little trunks they'd gotten for him that afternoon. Jonathan sat at the side of the pool, dipping the baby's feet in and playing with him a bit before passing him to Shay. Sienna got in the whirlpool tub, and he joined her there.

"Looks like you are moving around a lot better, love," he said.

"I am. I think I'm pretty much there. I have a final x-ray tomorrow, and if they clear me, I've got to start riding Ira again, or at least start working with him on the ground."

They watched as Aurora played with Bell and Shay dipped Justice in and out of the water. The baby's laugh echoed across the room; it was one of Sienna's favorite sounds. Bella started playing with him, tickling his toes.

"Those two are going to be great parents," Jonathan observed. "I have to admit, I always knew Shay would be. He would adopt anything and bring it home when he was a kid—dogs, frogs, crickets—whatever. One time I was giving him a driving lesson, and he stopped the truck in the middle of the road to let a bug off the windshield."

He laughed at the memory.

"I could see him doing that." Sienna chuckled. "And Aurora has grown up overnight, it seems. She's going to be a great mom. I am so proud of her."

Jonathan watched her and her pink hair for a while. Aurora caught him and stuck her tongue out at him and smiled. He winked back at her sweetly.

"You know . . . she really showed how tough she is," he said. "Not just that she stepped in when she did and saved your life—I mean, thank God for that—but after everything happened. Shay said she was completely calm at the police station. She didn't get rattled at all. I guess I figured she'd crack after a few days or something, but she never did. I waited for her to cry, get angry, something... but she just didn't. She even told that nosey child psychologist where to go. I can remember...Aurora told her, 'We've got it handled, Bella's already in therapy.' And the psychologist asked what type, and Aurora said, 'Equine Assisted Rehabilitation for Post-Traumatic Stress Disorder.' That lady shut her mouth so fast... and she never came back."

"It worked though, didn't it...with Bell," Sienna said. "I knew it would. Barbara rescues these horses from abuse and rehabilitates them, but then she pairs them with hurting people. It's amazing what she has done over the years. Divorcees, abused kids, widowers, you name it, she's helped them. She helped me when I first moved here."

"Yeah, that's what Aurora said," Jonathan went on. "She was adamant about it. If I didn't take Bella riding, even for one day, Aurora did. Barbara said she just told Bella how hurt Peanut had been, how scared he was, and she told Bella if he could make it, she could. And it worked. I was worried at first. Bell wouldn't say anything, and she had a lot of nightmares, but after a few days with Peanut, she came around."

"Thank God," Sienna said, watching Bella laughing as she played in the water.

"Yes, thank God," he wholeheartedly agreed, gently rubbing Sienna's shoulders and her sore back for awhile before continuing. "You know what Aurora said to me?"

"I could only imagine," Sienna kidded as she rolled her eyes.

"She came into the kitchen one morning, about a week ago, just strolled in and said, 'I see you eyeing me, Driscoll. I see you waiting for my feminine side to ask you for your strong, manly shoulder to lean on. Well, you're gonna be eyeballin' me for the rest of your life cuz' it ain't gonna happen. Welcome to woman power, my friend. You might not want to play ball with me because there will be a smack down of some sort.'"

Sienna laughed at his impersonation of Aurora, and he was pleased because he thought he was quite good.

"But more seriously she said, 'I bet you think I'm cold for laying the guy out like that and not shedding a tear, but I knew from the moment I came back with Sienna, that first day. I knew I was supposed to save her life, even if it meant losing mine. And I've always been okay with that. I was just waiting for it. And it finally happened, that's all. And I don't feel one bit bad about it, not at all. And I never will. Don't ask me how I knew that, how I was supposed to protect her and all. I just did.' She just told me that, got a drink of water, and left."

"She's pretty dramatic that way. She certainly knows how to make an entrance and an exit to emphasize her points." Sienna gazed out over the pool, feeling very proud of Aurora's strength.

"I asked them to come to Ireland with us," Jonathan said.

Sienna looked over at him and kissed him on the lips.

"Thank you," she said.

∞∾

"My book publisher just called," Sienna was barely keeping her feet on the ground. She was waving her hands up and down excitedly.

"Well, what did she say, love?"

"Movie!"

She nodded her head up and down.

"Yeah...?" He encouraged with a smile.

"They've asked me to help write the screenplay, and they wondered if I had any ideas for cinematography, which I most certainly do...."

"And...?"

"And *music!*"

She squealed and jumped into his arms. He spun her in a circle, his smile buried in her hair. When he let her down on her feet, she hit the ground talking.

"I didn't even have to ask them, Jonathan. I didn't have to say a word. This is all just falling together—it has to be God."

He leaned back against the kitchen counter to take it all in—his love, their new life together—standing in the very room where she nearly lost her life forty days before. They had a daughter—happy, healed, free, and praying like she was born to do. They had a son, a little baby Sienna could call her own. They had the beginnings of a lifelong united career, a creative avenue through which they could share their love of God with the world. They were about to be married, about to start a new life in a new country. They were about to be an aunt and uncle. Life simply could not be any more perfect, and it was hard *not* to see God's hand holding it all together.

Yet, before they could get started, there was one more thing they needed to do...

Alex drove them to the cemetery and then walked them out to Cheney's stone. It read, Gifted Musician, Too Many Songs Left Unsung, and the dates of her time spent here. Sienna didn't have to ask if Jonathan determined the inscription. She knelt down, holding a quiet conversation between two college friends, ending it by placing a dozen yellow roses upon the ground.

The next stop was equally difficult.

Alex helped Jonathan load up his gear, informing him of the details of the sale. Sienna took a last walk along the beach, ending on the steps where Jonathan first saw her as his partner, gave her a first kiss. She ran her hand along the wooden railing, touched the spaces that he touched when she looked up at him and first noticed how beautiful he was. She wiped a couple tears off her cheeks and turned to look out at the sea. She heard the screen door open and close behind her and felt his love surrounding as his arms wrapped warmly around her waist. He rocked her gently, kissed her hair, and whispered, "I've got the best thing about this place right here in my arms. You're all I want and all I ever will."

She leaned back against his chest and received his sweet intention until the wind changed, until the sea shifted.

"Are you going with me?"

He asked her the question with grave seriousness, a defensive hardening to his voice which indicated that he was about to go into Roger's house. It was a house, ironically, willed back to Jonathan in the event of Roger's death. Jonathan was going into the house to remove anything left over by the police regarding Roger's obsession with Sienna.

She nodded she would join him.

"Are you sure?"

"Yeah, I'll be fine," She tried to reaffirm her statement with a smile, but it was delivered too weakly to convince him.

They walked hand-in-hand into the house; neither of them could speak. Alex was following behind, quiet as a ghost. The door creaked as he closed it, and no one said as much, but they each felt like they'd just entered a morgue. Jonathan's hand moved to the small of Sienna's back as he introduced the wicked mess to her. She shivered slightly with chills traveling her spine and circling her healing ribs, taking a moment just to take it all in. She stepped in closer, eyeing certain photographs and wondering how he'd gotten shots of her at this location, or that. She eventually pulled up a chair and sat down, turned on a desk lamp, put on her reading glasses, and calmly began skimming the notes he took as he was studying her book. Jonathan stood beside her, patiently waiting, glancing every now and then to Alex who simply shrugged his shoulders. Finally, Sienna pushed her chair back a bit and asked, what sounded like a trivia question, toward the ceiling.

"Which group seemed to trouble Jesus more, Pharisees or sinners?"

Jonathan glanced toward Alex.

"Don't look at me, man," he said quietly, physically backing up a step.

"Pharisees," Jonathan answered.

"Yeah...the Pharisees," Sienna affirmed thoughtfully, then asked, "Why do you think that is?"

"I don't know...," Jonathan said, "I guess I've never thought about it much."

"I think it was because they tried to limit man's perception of God. They tried to limit what God could do, and how God could do it, by limiting the thoughts, and therefore the prayers, of man."

"Yeah," Jonathan said, trying to get her point.

"God can do anything, anyway, anywhere, through anyone. In other words, God has no limits. None."

She looked down at the hundreds of notes scrawled in red across her book's pages, *Doctrinally incorrect*! and *Blasphemy*!, and she seemed deeply saddened.

"What are you getting at, sweetheart?" he prompted her gently.

"He meant well."

"What?" Jonathan stammered. "How could he have meant well by stalking you...by attacking you, Sienna?"

Sienna reached up and took hold of his hand, waiting for the tension in it to release before she began.

"Roger was advocating for God because I think he really loved God. But he missed one very important thing. God doesn't need an advocate. God is big enough to take care of Himself, His own reputation, and all our mistakes besides. God can see the heart; man can only judge what he thinks he sees.

And to judge someone's work as it is delivered hand-in-hand with their interpretation of God, is to judge God in them.

"What I mean is that Roger and I were actually on the same side—we both loved God. But Roger didn't understand that my version of God has the capability to save souls similar to mine, not necessarily those similar to his. And my so-called success doesn't mean I'm one hundred percent right in my interpretations of Him. I know, and God knows, that if I didn't make a dime at it, I'd still be doing what He put me here to do. My heart is right. God created me this way to use me for His unique purpose. He created me to interpret His Word in the way that I do, on purpose. He has revealed His Word to me in a particular way for a particular reason that only He knows. And I'm sure He was trying to do the same with Roger. Unfortunately, he got off track and missed the mark."

"Way off track, man," Alex commented quietly.

Sienna looked up at Jonathan with a dreadful darkness in her eyes. "Do you see the danger in Christians judging other Christians? Can you start to see that?"

"I think I can," he said remorsefully, considering everything from countries racked with devastating wars, to churches, to families, and individual souls being torn apart right along with the work God was trying to do in the earth.

Sienna stood up slowly as if shouldering a universal burden, "Christians fighting Christians, Christians judging Christians, must be a most disappointing thing to God. Roger was a Christian musician, right?"

"Mostly, yeah, but he actually spent the first part of his career as a pastor," Jonathan answered quietly, shaking his head and keeping certain details to himself such as the pornography the police found on Roger's computer and the massive amounts of drug paraphernalia hidden in the man's home. To say that Roger was severely conflicted would be a gross understatement.

She turned around and scanned the room one last time, "George MacDonald stated it well when he wrote that men in their theology forget the very Word of God. I wish Roger would have just sat down with me and talked to me. I wish he would have just asked me what my motives were."

She turned to leave the room, passively ending with this, "We probably could have been good friends." To which Jonathan raised his eyebrows and then rubbed his face with both hands as if to erase the preposterous suggestion because in his mind Roger deserved no explanation other than he was a lunatic, plain and simple. And if Aurora hadn't killed him, Jonathan would have.

Plain and simple.

And how could it possibly be...that to some degree, both of them were right?

chapter thirty-eight

*T*HEY HAD CARVED in her Ireland church, in an ivory stone pillar, these words...

Learn to do these things;
Seek Justice,
Reprove the Ruthless,
Defend the Orphan,
Plead for the Widow.

—ISAIAH 1:17

They, Jonathan's family and friends, had restored the amazing structure completely, and it was absolutely every bit as beautiful as it was initially intended to be. It was a church standing at unwavering attention with a most holy reverence to the God above and within it. It was a library unique, unmatched by any other on the earth and called into being as if by Sienna's dreams still undreamt. Its walls were lined with mahogany shelves and old—very, very old—books: Bibles of some of the rarest translations, early legal depositions of the court, primitive medical journals with the original hand-drawn illustrations, and architectural blueprints of some amazing historical structures. It was a writer's earthly heaven for certain. On one side of the church, they had left the pews, refinished in rich tones and lined up in perfect rows facing the altar, and, on the other, a stunning, hand-carved bed layered with ivory linens and wool, and behind it, an actual, antique, fully restored grand piano.

Jonathan had asked Jude to get it ready for their arrival. He hadn't seen it yet himself. He sent Sienna on ahead, wanting her to arrive there alone. He wanted to let her experience his family's welcoming and acceptance of her. He wanted her to feel their love without him standing in the middle, blocking it. So he followed behind slowly, lollygagging, as it were, listening to Bell bring forth her stories as she plucked them from the green and sent them toward the sky. His eyes were full of light and a soft-moving joy as he watched over the baby in his arms, watched the expressions of learning and listening as he paid full attention to his sister's ramblings with an inherent wonderment and awe. His big babyish eyes he held open widely, the thoughts emerging behind them seemed to be taking it all in. Jonathan gazed restfully out across his meadow, absorbing the colors as strength and avenue, and releasing his soul freely forth in layers and unto the vapors floating over the peaceful sea, and he felt, he *knew* actually, that the person he held in his arms was a sacred and a most precious one, and that, in his barely begun little life, he was already being watched over unlike anyone ever had been before, save Jesus Christ Himself.

"Baby Justice," he said, holding him up and kissing his forehead.

The wee boy looked directly into his father's eyes and gently touched his father's chin with tiny fingertips and thumb.

"What am I to expect from you?" Jonathan asked with an inquisitive smile.

"Justice is coming down to the earth," Bella answered loudly, bending over deep as if preaching to a wishing stone or a certain small bug that had caught her eye. "Justice will see all things hidden in this world. Justice will see things clearly like the all-seeing eye of God. Justice will not rest until the very nature of evil has been stopped."

She then went back to whatever she was saying before, bringing up a four-leaf clover and holding it toward her dad to show him. Jonathan looked again into the face of his son.

"God help us, then," he said, and he smiled as he set the boy at his hip, gesturing his daughter to take hold of his hand, and they walked on toward their church, a little thrown together family held by the power of One.

∞

With the money from the sale of the American houses, Jonathan did four things. First, he prayed about it, and second, he obeyed the Lord's suggestions. Thirdly, he presented his father with an offer to manage a fleet of brand new fishing boats owned by a company put primarily in Bella and Justice's names.

"You'd be doing my kids a favor, Dad," he explained, "If they want to go to college or start a career or whatever they want to do, they have something that's been making some money for them over the years. I'd really appreciate your help with this...I know it's a lot to ask..."

Jude had been standing by the kitchen table listening to all this, staring out the window, toward the sea, with a set and defiant chin. He became a tad bit misty-eyed as his pride began buckling down on the inside of him. He hadn't said anything to anyone yet, but his business was falling apart. It was sustaining too many families, the boats and the equipment were old, the price of fuel was rising, the price of fish, dropping. They'd been docked since Jonathan had left. They'd done nothing but work on that church because they'd have been losing money for certain had they gone out to sea.

So when Jonathan said, "I know it's a lot to ask...," Jude grabbed his son around his neck and patted him hard on the back in thanks. And rather than let him see his old man cry, Jude headed out the door and disappeared for an entire day.

With the new boats, with the better equipment, with each man being captain of his own vessel, they could make a decent go of it, as well as live in peace with each other. It's what Jude had been praying for for more than five solid years.

Fourthly and finally, Jonathan took the remainder of the money and gave it to Aurora and Shay so they could find a decent home, prepare for the new baby, and open the domestic abuse shelter for rural Ireland that she wanted to. And he was also building a recording studio, somewhat for himself, but mostly for her. He'd asked her if she'd sing on his new record—she was actually speechless.

Jonathan, Sienna, and their children would have to make due for a while, living between their church and Jude and Ciara's home until they could get enough funds together to build their own house. First priority would be the wedding and, shortly thereafter, a barn for Ira and Peanut and the dogs and the small herd of cattle Jonathan had inherited with the land.

One quiet evening, while the grandparents were watching the children, they were resting on the bed in their church.

"What would go there?" Sienna inquired, tilting her head and gazing thoughtfully at a prominent blank space on the far wall.

"A Kinkade," he answered.

"Yeah?"

"Yeah."

"It would...," she said dreamily, envisioning the vibrant colors. "You know I always wanted to live in one of those."

"In a Kinkade painting?"

"Yeah, I mean they're so beautiful. You wouldn't want to live in one of those thatched-roof cottages by the water? You know, as long as someone else did all that landscaping..."

He chuckled at her.

"When I look at those lighted windows, I always wonder what the people are doing inside that house," she continued.

"I know what I'd be doing," he said, looking at her a certain way.

She smacked him playfully on the arm and they both laughed.

"Every time I tried to live that peacefully—I'm talking in reality now if you are having trouble keeping up..."

"Sometimes..." He teased her.

"I'd try to envision my life that perfect, and I swear it was like—everything would blow up in my face and I'd see my beautiful life-sized painting with a stick of lit dynamite in the center of it. Kaboom!" she said dryly, her hands floating in the air indicating the aftermath of an explosion.

"Not talking reality now—right?" he jested.

"You're quick." She grinned.

He smiled to himself as she looked at everything around her and finally said, "It's hard to believe that this is real. This is so much better."

She looked into his eyes and turned toward him. "This is better than anything I ever imagined. This is as close to heaven as I can get. And it's because of you."

He looked at her sweetly and reached over to brush her cheek and kindly hold her chin for a moment. Now he knew what to get her for a wedding gift.

"Cottage by the water, huh?" he said.

"Thatched-roof and private," she answered. "I feel like I finally have the life to go with that painting. And you're right," she said rolling onto her back and eyeing the empty space again, "it would go perfectly there."

chapter thirty-nine

*M*OST OF THE horses in County Donegal, along with repaired, shined, and polished carriages or carts, were employed for the wedding of Jonathan Driscoll and Sienna Emory. The ceremony was held in the newly restored church in Jonathan's Meadow, as the grand parcel of land has since become known. Only select friends and family were invited to the private event, with a massive reception and all-night party at the home of Jude Driscoll to follow, in a drunken attempt to make up for it.

The ceremony itself was beautiful. The men lined up behind Jonathan were not only his brothers, his life-long friends, they were his band of loyalty. They were all equally proud of the man standing ahead of them, and they couldn't help but let it show on their ruggedly handsome faces. They carried their love of him confidently in their tailored woolen jackets and crisp ivory shirts, each one ranking Captain because of him. And this day they honored him because he was an honorable man.

Jackobie, Katarina, Mia, and Aurora were gleaming with joy beneath their matching up-dos and flowing champagne dresses with chocolate sashes at their waists, which tied in the back with a bow. They each carried dark burgundy roses and a priceless smile. Bella was beautiful in her dark burgundy dress, dropping petals from roses on the floor all around her as she walked down the aisle toward her dad. When she reached him, he bent down to kiss her gloved hand and give her a special smile. Then Ciara, beautifully dressed and already dabbing tears, carried a suited Justice down the aisle and sat with him in the front pew beside great-grandpa Brody.

When the pianist changed songs, everyone in attendance stood up to turn back toward her. She was, simply and elegantly, the most amazing person, the most beautiful woman Jonathan had ever seen, and she was smiling directly at him, walking directly to him. He never looked away. Neither did she. Jude was walking proudly at her arm, and when he presented her to his son he said, "Love her forever. Guard her with your life," and he reached up to embrace his boy, considering him a man he was privileged just to know.

After the sweet exchange of rings, after endearing smiles offered to each other and intermittent sighs released toward the heavenly realm in thanks that it finally be true, after Bishop Jacobs officially declared them husband and wife, they chose to do a most precious and holy thing, unrehearsed but between the two. Jonathan held on to each of her hands, he brought his forehead to hers, they closed their eyes and they prayed with each other, "Dear God, as we start our lives together as husband and wife, let no one come before the other but You."

They said these words most reverently to their Lord and slowly they each smiled while pulling back and looking into each other's eyes. He then planted a kiss on her that made everybody want a love like theirs.

The party that followed began at the bottom of the meadow, Sienna and Jonathan could hear the crowd that had gathered—a swarm of people from several counties and multiple countries that had obviously found no good reason why they shouldn't start the merriment without them.

"Holy—" Jonathan started.

"—Spirit!" Sienna finished for him, both of their jaws dropping at the vast number of people.

Jonathan shouted to his mum, one carriage behind, "Who are all these people?"

"I guess you two are celebrities. Your wedding date was in all the tabloids at the market, but I don't think we have enough fish for this many, do we Jude?"

Jonathan looked apologetically at Sienna, "You ready for this?"

Just then some man hollered, "Here they come!"

Sienna saw the mass of people moving toward them with their plastic glasses sloshing, and their colorful handbags waving, and their wrinkled ties flitting in the breeze, and she was wise enough to order the driver to stop the carriage, and to tell everyone down the line to get out before the horses spooked or bolted.

And a party it most certainly was. After the liquor and the food ran out—in that order—the mob seemed to make its way to the bars in town which must have made more income in that one night than they had the whole fiscal year. Mostly friends and family and locals remained as Jonathan gave a final toast, thanking them for sharing in the best day of his life. He made sure Bella and Justice would be well taken care of and that his brothers and his friends would keep strangers from traveling up the far road, then he whispered in Sienna's ear, "Are you ready?"

They snuck out the back way to a predetermined horse and carriage. He draped his jacket over her bare shoulders, and they slowly made their way back through the black and dripping meadow, back up the long hill toward their sacred and humble church of warmth. The darkness was thick with fog, the ground all around them heavy with blossoming midnight dew. A few moments into the journey, the cloaking distance delivered them into the soft folds of silence and romanced them way back into a simpler time. She could hear nothing but the hooves and wheels working the murky ground, the sweet night noises of shore and frog surrounding, and if she listened close enough, she could hear him smiling. And it was that sound only that soothed her as it rested upon her spirit as she rode along there with him.

He didn't say anything, not a single word. He just steadily drove that jet black horse with his hands woven in and strong upon the leather reins.

When they arrived at their church, he jumped out quickly and tied the horse. He came back offering his hand to help her down. Closer to his body, she felt his warmth and looked up into his face. She felt his arm beneath her and was resting in his arms, cradled against his chest by the time she realized he was picking her up and walking. She'd never felt his raw strength surrounding her like that before. Once into the church, he placed her back on her feet and he left her to light a single candle.

She watched him as he stood beside the bed, unbuttoning his shirt. She watched him take it off and turn to toss it on a nearby chair. She watched the light play across his back, his shoulders, muscle, skin, tattoo…, and finally his chest as he turned to walk back toward her, a comforting smile on his beautiful face.

He took the jacket off his bride, letting it gently swing and fall into a neighboring pew. It slid to the floor, but he didn't notice. He brought both hands to her face and moved in to kiss her. Then he pulled her into him in a loving embrace as he told her, "Thank you for marrying me."

He moved back from her, gazing into her eyes with such depth, need, and want that she swore she felt their souls connecting…and they did so with such complete unity, such a giving love, that it was on a level she never knew existed. She'd never even considered the possibility before now. She'd never imagined that a love like this was truly possible, not until the very moment that it happened. And she felt it.

He was speaking directly into her soul, bringing these amazing things forth and into their world, when he whispered, "Thank you for putting that much faith in me."

He gently held her hand in the air, guiding her into a turn away from him. He kissed the base of her neck, moving in close behind her, his hand gliding across her waist, the other across her back and then comfortingly stilling beside her neck, moving hair away to kiss her cheek tenderly, sweetly. He started unbuttoning her gown, patiently, with confidence in his unguarded touch. She looked up at the cross above the door. As if reading her thoughts, he whispered, "I think God understands. I think He's understood since He created Eden."

What he didn't see was the smile that spread across her face, but he knew it was there. He could sense it emanating from her whole body. He could feel it move beneath his hands.

∞

And a sacred silence filled that valley as it reverenced the truthfulness found in love, from the stillness of the lark in the highest canopy to the smallest cricket resting its wings on the lowest singing stone. The sea with wickedness filled was at its rest, and not a blade of grass rustled against it a warning. There was nothing in the night season for that ominous horse to swivel a telling ear toward, nothing but the lazy flicker of the candlelight and flitting bug against the wavy glass windows of the church. And though invisible but to God, to Bella's heavenly dreams and so held forward in a darker time within the future of Justice, there were mighty Angels surrounding that building of Cornerstones. They guarded it high in thick circles layered deep as in a legion or a fortress wall, standing firm in worldly movements and yet immovable from here, fierce as any force of any reckoning ever told and yet contained. They stood solid and yet were phantom-like spirits lined up and floating in a holy order, impenetrable by and against all evil throughout this valley of peace, risen amid this meadow of things left unseen and stories, as of yet, gone unwritten, with purposes left unfulfilled... *what be yours...*

Wherever two on earth agree, there I am with them.
　　　　　　　　—The Gospel According to Matthew, 18:20

epilogue

WHEN I SAID I needed someone breathing beside me, I meant you.

"When I said I never wanted to be left alone again, I meant by you.

"When I said I can't survive on anything less than a love that lasts forever, I meant that I would die without the love between me and you.

"And when I said I could never love anyone like this again, I meant after you there simply wouldn't be anything left of me.

"In the sweet name of God, don't leave me...please, don't leave me now...."

These words were spoken out loud in the back seat of a patrol car but no one ever really heard them, apart from God. And He took them as a righteous prayer, and He answered them back righteously. Therefore, Sienna didn't die on her kitchen floor from a rambling and floating bone which was about to puncture her lung. Instead, the hand of God slowly, gently, put it back in its place and set things aright as if nothing had happened at all but for a man coming to know how deeply he could love a woman.

And so, for enduring satanic tests and trials, for surviving plots thrown against light and love with a crooked hand, there are outcomes glorious. In the hanging on rides the breakthrough prayed and pleaded for, for our God is a God of justice—a word which is an utter impossibility without the purest form of love holding the balance, tempering the scales.

Collectively, through the writing of novels, the singing of songs, and the speaking of prayers, the little family went on together fulfilling their offices and in so doing saved one hundred thousand souls. Including a most precious one, a most special one, the only one of his kind set loose upon the earth—a little boy named Justice and soon to be a man.

references

The Amplified Bible. (1954, 1958, 1962, 1964, 1965, 1987). Grand Rapids, MI: Zondervan Publishing House/Corporation; La Habra, CA: Lockman Foundation.

MacDonald, George, (1824-1905). (1990). *Knowing the Heart of God: Where Obedience Is the One Path to Drawing Intimately Close to Our Father;* compiled, arranged, and edited by Michael R Phillips. Bloomington, MN: Bethany House Publishers. Quoted material used by permission of Sunrise Books, P.O. Box 7003, Eureka, CA 95502, as well as, Bethany House Publishers, 11400 Hampshire Avenue South, Bloomington, MN.

Frost, Robert, & Holt, Henry. (1959). *You Come Too: Favorite Poems for Young Readers; Stopping by Woods on a Snowy Evening.* New York, NY: Henry Holt and Company, Inc.

Cibot, Francois-Edouard, (1799-1877). French. *Fallen Angels (Anges Dechus).* (1833). Oil on canvas. Museum Purchase. Omaha, NE: Joslyn Art Museum; website: www.joslyn.org.

Killybegs: Na Cealla Beaga. (2009, July 08). In *Wikipedia.* Retrieved July 31, 2009, from http://en.wikipedia.org/wiki/Killybegs.

Federation of Irish Fishermen. (2009, June 28). In *Wikipedia.* Retrieved July 31, 2009, from http://en.wikipedia.org/wiki/Federation_of_ Irish_fishermen.

also by *Dawn Dyson*

MERCY SKY

Available Through

iUniverse.com

Barnesandnoble.com

Amazon.com

VISIT THE AUTHOR'S WEBSITE

www.DawnDyson.com

EXCERPT FROM THE SEQUEL TO *BELLA MAURA* CALLED, *JUSTICE QUINN*. LOOK FOR IT IN THE FUTURE. . . .

*J*USTICE HAS NOTHING if not the end.

Justice has no one if not everyone.

Justice heard, Justice seen, cannot inflict anything but the most horrific terror, the highest order of all Holy fears, in those who call themselves too strong to believe, too ruthless to be taken advantage of, or too intelligent to be wise.

And yet, God's sons, His daughters, are the only ones told, "Fear not. God is a god of Justice."

Who then, would remain . . . ?

Would it be you, oh perfect religious one, calling forth Mercy with Jesus' name?

It will all come apart to finally be put right. I will not be controlled. Not by anyone but my Lord. I will not bend a knee but for Him and by my choosing. Curse me for the life He has given me, blame me for the Confidence to walk it genuinely out. Oh . . . , if I were you, I'd so shut my mouth.

Because someone might be better connected than you, might be praying right this moment, saying, "Justice come, Justice come down. And let me rise to know my first taste of fairness upon the lips you gave me, sweet and utter purity dripping down in a land of milk and honey, and of rest and peaceful quiet eternally unmolested.

"Justice, turn my eyes from Your wrath as You move in ways mysterious, and let me trust that You have done everything in secret, in the dark, which needed to be done—that with Your left hand. And You have made me whole, restored and righted me once again—that upon Your right. I smile in a bliss unbothered while my enemies tremble and turn to dust and the last thing they know of be me and my blessed name whispered with fondness in welcoming and recognition of character as it is released forth from the smiling lips of my God; that, and their twisted regret for misusing, misjudging all that is within me. For it is You they used, You they judged. And dare we be judging You, Lord.

"Justice come.

"Justice come down.

"For I am tired of winning battles I never cared to start. I am tired of wiping blood from my side while praying, 'Father, forgive them for they know not what they do,' finished just in time to feel the cut from another blade. Is it not due time that ignorance should depart them and leave them with vacant mouths, vacant minds, empty hands?"

But sweet patience, You have given it to me…, to hold beneath eyes designed to look up because I see things in You. Patience is not a pardon, it is a precursor to whatever You will do. Vengence is Mine, sayeth the Lord. And I know Your Word will not return to You void.

Justice…what a powerful word. You see, my mother was angry; my mother was tired. My mother was twenty-three the day she died by me own father's hand, and this note is all I have left of her; it's the only part of her I ever had at all. It was something she had written down with a hurried fervor, a secret prayer stuck in the darkened folds of her Bible. Aunt Aurora had managed to snag it—that and a couple toys—when she snagged me as a baby boy, and I am eternally grateful. And I am what I am. And for that I can never be sorry.

My name is Justice. And I'm comin' down. And I'm not for the weak-hearted nor the fainted saints.